BIANCHI

SINFUL NEW YORK SERIES BOOK ONE

ADDISON TATE

Bianchi

Sinful New York Series
Book 1

Addison Tate

KASTLEMORE
PUBLISHING LTD

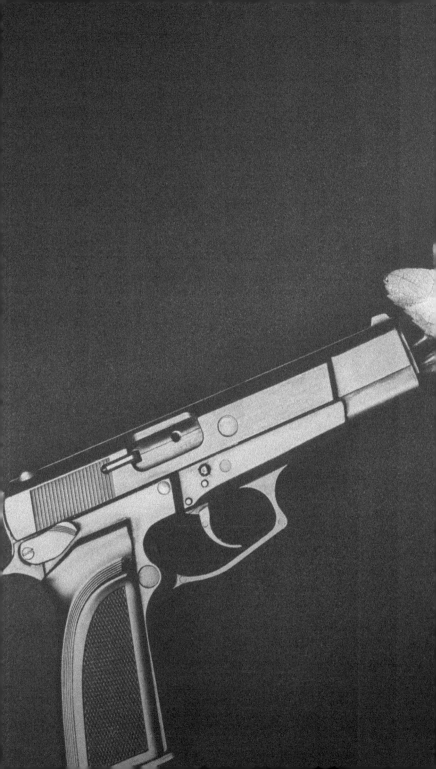

Dedication

This is for all the dark romance baddies who dream of being kidnapped and fucked by a Mafia Don and eaten out until you're clean...

Romeo Bianchi is ready and waiting for you...

Ten years ago, I told my father to stay out of my life. I thought it would keep me safe, but now he's the reason my life could be taken.

For too long, I've barely been existing, coasting through life and waiting for the inevitable end. Perhaps that is why, when I return home from work and find Romeo Bianchi waiting for me in the shadows, I accept my fate, wholeheartedly.

I expect him to take my life without a thought, but he takes me captive. To him, I'm nothing but a pawn in his dangerous game of retribution. But weeks pass and the moments we share weave a tangled web of connection between us, burrowing deeper into my heart with every touch, taste, and look.

When faced with a choice that could save his life, I ask myself one simple question:

Who protects the man that has spent his entire life protecting everyone else?

Authors Note

As with any book I write there will always be a happy ever after, however, to get there we go through a lot of turbulence and trauma.

This book contains some themes that may be triggering and in the interest of putting your mental health first, please scan the QR code below for the full list of triggers.

Signorina - Miss
Per i bambini - For the children
Tua madre - Your mother
Mia amata - My beloved
Fatto l'amore - Made love
Buon appetito - Enjoy your meal
Cornetto - An Italian pastry
Bambina - Little girl/Child
Zio - Uncle
Cara - Dear
Quei figli di puttana - Sons of bitches
Amore mio - My love
Amore - Love
Mi sposi - Marry me

Russian Translation
Durak - Fool

BIANCHI

ADDISON TATE

SINFUL NEW YORK SERIES

powerful men brought to their knees-

Chapter 1

Romeo

My body aches. It's the deep, all-consuming ache that I could put down to lack of sleep or the thirteen-hour flight. My *nonna* would say it's because of the stress—she'd be right. It's been there for years, slowly getting worse, hovering in the periphery of my existence.

To some extent, it's expected, especially given the world that I live in. But today, it's overwhelming; consuming me and making its presence known in the most ostentatious way. Every muscle in my body is tense. A headache pounds at the base of my skull, and I roll my shoulders to ease the pressure that's been building since I got the call.

La mia famiglia è sotto attacco.

Yesterday, I was back home in Palermo. I was putting plans in place to expand our operation abroad when

1

Massimo called. I was in the middle of a meeting but something had my hand snatching up the phone as it vibrated across the table. When the call connected, a chill ran down my spine. As Massimo uttered those fateful words, for a second, I wished I hadn't answered and yet there was no hesitation in my response.

Massimo is the head of La Cosa Nostra—or the American Mafia, as most people know it. He has a larger-than-life persona about him so doesn't ask for help with trivial matters. And especially when he's been running the operation without a hitch ever since he took over ten years ago. I know that Massimo can take care of business, dealing with issues in the way our fathers taught us—with little or no compassion. But he's my cousin, and in his thirty years of existence, I've *never* heard him sound like he did on that call.

We've been attacked, Rome. It's the third in two weeks. We need you here. Massimo's words bounce around in my mind, replaying like a broken record. *This is war.* But there will only be *one* family that comes out on top. For decades, ours has asserted its dominance in this world. Enemies have come and gone, but there are always players in the game, looking for what they think is an easy way to the top.

There are no limits to the lengths people will go to in order to get more.

To have more power.

Whoever is behind this has too much knowledge of

Massimo's operation. Yes, it could be that they've made some well-calculated guesses, but to make three and have them all hit the mark, seems too coincidental.

Daniele, my underboss, is sitting opposite me, reviewing a contract for a building I'm purchasing. Yellow tabs dot the edge of the paper indicating points for me to review. It's just the two of us for now. I'll send for more men once we've assessed the situation, *if it's needed*. The operation doesn't stop just because I've left the country.

I scrub a hand over my jaw as I look out of the rain-spotted cabin window and over the slick black tarmac. *I'd rather be anywhere but here.* Resting my head against the leather headrest, I tap a finger on my knee under the table as I go over what we know so far.

A bomb went off as a shipment was arriving at the docks and Massimo lost *five* men. It could have been more. *It could have been him.* After losing my parents to a car bomb when I was twenty, I refuse to lose my only other living relative that way. And that's another reason for my visit; Massimo has been present at all the attacks. There was a shooting as he was leaving a restaurant. A car that tried to ram him off the road. And now this. My body tightens and I clench my fists to control the waves of fury that have been coursing through me since the call.

Whoever is trying to take out my family will die.

"Mr. Bianchi, we are ready for you to disembark. Thank you for flying with us today." The pilot's voice fills the cabin, and I drag myself out of my seat.

My muscles feel heavy, and I crack my neck from side to side in an effort to force my mind to focus. As the blonde-haired flight attendant opens the door, her red-coated lips spread into a grin that's bordering on flirtatious rather than professional. The glint in her eyes as they rake over my body tells me she knows exactly what she's doing.

"Thank you for flying with us, Mr. Bianchi. I hope you enjoyed your flight."

When I approach her, she holds out her hand, a piece of paper in her palm. I look down at it dismissively before brushing past her and out of the plane. This is why I should buy my own damn plane. If she really knew who I was and what I do, I can guarantee that she wouldn't be so willing to give me her number.

Crossing the threshold, I come to a stop at the top of the stairs, a cold breeze hitting me. I tip my head back, drops of rain dotting my face as I look up at the sky of gray clouds. The weather matches my mood perfectly. Perhaps it's a foreshadowing of what's to come.

I pull in a lungful of air. It smells of earth and gasoline. Blowing my breath out, my eyes roam around the tarmac of the private airport. Silty puddles form on the ground, and hurried figures race through the light rain.

A hand lands on my shoulder, pulling my attention to Daniele as he comes to a stop behind me. He inclines his head toward the three black SUVs strategically parked at the bottom of the steps. "We should be at Massimo's within the hour, boss."

I amble down the stairs, my gaze roaming the landing strip. Getting lost in my thoughts will only get me killed. If somebody is trying to take out my family, then I'm a prime target. It's a natural hazard of the job and one I'd be a fool to ignore.

When I reach the bottom of the steps, I stuff my hand into my pocket, palming the pocket watch my *nonno* gifted me. I was sixteen when he died, but he taught me so much—along with my father—about this life.

I can hear his voice so clearly, as if he's standing in front of me. *"Always have your guard up, Romeo. Never let anyone get too close, because they will use that against you in the most brutal of ways."*

He was on his deathbed when he shared that nugget of wisdom. My mother pulled me away as quickly as she could, but the words have always hovered on the periphery of my mind, guiding me in everything I do. His guidance has got me this far, which, given my lifestyle, is a miracle.

One of Massimo's men steps out from the driver's seat of the middle SUV. He holds the door open as I approach, inclining his head as I climb into the heated car. "Good evening, Don." He closes the door, before climbing behind the wheel.

The rain intensifies, drumming on the roof of the car as I pull on my seat belt. I'm not in the mood for making small talk, and based on the heaviness hanging in the atmosphere, neither are Massimo's men. With our bags stowed into the cars and our passports checked, Daniele climbs in beside me. The only sounds as the car travels across the airfield are the low hum of the engine and the occasional splash of puddles we hit. The gravity of the reason for my visit is felt by us all.

I watch the landscape pass by in a blur as we pull out onto the highway. Massimo's estate is in Stony Brook, about an hour and twenty from JFK's private terminal. He has a penthouse in New York, and although he used to spend most of his time in the city, recently, he's spending more and more time in the house our *nonno* built.

A familiar burning desire claws at me, urging me to turn around and go home. It's why it's been years since I last visited the States. In fact, the last time I was here was for Massimo's mother's funeral, twelve years ago. I couldn't make it out for Dario's—Massimo's father—funeral five years later. Too much was happening back home. *He would have understood.* I swallow down the thickness in my throat and focus on the reason I'm here now.

Smoothing a hand over my black Oxford shirt, I pull open my coat, the heat in the car making a bead of sweat run down the center of my spine. My tone is clipped and to the point when I ask, "Do we have any updates?"

I feel Daniele shift in his seat but he continues to look out the window as he speaks. "No, boss. The last comms I had with Aldo were that they were close to figuring it out, but as expected, there was a buzz around the dock and it hampered our investigations."

It might be more challenging to take action with no name, but it won't be impossible. We won't rest until we find them. In targeting us, they have only fueled our fire and *when* we catch them—because we will—they will wish they had the sense to never be born. As the head of the family, it's my job to make sure a message is sent.

Chapter 2

Romeo

The remainder of the journey to Massimo's is spent in silence. Every enemy we've ever faced flashes through my mind on a supersonic carousel. I can't pinpoint which one is more likely to have pulled this off.

With my thoughts occupied, the drive passes quickly, and before I know it, the three cars pull into the driveway of Massimo's estate. We speed down the gravel road. Dust swirls into a cloud from the car in front of us, hitting the windshield and dissipating into the air. The car ahead turns left as we go right and swing around the fountain that hasn't functioned for years, coming to a stop at the foot of the steps.

Aldo, Massimo's *consigliere*, is waiting for us. He holds my door open as I step out. My heart hammers in my chest, and I crack my neck as I school my features into my usual mask of indifference. His posture is stiff and there's a light sheen of sweat on his forehead despite the cool climate. He holds my stare before his eyes dart to Daniele when he rounds the car to join us. Aldo stands taller, his chin jutting out, as Daniele comes to a stop beside me.

"Romeo, Daniele. It's good to see you." He pauses, tugging on the hem of his blazer as his eyes bounce around on the landscape. I eye his fidgeting movements suspiciously. Clearing his throat, he brings his attention back to us and adds, "If only it was under better circumstances."

Brushing off the wariness that has no place with family, I clap Aldo on the shoulder and shake his hand with the other. "If it was under better circumstances, I wouldn't need to be here, Aldo."

Ignoring the adrenaline rushing through me, I stroll past him, up the stairs, and into the house, certain they will follow. At first glance, not much has changed about the place. Although the furnishings seem to have been updated, there is still a grandeur to it. Money and status are clear in every room I pass on my way to Massimo's office.

Our *nonno* purchased the land over fifty years ago. He built the house for our *nonna*, paying homage to the villas in Sicily. Except it's a fortress, with bulletproof windows and armed guards walking the perimeter day and night.

I pass five of Massimo's men on my way to the back of the house. Their expressions are grave as each of them bows their head and clears a path for me. The mood is somber. I have no doubt that these men are just as angered by these attacks as I am. We'll need that passion for when we find these bastards.

Massimo's office door is open when I arrive. His laptop is open in front of him and a pile of files sit to his right in a neat stack. The sleeves of his crumpled white shirt are rolled up, exposing his tattoos.

"*Cugino*, it's good to see you," I greet, walking into the room.

His head darts up, and I'm hit by a familiarity I haven't felt in years. *It's been too long.* Of course we keep in touch, but considering Massimo is the only blood family I have left, we don't visit like I imagine a 'normal' family would.

Massimo smiles, and although it quickly fades, for a moment, the tiredness that was evident on his face was wiped away by the simple act of baring his teeth. Looking at him, I'm reminded of our mischief-filled childhood, safe under the security blanket that covered us before responsibility and the dangerous life we lead was thrust upon us.

A creek sounds around the room as he leans back in his chair. His calm posture is a contradiction of the mussed style of his hair. It speaks volumes as to the frustration I'm sure he feels. He will have pulled an all-nighter, working relentlessly through the night to find us answers as to who is behind these attacks. "Rome, it's good to see you."

Taking a seat in front of his desk, I lean back, cutting straight to the point when I ask, "What do we know?"

Aldo moves to stand behind Massimo's desk while Daniele sits in the chair beside me. I inhale deeply, trying to center myself and clear the blood rushing in my ears. The collective weight of our need for vengeance hangs over us like a cloud, darkening the mood of the room.

Opening a manila folder, Aldo pulls out it contents and places it on the desk in front of me. A report is clipped to the right, but my eyes are instantly drawn to the picture of a woman. She's dressed in yoga pants and a sports bra, with her jet-black hair tied back in a high ponytail. She looks like any New York Upper East Sider off to a yoga class. Her face is partially obscured, but it doesn't stop a tightness gripping my gut as my eyes roam over the grainy black and white image. She looks familiar and yet I'm sure I've never met her. *I'd have remembered.*

I clear my throat before asking, "Who is she?"

"*That* is Aurora Costa." There's a hint of venom in Massimo's tone when he says it. "Her father, Francesco Costa, is the one behind the most recent attack."

My brows pull together, a deep groove forming between them. The names sound familiar. I wrack my brain for why, but come up empty.

"Who is he, and how can you be sure he's responsible?" Daniele asks.

Massimo flexes his fist atop the mahogany desk and Aldo steps forward, updating us further. "Francesco was Dario's underboss. His signature was on the device that exploded at the dock. One of our guys from the police department shared the evidence they've collected. As you can see..."

Aldo spreads three more photographs across the desk, hiding the one of Aurora from view. He points out the remnants of the device surrounded by dirt and debris. The infinity symbol with 'F' and 'C' in the loops is visible under the thin layer of dust. "This is Costa's signature. There's no doubt in my mind about it. This was his MO, his calling card, whatever you want to call it. He would always leave an infinity symbol behind. Of course, we—*la famiglia*—are the only ones who know this and can attribute it to him. I've asked for the police to stall in their investigations so we can get ahead of this with our own."

"It sounds like you've made good progress." I pause, considering everything that's laid out in front of me. My hand lifts, pushing away the photos of the device and picking up the one of Aurora. I stare at it, silently urging her image to turn toward the camera so I can see her properly. Realizing I'm being ridiculous, I drop the photo back onto the desk and sit back, before asking, "What does the daughter have to do with this?"

With a defeated exhale, Massimo leans forward, resting his elbows on his desk. "The only lead we have is *her*. It seems Francesco has managed to go into hiding. We've spoken to everybody who knows him or could have a possible lead to his whereabouts and have come up empty. It seems that nobody knows where he is." He pulls in a breath, running his tongue over his teeth as he exhales. "Of course, it's possible someone is covering for him, and if they are, we will deal with them, but I think we need to go after her. She's the only lead we haven't chased down." He pauses, his gaze firmly on me when he implores, "Going after her, *his family*, will bring him out."

A cold weight settles into the pit of my stomach. I know exactly what Massimo is asking. In order to seek retribution, we need to sink to a level I swore I never would. To a level that no man—as far as I'm aware—in our family ever has. I chew at the flesh on the inside of my cheek. There has to be another way, one that doesn't involve *this*.

"We've stayed up all night, Rome. Every possibility has been considered and I'm telling you, *this* is the only way to draw him out." Massimo's words are meant to soothe, but all they do is add to the unease.

"So why not just kidnap her?"

In my sixteen years as head of the family, I've never had to give an order to kill a woman, and the thought of doing so doesn't sit right with me.

"An eye for an eye. He's killed our men; we need to hit him where it hurts."

Resting my chin on my fist, I reply, "What if we kill her and he still carries on?"

"Then we think of a new plan."

"Massimo, we need to think with our heads, not our hearts. If we kill her and he carries on, then it was for nothing."

Drumming his fingers on the desk, he leans back, regarding me. "It would never be for nothing. We kill her and we lure him out. *She* is the key to finding him and if that makes her collateral damage, that's on him, not us."

I regard him for the longest time. My family—*the mafia*—will always come first and if killing Aurora Costa is the only way to protect them, then it must be done.

Reluctantly, I reply, "Okay." Picking up her photo, I allow myself one last look before dropping it face down on top of the others. "The gravity of this decision can't be lost on us. If he cares for her as deeply as we suspect, then we need to be prepared for the consequences of taking her life. Because Francesco *will* come out on the attack."

One by one, I make eye contact with the men I trust the most. They nod in agreement, and when my eyes meet Massimo's, I say, "I don't expect any of your men to break the oath they made. As the head of the family, it's my burden to carry."

Women and children have been off-limits for as long as the mafia has been around. We do not touch them. They have always been considered innocent, unsullied by the heinous acts we carry out. In making the decision I have today, I'm effectively saying that a rule we have abided by for centuries is null and void, opening us up to repercussions we might not want.

Chapter 3

Aurora

There's a faint lingering of death and destruction permeating the air as I hold my apartment door open. The light in the hallway flickers as I stand with one foot in the entryway of my apartment and the other still in the hallway, considering my options. Whoever he is, I knew he was here before I unlocked the door. Yet, I didn't do what any sane person would. *I should turn around and run. It's not too late.*

I knew this day would come. The world my father occupies was always going to find me, no matter how far I tried to distance myself from it.

It would be easy to blame my lack of self-preservation on working sixteen-hour shifts as an emergency dispatcher, but deep down, I know I can't. Something much darker that's been festering inside of me for years is in control of me now. It twists and turns in my gut, propelling me forward with a bravado and acceptance of whatever my future holds. Crossing the threshold, I brace myself, ready to come face-to-face with the devil who's waiting for me.

Just like I've been waiting for him.

An awareness ripples through me, my body warming as I kick the door closed behind me. From my position by the front door, I have a view of my living room and kitchen. There's no sign of him. He must be hidden in the shadows, because I *know* he's here. I can feel him, like the ground beneath me.

Adrenaline courses through my body, and although I don't know why he's here or what he might be after, I'm ready for the confrontation. *For the excitement.*

Hanging my keys on the hook by the door, I go through the motions of taking off my jacket and putting it in the cupboard by the door with my bag. It's been raining pretty much nonstop for the last four days, and although my feet are soaked and cold in my sneakers, I keep them on. Hopefully, they'll give me an advantage should I need to fight him.

Moving in the direction of my bedroom, the squeak of my shoes punctuates the air. The hairs on the back of my neck stand on end. I can feel his eyes on me, slowly hunting his prey.

My breathing is steady, portraying none of the panic that's now bubbling beneath the surface. *Maybe this wasn't such a good idea.* I don't bother with the lights, allowing the darkness to envelop me as I navigate the familiarity of my apartment, praying to God that he doesn't make himself known before I'm ready.

My mind goes to my bedside table and the 9mm gun I have taped to the inside of the top drawer. I've never had a reason to use it, but after the couple who live in the apartment above me were robbed, I figured it was better to be safe than sorry. I'm not sure what use it will be to me now but it might buy me some time.

I clench my jaw, annoyed at the invasion of *my* home. *Who does he think he is?* Breaking into my apartment, waiting to... to do who knows what. Pressing my lips together, I slip into my bedroom at the end of the hallway.

Moonlight floods the space, a beam guiding my path to the bedside table. I don't bother to close the door behind me. It creaks from where I haven't had time to grease the hinges and I don't want to give him a reason to come and find me just yet.

An urgency overtakes me as I open the drawer, my hand diving in and coming up empty, before my movements turn desperate as I search for the unused object. My mouth goes dry, and I shake my head in denial. Realization makes my shoulders slump, and I exhale heavily, staring at my empty hands like the weapon may appear if I wish for it hard enough. The reality is, he's found it. *Of course he has.*

I'm going to die.

A sick, yearning smile pulls at the corners of my mouth before falling away when the hard nozzle of a gun is jabbed into the back of my head. I feel his heat at my back, warming my body, and curse myself for not leaving when I had the chance.

"Looking for something, Aurora?" His slightly accented voice sends a flutter of need to the pit of my stomach. There's a dark and dangerous edge to his tone.

I close my eyes, forcing my body to sink into the anticipation of what's to come. *This is how it ends? A bullet through the back of the head from a man I don't know? Maybe that isn't his plan at all. He could have killed me already.*

Scenarios run through my mind, each one becoming more and more violent. *Can I get out of here alive? Do I even want to?* I dismiss the last question before it fully forms. Obviously, I want to get out of here. But trying to fight him will use up strength that I might need to preserve, because even without seeing him, I know he'll overpower me. The thought sends a ripple of awareness down my spine, but I fight against it, holding my body still. A light sheen of sweat coats my upper lip, and I dig my fingernails into the palms of my hands, the pain a welcome distraction.

The cocktail of fear and powerlessness slides its way through my body, stiffening my limbs and crushing my posture. There's going to be no way out of here alive.

I harden my expression, unwilling to show him any fear, and wait for his next move. Fighting him might make the end come quicker, but there would be no dignity in it, and although I could scream, in this building, nobody would come. *I'm on my own now.* I'll meet my maker with peace in my heart, even if the devil is the one pushing me out of existence.

I thought I'd have more uncertainty; more of a will to live when the end came. All I feel is acceptance and a desire to be free. I push my head back onto the barrel, silently begging him to pull the trigger.

A dark chuckle reverberates in his chest. *He's teasing me.* The pieces slip into place like dominoes falling. Killing me quickly doesn't give him what he needs or what he came for. He's going to drag this out until I'm begging him to end it.

I refuse to give him the satisfaction.

He might have orders, but there will be no pleas falling from my lips today. Whoever has sent this *mobster* will be sorely disappointed.

Inhaling deeply, his expensive cologne sends a frisson of awareness to my core. *God, what is wrong with me?* I hold my breath, refusing to dwell on the fact that his scent is both arousing and comforting at the same time. It's irrelevant to my life being taken.

He moves closer, but still manages to keep his body away from mine. The movement pushes the gun harder against my skull. The baritone of his voice feels deeper now, commanding and calm, when he says, "No sudden movements, *bella*. We're going into the living room."

I swallow thickly, turning toward the door. He remains out of my eyeline as he follows behind me. My movements are slow and cautious, as if I'm pushing through treacle; each step harder than the last as we walk.

Frowning, I tilt my head as I come to a stop on the edge of the living room. One of the chairs from the table in the kitchen is positioned in front of the large bay window. I rented this apartment for that window and how the morning light spills in through it. It doesn't make much sense to kill me there, not when anyone could potentially witness it. Maybe that's the point. He *wants* to make a show of my death.

Biting down on my lip, my eyes dart over to the chair I usually sit in to read—*my mom's armchair*. It's been carelessly pushed to the side, and now, instead of facing the window, it's pointing into the room. Heat flushes through my body, and I noisily blow out a breath. His lack of care for my possessions is angering me more than his presence in my home.

A nudge to my back propels me forward and out of my own head. I stumble over my feet, but his large hand wraps around my elbow, halting me. A zing jolts through me from the contact, and I suck in a breath before snatching my arm back. *What the fuck was that?*

I move through the room, my chin held high. Sliding into the chair, I focus on the rain falling just beyond the windowpane. The sky is gray and overcast, adding to the ominous feeling filling the room and threatening to suffo-cate me.

Moving into my line of sight, he blocks my view. The glow from the street lamps outside illuminate the room enough for me to see his face for the first time. I blink rapidly, trying to reconcile the handsome man standing in front of me with the acts I know he's here to commit.

His hair is slicked back, curling at the collar of his shirt and his intense dark eyes—they almost look demonic —are framed by the longest lashes I've ever seen on a man. We hold each other's gaze until I can't take anymore and drop my focus to the muscle ticking in his stubbled jaw. My eyes move to his mouth and the fullness of his lips before I force myself to look away.

Even the clothes he's wearing are very fitting for the role he's here to fulfill. A black shirt, with a silk-looking waistcoat covering his torso. His sleeves are rolled up, the corded muscles of his forearms a further reminder of the power he exudes.

His movements are meticulous as he picks up a roll of duct tape and begins to secure me to the chair. I consider making a move to try and take the other gun from the black leather holster secured to his chest, but think better of it. Instead, I return my attention to the window, a million questions on the tip of my tongue fighting to be voiced.

Who is he?

What does he want from me?

How did he get into my apartment?

Will he take his time or put me out of my misery before I've had a chance to say a word?

The sound of tape being pulled brings my attention back to him, and I watch, fascinated, as he puts it between his straight, white teeth and rips. A smirk lifts the corner of his mouth, and I look away, huffing out a breath. *This isn't even remotely funny.*

Without a word, his fingers thrust into my hair, and he jerks my head back. The sting remains, even after he's released me. He covers my mouth with the tape and moves to the armchair, sinking into the cushions. His posture is relaxed and sure, like he has no qualms about his reason for being here.

I might be in a compromised position, with my feet and hands bound, and tape covering my mouth, but I'm still feeding off his energy. *I'm not fearful.* My heart isn't racing and the adrenaline that was there when I first got home is now gone. I feel almost serene.

When I was a kid, I had moments of wondering what death would feel like. The thoughts alone would terrify me, but right now, I'm not scared. I'm not worried about the agonizing murder this monster no doubt has planned for me. *No.* I embrace it.

I welcome him dragging me into the pits of hell and ending my nonexistence. Ending the life I've wasted, running from my demons, and hiding like a coward. Perhaps I should be promising to do more, *to be more*, if I can just get out of this mess, but there's no point.

The end is inevitable, whether I go today or in fifty years.

For the longest time, he sits quietly in the corner of the room, hidden in the shadows. *Watching me.* I try to block him out, using the time to make peace with myself.

The gentle patter of rain against the window soothes me as I reflect on my life. There are so many things I could have done differently, but what's done is done. There's nothing left for me to do but accept where I went wrong and let go of the hate and resentment that I've held on to for far too long.

The sound of the rain and the city beyond the window are like a lullaby to my exhausted mind. My eyes flutter shut and my breath becomes labored as I try and fail to fight against the fatigue.

He stands, cracking his knuckles as he moves around the room and behind me. When I open my eyes again, I stare ahead at the inky black sky, trying my hardest to switch off my body's awareness of him.

I shuffle back in the chair, the hairs on the back of my neck standing to attention at his proximity behind me. His thick fingers take hold of my nose, cutting off my air supply as he forces my head back so my gaze connects to his.

This is it.

My heart beats an erratic rhythm in my chest and my pulse pounds in my ears. Digging my fingers into the armrest, I force the panic flooding me to subside. His grip slips slightly from the slick sweat forming on my face. My mouth fights against the tape, the sting of my skin being pulled doing nothing to dim the smile that's forming on my lips. *I've been looking forward to this moment for the longest time.* My lungs burn. The natural instinct to fight wages an internal war with my mind's desire to give in.

His voice is gruff, something akin to admiration shining in his eyes as he asks, "You want to die, don't you, *cucciola?*"

If only you knew.

I drink in his reaction to what he's doing to me. Full lips lift at the corner, his strong jaw clenching and grinding in a hypnotic dance. Now that he's closer, I'm drawn to the darkest blue eyes I've ever seen. I'm starting to realize this isn't a mobster. He's definitely in the mafia, but everything about him screams power and control.

Has he had to do this often?

It doesn't matter. There's too much noise in my head, and I close my eyes in an attempt to shut him out. Like coming home, I sink back into the darkness that twists and turns as it envelops me. Nothing matters now.

I'll see you soon, Mama.

My chest loosens, and I drift into a cloud of relief. A curtain of peacefulness descends on me and then... he releases me. Instinctively, I inhale a desperate breath. My lungs scream as I suck in heavy breaths through my nose, my eyes darting open and searching for him. Demands I know I have no right to make are at the forefront of my mind: *Finish me, dammit.*

The pad of his thumb strokes over the apple of my cheek in a move that seems far too tender for a man like him. Yet, I watch, intrigued, as he lifts it to his mouth, sucking on the flesh. There's something almost possessive about the act and it has a pool of warmth flooding my core.

My brow furrows, unsure of what to make of him or my reaction. Forcing my gaze away, I curse myself when I register the wetness on my cheek. *Great.* No doubt he's taken my tears as a sign of weakness.

"Costa women don't show weakness; unless it can be used as a strength." My mom's words ring in my ears, and I set my shoulders back, determination stiffening my spine.

He stands tall, moving to lean against the wall, crossing his arms over his broad chest. "My name is Romeo Bianchi, and I am the head of The Sicilian Mafia. Your father has committed a crime against *la mia famiglia* and he must pay."

Chapter 4

Aurora

Shifting my attention away from Romeo Bianchi—head of the *fucking* mafia—I fight against the rising tide of emotions threatening to suffocate me. The weight of my circumstance sits squarely on my chest; *heavy and painful*. He doesn't say a word, the only sounds around us that of the storm outside and the creaking of the old building.

My eyes flutter closed and I huff out a bewildered laugh. *I'm going to die because of the actions of a man I haven't seen or spoken to in over ten years*. My last words to Francesco Costa—*my father*—were screamed with all the hatred, sadness, and anger I couldn't hide as he *walked away* from me. I told him that he was dead to me, and if he left, I didn't want to see him again. Despite my threats, he went without so much as a backward glance. Without an ounce of remorse.

There is no hope of him coming to my rescue.

Romeo clears his throat and my eyes pop open. My *executioner* moves into my line of sight, scrubbing a hand over his jaw. Following the motion, my focus lands on the black gloves adorning his hands.

"Perhaps you need a reminder of the gravity of the situation you're in, Aurora, because I don't think you get what my presence here means."

Oh, believe me, I do.

I tighten my fists and hold his intense stare, ignoring the way my muscles tense and a thread of trepidation weaves its way through my body with each passing second. I work like crazy to keep it hidden from him. Showing any weakness will only mean he's won.

He takes a step forward, followed by another, until his legs are less than an inch away from me. I keep my attention on that tiny gap. In my periphery, I see him lift a gloved hand, and I brace for the impact. He's probably frustrated, angry even, by my lack of fear.

But instead of hitting me, he peels away the tape. Air hisses through my clenched teeth at the sharp sting left behind. He meticulously folds the strip before dropping it on the windowsill. "Do you understand the predicament your father has put you in, *cucciola*?"

I nod. Even with my limited knowledge of what my father was involved in and who this man is, it's easy enough to grasp. And yet I can't seem to make myself care. My shoulders slump and my breathing evens out. I welcome the numbness that's invading my body, pulling it into my embrace until I feel nothing but peace.

Will the sun still shine when I'm gone?

Of course, I know it will. Even if it hasn't made an appearance for me since the day my mom died. Darkness has been the only thing I've known for twelve long years. It's probably why nobody will notice when I've gone.

I've coasted through life with little to no human interaction. I should have made friends. Hell, I should have *tried* to live my life instead of wallowing in my grief. *Would she be disappointed in me because of it? Or would she understand that nothing made sense and I just couldn't cope without her?*

Either way, the sun will still rise and set, the world will keep spinning, and people will continue to come and go.

"Aurora."

It's a command that rolls off his tongue in a way it never has with anyone else. A jolt of something that has no right to be there passes through me, settling in my core with ease. As I'm sure he intended, I lift my wide eyes to him, my mouth slightly agape and unspoken questions hanging in the air between us.

"Speak."

My head rears back and my brow tugs together. *Someone should teach this guy some manners. Who the fuck does he think he is?* I don't bark just because he—or anyone, for that matter—demands that I do. In fact, he can shove his question up his ass. I look away, my teeth grinding as I fight against the desire to tell him to do just that.

His hand darts out and seizes my chin, forcing me to look at him. There is no gentleness in his hold. No, he's showing me a glimpse of his power. *Well, I didn't need it.* His fingers dig into my jaw so tightly I'm surprised it doesn't crack in his grip. He dips until his forehead presses painfully onto mine.

Despite the physical discomfort he's causing me, I can't stop myself from pulling in a breath at his proximity. My senses are assaulted by his clean, woodsy scent as his cobalt-blue eyes meet my sea-green ones in an almost volatile moment.

Easing up on his assault, he smooths his thumb over my jaw as he demands, "Use your words, Aurora." He pauses. "Do you understand?"

I swallow thickly, my voice betraying me and coming out as nothing more than a croak. "Yes, I understand but—"

Romeo steps away, dropping my chin like it's on fire and cutting me off as he says, "Good. Now, where is your father?"

Rolling my eyes, I blow out an exasperated breath. "If you'd let me finish." My reply has too much sass coating the words, especially given the interaction we've just had.

He bares his teeth in a snarl before raising a brow while he waits for me to continue.

I tell him the truth. That's all I have. "I don't know where Francesco is because we haven't spoken in years."

A shadow passes over his features, and when he finally speaks, his voice sounds even darker and deeper than it did moments ago. "What should I do with you, *bella*? Should I take you until your weasel of a father comes crawling out to save you? Or should I send a message to him now? Maybe cutting off a finger for every lie you tell will be enough to draw him out."

My fingers flex on the arms of the chair as I grip them. He stuffs his hands into the pockets of his black slacks. His stance is relaxed and deceptively calm, given he's just described how he plans to dismember me.

He moves to lean against the arm of my mom's armchair, before he continues, "No. I think perhaps I should skin you alive. Send your father a video to commemorate the process. Your screams of terror will haunt him every day until I track him down and show him *il vero diavolo*. It would be the least the pair of you deserve because thinking I am stupid seems to run in your family. I know he's been watching you, *bella*. I found the cameras and the empty apartment across the street."

My mouth falls open before I catch myself and snap it shut. *What is he talking about?* A groove forms between my brows and my eyes dart around the room, wondering if the surveillance made its way into my apartment.

Stretching his neck, he looks around the curtain, directing my attention to the building across the way. I haven't paid much attention to it. *Why would I?* A shudder races down my spine when my eyes land on the only floor in the building that's pitch black. Romeo lifts his hand in what looks like a signal to someone in the other building. A light from a torch shines in one of the windows and I can just about make out the silhouette of a man. The beam of light lands on a metal rod, moving upward until a small camera atop a tripod comes into view.

Somebody has been watching me?

For how long?

For the first time since I walked into my apartment today, true fear takes hold of me, creeping into my blood and turning my skin cold. I can feel it rushing through my body, sucking the life from my being. My body revolts, fighting against the tape on my wrists.

I never asked to be a part of this life.

Dropping my focus to the floor, I pull in a breath and blow it out, accepting the fact that Romeo Bianchi isn't the man to give me any answers. There's no use in me losing my shit over this. Closing my eyes, I swallow thickly, pushing down the panic that's simmering beneath the surface.

When I open them again, I find Romeo watching me. "Not that I get a say, but my preference would be for you to kill me as quickly as possible. And for what it's worth, I am sorry my father wronged you."

He takes the three or so steps it takes to come to a stop in front of me. I steel myself against the effect his proximity has on me. I expect him to do what he's done each time he's made this exact power move, because that's what this is. *A power move*. A way for him to instill fear in me and make me more pliable. But he's in for a surprise, as I refuse to do either.

Pulling a hand out of his pocket, he brings it toward me. There's no emotion on his face. In fact, he looks cool, calm, and collected when he tightens his hand around my throat. The pressure isn't enough to cut off my air supply, but it does give me a stark reminder of the power he has over me... the power to take my life with one squeeze of his hand.

What feels like a current of electricity passes between us, as he strokes his thumb down the column of my throat. I fight against the overwhelming urge to swallow thickly, worried that he might take it as a sign of weakness. My eyes get heavy each time he touches me and moisture floods my mouth.

Begging is beneath me.

But what would I be begging for?

Romeo drops his hand. I fist mine, grateful they are tied to the chair and unable to hold the heated skin on my neck. Forcing my breathing to remain even, I keep my eyes ahead as he walks behind me. I watch his reflection in the window as he picks up something from the coffee table. When he turns, the glint of metal is hard to miss, even in the dimly lit room. A fluttering of anticipation zaps through my chest before it's gone. Wetting my lips, I search for the words to beg for my life but come up empty. Even as I open my mouth to speak, nothing comes out.

He stands behind me, the knife in his hand and his

head tilted. I sit back in the chair. The tension I've been holding on to for far longer than tonight ebbs away, leaving me feeling relaxed. I accept my fate at the hands of what I'm sure is one of the deadliest men I've ever met. My eyes flutter closed, and I hone in on the feel of every breath. Each inhale and exhale is a gift about to be taken away.

The cold metal presses gently on the exposed skin at the base of my neck. *This won't be quick.* It can take anywhere from six to ten minutes to bleed out from cutting the carotid artery. He drags the knife across my shoulder and down my right arm. Goosebumps follow in its wake and my nipples pebble from the excitement that comes with the danger. The pull of the tape being cut has me sucking in an audible breath as surprise steals my fear.

"If you try to run, I will break both of your legs. If you cooperate with me, *cucciola*, well, then I'll set you free. *Capisci*?" His voice is dark, but there's a note hidden somewhere in the depths that sounds like he might regret the words he utters.

I don't want to be free.

Not in the way he means, at least. Yet I still find myself nodding, despite the dark, twisted side of me wanting to test his threat.

With the tape removed from my wrists and ankles, he straightens, throwing the knife onto the couch behind me. "Stand in front of the window."

Getting out of the chair, I do as he demands. This has

to be a trick. There's a camera across the street, one Francesco supposedly set up. *Is he going to kill me in front of it?*

All thoughts leave me when Romeo's heat engulfs me from behind. My body tenses, and I force my attention down to the street below. Anything to not meet his captivating stare in the reflection of the windowpane. A row of black SUVs line the street, abandoned in the middle of the road. *How did I miss those when I came home?*

Romeo places his now bare hand on my hip and presses his body into mine. His solid build is almost comforting, begging me to lean back into him. I know I shouldn't, but I crave the intimacy that I think he could give me. But that's another version of us; one that doesn't exist and never has. Standing rigid, I ignore the feelings stirring in my gut from his proximity. "Smile for the camera, Aurora," he murmurs, his warm breath dusting my ear.

As if I'm a puppet to his every command, my eyes lift, finding the window across the street from earlier. Looking in from the outside, the way his hand is resting on me and the closeness of our bodies, it might look like an intimate embrace.

When his hand moves under my T-shirt, the roughness of his palm grazing my stomach has me suppressing a primal moan. The sensation his fingers leave behind on my heated skin has my head sagging and my body melting into him as his hard length against my back drags the moan from my mouth.

I need more. My hips grind in small, slow movements. I feel wanton. Bracing my hands on the window frame, I dig my nails into the wood to keep from touching myself. It would be so easy to give in to this attraction I feel for him.

He fists my hair with his free hand, yanking on the strands as his grip on my hip tightens to the point of pain. He jerks my head to the side and buries his nose into the crook of my neck. Instinctively, my back arches, and my eyes close, my body craving *more*.

With his hand still resting on my bare skin, burning into the flesh with a heat I haven't felt in a long time, he licks the column of my throat, nipping my earlobe. A dark chuckle falls from his lips, echoing around the room and penetrating the haze that I was happy to drown in.

Heaving my eyes open, I meet his in the reflection of the glass. A smirk pulls at the corner of his full mouth, amusement dancing in his eyes. *I've played right into his hands*.

"*Bella,* you put on an even better show than I could've asked for. You just might be of some use yet."

Chapter 5

Romeo

We hit traffic almost as soon as we pull away from Aurora's apartment building. Cars are travel slowly, mindful of the slick, rain-covered streets. *City living isn't for me.* There are too many people. Too many chances of someone stumbling onto something they shouldn't. The air is pungent with the smell of a million people and *nothing* is clean.

Although there are *some* positives. People tend to turn a blind eye to anything that might give them trouble. And, on the rare occasion someone wants to play the hero, a hardened stare works well enough to send them away.

I turn my attention back to the woman in the backseat beside me with her stiff posture and body turned toward the door. Her jasmine scent has been teasing me ever since I walked into her apartment. The plan was simple: get Francesco's location and then get rid of her.

Make it look like an accident or suicide, scrubbing away any trace of me in her apartment.

But there's something about Aurora Costa that intrigues me. I could chalk it up to being used to the energy shifting in a room whenever I walk in, or people cowering and there being none of that with her. But she's like nobody I've ever met before. The fact that she was fucking *smiling* at the idea of me killing her, well, that fascinated me.

Watching the peace that came with her acceptance had me making a decision that could go one of two ways. Either it will be detrimental to my family or work exactly as I think it will in luring Francesco out.

Her lifeless body should be back in her apartment. She shouldn't be sitting here, bound and blindfolded, as we head back to Massimo's.

It takes us nearly two hours to get from Aurora's apartment in Brooklyn back to Sandy Brook. The rain slowed us down, but once we left behind the city and apartment blocks turned into mansions with acres, the drive flew by. I expected Aurora to put up more of a fight as the journey went on, but the quiet has been soothing.

Daniele navigates the car, his attention occasionally shifting from the road ahead to the rearview mirror. He wants to know what my plan is, but he should know by now that whatever it is, I've thought it through. Bringing Aurora with us was the right move. If I'd killed her, we'd be back to square one with no clue where Francesco is. At least now we have *something*.

Aurora's soft voice cuts through the quiet of the car. "Where are we going?"

My eyes roam freely over her, mentally tracing the contours of her body. There's no reason for me to share that information with her. She's my prisoner, my enemy. And yet, I still find myself replying. "To my cousin's property. You'll stay there until your father gives himself up."

Her head dips, before she thinks better of it, and squares her shoulders, turning toward me. Even without her eyes on me, my body heats to an almost unbearable temperature. Just knowing that her *intention* is to give me her full focus is enough.

Aurora licks her lips. The sight of her pink tongue and the trail of wetness it leaves behind is a distraction that sends a shameful bolt of lust into my gut. Unfazed, she declares, "I've already told you, Francesco won't come for me. You're just wasting your time and delaying what we both know is going to happen to me."

She's adamant that death will be the inevitable outcome for her. I want to prove her wrong, but given that will most likely happen, I can't. Instead, I rip my eyes away from her and reply, "We'll see about that, *cucciola.*"

Aurora sighs heavily. The dull thud of her head dropping onto the headrest echoes around the car, and she mutters something to herself that I can't quite make out.

Running my tongue over my teeth, I pick at a piece of lint on my pant leg. Lifting my eyes to her again, I say, "I'll offer you some friendly advice, Aurora. If you want to make it out of this situation alive, get rid of the attitude. It's a surefire way to end up at the bottom of the river."

She flinches, and my brows pull together at the slight quiver in her jaw. It's at odds with the strong-willed woman she portrays. When she turns back toward the door, I shake off the ache that settles in my chest. Pulling out my phone, I bring up the message thread with Massimo.

ROMEO

We're five minutes out.

MASSIMO

It would have been quicker if you took the helicopter. Just saying, cousin.

I don't acknowledge his comment because, although it would have, I thought I needed the drive to clear my mind for the task at hand. My phone buzzes.

MASSIMO

Is it done?

The news of our guest will be best delivered in person. Massimo is the type of person to react, then ask questions. It's served him well this far in life but, right now at least, it isn't the kind of leadership we need. If I'm in front of him, he can let his frustration out on me and won't make any rash moves.

I swipe left on the notification and open up my emails. Since touching down yesterday, I haven't had a chance to filter through them. My legitimate businesses in Palermo are what keep me clean. Certain people that I do business with—typically politicians and police officials —prefer to operate under the guise of legality. It's common knowledge what my actual job is, regardless of the front I put on.

When the convoy of cars pulls into the circular driveway of Massimo's estate, I climb out before Daniele can bring the car to a complete stop. Rain pelts down, quickly soaking my hair and clothes. *Does it only ever rain here?*

Daniele doesn't hesitate, stepping from the car and meeting me by the back passenger door. His shoulders hunch, and he lifts the collar of his jacket to cover his neck.

Speaking in Italian, I instruct, *"Take her into the house through the side entrance. Put her in the basement and leave the blindfold and restraints on. I'll deal with her myself once I've updated Massimo."*

"Yes, boss." His words trail after me as I stride toward the house.

The sound of shoes crunching on the gravel mixes with the downpour of rain as I jog up the front steps. I'm intent on finding Massimo and getting a plan figured out on what our next move is, but there's still an awareness of her. No matter how much I try to brush it off, it's still there, burying itself under my skin and into my blood.

I push through the front door, coming to a halt at the eerie quiet that greets me. There's a different atmosphere to the house now than there was yesterday. There's no low murmur of chatter and people going about their jobs. You could hear a pin drop.

My hand itches to reach for my weapon, but with my guard up, I cross the lobby and head in the direction of Massimo's office. The squeak of my dress shoes on the white marble floor echoes around me.

With a knock to announce my presence, rather than born out of manners, I push open his office door. I'm fully prepared for a shit storm when I break the news to him. Despite there being a clear hierarchy, sometimes Massimo forgets that *I* have the final say over things. The lines have blurred and been crossed many times between us and perhaps I've been too soft on him, given he's my family.

I stroll into the room, not caring that droplets of rain are falling onto the cream carpet. Warmth hits me, closely followed by the stench of a man who hasn't showered in a couple of days. I divert to the window, pulling it open a little before I take a seat in front of his desk. Aside from his laptop and a few manila folders, the desktop is clear.

My face twists, and I wrinkle my nose as I admonish, "*Dio*, cousin. Would it kill you to shower? It smells like something died in here."

Massimo ignores my question. His bloodshot, tired eyes are wide and pleading for information. "How did it go?"

I huff out a laugh, turning away to look out the window. Rolling hills fill the view, the animals grazing, reminding me of home even with the downpour that is yet to ease up. Scrubbing a hand over my jaw, I try and fail to come up with the right words to ease him into our new circumstances.

At my continued silence, Massimo urges, "Come on, Rome. Now isn't the time to block me out. Not when there's so much at stake. What did you find out from her? Does she know where he is?"

He's misinterpreted my silence for teasing. He should know better than anyone that I don't need reminding of the gravity of the situation.

Shrugging, I fix my gaze on him and reply, "She's in the basement."

Massimo jolts up from his chair before I've finished my sentence. It rolls back, crashing into the bookshelf and rattling the items on display from the force.

"She's where? Are you stupid, Romeo?" Indignation fills his voice, quickly followed by panic. "You can't bring a dead woman back to my *home*."

I stand, leaning my hands on the desk and holding his wide-eyed stare with mine. "Watch how you talk to me, Massimo. I'm still the head of this family and if I want to bring a fucking cemetery back to your house, I will. If I want to crucify a guy on your front lawn for your neighbors to see or paint your walls with the blood of our enemies, then *I. Will.* And there's nothing you can do to stop me."

He glares at me before reaching for his chair and

collapsing back into it. He drags a hand over his face, his exhaustion clear.

I smooth a hand down my chest before taking a seat. Crossing a leg over my knee, I reply, "I know this is difficult for you, Massimo, but questioning me is only going to end one way. Besides, I didn't say she was dead."

We stare at each other for a moment. I know he wants to question why I didn't go through with the plan, why I brought her here, and what's next. The muscle in his jaw ticks before he visibly forces his body to relax and asks, "So, what's the plan with her now?"

My tone conveys authority when I reply, "She doesn't know where he is, but I do know he has eyes on her. If he's as smart as we're giving him credit for being, I'm certain he will show up soon enough. And when he does, we'll take care of them both. For now, she will stay in the basement."

Massimo eyes me skeptically, but he's taken the reminder of our hierarchy and I know he won't argue with me, no matter how frustrated he is. "And how will we draw him out?"

Scrubbing my hand over my jaw, my gaze bounces around the office. Dark furniture fills the space, with a couch along one wall and two chairs against the opposite one. It suits Massimo. He's never been a *sunshine and light* kind of guy. Even as a kid, he was always about the darkness. It's what makes him so good as a don.

"By now, he should be aware that we have her. There was a live feed camera set up in the apartment across the road. Daniele and Leonardo went through the place, but it didn't look like there was any sign of anyone having been there recently."

Massimo nods distractedly. He tilts his head, asking, "If there didn't look to be anyone there recently, how do we know he's been watching her and it's not some other creep?"

"The simple answer is, we don't. At least not yet. Leonardo took the equipment and is on his way over to Callum's for him to put a trace on it. See who it belongs to."

Leonardo is Massimo's underboss, and aside from Daniele, the only one who can handle Callum and his... unpredictable ways.

"Irish Callum?"

I nod. "He's out of it."

"You and I both know there is no out of the mafia, Rome. Whether that be the Irish, the Italian, or even the fucking Russian."

Shrugging, I reply, "He's as out of it as he can be. He knows how important this is, so we should have some answers in a few hours."

A knock on the door halts our conversation. Massimo calls out for them to enter, and Daniele steps into the room, closing the door behind him.

"Romeo, Massimo." He nods as he comes to a stop in front of the desk. "She's in the basement. If you don't need me, I'll go get showered and pick up with Aldo on what he's got."

"Get some rest before you do. We need everyone to be on their A-game." A plan forms in my mind, and as Daniele turns back toward the door, I call out to him. My eyes are on Massimo when I say, "I'll be out for dinner this evening and I'll need you with me."

"Yes, boss."

At least someone isn't constantly needing a reminder of his position in this family. Massimo is staring back at me, his chin resting on his thumb and his fingers on his top lip. He cocks a brow.

"What?"

Sitting back in his chair, he moves a file from one side of his laptop to the other, replying, "Nothing."

"Come on, Massimo. You didn't have a problem questioning me a moment ago. What is it?"

He shakes his head, moving another file across, his focus on the task rather than me. "It's not my place to question you, Rome. You've made that damn clear today."

"And yet you're going to. Say whatever it is you've got to say."

Rolling his eyes, he finally brings his attention back to me, his fingers drumming lightly on the desk. "Fine. Do you really think now is the time to be going out for dinner with your US flavor of the month?"

Chuckling, I pull on my cuffs. My demeanor shifts, and I sit forward, resting my elbows on my knees. "I'm taking my *hostage* out for dinner. We might not know for certain that it's her father watching her, but we need to be seen if my plan is going to work."

Massimo shakes his head in what I'm assuming is disbelief, huffing out a breath. "And showing her off for the world to see is how you're going to achieve that? I guess that's one way to get it done."

"Exactly. And *when* we dispose of her, it will look like a rival has tried to exact revenge on me by killing 'my woman'. It's a win-win, really."

Stifling a yawn, Massimo rests his elbows on the mahogany desk. "If you think this is the best way to get to Francesco, then I trust your judgment. I just hope it's the right call, Rome, because he's still out there and willing to take risks to get to us."

Standing, I stuff my hands into my pockets and rock back on my heels. "I know what I have planned is risky and that leaving the estate could come with an array of problems, but we won't find Francesco stuck behind these walls."

What I don't add, but hangs in the air around us, is that the sooner we get this resolved, the sooner I can leave.

Sincerely, Massimo replies, "I know. Just be careful, cousin."

My lips curl upward and I throw him a wink. "Aren't I always? I need you to get me a reservation, arrange for some publicity and then get some sleep. I meant what I said to Daniele; we all need to be on our A-game and we can't do that if we're exhausted. Oh, and I'll need her to look like a woman I'd date."

Without another word, I leave the office, moving on autopilot to our guest. Our entire existence comes with a level of danger at every turn, but the most dangerous person I've ever faced is bound and blindfolded in the basement.

Aurora is a distraction.

One I should spend as little time with as possible because she's likely to get me killed.

Chapter 6

Aurora

With my eyes covered, my other senses are heightened as I sit in the room I've been brought to. There's a strong damp smell, mixed with a hint of metallic that could only come from the spilling of blood, and a haunting chill to the air that sets me on edge.

I think I'm alone, but I haven't had the courage to bring myself to move, just in case. Surely, if I wasn't, someone would have made themselves known by now? It feels like hours since I was unceremoniously dumped in here.

Hesitantly, I test to see if my theory of being alone is true, twisting and pulling at the tape Romeo used to restrain me before we left my apartment. I hiss out a breath when the tape pulls at the hairs on my wrists.

I've barely moved before footsteps sound in the hallway and I freeze. *Fuck.* I should have removed the

48

blindfold when I had a chance. The sound of a key turning in the lock echoes around me, and a shiver races down my spine at the unknown. Goosebumps break out over my exposed skin and I shift in the uncomfortable metal seat.

Okay, whoever it is, is going to come in and do whatever they have planned for me. All I can do is fight like hell. I close my eyes and focus on my breathing. One. Two. Three. Four. *Box breathing*. My therapist taught me the technique as a way to focus and relieve stress after my mom died. It does little to ease me now. In fact, breathing in the stale air does nothing but make me feel nauseous.

My heart races as the true reality of my circumstances dawns on me. Back in my apartment, I had a sense of bravado that came from knowing my surroundings and hoping that whatever he had planned would be over quickly. Here, I don't know how long he's going to drag this out for, how much my body can handle, or if he'll be the only one.

I should have fought more.

Who am I kidding? I should have fought, period.

I've been submissive and gone along with whatever he's demanded. What's worse is that I can't say *why* that is. From his first command, I've been his puppet. Doing whatever he demands, and for what? So I can be used and abused until my final breath? *I don't think so.* I'm ashamed of myself for being a coward. This isn't how I was raised.

The door creaks as it's pushed open, and I listen

intently, tracking his movements. Much like back at my apartment, I sense that it's *him* as soon as he crosses the threshold. My mind and body are attuned to his presence in a way they have no right to be.

A weighted, tense air fills the room, pulling any oxygen into its bubble and making it hard to breathe. There can only be two reasons for him being here. Either he's going to put me out of my misery—which isn't likely, considering he could have done that at my apartment—or he's going to get started on making those threats he made earlier a reality.

I wait for him to make a move. To say something. But when the only sound is the heaviness of my own breathing and the blood rushing in my ears, my brows tug together.

Am I imagining that he's here?

Have I lost my mind?

I push myself to focus, listening intently for any sign of him. He appears in my mind like a picture. His hands touching my body. His breath on my neck. His warmth wrapped around me. I clench my thighs, my body taunting me at the faint memory of his skin on mine. A pool of warmth floods me, and I bite down on the soft flesh inside my mouth in an attempt to keep my body in check.

What is wrong with me? I tense, my whole body turning to stone. There's no way in hell that I am attracted to... to a *mob boss*. I clench my fists, determined to remain defiant and not make this any easier for him than I already have.

I shiver when he picks up my bound hands. The contact of his skin on mine is unexpected and yet that warmth from moments ago only intensifies. I could lie and pretend that my body's reaction is because he took me by surprise, but we both know that has nothing to do with it.

Holding my breath, I push down the feelings bubbling beneath the surface and wait for his next move. The brutal contact of his fist or the press of his gun against my temple. Now more than ever, I wish I'd taken off the blindfold. So I could observe him and show him, with my eyes, that I'm not afraid. Instead, I jut out my chin in the direction I think he's standing and show him with my body language how unafraid I am.

The relief I feel is palpable when the tape that was binding my wrists is released. I soothe the skin that I'm certain is red and marked. Romeo removes the blindfold next, his touch surprisingly soft. Blinking, my eyes adjust to the brightness of the room before settling on him. He stuffs the material in his pocket as he stares down at me. His face is covered in shadows created by the dim light of the room, but it does little to hide the handsome contours.

"You'll be staying here for the foreseeable future. There's a shower, toilet, and basin for you to wash up in and you'll be sent three meals a day. Whether or not you eat them is up to you. We're going to take some pictures later, so get cleaned up. I'll be back in a few hours." His tone is a cocktail of frustration and boredom, as if he'd rather be anywhere than standing in front of me.

My voice comes out as a croak, and I clear my throat. "Are there cameras in here?" If this room is used for what I think it is, they must have a camera, even if it's hidden.

"Yes."

The finality in that one word has my body collapsing back into the chair as Romeo turns his back to me and leaves the room. The sound of the key turning in the lock serves as a reminder of my current predicament. My eyes sting as I look around.

There's not much to see. Gray cinder block walls surround me—I'm guessing the room is soundproof. A dim, bare light bulb gently swings overhead, casting the room in shadow. The floor slopes into the center, where a drain sits directly below the chair I'm seated in. In one corner is a cot and in another is the shower and toilet. If I wasn't so accepting of death, I'd be grateful that I've been granted a few more moments of life; even if it's in a room as gloomy as this one.

On unsteady legs, I stand from the chair and move to the cot. A blanket is folded up at the bottom of it, with some basic toiletries on top. *Ha. A five-star experience.* I reach out to pick up a bottle of shower gel before dropping my arm back to my side. Like running full force into a wall, I'm hit with the enormity of my situation. I'm a prisoner, trapped in a cell with no escape.

Wrapping my arms around my waist, I turn in a

circle. There isn't a hope of me making it out of this room without a fight. There are no windows and the door is the only way in or out. My brow furrows as I chew over what Romeo said moments ago. *"We're going to take some pictures later, so get cleaned up. I'll be back in a few hours."*

Sorry to break it to you, Mr. Bianchi, but we don't always get what we want. I won't be getting cleaned up and I sure as hell won't be taking any pictures with you. Why does he need me to be cleaned up? Surely it would look better if I was disheveled and dirty? His whole plan makes no sense. First, the show for the camera at my apartment and now...

It's like a light being switched on. He wants to make it look like we're *together*. I'm sure he thinks that my father will be so *incensed* that he'll come out of hiding and try to track me down. It'll be the perfect ruse to lure him to his inevitable death. Except Romeo didn't plan for me to *not* go along with his plan. He's going to kill me either way, and I'll be damned if I do as he demands. I won't be used like that.

You don't have much choice, Aurora.

Yes, I do. I'm a person. I have a say in what I do or don't do. And *Romeo Bianchi* has no control over me.

Turning back to the bed, I sweep the toiletries onto the floor. They land with a clatter, echoing around the room. I lower myself onto the brown-stained mattress, curling into the fetal position. With my back to the room, my eyes trace over the cracks in the wall and the faint scratch marks of past prisoners before I close them, shutting out my surroundings. I blow out a breath and force my body to relax, hoping that with a little sleep, the dull throb behind my eyes will be gone. Even if the rest of my problems and reminders of the day I've had are still there when I wake up.

Chapter 7

Romeo

Steam billows around me as I walk out of the bathroom. Using the towel around my neck, I dry my hair. The grime of traveling is gone, and after a nap, I feel *marginally* more awake than I did when I came upstairs. My cell phone vibrates across the bedside table on the other side of the room.

The room I'm staying in is like any of the other guest rooms in this house. There are two large windows, one of which has a window seat. The furniture comprises a bed, two bedside tables, a mirror leaning against the wall, an armchair, and a small table. It's more than enough for what I need.

Swiping up my phone, I frown when a name I'm not expecting to see for a while flashes on the screen. I connect the call and bring it to my ear. "Callum?"

"I have some news for you."

My brows reach for my hairline, and I take a seat on the edge of the bed. "That was quick."

Callum chuckles, the sound mingling with the clattering of his keyboard. I can picture him, somewhere in a basement, surrounded by screens, his fingers flying across the keys as he hacks into something he shouldn't. "Leo expressed how important this one was, so I moved it to the top of my list."

Rubbing my eye, I ask, "What have you got for me?"

"Whoever set up the camera doesn't know much about IP addresses or tracking, for that matter. The computer has a record of every time they logged onto the live stream and I can give you an approximate location for where they are. Or were."

Dio, that sounds almost too good to be true. "What's the catch?"

Callum sighs heavily. "Whoever has been watching her hasn't been online for the last few weeks. It could be that they've lost interest or they've moved away, but unfortunately, it doesn't look like you'll find anything when you get there."

Great. It's effectively a dead end unless there's something at that address. *Would he be stupid enough to still be there and not have eyes on her? Is he the kind of man that would leave her for the wolves?*

There's too much that we don't yet know, but starting at that address is as good a place as any. Right after the show I need to put on with Aurora. He might not be accessing that feed, but it'll be a little hard not to notice her face splashed across the internet.

Pushing a hand through my damp hair, I reply, "Send over the details you have, and we'll reach out if we need anything more."

"Got it."

The call disconnects and I throw the phone on the bed. Leaning forward, I hold my head in my hands, the beginnings of a headache throbbing behind my eyes. In the solitude of my room, I can let my guard down, even if it's only to show myself how exhausted I am.

Running my hands down my face, I exhale heavily before standing. The last thing I want to do is go out tonight. Not when there are so many more important things to be doing, like going to that address and finding out what's there. There *has* to be something.

I stand, heading in the direction of the closet as I replay the conversation with Callum. What he's found might not be the lead we were looking for, but it's more than what we had before I took Aurora. Maybe she was telling the truth when she said she hadn't heard from her father in years. *Right, and people always tell the truth when their lives are on the line.*

I go through the motions of getting dressed, and as I'm buttoning up my black dress shirt, there's a knock at the bedroom door.

Massimo walks in as I stride out of the closet. He inclines his head before moving over to the armchair by the window. He sets two glasses and a bottle of scotch on the small table.

Fastening my cuffs, I come to a stop next to him. "Have you slept?"

He finishes pouring the amber liquid into each glass before he turns, holding one of them out. I take it from him and he collapses into the chair, tipping his head back and exhaling a long, tired breath.

His eyes are small slits, giving me my answer before he even speaks. "Not yet, but I will later. You have a reservation for two at eight. As requested, the paparazzi will be there to welcome you. And two girls will be here at six to do her hair and make-up." He takes a sip of his drink before he asks, "Do you own any clothes that aren't black?"

Cocking a brow, I tease, "Are you trying to give me fashion advice?"

"I mean..." He looks me up and down. "Someone should."

"Right, because you're one to talk. We're practically wearing the same thing."

Massimo shrugs, smothering another yawn. "Right, but mine goes with the name."

I can't help but chuckle at that. Massimo has the nickname 'The Crow'. He picked it up when he was younger and would take shiny things that caught his eye. It's a badge of honor for him now, even if he doesn't steal things anymore.

"So I should try out some pointy horns and wear all red?"

"Some color wouldn't hurt," he quips back.

I've missed this. Having someone to be myself with and not constantly on guard. Every interaction I have is shrouded in darkness. And even though I can accept that it comes with the territory, sometimes there needs to be a hint of light.

Brushing off the melancholy thoughts that have no place in my world, I step in front of the mirror. I tuck my shirt into my pants and fasten my belt before meeting Massimo's gaze in the reflection and replying, "Maybe another day."

With my suit jacket on and my phone in my pocket, I walk to the bedroom door with Massimo trailing behind. I hold it open and when he's on the threshold, I say, "Callum called. He's got a lead, but it might come to nothing. I've asked him to email it over."

Massimo's eyes widen and he stares at me with accusations in his gaze. "You could have led with that, Rome. I'll get started on it tonight."

I clap him on the shoulder, applying a light pressure that gets him moving. Closing the door, I fall into step with him as we walk down the corridor and toward the stairs.

My tone is authoritative, brokering no argument when I say, "You won't. I didn't tell you this so you can do something with it. I told you so we have the same information. Get some sleep. We can pick this up again in the morning."

Massimo stops at the top of the stairs, turning to face me. A look of determination fills his face and he takes a step forward, his jaw set. "Rome, I appreciate you looking out for me, but I won't rest until we find out who did this. It's the least I can do for the men we lost."

I blow out a breath, smoothing a hand over my jaw. "All that will lead to is your death, and that's the last thing we need. You can't protect your men when you're dead. I say this as your don, Massimo, and I won't tell you again. Get. Some. Sleep."

Disappointment rounds his shoulders, a stony expression coating his features. I get it, but he's only likely to make mistakes if he's not rested. Huffing out a breath, he inclines his head before stalking off in the direction of his room.

The banging of a door in the distance concludes Massimo's exit, and I flick my wrist, checking the time. With one problem person solved, it's on to the next. We have an hour until her clothes arrive and if I've read Aurora right, she won't have showered like I asked her to.

It's about time I show her exactly who she's dealing with.

Chapter 8

Aurora

Waves of hostility crash into me, pulling me from my dreamless sleep long before the creak of the heavy door penetrates the haze. My eyes flutter open and I stare at the gray brick in front of me, confused as to where I am.

You're in a prison cell, Aurora.

Right, because I got kidnapped by some insane mafia don, who seems to think I know where my father is. Maybe if I go back to sleep, I'll wake up in my own bed and all of this will have been a dream. *Or a nightmare.* I squeeze my eyes shut, but his angry breathing and the hostility choking the air don't dissipate.

"What are you doing?"

It's a growled question, full of threat and meant to intimidate. I'm sure it's had the desired effect on others; people who have wanted to fight for their lives. But I want nothing more than for him to make good on his threats. For him to put me out of my misery.

At my silence, he closes the gap between us. His footsteps are light, and I imagine him prowling toward me like a majestic lion. Every fiber of my being comes alive when his thick fingers grab my arm, rolling me onto my back. There's a touch of hesitancy in his cobalt-blue eyes, as if he, too, can feel the energy passing between us. A shiver skates down my spine and my breath hitches as tingles race down my arm.

He releases me, and I fight against the urge to rub the spot that feels scarred by his touch. When he kneels on the bed, it creaks under his weight and I hold his stare as he brings his face to within an inch of mine.

My tongue darts out to lick my lips. His nostrils flare and he bares his teeth to me. Even as he pins me to the bed with a look of anger—red and flaming, burning into my soul—I can't stop the defiant curling of my lips.

Do your worst, Romeo Bianchi.

He grips my chin in his fingers like a vise. Fear bubbles to the surface before I push it down, compelling the numbness I'm too familiar with to take over. *Fear has no place in my emotions.*

"You think this is funny? That you have a say in *anything* that happens to you? Your days of freedom are long gone, Aurora. I own *every* inch of you. When I say jump, you don't ask how high, you just fucking do it. The sooner you realize that, the better."

His words send a confusing mixture of excitement,

powerlessness, and anger hurtling through my body, heating the nape of my neck. And yet, I don't move or show him any sign of the emotions warring inside of me.

Forcefully pushing my face away, he grabs at the collar of my T-shirt, lifting my limp body from the mattress. I stare at the wall. The throbbing in my jaw from where he grabbed me is unbearable, and I blink away the tears that threaten to spill.

He drops me back onto the mattress, ripping the cheap cotton of my shirt down the middle. A gasp is torn from my lips when his knuckles graze my pebbled nipples as he exposes my bare chest. My eyes snap to his, and I bite my tongue to hold back a moan.

How can I want him when he's behaving in such a vicious way?

I should be feeling *humiliated*, not turned on and... needy.

Shocked at what he's done and my body's betrayal, I make no attempt to cover myself. The cool air has goose-bumps forming on my exposed skin and I search his face for a reaction to my nakedness. There's no hint of regret or remorse in his striking gaze. The anger is still there, bubbling beneath the surface, but there's also heat.

Holding my stare, he brushes his hand down my stomach. Instinctively, my hips lift a fraction, and I bite down on my lip to keep from begging him for more. The silence is deafening and I'm acutely aware of each breath I take as I wait. He moves in slow motion, popping the button of my jeans and lazily dragging the zipper down. I swallow thickly, anticipation and arousal heightening my senses.

Suddenly, he steps back, his height magnified from where I lie on the bed. It's as if the moment never happened when he tugs on the cuffs of his shirt and snaps, "Get up, Aurora. I expect you to be showered and dressed in the next twenty minutes."

The 'or else' remains unspoken, hanging in the air, as he strides out of the room, slamming the door behind him.

I allow myself two minutes to process what's just happened before I move on autopilot, swinging my legs over the edge of the mattress. My concern about being watched is long gone, along with any modesty I had. He's ripped them both away with my T-shirt, leaving me to feel wanton and dirty.

I undress, leaving what's left of my clothes in a pile on the end of the bed, before grabbing the bottle of shower gel I threw on the floor earlier. Naked, I walk to the shower in the corner of the room. I have no clue what I'm going to wear now. *Does he think I'll walk around naked for his pleasure?* No, he can't be that callous.

Christ, Aurora. You don't know this man or what he's capable of.

I've worked so hard to keep myself out of this life. If I want to live, I should keep my head down and do as he demands. *But I don't want to live.* Dismissing the dark thought, I reach into the cubicle, twisting the rusted faucets. They're stiff and creak as I force them to move.

Just beyond the wall, I hear water rushing as it makes its way through the pipes.

Cold water spurts onto the stained tile floor. After a few minutes of it not getting any warmer, I step under the spray. *Of course there won't be hot water in their torture room.* Icy water pelts down on my goosebump-prickled skin. Tremors wrack my body, and despite the freezing water, I dip my head under it, holding still as I give in to the silent sobs.

There's a safety to the water because I know that it will hide my fear, hurt, and humiliation from the world. *It always has.*

When my tears have dried up and I can't take the torturous temperature anymore, I take a step back. Shutting off the shower, I turn in search of a towel. I don't know why I'm surprised there isn't one. *It's not a damn hotel, Aurora.*

Swiping up the blanket, I use it to dry off my hair before dabbing at my body. The coarse material doesn't absorb the water like I need, but it does a good enough job. My eyes fall to my torn clothes in a pile on the bed. I don't have much choice. I'm going to have to put them on again.

Wrapping the blanket around my body, I tug my jeans back on; the denim clinging to my damp legs as I wrestle them up. I'm slightly out of breath by the time I push the button through the hole and pull up the zipper.

I hold up the my shirt, twisting and turning it as I try to figure out the best way to use it to cover myself. In the end, I slide my arms through the sleeves, putting the back at my front and tying the tattered edges behind me. It's not perfect but it will do.

My body tenses at the reverberation of the door being unlocked and pushed open. I don't turn to face him, but the way my body reacts, I know it's Romeo. His frustration from earlier seems to have gone. I guess I should be thankful for that.

When he doesn't speak, I finally turn. He's leaning against the wall, observing me as I comb my fingers through my damp hair. Trying to be as covert as possible, I take him in. He's dressed all in black with his hair slicked back, but still curling at the collar. My fingers itch to fiddle with the strands, and I tug on my own a tad too firmly. His jaw is smooth where he's shaved, but it doesn't take away from his handsome features. I still want to run my fingers over his full lips and trace the contours of his cheekbones and nose.

God, what is wrong with me?

"I'm glad to see you can follow instructions, *cucciola*." He pushes away from the wall, stuffing his hands in his pockets. There's an edge to his voice when he adds, "I'll only say this once, Aurora, when you go upstairs, don't try to run. Should you so much as *think* about it, I won't hesitate to put a bullet in the back of your head."

Folding my arms across my chest, I tilt my head. "So, if I don't want to be held down here against my will," I look around the room, my lip curling in disgust before I meet his hardened stare and continue, "I should just make a break for it and you'll put me out of my misery? Got it."

Crossing the room, I move to step past him, but he grabs hold of my arm, slamming me against the wall. My head knocks against the brick and I flinch at the contact, my nostrils flaring, before Romeo crowds me, forcing my chin up. There's so much anger and... lust in his gaze that I'm surprised I don't combust on the spot.

Don't show him any weakness. It's what he wants.

"Don't test me, Aurora. You might put on a brave 'I don't give fuck' front, but that's all it is. *A front.* I can see right through you, and I know that when the time comes, you'll be a whimpering mess, begging for your life. Hell, you might offer me your body."

His thumb swipes over my bottom lip, and my breath hitches as he pulls it down, leaving a trail of wetness on my chin before he pushes his thumb into my open mouth. I fight against the desire to close my eyes and swirl my tongue around it. His voice is thick and dark when he continues, "Believe me, *bella*, you won't be *that* good. Nobody ever is. You'd do well to remember that even when you think you have it, the control will always sit firmly with me."

He steps away, seemingly unfazed by our interaction, holding out his arm for me to exit the room. My heart races, and a heat rushes through my body. Twice, in less than an hour, he's elicited that kind of reaction in me. I need to get my body under control, because giving into this man is completely reprehensible.

I break eye contact with Romeo, turning away as I head for the door. All the while praying that my internal reaction remains just that—*internal.*

There's laughter in his voice when he says, "Daniele will take you upstairs. There are people coming to do your hair and makeup. They won't care for any tales you might tell, Aurora. And even if they did, it would be *you* with their blood on your hands."

His words are worse than the cold shower and I swallow thickly. I get the impression that Romeo would have no issues with making *that* threat a reality. Keeping my attention on the path ahead, I move down the dark corridor. Daniele, the guy from earlier, is waiting at the bottom of a set of steps. When I reach him, his hand wraps around my arm and I flinch at his harsh grip.

Romeo's tone is biting when he calls, "Ease up, Daniele. I don't want my date covered in bruises."

His date? My brows pull together as I process his words. *What the hell does Romeo Bianchi have planned for me?*

Whatever it is, I'm certain that it will only end one way.

And it won't be in my favor.

Chapter 9

Aurora

Daniele doesn't release my arm until we reach the living room. He swings open the heavy door and pushes me across the threshold, closing it before I've had a chance to turn around. The sound of his footsteps getting further and further away fuels an idea in my mind.

Maybe now's my chance.

My eyes dart around the room, searching for an escape, or a weapon, anything that might help get me out of here. Two cream couches, big enough to fit at least twenty people, take up most of the space, and a large flat screen TV hangs on the wall that they're pointed at. This is not what I would have said the decor would be like, given the whole mafia thing. If I wasn't being held hostage, I could definitely curl up on one of the couches and watch a movie.

I've barely taken five steps when the door opens

again. My hand flies up to cover my racing heart. I bite the inside of my cheek when I turn to face the tall, good-looking guy who's just walked in. The collar of his shirt is open and the dark ink of his tattoos peeks through, wrapping around his neck.

An air of danger surrounds him, as if he could snap my neck with one hand and be unfazed by the action. A chill races down my spine and I fight against my natural instinct to run. I don't know who he is and I don't want to.

Neither of us speaks. Instead, he regards me with a cocktail of curiosity and annoyance swirling in his dark brown eyes. His hair is messy and makes him look almost unhinged. I can't help but compare it to Romeo's and how his is always so neat and styled.

His tone is calm and dismissive when he says, "I expected more."

Tilting my head, I wrap my arms around my waist before dropping them and standing taller. The last thing I want is to show him *any* sign of weakness. Keeping my tone as indifferent as his, I reply, "I don't follow."

He pushes away from the doorjamb and walks toward me. There's a casualness to his body language and the way his hands are tucked away in his pockets, but it doesn't match his harsh and biting words. "I expected *you* to be more. Clearly, Romeo sees something in you. I'm just not sure what or why." He pauses when he comes to a stop in front of me. "A bit of friendly advice, Aurora. Don't think you can stop what's going to happen to you. I know my cousin well enough to know that when this is all over, he'll have no issues putting a bullet between those pretty little sea-green eyes."

His words drip in malice, but I can't help but laugh at his threat. "That's funny."

He frowns, swiping his thumb over his bottom lip as he takes another step forward. I take two back, needing to put a little space between us. "You think I'm lying? Do you have any idea who you're dealing with?"

"Oh, I know. I just don't care. It's funny that you think I want *any* of this. That I want to live or even care about whatever happens to me."

We stare at each other in silence until a knock on the door breaks through the quiet. Unwilling to break eye contact first, I hold his stare. He might have been intimidating before he opened his mouth, but this guy is a dick.

A throat clears. "Sorry to interrupt, Massimo. The girls are here."

So that's his name.

Massimo's eyes flit down my body, from head to toe, but unlike when Romeo's eyes are on me, there's no hedonistic reaction. I don't crave more of him from something as simple as his focus on my body. In fact, Massimo's attention only makes me wish I didn't exist.

Without a word, he turns and stalks out of the room. The man who interrupted us waves his arm to someone I can't see in the corridor, calling, "This way, ladies."

Fuck. My opportunity to find a way out of here has gone.

Two women enter the room. My brows raise at their short bubblegum pink dresses and overdone hair and makeup. They kind of remind me of the sisters from *Hocus Pocus* and if they aren't twins, they sure could pass for them. Everything about them, except for their hair color, is the same.

"Thanks, Leo, baby," the blonde purrs. She holds his stare before dragging her hand down his chest and resting it on his belt buckle. I'm not sure why, but I feel a sense of victory when he picks it up and drops it by her side. She shrugs his rejection off and flounces into the room behind the brunette.

Like two slender giant vultures, they start circling me, pulling at my hair and gripping my face too harshly. Their fake nails dig into my skin. With Leo at their back, they don't try to hide their sneers of disgust.

"What do you think, Francesca?" the blonde asks.

Francesca grabs a handful of my hair and yanks my head back. I bite down on my tongue to keep from crying out. *Show no weakness, Aurora.*

"This one's going to need a lot of work. How long do we have, Leo?"

In the small gap between them, I can see Leo still standing in the doorway. He flicks his wrist and grunts, "Forty-five minutes."

Francesca tsks, before gripping my arm tightly, dragging me to a small table by one of the windows, and pushing me into a chair. They get to work, muttering things between themselves in Italian and then giggling. It doesn't take a genius to figure out they're talking about me. Now, more than ever, I wish I'd not rebelled so hard against my father and taken the Italian lessons my mom wanted me to. What I wouldn't give to wipe the laughter from their faces.

Blondie yanks a strand of my hair, and I get jabbed in the eye with the liner Francesca just so happens to have positioned by my eyeball. I rear back, my hand instinctively going to my eye as it waters and runs down my cheek.

"Come on, Martina, you've got to be more careful than that," Francesca admonishes. If it wasn't for the smirk she can't hide, I'd think she was being sincere.

A gentle knock sounds at the door, and I breathe a sigh of relief for the reprieve it will give me. Francesca and Martina share a look before my hand is yanked away from my eye and Francesca dabs at it with a ball of cotton, her attention fixed on the door. It creaks open, and a mousy blonde steps through, her head bent as she struggles in with a box that looks like it weighs more than her.

Francesca throws the cotton ball onto the table and rolls her eyes. Her top lip curls when she turns to face me. Gripping my chin, she lifts it and goes back to applying the makeup. "What do you want?"

I grind my teeth and blow out a breath. *This is not my fight.* All I need to do is keep my mouth shut, let them do their damage and then maybe, just maybe, I can figure out a way out of here.

"I'm so sorry to interrupt. Mr. Bianchi asked me to bring this in. It's just arrived."

Martina tugs at my hair so hard I'm surprised she doesn't break my neck. With my gaze fixed on the ceiling, I dig my fingers into the wooden armrests and slowly exhale. Her tone is curt and dismissive. "Okay, well, leave it on the couch and get lost."

It's one thing to talk to me like this when I have no place in this world, but she's just doing her job and they're just being plain rude. "You don't have to be such bitches to every person you come into contact with."

Quiet falls over the room, the gentle ticking of a clock the only sound. It feels like an eternity before they choose to ignore my outburst and continue with their conversation. The woman who bought my dress scurries from the room, quietly closing the door behind her. Rapid-fire Italian flies over my head as I get yanked and prodded until they are satisfied with their work.

———

He's dressed me up like a fucking *sex doll*. For what reason—other than to embarrass me—I'm not entirely sure. I would have thought he'd want me to look semi-decent, especially if it's to be believed that I'm with him.

I feel like... I don't even know. I'm speechless. The white dress is a size too small and barely covers my ass. If there's even a chance of a gentle breeze, I can guarantee that whoever is looking is going to get more than they signed up for.

Martina and Francesca sure had fun making me look like a clown. The makeup is a layer too thick and my hair has been backcombed, making me look like I've been well and truly serviced. If the giggling and nudging were any indication, they wanted me to be an embarrassment for Romeo.

Well, I can't do anything about the dress, but I can try and at least fix the rest. My eyes zero in on a box of tissues in the middle of the coffee table and I teeter my way over in heels that are way too high. Plucking out a handful, I use the TV screen as a mirror and swipe off a generous layer of foundation. The once-white tissue comes away orange. As happy as I can be, I throw the used ones on the table.

I just know that however I try to fix my hair, it's going to hurt, but there's no way I'm going out, having pictures taken and looking like I've been dragged through a hedge. Gently, I run my fingers through the tangled tresses, teasing at the clumps until my hair is back to a normal height.

It's all in vain because I know that regardless of what I look like, Romeo will still go through with his plan.

My eyes land on the clock, watching as the hands move at an excruciatingly slow pace. I've been in this room, alone, for the last thirty minutes, waiting for Romeo. So far, I've come up with a million ideas on how to escape. I've put into action precisely one. On high alert, I tried the window, my stomach a mess as I pushed to open it. There was no time to process the disappointment when I found it locked, because a phone rang in the corner of the room and I nearly jumped out of my skin.

I haven't dared to try to find another way out, especially because the girl from earlier came to answer the phone and left the door slightly ajar. It was stupid of me to try in the first place. What I need to do is bide my time and observe my surroundings. Running out blindly will only end one way.

My forehead rests against the cool glass pane as I stare out of the window I tried to escape through moments ago. It's finally stopped raining and the green lawn that stretches for miles looks dewy and vibrant. I can't see another building for miles and the reminder of where I am and who has me sends a frisson of awareness racing down my spine. *If I do get out of here, where do I run to? How far will be far enough to get me to safety?*

When the door opens, I force myself to keep still. I know it's Romeo by the way the hairs stand on the back of my neck and goosebumps form a trail across my exposed skin. He doesn't say a word, and I can't see him in the reflection of the window, so I turn to face him, blowing out an exasperated breath.

Of course he looks good. I think it would be impossible for him not to. I'm yet to see him looking ruffled, and for some reason, that pisses me off. I want to push him closer to the edge, to see him lose control, because it's not fair that he can be so unbothered by me when I notice every minute detail about him.

"Have you had those women dress me up like one of your favorite sex dolls?" I accuse. "You might be forcing me to go along with your plan, *Mr. Bianchi*, but there's not a chance in hell I'll be giving you anything in return. At least not willingly." I fold my arms under my bust. The sweetheart neckline of the dress barely contains my breasts, and when it hits me that I'm giving some *very* mixed signals, I drop my arms to my side.

Romeo huffs out a laugh as he prowls toward me. I take a step back, then curse myself when I hit the window ledge. Staring at him down my nose, I close the distance between us, determined to show him that I'm unaffected by him, even if it's not true.

My voice comes out strong and sure, despite the uncertainty and anguish swirling in the depths of my gut. "As much as you might try to scare me, it's not working." I clench my fists at my sides to hide the trembling that contradicts my words.

A darkness has been hovering over my existence for too long and I'm ready to face it now. For months, I've been trying to keep my head above the water and... *I'm tired*. The day Romeo walked into my apartment, the possibility of everything ending became a reality and I'll keep holding on to that hope until I take my last breath.

Romeo runs a finger down my cheek, keeping his voice soft when he says, "I have no doubt, *cucciola. Dio,* even though you know what I am capable of, you still test me at every fucking turn."

Inspecting my nails, I try to convey an air of boredom, as if my entire body isn't alight at his touch. My voice sounds gravelly, but I don't clear it for fear that he might see through the front I'm putting up. "If you were going to go through with your threats, I'd be dead already. I'm just trying to figure out how much more I need to push you before you *finally* do it. I'm tired of this cat and mouse game you seem intent on playing."

His hand darts to my hair, grabbing hold of the strands at the back of my head. The sting at the base of my skull has my eyes watering in a matter of seconds, and I blink rapidly in an effort to keep my reaction hidden from him. Romeo pulls harder, the force making my back arch, pressing my body into his, and I fight against the urge to melt into him. His tongue lazily rolls across his bottom lip. The words to implore him for a taste are begging to be spoken, but I dare not utter them. Instead, I bite down on the inside of my cheek, the metallic tang of blood filling my mouth.

"*Aurora.*" So much is said in the way he murmurs my name. Most of it is in direct contrast to the aggressive way he's holding my hair. A small part of me wants to believe that maybe he's as affected by me as I am by him, but I know that can't be true. His fingers ease up before he releases me and moves his hand to my throat. Dark eyes dare me to protest. "If you behave, you just might make it out of here with your life. But if you keep acting out, I'll have you begging for death, while I force you to watch the life drain out of the eyes of the person you love the most."

I huff out a laugh and roll my eyes, still pushing him. "Then the joke's on you, Romeo, because you can't kill a dead person."

With a heavy sigh, he shakes his head and releases me before he walks away. He comes to a stop in front of the door, his annoyance clear in his tone when he says, "This is becoming tiresome, Aurora. I only have so much patience and you're testing it at every turn."

I call after him, "Just end it, Romeo. I won't be any help in luring my father out, because he doesn't care for me how you want him to. The sooner you get that, the sooner you can move on to a different plan."

He looks back at me over his shoulder. The air between us is stifling, but neither of us wants to give in. *We're at a stalemate.* Shaking his head, Romeo replies, "Come, we're going to be late."

I guess we're still going to take the pictures then.

Chapter 10

Romeo

A urora's parting shot plays on my mind. Even now, an hour later, her words are plaguing me. I'm not a man who tends to second-guess his decisions, but she's so *goddamn* adamant her father won't come. I guess time will tell which one of us is right. And if *I'm* wrong, then I'll have no issue tying up the loose ends and killing her.

After arriving at the helipad, Daniele scanned the cars for any GPS trackers. They came up clear and we've circled the block twice. The SUV rolls to a stop at the curb outside the restaurant. *Massimo came through with this reservation.* The place is a hive of activity, with a barrage of paparazzi camped out front waiting to take pictures of the rich and famous.

I guess for the right price, anyone can make the front page.

My hand reaches for the door handle and I instruct

Daniele, "Find somewhere to wait, or grab some food. We'll be here for a couple of hours to make sure the message gets out there."

His eyes meet mine and he nods. "Yes, boss."

I step out onto the sidewalk, the quiet of the car replaced by the sounds of the city as I button my jacket. On my periphery, I catch two of our men climbing from the car behind us and taking up residence on the sidewalk. Camera bulbs flash and my name is called out as I turn to offer Aurora my hand. There's no mistaking the fire in her eyes, and I raise my brows. My warning is clear: *make a scene and you'll regret it.*

With anyone else, my threats would have been enough. *But with Aurora?* Well, she's shown a clear lack of caring about what happens to her. I've never had someone so willing to die that they push me to pull the trigger.

Aurora huffs out a breath before delicate fingers slide into my palm—the warmth and softness has my chest puffing out as a strange surge of protectiveness shoots through my veins.

Her black hair falls forward, partially hiding her face as she climbs from the car. When she has one foot on the sidewalk, I tug her toward me. She falls into my chest, her hand instinctively resting there between us as she finds her balance. Jasmine assaults my senses, and for a brief moment, I wonder how she still smells so good.

From the outside, the moment must look intimate and it feeds the press the scoop we planned. What I don't expect is the dart of lust that shoots to my gut, driving me to imagine what her full, slightly parted lips would feel like if I dipped my head and stole a taste.

For half a second, I wonder if kidnapping her was such a good idea. She's a temptress. A siren, calling to men in a way that she's seemingly oblivious to. But there's not a doubt in my mind that she could drown a man in her allure. *Dio.* When I walked into the room earlier and saw her in that dress, I was seconds away from bending her over the back of the couch and fucking her senseless.

Click. Click. Click.

"Who's the lucky lady, Mr. Bianchi?"

Click. Click. Click.

"Can we get a kiss?"

Click. Click. Click.

"What's your name, sweetheart?"

Click. Click. Click.

The barrage of questions pulls me back to the moment, reminding me why I'm here and what is at stake. *I won't allow her to compromise my family.* Grinding my teeth, I snatch up her hand, angry at myself for being preoccupied. I'm not a man who gets easily distracted, and yet for a moment, she'd sucked me into a bubble.

It won't happen again.

Ignoring the questions still being fired at us, I yank Aurora into my side and walk along the red carpet that leads toward the entrance of the restaurant. A valet holds the door open, a strange look I can't quite define on his features. My grip tightens on Aurora's hip before I usher her in ahead of me.

When the door closes behind us, it's like being submerged underwater. The muffled shouting of the crowd outside is unintelligible as it bounces off the glass. Instead, soft classical music plays over the speakers, providing a background to the busy chatter of the restaurant. Dark lighting offers up an intimate atmosphere, perfect to feed the illusion we're selling.

The maître d' greets us with a beaming smile that doesn't quite reach his eyes. He's staring somewhere over my left shoulder when he greets me. "Mr. Bianchi, it's a pleasure to host you this evening. Please, this way."

It's nothing new for people to be afraid of me, but I don't like the way his eyes flit down Aurora's body before lifting to her face and flaring in surprise. A muscle ticks in my jaw, and if we weren't in a restaurant full of people, I'd put a bullet in his kneecap and make him apologize to her before I put one in his head.

Clearing my throat, I unbutton my jacket, pulling back the lapel. The action draws his attention, and when his eyes land on my holstered gun, the color drains from his face. He shakes his head before swiping up two menus from the host stand with trembling hands before turning to show us to our table.

My hand rests on the curve of Aurora's lower back as we're shown to a booth in the back corner of the restaurant. From here, we won't need to keep up the charade for the entire dinner as the booth hides us enough to afford us some privacy, but I'll still have a good view of the restaurant.

With a light pressure, I urge Aurora to take a seat. She glares at me over her shoulder before shuffling into the booth, tugging at the low hem of her dress. I slide in next to her, making sure to face the restaurant. It looks like we've caused a frenzy; the restaurant is filled with flashes from where their lenses are pressed to the glass.

The maître d' squirms under the intensity of my stare before handing out the menus, obviously misinterpreting it as annoyance at the paparazzi beyond the window. He runs a finger around his collar. "I will get them moved right away, Mr. Bianchi. Carlo will be your server this evening. He'll be with you momentarily, but can I get you anything to drink whilst you wait? Perhaps a bottle of champagne? On the house, of course."

I turn my attention to Aurora; a brow lifted in question. She's gazing out of the window, a pensive look on her face. It's only when the quiet drags on that she shifts her focus to me.

Out of nowhere, the familiar sound of a gunshot echoes around the room, quickly followed by blood and brain matter exploding over us. Aurora's wide eyes latch on to mine as the maître d's body hits the table. The green depths are somehow starker with the red now marring her face. If I'd had time to take in her reaction properly, I might have noticed the way she's frozen in shock or the terror in her expression. Instead, I take cover, pulling out my weapon before the screams of the other patrons ring through the room.

An avalanche of glass cascades to the floor as the front window shatters, leaving a clear line of sight to the street outside. Sucking in a breath, I block out the screams and sounds of plates smashing, focusing on where the gunfire is coming from. *Cazzo.* Bullets are flying at us from all directions. There are multiple shooters, that much I'm sure of.

I peer around the booth, taking in the once-bustling restaurant. Bodies litter both the sidewalk and the restaurant floor. I don't have time to wonder if they're all dead or simply taking cover, but they allow me to see out onto the block and find the man half-hidden behind a vehicle across the street. His automatic weapon rests on the hood of a car as he sprays bullets unforgivingly into the restaurant.

I'm thinking through my next move, wondering if the men we had stationed outside are dead—most likely—when a pained whimper sounds behind me. For a heart-stopping second, I brace myself for the fact that Aurora might have been hit. When my eyes seek her out, I find her sitting, motionless, in the exact spot she was moments ago. Her mouth is slightly agape and her eyes are wide as she stares, unblinking, at the blood that's pooling on the white tablecloth from the gaping hole in the maître d's head, his lifeless eyes fixed in her direction.

"Get the fuck down," I shout in Italian, reaching over to tug her down onto the bench, out of the firing line.

A bullet whizzes past my head, piercing the back of the booth, sending padding exploding into the air. *That was too close for comfort.* My heart thumps wildly in my chest as I bunker down onto the bench. This isn't my first gunfight, and I'd rather it not be my last, but I'm massively outnumbered. Keeping low, I pull out my phone and shoot off a text to Daniele in the hopes that he's in the vicinity.

ROMEO

> Restaurant. Shooter. Auto. More
> than one.

I wait until the bubble shows as delivered before pocketing my phone. Wood and plaster splinter around us as the heavy gunfire ensues. There's no letup in the ammo raining down on us, which tells me whoever they are, they came here to kill and they don't care who gets caught in the crossfire. This isn't a warning, it's an assassination attempt. I've seen enough to know that they won't stop until their target—me—is taken out. Although anyone worth their salt would have taken me out with the first shot, not the fucking maître d'.

Somewhere in the restaurant, a cell phone rings, barely audible over the gunfire. Nobody picks up and when the ringing stops, it quickly starts up again, this time followed by several other ringtones.

Shuffling along the bench, I look back to silently tell Aurora to stay hidden. The last thing I need is the only connection we have to Francesco Costa being taken out.

Her eyes are shut and her lips are moving as she mouths something to herself. I rest my hand on her arm and wait for her unfocused gaze to meet mine before I motion for her to stay. She dips her chin in acknowledgment.

Another peek over the edge of the booth, and I can see the gunman aiming his weapon down the street.

Thank fuck for back up.

With adrenaline coursing through my veins, I move out of my seat, keeping as close to the wall as I possibly can. There's no way I can make a kill shot from where I am and this *figlio di puttana* doesn't get to go home today.

The unmistakable stench of death is in the air. Bodies litter the restaurant, and as I move through it, terrified, wide eyes meet mine of the patrons who have survived and are taking cover.

Blood rushes in my ears and my heart beats a rhythm of rage in my chest. When I reach the window, I take cover behind the wall and lift my gun, bringing him into the line of fire. I flex my finger over the trigger and, without a second thought, I apply a light pressure. The bullet meets its intended point on his head, and he crumples to the ground, his weapon falling to the floor.

The block is now eerily quiet, and as I step from behind the wall, the unmistakable click of a magazine being loaded echoes around the buildings. I don't have time to react and move before a bullet flies toward me, grazing my arm.

Cazzo!

My hand lifts to the wound, and when I pull it away,

blood drips from my fingers. The deafening sound of gunshots doesn't ease up. The plaster and brick around me splinters and sprays as the unknown attacker continues their assault.

Pulling out my phone, I open up the camera and maneuver it around the wall. The shooter is there dressed all in black, a balaclava covering his face, carrying himself with all the calmness one would expect of a hitman. If the fire wasn't being aimed at me, I'd be in awe of his brazenness. Instead, it's just pissing me the fuck off.

Sliding down the wall, I lie on my stomach and army-crawl across the floor toward the opening. The shards of glass slice through the fabric of my suit, painfully digging into the flesh of my forearms and knees as I go. The slicing pain is almost unbearable, but I do what I do best; block it out and focus on the task at hand. In position under the small window ledge, I send up a silent prayer that whoever is shooting at him from the other end of the block is distracting him.

It's not ideal, being this low on the ground, but at least I've got a shot. When he gets within range, I aim for his head before squeezing the trigger. He drops, silence filling the air before he's even hit the ground.

Rolling to the side, I lie on my back staring up at the destruction, counting down from ten. My chest heaves with each labored breath, and I flex my fingers on the handle of my gun, ready to attack again if needed. When the only noise is that of sirens in the distance, I stand. There's a tightness in my chest that I force to loosen as I brush off the fragments of glass from my suit.

Holstering my weapon, I keep to the outskirts of the restaurant as I walk back to the table, calling Daniele. Who knows if they're the last of it, but we're sitting ducks in this restaurant. I need to get Aurora and get the hell out of here.

Daniele answers on the first ring, his worry evident when he asks, "Boss. You guys okay?"

"We're fine." I seethe. "How's it looking out there?"

Daniele blows out a breath before responding. "There's going to be a lot of heat here soon." I hear the clunk as the car door shuts, and the engine roars to life as he continues, "I counted three. You took two out and one ran as I was pulling up. It's best if we don't stick around though, I'll bring the car to the back."

Fuck.

Without a word, I end the call, pocketing my phone as I crouch in front of our table. Using my body as a shield from the destruction behind me, I gently whisper her name. Glassy, wide gaze moves to me, bouncing around my face. "We have to go. Keep your eyes on me and do exactly as I say."

She sits up and stumbles out of the booth, her eyes not leaving mine even when she's safely in my arms. Blood and brain matter stain her white dress. Her body vibrates with fear, and I tighten my hold around her waist, moving us to the back of the restaurant.

We come to a stop next to the fire exit. "Wait here. If

you hear any more gunfire, run for the bathroom. Lock yourself in a stall, stand on the toilet seat, and don't make a sound until I come for you. Okay?"

Her jaw quivers before she visibly clenches it and gives me a firm nod. Pushing down on the door's release bar, I lift my gun and ease outside. Daniele has the back door of the car open, his gun trained on the end of the alleyway.

I turn back to Aurora, ready to grab her hand and make a dash for it, but my focus lands on the masculine hand clamped over her mouth and the other holding a gun to her temple. Aurora's eyes are squeezed shut and her nostrils flare as silent sobs wrack her body.

The valet.

I should have seen this coming.

Stepping to the side, I allow the door to close before lifting my gun and aiming it at his head. The soft glow of the emergency exit sign is the only illumination, but I see him as if we're under a spotlight.

"There's only one way you get to go home today." My voice is deceptively soft as the lie falls from my lips.

We both know he won't leave here alive.

A bead of sweat forms on his brow, and he rasps, "Drop your weapon and put your hands on the wall or... or I'll kill her."

Aurora's eyes fly open, fear dilating her pupils. *So she's not as accepting of death as she's been making out.* I file away the thought before replying, "That's not going to happen, *stronzo*."

He squeezes his eyes shut, his rasping breaths filling the quiet. With a jerk of my head, I indicate for Aurora to move. She pulls in his arms, moving just enough for me to take aim, and as he opens his eyes, I pull the trigger. The bullet penetrates his skull, splattering blood and fragments of bone over Aurora and the wall next to her. She flinches, her throat working as if she's trying to suppress a scream.

Not wasting a second or giving her time to dwell on what's just happened, I grab her hand and push through the door, urging her to get into the car. When Daniele is behind the wheel and we're racing through the city, I rest my head on the headrest and blow out a heavy breath.

"To the helipad?"

The question is loaded with concern, and after what we've experienced this evening, I don't blame him. "If you're up for it, drive us back to Massimo's."

This is bigger than we could have anticipated and without knowing when the next attack could come, every step we take needs to be well thought through.

Chapter 11

Romeo

Daniele navigates the car through the back streets until we reach the highway. Every mile has been fraught with tension and the storm raging inside of me has only grown. I have no desire to dampen it out. After all, it's going to fuel me for days. We may not have any information—aside from Francesco's signature on the bomb—but heads will roll for what has happened tonight.

That's the *one* thing I can guarantee.

We have an enemy trying to extinguish us, and yet we're no closer to finding him than we were before I arrived in the States. Massimo is certain that Francesco is behind this and although the evidence—Francesco's signature—points to that being the case, I just don't understand why.

He was part of the family.

Could someone have set him up?

It's no use speculating on the why right now, we need to find him and put a stop to these attacks. I blow out a breath, refocusing my thoughts. Tonight, they got close. *Too close.* We need to get ahead of them, figure out what their next move will be before they make it. If we don't, then there will only be more bloodshed.

My mind replays the events of the evening.

Nothing looked out of the ordinary.

The shooters waited until we were seated in the restaurant and seemed to know where we were sitting. They very easily could have taken us out while we walked in. There would have been a lot fewer casualties if they had.

Very few people knew we were going to that specific restaurant tonight, let alone the finer details of our seating arrangements. In fact, the only people that knew who our reservation was for were me, Daniele, Massimo, and his men.

Do we have a rat?

Fuck. It's the only explanation for all the attacks and certainly for tonight's. Somebody must have told Francesco about our plans for the evening for him to have that much detail. If he was following us, he wouldn't have known as much as he did, or have time to infiltrate the staff.

But why would he risk Aurora's life?

Was she telling the truth about him not coming for her?

Is *she* the rat? As soon as the question forms, I dismiss

it. She has no way of communicating with the outside world. *And she could have been killed.* I stare blankly at the scenery as it passes us by in a blur. The ghost of her, hidden underneath the table with fear cloaking her like a blanket, haunts me.

Aurora's soft voice penetrates the fog in my mind. Her fingers brush over my arm as she murmurs, "You're bleeding." Her concern for me is laughable, but it makes my chest tighten, nonetheless.

As the adrenaline wears off, the throbbing ache from the gunshot wound makes itself known. I flex my fingers and reply, "It's nothing, just a graze. I'll survive." It's not like this is the first time I've taken a bullet.

Daniele's eyes meet mine in the rearview mirror. "Are you injured badly?"

Daniele and I grew up together when my family moved back to Sicily. He's more like a brother to me than an employee, but for a man in his position, he worries about me more than he should. If I die, I die, and there's nothing either of us can do about it.

Aurora sighs heavily when I respond to him in Italian. *"I'm fine. But if it makes you feel better, have Doc ready for when we arrive."*

The final thirty minutes of the drive back to Massimo's are filled with a tense silence. It's the kind that sucks the air out of the space and allows my mind to focus on the fury that's twisting inside of me.

We come to a stop at the bottom of the steps outside the house, and I issue a command to Daniele to take

Aurora to my room before jumping out of the car, taking the steps two at a time. Bursting through the door, it swings open, banging against the wall and nearly knocking Aldo over. If there isn't a mist of rage swallowing me whole, I'd ask if he was okay. Instead, I roar, "Where is Massimo?"

Aldo's brow furrows before he steps aside and drops his head, pointing toward the back of the house. "He's in the kitchen."

I stalk in the direction of the kitchen, my fists clenching and unclenching as I close the distance. The sound of voices and radio chatter fill the air. There's a level of comfort to the noise that reminds me of home, but right now it's doing little to dampen my ire.

Massimo is seated at the kitchen table with a spoonful of what looks like *gnocchi alla sorrentina* raised to his lips. The spoon clangs to the bowl, splashing the sauce onto his black shirt. When he sees me, he pushes back from the table, his chair clattering to the floor. His brows reach for his hairline. "Holy shit. What happened?"

"You've got a *fucking* rat, is what the fuck happened, *cousin.*" I sneer. "Mark my words, Massimo, I'll kill every single one of your men to find out who it is. And when I do, I'll skin the *ratto,* before I hang him from the tree by the front gate as a warning to anyone else that thinks it's a smart idea to betray us."

Holding up his hands, Massimo approaches me timidly. "Come, Romeo, we'll have a drink and you can tell me exactly what's happened." He turns to Alma, his chef, and instructs, "Bring us two glasses and the whisky."

There's a pounding in my ears and when he gets close enough, I fist the front of his shirt, moving forward until his back hits the wall. He doesn't fight my hold. The only sign of his frustration is in the narrowing of his eyes.

Tightening my hold on him, I bare my teeth and spit, "I don't need to sit down and have a drink, Massimo. What I *need* is to find the person who is in communication with the man who just tried to kill me. No amount of talking will stop me from finding him. So, you either cooperate, or I'll be inclined to believe that you're involved."

As the words leave my lips, I know they aren't true. There's no way he's involved. Massimo has always been a silent, broody type, waiting until the perfect moment to unleash his unhinged attacks. He'll strike when you least expect it, not plot secretly in the background.

Releasing him, I step back and run my fingers through my hair. I force some of the tension out of my shoulders before I speak. "You have a rat, Massimo, and the last time I checked, you answer to me, not the other way round. Have your men lined up in the backyard in the next twenty minutes."

Massimo waits until I'm on the threshold of the room before calling out, "If you're going to start taking out my men, then I should at least know why, Romeo. This could be exactly what they want you to do; make us weak so they can plunge the knife in and finally finish us off."

I twist abruptly toward him, and when I speak, my voice yields no emotion. "There were three gunmen at the restaurant." I scrub a hand down my face while I try to calm my anger. "Civilians were killed, Massimo, and the only people who knew it was me going to *that* restaurant are in this house."

Heaving out a sigh, Massimo says, "Anyone could have tipped them off, Rome. We called the fucking press—"

I can't contain my fury, shouting, "They could have fucking killed her, Massimo. She's mine." I jab my finger in my chest before dropping it and stalking toward him. There's too much energy flowing through me, and I need to get it out.

Massimo quirks a brow, a smirk on his lips as he rolls his tongue around in his mouth. "She's yours, yeah?"

"To *fucking* kill. And *only* once we've got what we need from her. You and I both know the leak has come from inside your house and if you can't fix it, then I will."

"I trust my men, Rome. But—" He exhales sharply before continuing, "If you say we have a rat, everything moves to a need-to-know basis. We'll find out who it is without needlessly killing people. Go and get cleaned up, *then* we can figure out a plan of attack."

Deep down, I know that he's right, but the dark and dangerous beast inside of me doesn't want to listen. I've killed three men tonight, but it's not *enough*. There's a craving to do some damage pulsing under my skin.

A knock on the kitchen door pulls my focus away from Massimo. Doc walks in, closely followed by Daniele. "I heard there was a bullet wound that needed tending to?"

Massimo huffs out a laugh, muttering something under his breath that sounds suspiciously like, *you could have fucking led with that.*

I grunt an acknowledgment to Doc before moving toward the table and shrugging out of my jacket. I lay it over the back of a chair before getting to work on the buttons of my shirt. "It's just a graze."

With my shirt discarded, Doc picks up my arm, perching his glasses on the edge of his nose as he twists and turns it under the lights. "Yes, it looks like a graze and the scratches on your arm appear to be superficial. We'll get you cleaned up to minimize the risk of infection, but it doesn't look like you'll need stitches. You'll be pleased to know that you'll survive."

"I'm sure my enemies will be thrilled."

Alma hands me a glass of amber liquid before she walks back to the counter, seemingly unfazed by the interaction I had earlier with Massimo. A headache pounds at the base of my skull as I silently urge Doc to work faster as he moves to get the first aid kit to clean me up.

I'm exhausted.

Both physically and mentally, but it's a hazard of the

job and I'll never walk away. Yes, you have to always be on your guard and there is *always* someone looking to take you out, but my family is the mafia and the mafia is my family.

This is all I've ever known.

At some point in their lives, every man in my family has been the head of the mafia. We have instilled fear in our enemies and that is why, whoever is behind this, is attacking us from the shadows. But no matter how long it takes, they won't be able to hide forever.

Chapter 12

Aurora

Unfocused, I stare at the wall in front of me, vaguely aware of the intricate gold floral pattern on the dark forest-green wallpaper. A heavy weight rests on my chest, making every breath harder than the last. I know that I *should* take off my dress and wash away the gore covering my face and body, but I can't move. Every fiber of my being is frozen. What makes it worse is the never-ending loop playing in my mind of the maître d' and his lifeless stare as blood poured from the hole in his head.

He was an innocent man.

In a split second, he no longer exists in this world. He was just doing his job and now he's gone. Who's going to break *that* news to his family? *Did he even have one?* Oh God, what about the other diners? I close my eyes to ease the ache behind them, but all it does is transport me back to the restaurant. Memories of screams of terror mix with the echo of heavy gunfire, but instead of it being crystal clear, it's muffled, like I'm underwater.

What is all of this death and destruction even for?

My eyes fly open and I blink rapidly, glancing around the room for an anchor to keep me in the moment. Rushing out a breath, I try in vain to focus my mind. Nothing is making any sense. If what Romeo said about my father being behind the attacks is true, then he wants Romeo and his family dead and he'll take out whoever gets in his way.

Even if it's his own daughter.

Why would he do this?

My parents split up when I was just a kid, but from everything my mom told me, my dad was loyal and loved us with his whole heart. It's why he walked away when I told him to. No matter how much I convince myself that he made a choice, I know it was one I forced upon him. *His life or mine.* I'd spent the better part of the evening begging him to walk away from the mafia, but he told me that wasn't an option. That they'd kill him if he tried to leave. And his sacrifice was all for nothing, because Romeo Bianchi has pulled me back into the life that I've tried so hard to stay out of.

I flinch when the door to the bedroom flies open, banging on the wall behind it, as a half-naked Romeo charges in. The exposed muscles and veins in his neck strain against his skin and dark, cold eyes meet mine. For the first time since Daniele left me in this room, I move, taking a step back.

Is this when he's going to kill me?

I see the moment he pulls himself from whatever trance he is in. Some of the tension seems to ease out of his body, the muscles in his bare torso rolling and releasing. A tattoo of a lion's head takes up pride of place over his pecs, leading to his solid abs. It's a majestic animal, teeth bared and the implied sound of its roar all too clear. There are other tattoos covering his body, but they don't draw my focus away.

Romeo strides across the room, purpose in every step he takes. I'm no longer afraid. Whatever he plans to do, I'd rather he just get it over with. His fingers wrap around my wrist, sending jolts of electricity up my arm at the contact. I'm powerless to resist him when he tugs me toward another door. Still in the stupid heels, I stumble over my feet before he steadies me with a hand on my hip, spreading the warmth of his touch to my core. For the first time since we got back from the restaurant, I feel *something*.

I squint as Romeo leads me into the bathroom. The brightness of the overhead lights is an assault on my eyes. A huge window behind the bath overlooks the garden and although it's pitch-black outside, the lack of privacy is still there. White marble tiles cover the walls and floor, with a walk-in shower along the far wall.

Releasing his hold on me, Romeo walks to the shower, turning it on. I wrap my hands around my waist, trying to keep the shivers from jolting my body. *How is it possible to feel so much and so little at the same time?*

Neither of us speaks and I'm not sure I could force a coherent sentence past my lips. The gravity of what happened today isn't lost on me. Innocent people died. I guess I can count myself lucky that, until Romeo Bianchi walked into my life, I'd never witnessed anything like this before. Truth be told, it's not something I thought I ever would. Sure, I've seen things in the news or guided people through difficult times as an emergency dispatcher, but I never thought the day would come when I'd be under fire in a fucking restaurant.

Romeo's hands land on his belt buckle, the sound of it being unclasped enough to pull me back into the moment. I turn my back to him, flinching when I catch sight of my reflection in the mirror above the basin. Splatters of blood and chunks of something I don't want to identify have congealed across my face and chest. The makeup that had been so harshly applied is now smeared and streaked and what I can only assume are skull fragments litter my hair. I rip my gaze away, unable to stomach the horrific reminders of the harrowing events of the evening.

I just want to get clean.

Romeo steps up behind me, the heat from his body like a blanket as his hands land on my shoulders. He smooths them down my bare arms before turning me toward him. I focus my eyes on the wall just past his shoulder.

He lifts my right arm, tugging down the zipper on my dress. Instead of fighting him, I allow him to undress me;

the fabric falling down my body and pooling around my feet. I should be making an effort to cover myself, to push him away and beg for him to not do whatever it is that he has planned, but I'm numb. My limbs are heavy and something as simple as moving my head to meet his gaze feels like an effort.

There's a scratch in my throat and an ache in my chest, but I clench my fists and swallow down the sadness. When he's done with me, I can cry, but not until I'm back in my cell and *alone*.

I'm stronger than my fear; than my emotions.

Bending, Romeo lifts my right foot to his knee and undoes the strap of my stiletto. He slides my foot free, placing it back on the heated floor before moving to the next. Even when his hands hold on to the lace thong—the only article of clothing I have left on—and he pulls the material down my thighs, I don't move. My mind is screaming at me to do something—to do anything to get away—but my body is refusing to cooperate.

When he stands, he follows my blank stare out of the window before blocking my view with his body. Smoothing back a strand of my hair, he soothes, "Nobody can see in, and even if they could, they know not to look at what's mine."

His.

What does that even mean?

What am I to him? A concubine? His prisoner? I don't feel like I'm my own person anymore and it's only been a day. *What will happen when he's kept me here for months? Or will my life be snatched from me before the week is over? Just like the maître d's.*

Oblivious to my spiraling thoughts, Romeo leads me into the shower and under the hot spray. Pin prickles assault my body as the water rains down on my cool skin.

With my back to him as he undresses, I allow my head to fall forward and watch the physical evidence of this evening flow down the drain, hoping the memories of tonight will wash away just as easily. *How did I end up in this position?* I thought my father walking away would keep me safe. That I'd be able to live a normal life.

Look how well that's turned out.

I can't help but feel that if I'd not forced my father to make a choice between me and his world, I wouldn't be in this position. I'd have had at least some protection, but instead, I'm alone and ill-prepared for a man with as much power as Romeo Bianchi. The magnitude of my circumstances coats me like the water falling from above me. It pulls me under, suffocating me as it crashes into me at lightning speed. A single solitary tear rolls down my cheek unchecked, and I brace my arms on the wall, trying with everything I have to push down the emotions that are consuming me.

It's too much.

A strong arm bands around my waist and I'm pulled into Romeo's warm, solid chest as he repositions us both under the spray. With his mouth close to my ear, he murmurs, "It's okay, *bella*. You can let go." His tone is soft, and as much as I search for an underlying threat, there isn't anything there.

His words ignite a fire, and I feel my fight return. I push out of his arms, turning to glare at him. The spray from the shower continues to pelt down on me from behind, and I push a hand through my hair to keep it away from my face.

My body tenses, and I snarl, "*No*. I don't need your *permission*. You have no right to comfort me when you're the reason I'm in this mess." I push forward, screaming, "I wish they'd killed me because you seem incapable of doing so. Even better, I wish they'd killed *you*."

A smug smirk lifts the corner of his mouth. "There she is."

I grind my teeth in an attempt to keep from exploding. *How dare he put me through all of this? Who does he think he is for taking me and using me as a pawn in his stupid game? For nearly getting me killed.*

I'll knock that stupid look off his handsome fucking face.

Unable to hold back, I launch myself at him. *At this six-foot-five wall of pure muscle.* Pulling back my arm, I push it forward toward his face. Dodging out of the way, his thick fingers grab my wrist, stopping me mid-air. He pins my arm above my head, wrapping the other around my neck as he shoves me back until my shoulders hit the cool tile. He pauses for a second before his mouth crashes down on mine. His kiss is dominating, and yet there is a softness to it as his warm lips plunder mine. I part my lips when he demands it, and our tongues tangle in a battle I'm happy to lose. There's something possessive and powerful in the hold he has over me. It sends shots of need to my core. A low growl in his chest vibrates through the palm I didn't realize I had splayed on him.

The air is robbed from my lungs and even if I had the ability to make him stop, I'm not sure I want him to. Currents pass through my body, and for the first time in what feels like forever, I feel *alive*. With my wrist still held in his hand above my head, I grab hold of his bicep with the other, digging my fingernails into the flesh as I try to stay grounded.

What is happening?

A whimper echoes around the bathroom, and it takes a second to register that the desperately needy sound has come from me. As our kiss continues, Romeo plunders my mouth, the light pressure on my throat a suggestion that his hunger is as ravaging as mine. Our mouths fight the war that started the moment we met. All the emotions from the past few days—defiance, strength, fear, and anger—battle to win. Neither of us needs air. We feed off each other, allowing life to pass between us with every swipe of our tongues.

Later on, I'll remember who he is and why I'm here, but right now, I want nothing more than to forget everything that isn't him. I want to forget that someone has been watching my apartment. That I've been taken prisoner by a man who thinks I can get my father to come out of hiding. Or what will happen when my father doesn't come out of hiding. But most of all, I want to forget all about the men who were killed in front of me tonight.

Romeo releases his hold on my throat and wrist. My body sags from the loss of contact, leaving me bereft. I don't want to acknowledge how much I like his hands on me and the way he makes me feel so alive.

My treacherous body almost rejoices when he wraps an arm around my waist, taking hold of my thigh with his other hand. His fingers dig into the flesh, but the pinch of my skin does little to bring me out of the sexual fog I'm sinking into. Like it's the most natural thing in the world, he hooks one of my legs over his arm, and I press my body against his naked chest like I belong to him.

Feeling bold and forgetting who this man is, my fingers dive into his thick hair, pulling on the wet strands and angling his head so I can deepen the kiss. I'm emboldened by the fact that he's allowing me this moment of power and control, when in reality, I have anything but.

An unmistakable cotton-covered hardness presses into me and a fleeting thought crosses my mind. *He never got fully undressed. Did he do that to protect me?* What that could mean is gone before I can think about it any further. My body's natural reaction takes over, and I rock my hips into him, seeking some sort of release for the need burning inside me.

Tearing my mouth away from his, I gasp for air as Romeo trails kisses down my neck and my gulps turn to moans. "I just... I need to... forget," I whisper, my tone breathy.

Romeo's only response is a grunt before he moves down my chest. His teeth graze over one puckered nipple before he flicks the bud with his tongue and sucks it deep into his mouth. The pop, as he releases it, echoes around the room.

His hand pushes the globe of my breast up and he swirls his tongue around my nipple again and again before pulling the bud through his bared teeth. The scrape is delicious and sends jolts of arousal through my body. He moves to the other, showing it the same attention.

God, I need more.

I buck my hips into him and move my hand to the nape of his neck, grabbing on to the hair, the movement not enough to ease the desire consuming me. I'm vaguely aware of the water raining down on us as the room fills with steam. Romeo's hand slips between my legs, finding my slick pussy. Moans tumble from my lips when he pushes his finger inside, stretching me gloriously. It feels like heaven, but it's still *not enough.*

Resting his head on my chest, Romeo growls, "So fucking tight, *bella.*"

My voice doesn't sound like my own when I speak; it's filled with need and... lust. "I need more. Please, move."

Adjusting his stance, Romeo widens his legs before sliding in a second finger. His eyes blow wide as he focuses on where his fingers fill me, watching as he thrusts and withdraws them again and again. I take the opportunity to catalog the perfection of his chiseled body as rivulets of water cascade down it. "Ride my fingers like you'll ride my cock, Aurora. Get that pretty little pussy ready to take me."

My body is at his command, my hips move without any thought, rolling and grinding on his fingers as I seek out my release. Tingles cascade through my body and my head tips back, knocking against the shower wall. With my throat exposed to him, Romeo grazes his teeth over the vulnerable skin, sending ripples of ecstasy up my spine.

It's all too much and not enough at the same time. My moans and whimpers bounce around the walls of the bathroom until the sound of the shower is completely drowned out.

"That's right, Aurora. Take what you need."

Oh God, I'm so close.

My nails dig into his shoulders as I lose all control. The walls of my pussy spasm around his fingers, and I know in a few short moments I'll be free falling into ecstasy. Squeezing my eyes closed, I race toward my completion, pleasure building to the ultimate peak. Then it falls away, leaving me breathless and frustrated when he eases his fingers out. I ache, my walls twitching around the emptiness, my hips still grinding the air as I seek out his eyes.

There's a hunger reflected back at me. He looks even

more dark and dangerous now than he ever has. I should be afraid, but that look is only heightening my excitement. It's turning me on even more than I ever thought was possible.

Romeo releases my leg so he can push his boxers down. His cock springs free, but I can't bring myself to look down. Just from that small bit of contact, I know he's big and I'm afraid that if I catch sight of him, I'll push him away and put a stop to whatever this is. *And that's the last thing I want.* I need to forget; to fill the void inside of me. I need him to help me do that.

My body tenses when he brings the head of his cock to my entrance. Our eyes connect and he soothes, "Relax, *bella.* You're strong, you can take it. All of it."

I don't know that I can, but I'm sure as hell going to try.

Blowing out a breath, I force my body to relax. My breaths come in short, sharp pants and I'm unable to look away from his dark blue eyes as he eases into me, one thick inch at a time. It feels like he's tearing me in half. He stretches me to the point of pain, but it soon turns to pleasure as he inches his way in deeper. When he's fully seated, expletives fall from between his clenched teeth.

As my body adjusts, I roll my hips, testing out the feel of him inside of me. Impaled but in the best possible way.

Using his shoulders and the wall behind me, I lift my hips, bringing him halfway out before I drop back down. Our moans fill the air, and for a moment, he gives me full control. I revel in it, riding him, getting my body acquainted with his size and the feel of him stroking my walls. It's not a hard or fast pace, but I'm taking what I need and he's willingly giving it to me.

A feral growl echoes around the room as he takes back control. Romeo's hips buck, pistoning in and out with a ferocity that alone brings me so close to tumbling over the edge.

Tension builds in my core, and I arch my back, pressing my body into his as the sensations consume me. Driven to the point where I can't take any more, I snap, and it sends pulses of pleasure throughout my body. My walls clench around him as the most intense orgasm of my life washes through me, and I cry out in ecstasy.

We're both breathless as the room comes back into focus. The patter of the shower running in the background is a reminder of where we are. A light sheen of sweat covers my body and tingles erupt in the leg holding me up. It feels like an eternity before Romeo pulls out, and steps away from me. He turns the shower head onto himself and squeezes some shower gel into his hand, lathering it up before he runs them over his body.

I slump against the wall, still in the midst of my orgasmic afterglow, with a mind that can't quite make sense of where I am or what just happened. As I'm sorting through my hazy thoughts and getting my breathless body back under control, a wetness that can't be attributed to the shower slides down the inside of my thigh and my mouth drops open.

"Did you..." I clear my throat before trying again, unable to hide my shock. "Did you cum inside me?"

Romeo stands in front of me, suds from the shower gel covering his body as he holds my stare. He rinses off a hand before smoothing it down my stomach until he reaches the space between my legs.

He swipes a digit through my slit before bringing it up between us. Our combined release glistens on his finger, and I watch, mesmerized, as he takes it between his lips and sucks it clean.

His tongue darts out, swiping over his bottom lip. "It sure looks..." He pauses, holding my gaze with a heat that has my body yearning for more. "And tastes like it."

I stand there, in a trance, as he walks out of the cubicle. His back is to me as he shakes his head and murmurs, "Fucking exquisite."

My eyes track him as he grabs a towel and wraps it around his waist, completely unfazed. *What the hell just happened? This has got to be a dream. A figment of my imagination.*

It has to be.

"Use the shampoo and shower gel and get cleaned up, Aurora. I'll leave some clothes on the bed and send Daniele to take you back to your room."

His parting words slam me back to reality. I've been a fool to forget who it is I'm dealing with. I might have needed him for a moment, but not anymore. The less time I can spend with Romeo Bianchi, the better.

When I walk out of the bathroom fifteen minutes

later, my hair is clean and any traces of him on my body—
and the people that died in front of me today—have been
scrubbed away. Laid out on the bed—just like he said it
would be—is a white oversized T-shirt. I pull it over my
head just as Daniele knocks on the bedroom door.

With one last look around the luxury of Romeo's
bedroom, my bare feet pad silently across the carpet, and
I swing the door open, ready to return to my new reality.

C *azzo!*

What the hell was that? The events of the day have really messed with my head if I thought it was a good idea to fuck Aurora. Yes, it's taken the edge off my frustration, replacing it with a lightness in my chest that only comes from having an explosive orgasm. But I can't allow it to happen again.

Aurora is only here because of who her father is and what he's done. And until I can rule out that she hasn't been sending him smoke signals, *she is my enemy*.

I stride down the hallway, putting some much needed distance between us. Even now, having had a taste of her, I crave more. Exercising some discipline, I pull my phone from my pocket and open the text chain with Daniele.

ROMEO

Finish up whatever you're doing and take Aurora back to the basement.

His response is almost immediate.

DANIELE

I'll be there in twenty.

It's best for all parties involved if she stays locked in the basement. Considering what has gone down tonight, it's safe to say that Francesco will be well aware of us by now. Besides, Aurora will be safe in that room.

Safe from who, exactly?

I stalk through the house in search of Massimo, coming up empty as I enter the kitchen. Our conversation remains unfinished, as far as I'm concerned. I won't rest until we find out who the fuck thought they'd be smart enough to take *us* on.

Massimo's moved to his office and when I enter, he's standing behind his desk, discussing something with Leonardo. I take a seat and Massimo lifts an eyebrow in question. We both know that there will be no apologies from me for my outburst earlier. They are for weak-minded men who can't stand behind their actions.

He straightens, readjusting his belt buckle before dropping into his chair. The look on his face is all my cousin, without a hint of my subordinate. It's reinforced when he asks, "Have you taken the edge off?"

Not even a little.

It's a question I would have asked him had he blown in like I did. But it sends a frisson of guilt skating down my spine and I fight to keep my face neutral. I slept with the enemy and that is a betrayal that would see a man killed in normal circumstances. It doesn't help that I can still taste us on my tongue and her unique jasmine scent lingers in my nostrils, or that there's a devilish desire clawing in my gut for more.

Every ounce of strength I possess goes into keeping my ass planted firmly in my seat. No good will come from me returning to my bedroom and pinning her to the bed, or filling her with cum just so I can savor the taste again.

Running a hand down my face, I silently vow that, when all of this shit is over, I'll return home and forget all about Aurora Costa. She'll be eight feet deep with a dead deer on top of her to mask the scent of her decomposing body and keep her from being discovered and I'll find myself buried in another warm, willing pussy.

It won't be as perfect as hers.

I adjust myself in my seat, dismissing the taunting thoughts. They have no place in my mind, especially when there are bigger issues at hand than a spectacular piece of ass. Ignoring Massimo's question, I ask one of my own to channel our focus back into the task at hand. "What do you have?"

Massimo's face morphs into his usual glower and he shakes his head. He shows me a photo of the carnage of bodies scattered around the restaurant I was in less than two hours ago.

My nostrils flare and I clench and unclench my hands. Any anger that was washed away by my moment with Aurora has come back with full force. I can barely hear Massimo through the mist of rage that engulfs me.

"You were lucky, Rome. The police have run facial recognition on the bodies of two of the gunmen. They were wanted and linked to an organization coming out of Brooklyn. Our insider has said they don't know much about them yet. From what we've managed to gather, we know that they're newly formed and there's no link to a specific family or outfit, but that's about all we know."

"And the valet I took out at the back?" I spit the question like poison on my tongue.

"A twenty-five-year-old, white male from Queens. Worked there for three years. Not sure what the connection is between him and the other two. He was a recent graduate from NYU, and if I'm being honest with you, Rome, it's just plain fucking weird that he did what he did."

Through gritted teeth, I ask, "What about the one that got away?"

Massimo runs a frustrated hand through his hair before answering. "He's gone underground. The police are searching for him and our guy knows to bring us the intel as soon as he lays his hands on it. They managed to track him to the subway station before he disappeared. I've got men out there running down every contact they have. He won't be able to take a piss without us knowing, let alone leave the city."

His statement provides little comfort, and he knows it. We have nothing new and what we do know, were clues we got from the bodies of the *figli di puttana* I killed.

I lean back in my chair, resting my elbows on the arms and steepling my fingers. "What about your men?"

Massimo inhales deeply, darting a glance over at Leonardo, where he's leaning against the wall. "I don't think it was one of them."

Pinching the bridge of my nose, I edge forward in my seat. My tone is calm and I allow my eyes to convey my frustration as I speak. "Until we've ruled every one of them out, Massimo, you don't know shit. Everyone has a price and somebody in your house has been offered theirs. There is no right or wrong way to figure this out, but I'm telling you now that my way of dealing with it will work. The end will justify the means."

"Respectfully, Rome, I disagree. Killing my men will do nothing but expose us. I am asking you to trust me on this. We'll figure out who is behind the attacks and who is feeding them information, but for now, we need all hands on deck."

I bolt upright, my chair falling back and thudding onto the carpeted floor. Fisting Massimo's shirt, I drag him out of his seat with the desk between us as I seethe. "And how the fuck do you suppose we do that? Because from where I'm standing, we don't have *un cazzo*."

Massimo exhales sharply. I can see the cogs turning behind his eyes, working on a plan. His shoulders fall, and he meets my gaze. "Give me a week and if I haven't figured out who it is, then we can do it your way."

A humorless laugh falls from my lips and I look out of the window before schooling my features. Turning my focus back to him, I release my hold on his shirt. "A week?"

Massimo shrugs. His fingers tap a light rhythm on the mahogany desk, betraying his nervousness. "Yeah. A week, that's all I'm asking for."

I move quickly, grabbing the back of his neck, pulling down until his face is inches from the pictures of destruction I faced today. My head follows him down until we're at eye level with each other and only then do I spit out, "And just how many attempts will be made before your week is over? Will we even make it that far? Look at what they've done and *then* ask me for a fucking week." I force his face to the pictures before continuing, "If you weren't going to follow my instructions, why the fuck did you call me here?"

Pressing his head onto the desk, I release him and stand tall. He straightens, smoothing down his shirt with a neutral look on his face as he masks his emotions. "You know why I called you here, Rome. And you know that I've never once asked you to give me more time. I've always followed your direction without question, but right now, I'm listening to my gut, just like *Nonno* taught us."

We stare at each other for the longest time, both unwilling to back down. An edge creeps into the room, sucking out the light and turning it dark until Leonardo clears his throat.

I narrow my eyes. "You can have your week, but just know, the second we're attacked, I'll be lining you up out there," I motion through the window, before continuing, "with your men."

Massimo nods his agreement, and I turn to right my chair. We still have things to figure out. Taking a seat again, I ask, "Does it still look like Francesco is behind all of this, or are we being attacked by two different organizations?"

Leonardo stands tall, clasping his hands as he pushes his shoulders back. "We know it was definitely him behind the bombing at the docks. The evidence was clear on that one, what with his signature on the device. It's hard to say for certain with the restaurant or the other two attacks. What was left behind at each scene hasn't led us anywhere, but we have an address from the bodies at the restaurant and I'm going to take three men to check it out tonight."

"I think it would be better for us to keep this as quiet as possible."

Massimo rubs his eye. "What are you thinking?"

"If we're just staking out the place, then there's no reason it can't be the three of us and Daniele."

Leonardo picks up a picture from the pile scattered around the desk. He stares at it before setting it down and asking, "I don't want to speak out of place, but do you think that's wise? You were just involved in a shootout and, for all we know, this could be a trap."

Standing, I brace my shoulders and lift my chin, incensed that he'd question my decision. "You, more than anyone, know that I never cower away from a threat. And the next time you open your mouth to question me, do yourself a favor and reconsider. Given our friendship and all you have done for Massimo over the years, I'll let it slide this time." Buttoning up my jacket, I add, "Be ready by 2 am."

Both know better than to question me further, although I'll argue they shouldn't have questioned me in the first place. I understand their frustration, especially when we're getting blocked at every turn.

Leaving Massimo's office, I head for my bedroom. I need an outlet for this pent up energy that doesn't involve a certain captive. As tempting as it is to fuck my frustration out, I need to remain focused, and that's only something I can get from a couple of hours in the gym.

The war is so close I can almost touch it.

Chapter 14

Aurora

The barrel of a gun is aimed at me from across the restaurant. From my position beside the table Romeo and I were seated at, I can't see his face, but we're the only two people here. Everybody else faded away when a single gunshot rang through the air. My body vibrates from the intensity of the tremors racing through me as he seems to glide across the room.

For a moment, I close my eyes, cataloging the sounds around me. Glass crunching under his black military boots; the wind howling through the open window and the pounding of the rain as it hits the asphalt outside.

I feel his presence get closer and as he crouches in front of me, I open my eyes, trying to make out the features of his face. My teary vision blurs him out and the shadows underneath his hood hide any discernible features.

He lifts the gun again and an evil chuckle echoes around the room. It sounds like it's coming from everywhere, not just from him. It reminds me of the scenes in horror films where the clown appears in all the mirrors. *Except, I can't see his face.* His shoulders shake with the force of his laughter, and he drops the gun to his side before tilting his head.

"P-pl-ease." The word comes out as a stuttered plea, as I beg the faceless man for my life. The tears that threatened to fall now tumble down my cheeks unchecked and snot runs from my nose, coating my top lip. When he lifts the gun again, I scream, "N-o-o. Please, I-I haven't done anything wrong."

Sirens howl in the distance, but they aren't getting any closer.

I'm on my own and nothing I do will save me, because it's now, when I'm faced with certain death, that I realize I'm not really ready. My eyes flutter closed and I mutter a prayer. Praying for something or someone to save me. I promise to be a good person, to do anything if I can just live *one* more day.

I flinch, a sob wrenched from my lips when he stabs the gun into my cheek, twisting and turning the cold metal against my skin.

"Eyes on me."

My eyes dart open, bouncing around the hollow black space of his hood. I search for any hint of familiarity, a hope that maybe I can understand why he's doing this, but I come up empty. There's nothing about him that I recognize, nothing jolts my memory.

"Like many things in life, death is inevitable." He pauses, looking over his shoulder. "But you should know, when the devil comes knocking, if you want to see *her* again, you need to hand over your soul. *Everything* will end when he comes for you, and then you'll finally have the peace you have been craving so badly."

What does that mean? It's on the tip of my tongue to ask, but my attention shifts to movement behind him. I scoot further back, my head knocking against the edge of the table.

The silhouette of a woman comes into view, her hands clasped in a prayer position. I rub my eyes, trying to clear the haze covering her face. It's as if she's a drawing that's been smudged.

The cold metal of the gun pressing into my cheek fades away until it's just the two of us. Her features slot into place like a puzzle until she's standing before me with a soft smile and love shining in her eyes that looks the same, but somehow different.

"Mama?" The word is ripped from me, both pained and disbelieving.

I move to my knees, uncaring of the shards of glass that dig into my bare flesh. The need to be near her, to touch her one more time, masks any pain I might feel. *I've missed her so much.*

She takes a step forward, her features filled with

anguish, and then, in the blink of an eye, she's gone and the faceless man is back.

There's a twitch in his hand when he raises the gun. It doesn't match the authority in his tone when he sneers. "If only you'd have listened, Aurora."

Before I get a word out, he pulls the trigger and I shoot up in bed. My breaths come in quick, shallow pants and I push away the covers as I scramble to press my back to the concrete wall. The brick is abrasive on my exposed skin.

No matter how hard I fight it, I can't quite separate what's just happened from my reality. They're both a nightmare, neither easy to escape from. My eyes dart around as I press a hand over my racing heart. The corners of the room are bathed in shadows, but I can see enough to know that I'm alone. My chest rises and falls in a rapid rhythm as I try to filter through the noise in my mind. One question pushes to the forefront; *why was my mom there?*

A bead of sweat trickles from my forehead, running down my face before dropping to the floor. Strands of my hair stick to my face and I push my fingers through it, wiping my damp palms on the front of Romeo's T-shirt.

I frown when every breath I take is an effort and tiny black spots fill my vision. For the first time since I was taken, I'm afraid. *Terrified, in fact.* Of what's out there and what's to come. I feel so out of my depth and there's nobody that can help me through it.

When a familiar stinging at the back of my throat

makes its presence known, I force myself to walk toward the shower on unsteady legs. Drowning in my panic isn't an option right now, and so I seek a familiar comfort in the solace that comes from the water. A lot has happened in such a short space of time and no matter how hard I try, I can't make sense of any of it.

How is this real life?

Three days ago—*at least I think that's how long it's been*—I watched a bullet pass through a man's head and saw his body crumple onto the table in front of me. That's three days since I felt a bullet rush past my ear and into the skull of a man holding a gun to my temple.

I turn a blind eye to the glaring fact that it's also been three days since I had sex with the man holding me captive. He hasn't been to see me since. *Why would he?* Daniele came to collect me, just like Romeo said he would, and that alone said everything I needed to know. And just like that, with the forced reminder of our dynamic, I dismiss the pull in my chest that amplifies my body's yearning for him.

Since being *banished* to my prison cell, I've only seen one person. An older woman who introduced herself as Alma when she dropped a tray of food off and the drawing materials I'd asked Daniele for. She comes three times a day with a homemade meal, collecting the still full tray from the previous time. I could lie and say the reason I haven't eaten is because I'm worried they'll poison the food, but what would be the point? I haven't eaten because I need to be in control of at least *one* thing in my life, and this is it.

Locked away in my windowless room, I've spent my days sketching out the memories that plague me. Some are happy, others are sad, but none are of the face of the man who showed up in my dream tonight. My favorites are the ones from when I was younger and my mom was still alive. We'd travel hours out of the city to a big house, and I'd play with the children that lived there while she... *I don't actually know what she did.* Once a month, we'd take three buses from the city and I'd get to play with three little boys.

The flashbacks are hazy and the boys remain faceless, but there are some things that I can see *so* clearly. Like the fountain and the garden of roses that are sometimes bright and red, but other times bleak and black. I don't know what any of it means, but at least the time seems to pass quickly when my mind is occupied with looking back on the past.

In a daze, I turn on the shower and immediately walk under the cold spray. The material of the T-shirt soaks through in a matter of seconds, sticking to the curves of my body. I fall forward, my arms heavy when I lift them to press my hands to the wall and keep myself upright.

The water pours over my head and I give in to the sobs that have my body convulsing. My chest aches, and when my knees give out, I collapse onto the grimy tiled floor, unable to stop myself. I curl into a ball with the water still pounding down on me and goosebumps forming on every inch of my skin. Even as my teeth chatter, I scream out in pain and anguish. Everything is just too much. *How do I survive any of this?*

It feels like an eternity before the water switches off. I stare at the cubicle wall, unmoving, with my arms wrapped around my waist, silently begging for a different kind of devil to come for me.

Chapter 15

Romeo

After three days of living in a car, we've achieved absolutely *nothing*. The information we were given was a dud and whoever was there was long gone before we even arrived. Either they were lucky, or someone told them we were coming.

We're back to where we were three days ago. *Con niente*. Every avenue we chase down leads to a dead end.

Massimo's exhausted voice cuts through the quiet of the car as Leonardo navigates the winding driveway back to the house. "Let's rest up. I'll have Alma fix us some food later and then we can figure out our next steps."

I bounce my knee and stare blankly out of the window. Despite the fatigue hovering over me like a dark cloud, there's an anticipation running through me as we close the distance to the house. Distracted, I reply, "Sounds good, cousin."

The car comes to a stop at the bottom of the steps and

we climb out, our exhaustion clear in our crumpled clothes and the way we're having to force ourselves to move. One of Massimo's men greets us, avoiding my gaze. "Don." He inclines his head before running a hand over the back of his neck. "We, uh, had a situation with the prisoner this morning."

My brow furrows, and I step between him and Massimo, forcing his attention to me. I'm at least a head taller than him as I get into his space. "What do you mean 'a situation'?" The venom in my tone is barely concealed. I ignore why it's there in the first place and grab onto his shirt, forcing him back.

Wide eyes meet mine before he corrects himself and masks his fear. When his heels hit the bottom step, I take his weight, pulling him until our faces are inches from each other. "You look at *me* when you're talking about her. If I have to remind you again, I'll have no problem gouging your eyes out."

His eyes widen and he stutters, "S-sorry, sir."

Releasing him, I straighten the cuffs of my shirt. Massimo's mouth pulls into a smug smirk and I clench my fists by my sides to keep from knocking it off his face.

"We found her in the shower…"

My stomach drops. He holds his hands up. "She's fine." The 'I think' hovers in the air before he continues, "The water was switched off as soon as we realized. We reviewed the video footage, and it looks like something spooked her. She gets into the shower—fully clothed—but then she—" He pauses, shuffling his feet as if he knows his next words will displease me. "Well, she collapsed to the floor, and when she didn't get up..." He trails off, shrugging as if the rest of the sentence should finish itself.

Massimo's hand lands on my shoulder, squeezing as he speaks for me. "Lorenzo, where is she now?"

Lorenzo's gulp is audible and echoes around the garden. I grind my back molars. He at least has the sense to look away when he replies, "She's still in her cell. We called Aldo, but he said you'd been clear on the instructions to leave her. That we were to only go in there if we were taking her food and Alma has been doing that."

He continues talking, rambling about how they were following my orders and that he was concerned because she hasn't been eating, but I'm not fully listening. It only takes a second before I'm racing up the stairs and into the house. My muscles tighten with every step I take and guilt gnaws in my gut. *I should have never left her for this long.*

Thankfully, the door to the basement is unlocked. I swing it open, uncaring when it knocks into the credenza behind. I race down the stairs, urgency fueling my movements. The key is hanging on the wall next to the door and I snatch it up before forcing myself to take a breath so I can unlock it.

The relief I feel when I get it open is short-lived when my eyes land on Aurora. There's an ache in my throat and a sourness on my tongue as I take in her lifeless body. She's curled up in the fetal position on the shower floor. Unblinking eyes stare straight ahead and if it wasn't for the tremors wracking her body, I'd think she was dead.

What have you done, Aurora?

My footsteps are hurried and heavy as I move across the room and snatch up the blanket from the bed. Striding toward her, I curse every single one of Massimo's men for having left her in this state. *Would she have still been alive if we'd come back in a day or two?*

She doesn't look to see who it is, and for some unexplainable reason, *that* pisses me off more. I never should have left her down here. If she dies... *Dio*, I can't think about that. She's going to be okay. Crouching down, I throw the blanket over her body and smooth a hand over her arm. She doesn't stir or move, instead, she continues to stare straight ahead.

There's a darkness under her eyes that wasn't there when I last saw her; it's amplified by the paleness of her skin. And despite having only been gone for three days, she looks like she's lost weight and is—if her blue-hued, cracked lips are anything to go by—dehydrated.

Securing her in my arms, I tighten my hold on her for a moment. Her body is limp and catatonic, even as I pull her into my warmth. Guilt assails me. It's my fault she's like this. If I hadn't left, she'd be okay. *I'll be damned if she's going to spend another night down here.*

Crossing the threshold into the main house, I come to a stop when I find Massimo waiting in the corridor. He regards me with a look of curiosity, his brows raised before he walks off in the direction of his office.

My arms flex around Aurora and I murmur soothing words as we continue through the house. When we reach my bedroom, I lay her on the bed, but there's still no sign of her behind the blank stare.

Cazzo.

I stalk into the bathroom to turn on the shower. Pent up energy rushes through my body and I move to stand in front of the mirror, staring at my reflection and urging myself to calm down. It doesn't take long for steam to fill the room. I rest my hands on the vanity unit, rolling my shoulders to ease the tension that's seeped into the muscles. If I go out there now, I'll demand an answer I don't think she can give me.

With one last heavy exhale, I return to the bedroom. She's still in the same position I left her in, staring at the wall. I take hold of her hands and pull her up. Banding an arm around her waist, I bend my knees to look into her eyes. She stares back at me, unseeing behind a dead stare.

I shake my head, before finding the hem of her T-shirt. My jaw ticks as I lift it, pulling the soaked cotton over her head. Her nipples are pebbled from the cold, and I force my gaze away from them. *Now isn't the time to be admiring her beauty.* I drop the soaked material to the floor, the dull, wet sound on the carpet loud in the otherwise quiet room.

Scooping her up in my arms, I carry her into the bathroom before seating her on the counter. I cup her cheek, stroking the pale skin as I urge her to look at me. She blinks, and although she's staring at me, I don't think she's really seeing me.

My eyes land on the reflection of her back in the mirror and it's then that I notice the scar running nearly the entire length of her spine. Although the line is thin, its raised appearance tells me it's old.

A memory of blood spilling into water fills my vision before I'm jolted back to the present, with a heavy weight settling on my chest. My brows tug together. *What the hell was that?*

I watch Aurora, trying—and failing—to catch another glimmer of the image that flashed through my mind. My concern forms a groove between my brows, and I pick her up, carrying her into the shower, uncaring whether I get soaked in the process.

Water covers us within seconds and I slide her down the length of my body, forcing my mind to think of anything but the temptation that she holds. *Getting a hard dick is definitely not appropriate when she's in this state.* Murmuring into her hair, I loosen my hold on her a fraction. "Aurora."

She flinches out of my hold, pushing her body into the corner, looking up at me with wide, terrified eyes. Her chin trembles, and I bend my knees to meet her gaze. "It's okay. You're safe."

Is she really?

As long as I have her, will she ever be safe?

Clearing my throat, I hold up my hands and take a step back. "Take your time, *bella*."

Running a hand over my jaw, I sigh before returning to the bedroom. I head for the closet, pulling out a fresh T-shirt for Aurora and making a mental note to arrange some clothes for her. Right now, we both need sleep.

———

After making sure she was okay, I gave Aurora some privacy to have a warm shower while I got changed and checked my emails. Twenty minutes later, she steps out of the bathroom as I'm staring out of the window thinking about the clusterfuck of a mess we've found ourselves in. In the reflection of the pane, I can just about make out Aurora's silhouette wrapped in a white towel. She remains on the threshold, her uncertainty clear as she clutches the doorframe.

The silence drags on and I turn to face her as I lean against the window ledge. "There's a T-shirt for you on the bed. Get some sleep, *bella*."

She bites down on her bottom lip, and it takes everything I have inside of me not to storm across the room and tug it free. She chews on the flesh, and I ball my hands into fists. "When will I be going back to the basement?"

Never. "You'll sleep in here tonight."

She appears to be thinking over my reply, her attention moving to the bed. Her voice is small when she asks, "Where will you sleep?"

I'm tempted to tell her that I'll be sleeping with her, but she's been through enough and I'm too tired to deal with her defiance. Although I'm not sure I'd get it in her current state. She might be talking but I don't like how quiet and meek she's being.

Straightening, I amble toward her, my movements purposefully slow and steady. Her eyes grow wide and I half expect her to take a step back at my advance. Instead, she catches herself and I watch the glorious moment the spark ignites in her eyes and she lifts her chin. The corner of my mouth kicks up and I brush away a strand of wet hair that's resting on her cheek.

"Don't worry, Aurora. You can have the bed all to yourself."

Her eyes flit back to the bed and I can see that she wants to say more, but I don't give her the opportunity. Stepping around her, I walk into the bathroom, closing the door behind me.

Chapter 16

Aurora

"P-p-lease," I plead.

A shadow, cloaked in wickedness, wraps around my ankle, turning the flesh black. It grips like a vise as it drags me across the restaurant. Its speed only increasing with each plea that tumbles from my lips. It doesn't matter how hard I fight, its hold is stronger and overpowering. Shards of glass rip into my body.

The faceless man from earlier has returned. This time, his head floats around me and his evil laugh plays out like a soundtrack to the torment of the shadow. They work in tandem, seeing which one can break me first, but that happened a long time ago. Now it's like a never-ending ride in the pits of hell and there's nothing I can do to get out.

My fingers dig into the concrete floor, trying to stop his momentum. Streaks of blood are left in my wake and my nails pull away from the bed of my fingers. The pain is unbearable, but I won't stop.

A woman screaming blares somewhere in the distance. The sound is gut-wrenching and foreign to my ears. I'm momentarily distracted from my own anguish as I search for her, even as the room continues to spin. My vision blurs, the restaurant unrecognizable as a space.

Suddenly, everything stops.

The sudden lack of motion throwing off my equilibrium. There's no more screaming, no more laughing, no more sirens, and no more shadows.

It's just me.

My chest is tight with every breath I greedily suck in. It feels like my heart is going to beat out of my rib cage and it's only when I've got my breathing under control that I allow the whimpers to fall from my lips. Tears stream down my cheeks and I wallow in the trepidation that's pinning me to the ground.

His black military boots come into view. The familiarity of them is clear, even through my blurred vision. My body tenses and I watch him come toward me, grinding the blood-covered glass into the ground as he prowls. I try to move, but my body doesn't cooperate.

He *tsks* as he walks around me and then, much like the first time I met him, he crouches in front of me. Shoving the barrel of his gun into my bloodied, bruised cheek, he sneers. "I didn't think you'd be this stupid, but clearly, I was wrong. You came back for more. There really is no getting through to you, is there, Aurora?"

I try to move away, but the force holds me still, wedging me between the ground and his weapon. With pleading eyes, I stare into the hollow of his hood and beg, "Please, I haven't done anything wrong. You have to believe me. I don't know why I'm here."

He ignores me, tilting his head to the side. "Maybe I need to do something *extreme* to get your attention."

The restaurant falls away and I'm tied to a chair in my apartment, the outside wall missing as rain pelts down into the space. It isn't lost on me that this is the same position I was in when Romeo took me. Or that I feel everything. The fear, the hopelessness, the panic. They're all there, battling to be the emotion that controls me.

My head is yanked back before bony fingers take hold of my cheeks and force my attention to the window across the street. Wide-eyed, my focus zones in on the only illuminated window. The same one that a camera was set up in for who knows how long.

The hooded man lifts his hand, pulling the building closer. When it's inches from mine, my eyes widen as they land on my mom. She's oblivious to us as she stares out of the window. I scream, but the gag that's suddenly appeared in my mouth muffles the words. She can't hear me. Helplessly, I watch as a shadow slithers up behind her. A knife appears at her throat, the light glinting off the metal before it moves, slashing from right to left. Her eyes flare, horror filling her face before she falls out of sight.

I bolt upright, screams of terror rushing past my lips as I look around the dark room. A warm body envelops me, and as I breathe in his familiar masculine scent, I try to calm my whirling mind. It takes me a moment to get my bearings and remember where I am and whose bed I'm in. *God, it felt so real.*

Romeo's hand soothes a hypnotic rhythm up and down my back as he murmurs into my hair, "You're okay. It's okay. I've got you."

For a moment, I burrow into him, taking the comfort I desperately need. I've not felt the warmth of another person's hug in so long. My fingers press into his bare back, urging him closer until I remember everything.

My brows tug down, and I try to pull out of his embrace, but he tightens it. It's somehow still comforting even as he exudes his power to keep me where he wants me.

He pulls me back onto the mattress, settling me into his arms as he says, "Go back to sleep, Aurora."

I'm too exhausted to fight with him. *What would be the point anyway?* If there is one thing I've learned about Romeo Bianchi, it's that you do as he commands. Fighting him will only make it worse.

Cocooned in the comfort of his hold, I blink slowly, my eyes getting heavier with each second that passes. *Please let me have a dreamless sleep.*

Chapter 17

Aurora

Pink and orange hues illuminate the skin of my eyelids, lifting the veil of a dreamless sleep. I stretch my arms, luxuriating in the cotton rustling around me, and my eyes flutter open, squinting at the brightness. Maybe if I stay here, I can pretend that I've had the best sleep of my life and that none of this is happening to me. Avoiding reality sounds pretty damn good right about now.

In the safety of Romeo's bed and with the calming quiet of the room, I allow myself to forget the events of the past few days. I turn onto my side, watching the branches of the tree just beyond the window rustle in the breeze. Water stains the windowpane and a lone droplet runs from one end to the other before being blown away.

On my periphery, I can see the empty chair just off to the side. I don't want to look at it or address the disappointment that's settled into my gut at him being gone. I should be relieved that he's not here. He saw me at my weakest and I have no doubt that he will use it against me. I need to reinforce my armor before I see him again.

Throwing back the covers, I climb from the bed, wiggling my toes on the soft carpet before standing. I pad across the room, toward the window. Instinctively, my hand runs along the arm of the chair, like I might be able to feel him there.

What is wrong with me?

The man held me in his arms and yet I'm obsessing over a chair he spent mere hours in. Redirecting myself to the window, I gaze out at the rolling hills. The gravel driveway seems to go on for miles and it dawns on me just how remote this place is. Resting my head on the cool glass, I squeeze my eyes shut, trying to understand my jumbled thoughts.

Is it too early for Stockholm Syndrome to kick in? I don't have that. Jeez. So what if he held me in his arms and soothed away my nightmare? He's still a cold-blooded killer and the reason I'm here and having bad dreams in the first place.

Movement near the edge of the tree line draws my attention. Two men with guns pass each other as they patrol the perimeter. A sharp tightness shoots through my chest. There one moment and gone the next.

Falling back into the chair, I'm hit with the scent of his woodsy cologne. It crowds me, cementing the fact that nothing will ever be the same. Even if I make it out of here alive, I'll be intrinsically changed, untrusting of anyone and everyone. My fate rests in the hands of a man who has made threats to kill me, and yet, no matter how much I don't want to, I can do nothing but surrender to him.

A knock sounds at the door, and I stand, instantly on guard for whoever may be on the other side. I soothe my hands down the front of Romeo's T-shirt, wishing I'd had the forethought to find a weapon. For some reason, I feel more exposed up here than I did in the basement.

I watch intently as the handle turns and the door is pushed open. Daniele stops mid-stride, averting his eyes when he says, "You're awake."

Nodding, I twist my fingers together before forcing my hands to my side. It's been a while since I've spoken and the act feels foreign when I stutter, "Y-y-yes."

He points toward the door he hasn't taken his eyes off of. "I—"

I cut him off. "What time is it?"

"Four-thirty."

Daniele has been nothing but gracious since I was taken. Maybe it's naïve of me, but I don't think he'd hurt me and so I think nothing of following him into another room. Besides, I have questions and he has the answers.

Daniele opens the door to what I now realize is the closet and I come to stop on the threshold. He pulls open a drawer, and I ask, "How long have I been asleep?"

He lifts a shoulder, pulling open another and moving around its contents. Over his shoulder, he replies, "I think it's been something like thirteen hours."

My eyes widen. *What? How is that even possible?*

I look around, my gaze landing on the bedroom door that's been left *wide* open. Gnawing on my bottom lip, I consider running for all of two seconds. The armed guards I saw outside shut down any idea I might have of making a break for it. And anyway, this is probably a test. Someone could be waiting in the hallway, eager to take me out.

Within seconds of me dismissing the idea to run, Daniele hands me a folded item of clothing. "Put them on. Romeo doesn't want you walking around the house half dressed."

Affording me some privacy, he leaves the room, closing the door behind him. I wait for a moment, listening intently for the sound of a key turning in the lock, but it never comes.

I spring into action, a fluttering in my stomach as I hold up a pair of soft, black sweats.

Quickly, I gather up one leg, stepping into it before I do the same with the other. Yards of material pool at my ankles and I hold the waistband to keep them from falling down.

Great.

It'll be more embarrassing to have them fall down than to not wear them at all, but who am I to go against Romeo's demands? With the hem of the T-shirt in my mouth, I pull on the drawstring before rolling the waistband down. When I let go, they slip down, riding low on my hips before I give up.

Darting into the bathroom, I come to a stop in front of the mirror. My reflection taunts me, reminding me of my lack of proper nutrition and self-care. Not wanting to dwell on it, I look away, splashing some warm water on my face and running some toothpaste around my teeth. Finger-combing my hair, I wince as I tug on the knots that have formed, wishing I'd asked for a brush instead of paper and pencils.

My shoulders slump, and my arms fall to my side. *Who am I preening myself for?* It sure as hell shouldn't be for any man in this house. They should see the mess I am in all its glory because if it wasn't for them, I wouldn't look like this.

Blowing out a breath, I roll my eyes and walk out of the bathroom. I hesitate for a second before straightening my spine and marching across the room to the bedroom door.

Pulling it open, I'm greeted by Daniele as he stands with a wide-legged stance, scrolling on his phone. He lifts his head and straightens before waving his arm for me to go ahead of him.

"Would it be possible for you to bring me some more drawing paper? And a hairbrush?" I ask as we start to walk.

"You've used the pad already?"

Chancing a glance at him as we approach the top of the stairs, I reply, "Yes."

Daniele's nostrils flare a fraction, but he doesn't say anything, only nodding as we continue down the stairs.

When we reach the bottom, I turn right, heading for the basement. It might be a journey I've only made twice, but I know my place and I know sleeping upstairs was a one-off.

Daniele cups my elbow, and my eyes bore into his fingers as they grip me and he steers me to the left. I blink up at him, my brow furrowed and a question on the tip of my tongue, but he shakes his head and continues moving us forward. *What is it with these men and shutting me down?*

We walk down the hallway in silence, passing a man with an automatic weapon who stands guard at a door. I divert my eyes until we pass him, taking in the paintings that hang on the opposite wall. When he's behind us, I turn to look out of the floor-to-ceiling windows that make up the other wall. Orange light spills through and onto the heated white marble flooring as the sun sets, reminding me of how long I've slept for.

At the end of the corridor, Daniele pulls me to a stop. I rest my hand on my fluttering stomach as I take in the intricate gold design of the double doors in front of us. Quietly, I blow out a breath, pushing down the nerves of the unknown as Daniele opens the doors. He steps back, giving me an unobstructed view of the room.

I gasp. The beauty and grandeur is like nothing I've ever seen before. There's a fairytale element to the space. With the ceiling and nearly every wall being made entirely of glass, it's like being outside but protected from the elements. *This would be a beautiful room to hold a wedding in. Woah. Where did that come from?*

My eyes bounce around the room, finally coming to rest on the large table that takes center stage. At the furthest end, Romeo sits with three other men. Two I recognize from the night of the shooting. It's hard not to remember the guy who barely contained his disgust at my presence. What was the other one's name? Leo. He showed the women in. Their presence sends a frisson of awareness skating down my spine.

Dark thoughts consume me, playing out in my mind. *Does Romeo need an audience to kill me? Is that why I've been brought here? Or are they going to...* Fear takes hold of me, wrapping around my throat like an old friend. The need to escape is more prevalent than ever.

I flinch when Daniele's hands rest on my shoulders, and he urges me forward. Refusing to move, I bear down, pushing back into him.

The conversation between the men halts and I'm aware of their focus turning toward me. "Sit, Aurora." Romeo's voice is a cocktail of impatience and empathy. When I remain where I am, he adds, "You're eating with us. Nothing more."

Daniele exhales heavily before he cups my elbow and forces me in the direction of Romeo. A snarl echoes around the room from the other end of the table and Daniele drops my arm, holding up his hands. Romeo's lip is curled up at the corner and there's a cold hardness in his eyes.

Romeo pushes out the chair next to him, inclining his head for me to sit. I slide into the high-backed chair, refusing to lock eyes with anyone. Power hangs in the air, and a desire to make myself as small as possible overtakes me. I fiddle with the material of the T-shirt pooled in my lap, needing something to distract me.

Daniele takes the seat next to me. He's barely in the chair before the tantalizing aroma of tomatoes teases my nostrils. I wrap my arms around my waist, trying to muffle the loud and garish gurgling sounds being omitted from it.

When a bowl of minestrone soup is placed in front of me, I close my eyes, subtly inhaling the tangy tomato scent. It's been at least four days since my last meal. I'm so hungry, but I *won't* eat. I stare at the contents of the bowl, the sound of cutlery clanging against china calling for me to pick up the spoon and have just one taste. My tongue darts out, swiping over my lips. Water from the shower hasn't really been cutting it, and the longer I look at the bowl in front of me, the less I remember why I'm not eating.

Because you want some semblance of control.

Right, and I guess it's one way to die. *Although doesn't it take months to die from starvation?*

"Everybody out." It's a booming and growled demand that forces my attention from the bowl in front of me. Daniele, Leo and the other guy—whose name I don't know—stand, grumbling as they walk from the room. My focus shifts to Romeo and his cousin who remain.

They're staring at each other, a silent conversation going on before Romeo pointedly says, "You too, Massimo."

I stand with him, my hand pressing into the table to steady myself as I stumble from my chair. Romeo's fingers wrap around my wrist and I pray that he can't feel my racing pulse. He holds me steady, even when I tug my arm, trying to break out of his grip.

"Sit, Aurora."

I drop back into the chair defeatedly and it's only then that he releases me. Folding my arms over my chest, I ready myself for whatever he's going to demand I do. I know that I won't like it, but I'll do it if it means I get to go home.

Romeo takes hold of the underside of my chair. The sound of wood scraping on wood is loud in the otherwise quiet room as he turns me toward him. The muscles in his arm strain under the weight and I watch, transfixed at the sight of his veins bulging. With his legs on either side of me and the heat from his body winding around us, I gnaw on my lower lip and fight the desire pooling in my core.

"Eyes up."

My head snaps up, and when I realize what I've done, my eyes shoot daggers at his arrogant face. *God, I'm a fucking puppet and he's the master*. He chuckles like he knows the power he holds over me, before turning his attention to my bowl of soup.

Carefully lifting the bowl, he swipes a spoon up from the table and runs it over the top of the red liquid. I expect him to lift it to my mouth, but he puts it in his own, pulling it back out clean. When his tongue darts out, I follow the movement as he wipes up a drop from the corner of his mouth.

I shouldn't want this man and yet my pussy throbs like it craves to be filled by him again. *Well, that is never going to happen again.* Crossing my legs, I shift in my chair to ease the ache and to put some space between us.

Romeo's voice is throaty, his attention on the soup when he asks, "Why are you not eating, *bella*?"

Brushing off my wholly inappropriate thoughts about what I want him to do to me, I inspect my nails, pushing for an air of nonchalance when I reply, "I don't know what you're talking about."

He huffs out a laugh before dropping the spoon into the bowl and leaning back in his chair. "Really? I have it on good authority that you've not eaten any of the meals Alma's prepared."

Apparently, Alma is a snitch. *Why does he care anyway?* Crossing my arms over my chest, I jut my chin out and hold his gaze. The lie falls from my lips with ease. "I don't know who told you that, but you've been misinformed."

The corner of his mouth lifts and the challenge in his cobalt-blue eyes is clear. "Okay, so eat the soup."

My response is quick. "I don't like minestrone."

"Everyone likes minestrone." The way he says it is so matter of fact, like whatever he says goes. I suppose in some ways it does, you don't become a man of his ranking by pandering to others. Romeo scoops up a spoonful of soup, holding it up and leaving me with no choice. I lean forward, closing my mouth around it. At the first hit of tangy tomato on my tongue, I close my eyes and moan. My stomach gurgles, demanding more. I look at the bowl and then to Romeo expectantly.

He clears his throat, shifting in his seat. "Don't like minestrone, *eh?*"

The lightness and teasing in his tone confuse me, and I sit back, a groove forming in my brows. *This isn't right.* He shouldn't be feeding me like we have an intimate relationship. He's holding me *prisoner*. I'd be a fool to forget the danger that follows this man. Especially when in the short time I've been around Romeo Bianchi, I've witnessed more death and destruction than I have in my entire twenty-eight years of existence.

The teasing has gone, replaced with a seriousness that appears to be born of concern when he asks again, "Why have you not been eating, *bella?*"

Everything fades away and I'm transported back to the restaurant with blood and broken glass surrounding me. Screams fill the air, but this time, they aren't mine, and I know that this isn't a nightmare. This is my new reality. *Unless I do something about it.*

Shaking my head, I force myself back into the moment. Praying he'll accept my non-answer, I murmur, "I wasn't hungry."

His eyes narrow, and I dig my nails into the palm of my hand to keep from squirming. Romeo shakes his head before moving his attention back to the bowl in his hand. My shoulders drop, tension releasing from my body as I watch him skim the spoon over the top of the soup. We fall into an easy routine as he brings spoonful after spoonful to my lips, ignoring my protests when I tell him I can feed myself.

It doesn't take long before the bowl is empty and the others return. Their conversation is coded, but it doesn't stop me from observing their dynamic from under my lashes.

What happens now?

I need to find a way out of here. As much as I can try to convince myself that bending to Romeo's will is the right thing to do if I want to live, the truth is; *I don't know him.*

Straightening in my seat, I wrap the hem of my T-shirt around my finger, ignoring the churning in my gut. So what if they kill me trying to escape? At least I'll have gone out partly on my own terms. Finding a way out of here has to be my priority. *What do I know about these men and where I am?*

One. They are the mafia. That much is clear.

Two. The place is guarded like a fortress and miles from civilization.

Three. The chances of being shot trying to escape are *extremely* high.

Four. They want my father and will use me to exact their revenge, even if it means I get killed in the process.

Five. When I am of no use to them, they *will* follow through on their threats to end my life.

My focus is pulled to Romeo when he leans back in his chair and speaks to Daniele in Italian. I study the features of his handsome face and the way his mouth moves as he talks. I need to be careful.

If I let him, Romeo will get under my skin until he's a part of my very existence. It doesn't take a genius to work out that it would be the worst possible thing that could happen.

Especially when he's going to kill me.

Chapter 18

Romeo

The door to Massimo's office hasn't even closed before he turns to me, a question in the raise of his one smug brow. If he wasn't family, that eyebrow would have seen a bullet between his eyes long before now. As it is, I'm starting to think he gets too much leeway.

Ignoring him, I cross the room, helping myself to a drink from the trolley. Pouring a finger of scotch into a glass, I hold up the canister, offering a drink to the others. As expected, they all decline.

We all know that I'm buying myself some time before the inevitable questioning around what happened at dinner starts. There's a heaviness in the air as I pick up the crystal glass and walk to the couch at the back of the room. Massimo falls into the seat behind his desk, huffing as he shakes his head. Leonardo stands beside it.

My *nonno* taught me that silence is golden in an interrogation. Human beings have a natural inclination to fill the awkwardness that comes with the quiet. Massimo is no exception to this rule, and I'd put my money on him speaking first. I sip my drink, looking over the rim at them both.

Massimo leans back in his chair, his chin resting on his fist. The open body language makes him appear calm, but I give it three more seconds.

One.

Two.

Three.

"Nobody else is going to say it, so I will. What the hell was that about, Rome?"

He's family.

The statement is a chant on repeat in my mind, reminding me not to kill him right now.

I throw back the remainder of my drink, discarding the glass on the coffee table in front of me. My legs are splayed as I remain seated on the couch and the voice of my *nonna* is begging me to keep the devil inside leashed. If our roles were reversed, I would be asking the same question, but I still find my fingers itching to unholster my gun and ask him who the fuck he thinks he is.

I roll my shoulders, the stiffness in them a reminder of last night's sleeping arrangements. It's swiftly followed by guilt at the reminder of Aurora's screams and the way her body trembled in my arms. *I did that.* I'm the reason for her nightmares and that doesn't fill me with satisfaction like it should.

Resting my ankle on my knee, I cock a brow and dare him to challenge me when I ask, "Which part exactly?"

He runs a hand through his hair, his frustration evident in the action. "You know what I mean, Rome. Why was the woman you've said is *our* hostage eating at *my* table?"

Holding his brown eyes, I order, "Out."

Leonardo leaves without protest. *At least someone knows their position in this house.*

With every second that passes, the air in Massimo's office becomes more and more charged, until his annoyance is rolling off of him in waves. He stands, pacing behind his desk, the energy he's holding onto spilling out into every bouncing step.

"I'm struggling to keep up with what the plan is, Rome."

Translation: I'm doing shit that doesn't make sense.

Scrubbing a hand over my jaw, I exhale heavily. He has as much at risk as I do. I should show him a little courtesy and be honest, but the truth is, I don't know why I'm doing what I'm doing.

Out of the two of us, I'm the one who considers every step before I take it. I calculate the risk and determine whether or not it's worth it. But when it comes to *her?* *Fuck.* I'm operating on instinct alone.

I should tell Massimo that I'll send her back to the basement. Even better, I should reassure him that I'll get rid of her because the likelihood of her being of any use to us is very slim.

Despite knowing what I *should* do, I still find myself opening my mouth, and with a tone that sounds bored, yet laced with patronization, saying, "She hasn't eaten for four days, cousin. We don't want her dead, *eh*?"

Massimo stares at me for the longest time before he drops back into his chair. Skepticism fills his voice, and he drags out each word. "Right, because she's the bait."

A muscle ticks in my jaw. Anger and disgust swirl beneath the surface at that word. *Bait.* She's more than that. Massimo looks at me expectantly, a brow raised, and I push down the feelings that I don't have the capacity to examine.

Grinding my molars, I unclench my jaw. "Exactly. Stop looking for something that isn't there and let's figure out what our next steps are."

I slide my phone from my pocket, shooting off a text to Daniele and Leonardo asking them to come to the office. When I move my focus back to Massimo, his head's still bobbing in agreement before he says, "I just have one question, maybe two, and then I'll leave it."

Staring him down, I wait. I already know what he's going to ask and if that *fucking* brow pops again, the fact that we're family won't mean shit.

"Why is she sleeping in your room? If she's our bait, shouldn't she be in the basement?" Genuine curiosity fills his voice.

She should, but she won't be spending another night

there. Last night, Daniele sent me the CCTV footage of her nightmare. I could hear her rasping breaths, even though there was no sound. A feeling I've never felt before settled on my chest and as I watched her sleep in my bed, I made her a promise. *If these are her last days, I won't let her die like a man full of sin, not when she's an angel of purity.*

Clearing my throat, I straighten my cuffs and look down my nose at him. "Massimo, if I have to remind you of your place in this family, you won't have one. I don't answer to you and you'll do well to remember that." There's a deathly calm to my tone that has seen many men piss themselves before I take their life.

I know he wants to demand an answer. He's grown too sure of himself with nobody to keep him in check in the years since his father passed. I'm to blame for that. The thought has a tightness forming in my chest and a heaviness settling in my stomach. *When this is all over, I'll have to make sure I visit more.*

"What's your other question?" I ask.

His eyes search mine, no doubt looking for a tell before he asks, "You'll be taking her to the gala next weekend?"

Fuck.

How could I have forgotten about that?

Sleep deprivation, that's how. I've barely slept twelve hours in the five days we've been here.

On day one of our stakeout, Massimo received a call from an associate who got their hands on the guest list of a gala being held by the Mayor of New York next Saturday. Francesco somehow managed to snag an invite, so of course, we need to attend. Which also means I need to take Aurora. Because she's our *bait*.

My hand balls into a fist on my thigh. "Maybe. For all we know, it could be a trap. Have we ruled out your friend who got us the reservation for the restaurant?"

The same 'friend' that got us the reservation is going to get us onto that guest list, but the idea is niggling at me. Very few people knew we would be there, and she was one of them. In fact, she was the only one that isn't a trusted member of this household. *I don't trust her.*

Massimo rubs at his eyes. "I don't think it was her, Rome. She didn't know that the reservation would be for you. All she did was put us in contact with someone at the restaurant and your name wasn't used."

I think over what he's said. I guess that does make sense, but I'm still going to have her looked into. Maybe Callum can do some digging for me.

A knock at the door halts our conversation and Massimo calls out. Daniele and Leonardo enter, dipping their heads to us before taking seats along the wall.

I'm staring at Massimo, waiting for him to take the lead, but he's watching me expectantly, waiting for my confirmation. Frustrated, I reply to his earlier question, "Yes, I'll be taking her. Have Maria arrange for a dress but maybe leave the hair and makeup. I don't need Aurora to look like a high-class hooker." *Again.*

Massimo smirks, and with too much sweetness

injected into his voice for a man of his position, he asks, "Are you sure?"

"Yes," I bite.

Pouting, he sits straighter in his chair and we get to work figuring out a plan for the gala now that we have a lead on Francesco.

Chapter 19

Aurora

Daniele holds Romeo's bedroom door open for me, inclining his head when I hesitate to enter. I don't understand why I've been sent up here again. Surely any courtesy I've been shown is over now? He's fed me, I've slept for hours and now I should be back in my cell?

Daniele sighs heavily as he stares down at me, his impatience clear in the way his jaw works with every second that ticks by. In the distance, there's a steady hum of chatter, reminding me that we're not alone.

When the dessert plates were cleared away after dinner, Romeo said something in Italian to Daniele. His chair scraped back, and he looked at me expectantly. My eyes darted to Romeo, but he refused to answer the questions my gaze bore into him.

I guess I have no choice but to cross the threshold and accept whatever fate lies in wait for me. My body tenses,

162

on high alert and aware of the danger lurking in the man behind me.

"Alma will bring you a fresh pad and a hairbrush in the morning."

I glance over my shoulder, a groove forming between my brows as I tilt my head, certain I must have misheard him. Facing the door, I open my mouth to speak, but he cuts off the attempt with a nod of his head before pulling the door closed. This time, the key turns in the lock, a finality in the sound as it echoes through the room.

Closing my eyes, I picture Romeo moving around doing things I've never seen him do. It's so real and intimate. The faint scent of him lingers in the air, and an anticipation hums in my core at the idea of being in his space. It feels all-consuming and... dangerous.

Blinking my eyes open, I cross the room to stand in front of the window, resting my forehead on the cool pane of glass. The sun has set, leaving the forest-green fields shrouded in darkness. My attention is drawn to the lights illuminating the driveway. If I wasn't being held captive, I'd be able to enjoy this view. There's something classic and elegant about it.

A golf cart speeds around the side of the house, coming to a stop at the bottom of the steps before two armed guards climb out of its back seat. They take up residence at the bottom of the steps, their guns cradled in their arms. I imagine the stony expressions on their faces as they settle in to protect the house and its occupants for the night. The cart races off down the driveway, kicking up a cloud of gravel as it goes.

Rolling my lips, I turn away from the window and face the bed. My teeth drag over my bottom lip as I stare at the freshly made sheets. *If I'm sleeping in here again tonight, will Romeo sleep in the chair again? Or does he expect something from me in exchange for his hospitality?*

I know he's set on using me to get to my father, but does he have his sights set on using my body too? What happened in the shower was a one-off. I was in shock and I know now, after the fact, that I should have pushed him away.

So why does my body ache to be filled by him again?

Massaging my chest to ease the tingling sensation taking up residence, I look around the room, forcing my mind to focus on why I'm here, how I get out, and *who* he is, to stop the yearning. He might have made me explode like nobody ever has before, but he's a murderer. And I'm going to be one of his victims.

For years, I kept myself out of this life and now I'm surrounded by dangerous men with very little regard for me. This isn't what I want and, the way I see it, I have *two* options. I can either stay and wait for them to kill me. Or I could find a way out. If I die doing that, at least I *tried*.

If a swift death is not an option, then I don't want to live here as a captive. My freedom is all that matters. And that's why I'm going to run.

A fluttering feeling passes through my chest and I

press my lips together, determined to get to work on finding a way out of here. My eyes dart around the room, bouncing from one spot to another. There has to be something in here that I can use. A phone or a radio; anything to communicate with the outside world. Christ, I'd settle for a carrier pigeon at this point.

I dart across the room to the bedside table closest to me. My movements are jerky as I pull it open. Disappointment settles into the pit of my stomach as I stare down at the empty drawer.

Think, Aurora. Where would you hide something that could get me out of here?

The moment my eyes land on the door opposite the bed, it's like a lightbulb flickering on and guiding me. *The closet.* An urgency takes over and I fly across the room, barreling through the door. The wood knocks against the cabinetry inside and I freeze as the loud bang reverberates.

I count down from five, staying as still as I possibly can. Only when I'm certain that nobody is coming do I move. I don't know how long Romeo will be downstairs, or if I'll get another chance to search for something that might help me make it out of here on *my* terms, so I need to be careful.

Closing the door behind me as quietly as possible, I pull in a breath, calming my body. Nausea swells in my throat and I shake out my hands to clear the nervousness racing through me.

I run my hands over the black and white shirts that

hang in a neat row on the right-hand side of the room. The other side is bare and for a brief, fanciful moment, I allow myself to imagine what it would be like to have *my* clothes hanging there.

Shaking my head, I huff out a disbelieving laugh. *Get it together, Aurora.* He's a mobster, and if I didn't want my own father in my life because of this world, why the hell would I want Romeo Bianchi when he's so much more dangerous?

I walk further into the closet, my eyes flitting around, searching. There has to be something here. A man like Romeo would have a phone or a laptop. Anything to conduct business on, especially in this day and age.

A set of drawers sits under a light at the end of the room. It calls to me like a siren, beckoning me over. I come to a stop in front of it, pulling open the top drawer.

Neatly rolled up ties stare back at me. Each one is a bright color, sectioned away in its own compartment. This doesn't add up and disappointment hits me. I would have expected expensive watches or sweaters, even underwear, but a bright purple tie was not on the list. In fact, I haven't seen him wearing anything other than black.

Pushing the drawer closed, I move on to the next one. Rolled up black T-shirts. *That's more like it.* How he managed to get so many black T-shirts in the same exact shade is a mystery and kind of impressive. I run my hands around the drawer, trying not to disturb the order. *Nothing.*

Desperation fuels my movements and I yank open the next drawer, searching with ferocity, uncaring about hiding my snooping this time. There has to be *something* here. I *need* there to be something here.

"What are you doing, Aurora?" There's genuine curiosity in his voice, but I'd be remiss to ignore the dangerous undercurrent idling beneath the surface.

I flinch, my eyes bulging before I drop my chin, needing a moment to compose myself.

Well, my attempt at escaping lasted a whole five minutes.

Pulling the shutters down and masking any emotions that might give me away, I turn to face Romeo. For a moment, I'm distracted by his open shirt and the dark ink gracing his beautifully chiseled chest. A dart of lust hits me in the gut, leaving me breathless. But then I remember what I was in the process of doing, and a smile forms on my lips that feels forced and weak. "Oh, nothing. I wasn't doing anything."

Romeo cocks a brow. "Really?" He moves closer, and I fold my arms over my chest, refusing to back down. "Because it looked like you were rummaging through my things."

My mind whirls, searching for a plausible explanation for what he walked in on before I stutter, "I... I was... I was looking for a clean T-shirt. I, umm, was going to shower. If that's okay?" I blink up at him, innocently.

He watches me, his eyes narrowed, before he steps around me. My body tenses, worry gnawing in my gut when he pulls open a drawer. The whoosh of it opening might as well be a guillotine for all I care. Subtly, I suck in a breath, but it gets stuck and a weird, panicked sound erupts from my parted lips.

This could very well be the beginning of the end.

His breath dusts my neck, the heat from his body setting off a whirlwind of mixed emotions. Lust fights with panic, but I keep my tense body still. When he hands me one of his black T-shirts, my shoulders slump. "You don't need to ask for my permission to bathe yourself, Aurora."

Grabbing it from his hand, I clench it to my chest. I take a step forward and then another until I reach the open door. Romeo calls out and I turn to face him, my eyes meeting his before darting to his full lips. I suck in a breath, blinking rapidly to keep myself rooted to the ground.

Unbuttoning his shirt, he says matter of factly, "We have a gala to attend next weekend. Maria will arrange a dress. I'll have her pick out some every-day clothes for you while she's at it."

His words take a second to register; my attention on the movements of his strong, capable hands. Lifting my eyes away from the tempting artwork that is his torso, I try but fail to process what he's saying. *Clothes? A gala?* He's taking me to a gala. A sense of dread fills me, panic clawing at my chest at the prospect of more gunfire. I rest my hand on my collarbone, swallowing down the bile.

Maybe I can use the gala to make my escape.

Clearing my throat, I push through the pounding in my ears and ask, "Can you at least ask her to get clothes that fit me?"

Romeo shrugs out of his shirt, dropping it onto the bench next to him. "What size are you?"

"A four."

Silence hangs heavy in the space between us and he looks at me expectantly with one hand resting on his belt buckle. "Are you going to shower?"

Crap. "Yes." I hold up the T-shirt, waving it in the air as I leave the room.

His voice floats through the air, following me when he calls, "Oh, and maybe when you're done, you can tell me what you were really doing."

There's a hint of danger in his words. One that has my thighs clenching in excitement at the same time as my heart beats an unsteady rhythm. I guess I'll be spending my time in the shower coming up with an excuse for going through his things because I'm not about to compromise the small bit of freedom he's given me.

For as long as I'm in this room, I'll spend my time wisely, searching for a way out.

My pencil glides with ease over the thick paper in the pad resting on my knees. I've been sitting in the window alcove of Romeo's room since I woke up alone this morning.

Disappointment churned in my gut when I tested the door and found it locked. I don't know why I felt like this but it shouldn't have been there. After all, nothing has changed between us for him to give me free rein to walk around the house.

The sun's setting now, pinks and purples filling the sky in a beautiful swathe of color. Aside from my clothes arriving this morning and two meals being delivered, I've been undisturbed.

I finished my search of Romeo's closet after lunch. Using the cover of putting my clothes away, I changed into a white T-shirt and navy jeans before digging around. There were no electronics or anything I can use as weapons—unless you count ties and belts, but they'd be no match for a gun. I was hoping that I'd get to leave the room for dinner and be able to scope out the rest of the house, but with each minute that passes, that idea seems less likely.

All of which means I've had zero opportunities to find a way out, so I've lost myself in the images that play out behind my eyelids. They come to life on the page, a familiarity to them that feels like home.

Pages of the same drawing are scattered around me. Determination fuels my movements as I try to *see* more. It's been hours, but I can't get past the roses and gray fountain that takes up pride of place among them.

The sketches are from memory, but I don't remember ever having seen anything like this place before. The grandeur is romantic, yet there's something cold and deathly about it in the dark shadows as my pencil flies across the page.

Exasperated, I rip another sheet out, throwing it to the floor. It hasn't even hit the ground before my pencil is back on the paper, moving with an urgency that flows through my veins.

When the tip of my pencil snaps, I exhale heavily, lifting my head to look out the window and roll my neck. A flock of blackbirds scatter from the trees in the distance, the sound of them crying out muffled by the glass. They disappear back into the trees and I look away at the made bed.

Last night, when I returned from the shower, Romeo

announced that we'd be sharing the bed going forward. A jolt of pleasure ran through my body, quickly followed by a flare of panic. There is no denying he's an attractive man, but the more time I'm spending in his company—technically bed—the more difficult it's becoming to separate the fact that he's a cold-blooded killer. *And I'll be his next victim.*

Heaving out a sigh, I shake my head and lay my pad on the bench in front of me. I need to come at this with a different approach. Clearly, going along with whatever he dictates isn't working anymore. If anything, I'm more likely to end up chained to his bed, satisfying his needs if I don't fight for my freedom.

Determined, I stand and walk to the tray on the small table next to the armchair. I'm going to demand answers to my burning questions, like how long does he intend to keep me. It's been over a week and nothing has happened. I don't know if they're any closer to finding my father. The gala isn't for another week, so when do I become redundant? I'm reaching for the pencil sharpener, my frustration bubbling beneath the surface, when the door swings open. I ignore whoever has entered, expecting it to be the housekeeper bringing dinner, before I realize there was no knock.

Adrenaline rushes through my body, my tongue darts out to swipe over my suddenly dry lips, and I hold my breath. Slowly, I turn, only releasing my breath when I catch Romeo's back walking into the bathroom before he kicks the door closed behind him. My wide eyes dart over to the open bedroom door.

This is my chance.

And yet I don't move. Now that the opportunity has presented itself, I don't think I'm ready. Inhaling sharply, I swipe my hands down my thighs, my breath leaves me in a rush and I force one foot in front of the other.

One step.

Two.

Three.

Four.

Steam envelops me when I push open the bathroom door. Water hitting the tile echoes around the room and although I can hardly see him through the misted glass, in my mind, his image is crystal clear. I see the water run over every toned inch of his body, leaving behind a glistening trail.

Rolling my lips together, I fold my arms over my chest, ignoring the way my pussy clenches when they graze my sensitive nipples. "I want to know what you plan on doing with me." The demand is clear in my tone and the words come out surprisingly strong, betraying none of the desire that's assaulting my body.

A large hand swipes the condensation from the glass that separates us. Sharp eyes meet mine, dropping down my body and setting me alight. I bite my tongue, digging my nails into my bare arms. *How does he do that with just one look?*

There's a hint of teasing in his tone when he says, "You're going to have to be clearer than that, *bella*."

Of their own accord, my eyes track the movement of his hand when he coasts it down his tattooed chest, getting lower and lower until it disappears from sight. The misted glass blocks my view, and that annoys me, nearly as much as him misinterpreting me.

Heat engulfs me and I drop my arms, moving toward the glass. His eyes get heavy and I add an extra sway to my step as I get closer. My eyes flit down to where his large hand is wrapped around his hardening cock. Keeping my face neutral, I lift my chin and spit, "Let's get one thing straight, *Mr. Bianchi*. The only way that"— my eyes flit down one last time and I inject as much venom into my tone as I can muster—"is going anywhere near me, is if I'm dead or unconscious. If you aren't going to put me out of my misery soon, then just fucking tell me and I'll do it myself."

No, you won't.

Romeo turns off the shower, stepping out of the cubicle and wrapping a towel around his waist. My body follows him, and as he crowds me in, I tilt my head back to hold his stare, forcing myself to stand taller. My back hits the glass of the shower wall with a dull thud.

He bends his knees, his face inches from mine as he brings his hands up to rest on either side of my head. A calmness fills his features but it does nothing to hide the heat in his gaze. There's such an intensity swirling in the inky blue depths that every fiber of my being comes alive at once. I hate that he can turn me on with his proximity. There has to be something wrong with me. Why else would I want a man like him?

His hand drops to rest on the skin exposed by my V-neck T-shirt. I pray he can't feel the pounding of my heart. A confident smirk lifts the corner of his mouth. He drops even closer, resting on his forearm as his hand moves to my throat. Applying a light pressure, he forces my head back.

"The blush of arousal on your chest tells me differently, Aurora. I guarantee if I dip my fingers into your panties, I'd find you soaking wet." His thumb swipes over my bottom lip and my gasp echoes around the room. He chuckles darkly, before continuing, "As for putting you out of your misery, why would I do that when there's so much more fun to be had?" He bares his teeth in a dangerous grin, tightening his hold on my neck a fraction before winking and releasing me.

The tension eases out of my body the moment he steps away and I sag against the cool, damp glass. It takes me a moment to organize my thoughts and rid myself of the inappropriate feelings that have taken root in my core. A different kind of heat flushes through my body, and the anger I should have held on to when I walked into this room returns.

In the reflection of the mirror, as it clears, I see him behind the door, crossing the threshold to the bedroom. I'm moving forward, launching myself at his back before I can think twice about what I'm doing. My legs latch on to his waist and I wrap one arm around his throat, grabbing my wrist with the other, applying as much pressure as I can.

This is a stupid idea.

No, it isn't.

This is plan B. Or maybe C. *Fuck it*. It doesn't have to be a plan *anything*, this is just me trying to get a reaction out of him. Forcing him to do *something*. Maybe if he shows me the mafia boss that I know he is, then this attraction I feel for him will disappear.

Taken by surprise, Romeo stumbles forward before righting himself. My arm aches, as I apply more pressure. *How long does it take to strangle somebody?* It's like being on a ride at the circus as he swings us around the room. *Am I doing this right?* He should be getting weaker, at least that's how it looks in the movies. Focusing back on my task, I don't realize where he's moved us until my back and head hit the wall with force. My grip loosens a fraction from the jolt, but it's enough for him to rip my arms away and throw me over his shoulder onto the bed.

I bounce a couple of times and my chest rises and falls in a rapid rhythm as I catch my breath. In the distance, I can hear a motor running somewhere in the garden. I expect Romeo to be on me, his hands wrapping around my throat, getting his revenge for my little attack, but there's nothing. Craning my neck, I look back at him from where he stands at the side of the bed above my head. His towel is gone and his cock juts out, hard and weeping.

I lick my lips, wide eyes meeting his. There's a dangerous glint in his, and it fills me with an excitement that has my entire body vibrating. It's an electrifying feeling of the unknown.

Romeo prowls closer, his cock close enough for me to see the bead of pre-cum on his tip as he growls, "I've killed men for less, *bella*."

Focus, Aurora.

I close my eyes, my limbs loosening as I relax back into the mattress. *I'm ready.* I have been for a while. Large hands grab under my arms and I'm yanked until my head is on the edge of the bed. My eyes dart open and my fingers clutch onto the sheet, curious more than anything as to how he's going to kill me.

His thumb presses onto my chin, forcing my mouth open before he continues, "The thing that stops me when it comes to killing you, Aurora, is that look of utter peacefulness you get on your face. Knowing how much you want the end to come only makes me want to withhold it from you."

My questioning gaze meets his heated ink-blue eyes. This isn't something he can edge me with. God, I've just attacked him. He should *want* me dead just as much as I want him to die.

Do I really want him dead?

The simple answer is no, but not because I care for him. I just want my *freedom*, whether that comes from death or being able to walk out of this house. Whatever happens to Romeo Bianchi is of no consequence to me.

Or at least that's what I tell myself despite the tug in my heart telling me differently.

His cock bobs above my face and my eyes greedily take in every detail. It would be so easy to open up and take him into my mouth. To get lost in him and distract myself from the circumstances I find myself in.

"Just do it." The words are nothing more than a croak. I don't know what exactly it is I want him to do, but I pray he understands either way.

He pulls my jaw down, pushing his thumb inside. Automatically, my lips clamp around it, and I suck, flicking my tongue back and forth over the tip. *This is wrong.* When he pulls free, a pop reverberates around the room and he smears my saliva over my mouth before forcing two fingers back inside. They hit the back of my throat and I gag before he eases up and I greedily bob my head on them. I shouldn't be so turned on by him or pliant to his command. And yet, I find myself willing.

Romeo's voice is hoarse when he commands, "Hang your head off the bed."

Without thinking, I do it. My movements hurried as I scoot toward the edge of the bed. He takes a step back, fisting his cock in one hand and holding the base with the other. When I'm in position, he moves forward, slipping the tip of his cock into my mouth with a hiss falling from his lips. Maybe I'm not the only one overcome with lust. The salty taste of him is mouthwatering.

Much like when he filled my mouth with his fingers, he thrusts forward, hitting the back of my throat.

I choke on his length, saliva spurting from the corners of my mouth. My hands reach up, holding onto his thighs, not sure if I'm trying to push him away or pull him deeper.

My body wriggles with the need for some sort of friction. Romeo takes hold of the hem of my T-shirt. He rips it from hem to collar with a force that I'm choosing to take as speaking volumes of his desire for me. Once I'm exposed to him, his large hands massage my breasts while I moan around his cock.

He pulls out of my mouth, straightening, and I follow him, sucking a tight ball into my mouth. Swirling my tongue around it, I release it with a pop before moving to the next. Romeo takes hold of my wrist when I reach for his cock. He shakes his head when I lift my disappointed gaze to his face in question.

"Take the jeans off, Aurora."

He releases me, and I immediately get to work on unbuttoning my jeans. An amused chuckle falls from his lips, but I don't let it deter me. The need to be naked and have my body touched by him outweighs any thought that he might be trying to humiliate me. My movements are hurried and desperate as I push my jeans and underwear down my legs, kicking them to the floor on the other side of the bed.

Shifting onto my knees, I crawl toward him, taking his cock in my hand. My fingers don't touch as I wrap them around his thick length. His hands fist by his side when I push his cock up toward his flat stomach and flatten my tongue on the underside, running it up his length as I stare up at him from under my lashes.

When I reach the head, I close my lips around him and he groans, grabbing fistfuls of my hair. My cheeks hollow when I suck as he sets the pace with gentle thrusts of his hips. I can tell he's trying to hold back and saliva pools in my mouth, dribbling down my chin at the thought that I'm testing his control. Slowly, I move my hand between my legs; the heat emanating from my pussy almost scorching. Wetness coats my fingers almost immediately as I glide them over my clit. The bundle of nerves sensitive to my touch.

"That's it. You're taking me so well."

Romeo thrusts and my eyes water, a single droplet running down my cheek and mixing with the saliva on my chin. I know I won't feel the same later, but right now, I want to feel him stretching the walls of my pussy. Even though there's a hunger inside of me that can't bear to drag my mouth away from his cock. He's on the verge of losing control, each thrust becoming more erratic as he slides further and further down my throat.

Suddenly he takes a step back, fisting his cock. I whimper at the loss and push up, ready to crawl to him. He's too far away for me to touch him, but we stare at each other, our chests rising and falling in tandem.

His eyes are dark, the pupils blown wide with arousal. "On your back. Ass on the edge of the bed," he orders.

My body heats, humming with desire, and I swallow

thickly before swinging my legs over the bed and lying back, desperate for his touch. When he wraps his fingers around my ankles, lifting my legs to rest against his shoulder, my body quivers in anticipation.

The head of his cock edges my entrance and I push my hips down, trying to urge him inside. He holds steady, and when he isn't forthcoming, I lift my eyes to his, a question in the depths. His jaw is tight and there's a look of what appears to be dominance shining in his dark blue eyes.

Gripping the bedsheet, I moan when he finally slams forward, stretching me and filling the void I didn't know was there. My breasts bounce from the force, knocking the air out of my lungs as I try to not combust.

I stretch around him in the most delicious possible way. *Like I was made for him.* Closing my eyes, I brush away the intrusive thought and instead concentrate on the feel of him, focusing on the cocktail of pain and pleasure that comes with his thickness filling me.

Romeo holds still for so long that my eyes dart open, searching his. He tightens his hold on my legs, a muscle in his jaw working beneath the surface. His mouth parts slightly, drawing my attention, and I'm overcome with an urge to feel his lips on mine.

Blinking, I whisper, breathlessly, "Rome. Please, move."

I've barely finished the sentence when he pulls out until only his head is filling me. I bite my lip, a stinging burning my eyes at the loss of him. Forcibly, he thrusts forward, his skin slapping against mine. I cry out, uncaring of who may hear. My fingers dig into the cotton sheets, anchoring my body to the bed as he pounds into me.

His pace increases, the time between each thrust getting shorter and shorter until his hips work in jerky, feral movements. Pleasure pools in the pit of my stomach, building until I feel like I can't take anymore. He stokes the fire inside of me until my body erupts and I convulse around him. My moans fill the room, mixing with his grunts as he chases his release. Little black dots appear in my vision and the air leaves my lungs in a rush.

Romeo stills, spilling inside of me and my pussy clenches around him, milking his cock for every last drop. Our eyes lock when he pulls out, a mask coming down over his face, hiding his emotions from me. A blanket of regret falls over me and I wrap my arms around my waist, turning my head to stare at the pillows.

A wetness pools at my entrance and panic claws at my throat. My legs fall to the side of him and I sit up, staring down at my pussy as cum spills from me. Disbelieving, I admonish, "You fucking came inside of me, *again*."

He growls, dropping to his knees and pushing my legs up and onto my chest. His voice is gruff when he orders, "Push it out, *bella*. Push my cum out of your pretty little cunt."

I blink, confused until he runs his finger between my folds, and a moan tumbles from my lips. Instinctively, I do as he demands and push his cum out of me. His tongue is there waiting, swiping over my entrance as the cocktail of our release slides free.

This might be the hottest and dirtiest thing I've ever experienced.

And I want more of it.

Romeo feasts on me, swiping our cum and spitting it back onto my pussy. I'm so turned on watching him. This powerful man, cleaning me up and then dirtying me again. Unintelligible words fall from my lips and a familiar tightening forms in my core. I can't stifle my screams as I enter euphoria, feeling everything and nothing as I come undone.

He stares at me, a heated darkness in his eyes before he stands, holding his hand out for me. "Let's get you showered or we'll be late for dinner."

I'm not sure I can move, let alone face other people. In a haze of post-orgasmic bliss, I slip my hand into his, falling into his chest as he pulls me up. He wraps an arm around my waist before dropping a fleeting kiss onto my lips that feels almost... intimate.

So much for staying clear of him and finding a way out of here.

Chapter 21

Romeo

I'm sitting at the bar in the entertainment room when Aurora floats in. My breath catches in my throat, choking me at the mere sight of her. The silky material of the red dress she's wearing clings to every curve of her body. From the front, it looks classy and demure, but when she turns toward Daniele who's standing behind her, I can see her exposed back, hinting at the lack of lingerie.

Fuck me.

In the two weeks since I took her, she's ingrained herself under my skin. Nothing more has happened between us since she tried to attack me, but we dance around each other each night, both aware of the other but unwilling to cross the line of captor and captive. It helps that I've kept myself busy, limiting our interactions as much as possible.

With the safety of a room between us and in the presence of an audience, I let my eyes roam over her freely. Ties hang over each shoulder, begging to be undone, and I clench my fist to stop myself from reaching for her. A simple pendant hangs around her neck, dangling down the length of her spine and touching the base of her back. *Will it hit against my hand if I rest it there?*

I look away, my jaw tight as I take a sip of my drink. The amber liquid burns as it travels down my throat. Like an addict needing a fix, my eyes find her again, bouncing over the image of her. With her hair piled on top of her head, she's exposed, and for a moment, I wonder if she chose the dress with the intention of driving me to distraction. From my position across the room, her scar is barely visible, but I know it's there and I wonder if she's as aware of it as I am.

Inappropriate thoughts fill my mind. Bodies entwined as I thrust into her from behind, my fingers tracing the scar and healing the only imperfection she has. *Except it's not.* There isn't an inch of her that could be considered flawed. I swallow the lump forming in my throat.

Dio.

I need to get the hell out of here. Standing, I demand my focus returns to the task at hand. Tonight, we come face-to-face with Francesco Costa. We have to be on our guard. We can't have a repeat of what happened at the restaurant. *Especially* when some of the city's most prominent players will be in attendance.

Throwing back my drink, I slam the glass on the

counter, the bang from my frustration drawing the attention of Aurora and Daniele. With a tug of my cuffs, I walk toward them, grinding out, "Come, we need to leave."

Inclining his head, Daniele responds, "Yes, boss."

Aurora's chin drops a fraction, her gaze moving to the garden beyond the window. Her dismissal of me irks more than I care to admit. I know her body in the most intimate of ways, and yet, I don't command her attention the way she does mine.

Frustration bubbles beneath the surface and my tone is curt and demanding when I continue past her and snap over my shoulder, "Now."

Maria holds the front door open as I step into the lobby. She offers up a polite smile as I approach, but I don't return it. My face is no doubt covered by a mask of indifference, despite the frustration bubbling beneath the surface. Through the door, I see Massimo on the stoop, his phone glued to his ear as he talks in hushed tones. When I cross the threshold, he nods before walking to the other end of the veranda. My brows furrow before I release them and reassure myself that Massimo isn't the enemy. *We'll meet him tonight.*

Coming to a stop at the top of the steps, I slot my hands into the pockets of my slacks, lifting my face to the sky. A light breeze blows through the air, bringing with it the smell of freshly mown lawns. Over the past week, there have been more days filled with sunshine and less with rain. It makes me hopeful that things might start going in the right direction for us.

The subtle hint of jasmine envelops me, alerting me to her presence along with the hairs on the back of my neck that stand to attention. I clench my hands in the confines of my pockets as she passes, heading toward the three black SUVs that line the driveway.

She keeps her attention on the stone steps, lifting the hem of her dress as she descends them. Six-inch black strappy stilettos adorn her feet and I'm assaulted with an image of her bent over the bed with nothing but her shoes on as I pound into her. The visual makes my cock twitch with excitement.

I track her as she moves across the gravel driveway toward the front car. With one hand out for balance and another lifting her dress, her hips sway in a slow and hypnotic rhythm. *Daniele must have told her which one we were traveling in.* The muscle in my jaw ticks when Nico holds the door open for her, his eyes lingering a moment too long.

I'm vaguely aware of Daniele coming to stand beside me, but it's not until his hand lands on my shoulder that I realize I've traveled down the first two steps. Pulled from the red mist, I look back, first at his hand and then to his face.

He removes it quickly, his face void of any emotion. "Massimo has an update for us, boss."

Inhaling sharply, I nod, returning to the top step. *I need to focus.* My attention can't be on the temptress that

I'm going to have to spend the evening keeping up appearances with. What matters most is *la mia famiglia* and Aurora Costa is not part of that. Nor will she ever be.

Massimo's fingers fly across his phone screen before he pockets it and joins us. "That was Dante. They've swept the venue. There doesn't appear to be anything suspicious, but we know that doesn't really mean much."

Leonardo comes to stand with us, holstering his gun. We're all armed, as always. Tonight, we might be surrounded by civilians, but based on what happened at the restaurant last week, we know that Francesco has no qualms with taking out *anyone* who gets in his way.

Running a finger under the collar of my shirt, I straighten my bow tie and reply, "It doesn't. But we *do* want there to be something. Ideally, Francesco. Without him, we have no leads." I pause, looking each man in the eye before I continue, "I know I don't need to say this, but I'm going to anyway. Be alert. If the slightest thing looks out of place or someone looks like they might be up to something, I want it looked into. I don't care if it's the next president, I want fucking answers. *Capisci?*"

A cocky smirk lifts the corner of Massimo's mouth and he inclines his head toward the car behind me. "No distractions, *eh?*"

This fucker. *He* was the one insistent that I bring her. It was *his* housekeeper that picked out that fucking dress. *But it was me that took her.*

Gritting my teeth, I spit, "I've never let a woman, much less one who's my captive, distract me from protecting this family, Massimo. I'm not about to start now over a pretty *cunt*." The word tastes like venom on my tongue because she's so much more, but admitting that is a sign of weakness that I'm unwilling to show.

Holding his hands up, Massimo shrugs. "If you say so, Rome."

With a chuckle and a shake of his head, he takes off down the stairs, closely followed by Leonardo. They jump into the second car, shutting the door behind them.

Tonight is going to be exhausting.

Chapter 22

Aurora

We arrived three hours ago, and after situating me at our table with a stony-faced giant called Angelo, Romeo left me. He's currently standing on the other side of the room, a handsome grin splitting his face as he talks to an older couple, who, I'm pretty sure, own the Mets.

I've stewed in my annoyance, drinking champagne and watching him like a stalker, unable to drag my eyes away. He hasn't looked in my direction *once*. As the hours have ticked by, he's moved around the room with a confidence most men lack, as a stiffness has crept into my neck and jaw with each passing minute.

It was naïve of me to think he'd *want* to keep me by his side. I thought I looked good in my dress and I'd taken the makeup Maria bought me and used every skill in my arsenal to make myself look beautiful. And yet, he's not spared me a single glance.

A woman in a gold dress, that probably cost more than my apartment, sidles up to him. She strokes her hand down his chest, leaning into his space. I wait for him to push her away, to take a step back, but he rests his hand on her lower back as he listens to whatever she's whispering to him. Fury envelops me, and I throw my drink back, the bubbles hitting the back of my throat before the alcohol seeps into my system.

I thought these things were supposed to have food served at them. There hasn't been a mention of dinner, and the sandwich I nibbled on earlier is the only food I've had since lunchtime. Drinking four glasses of champagne hasn't helped to calm the jealousy coursing through my veins and it does little to ease the ache in my chest now as I watch him with her.

Standing on unsteady legs, my chair scrapes across the wooden floor as it pushes back. The loud, brash sound is drowned out by the tinkling chatter of guests milling around the room. My eyes are fixed on them, boring a hole into the place where his hand touches her. I feel Angelo step up behind me, and I roll my eyes. *Right, mustn't forget that I need to be chaperoned everywhere.*

My strides are purposeful as I move across the room, my target in sight. It's not until I'm in the middle of the dancefloor, bodies swaying to a classical song and blocking my view that I come to a stop. *What am I thinking?* Am I really about to storm over there and demand he pay attention to me? *Like some jealous lover?* Shaking my head, I divert toward the bathroom, needing a moment to gather my disoriented thoughts. I'm not his. I have no right to be feeling this... *possessive* of him.

A hand reaches out of the crowd, snagging hold of my wrist and forcing me to stop. I look down at the fingers loosely gripping me before lifting my eyes to a set of cold, familiar brown ones. Massimo lifts the corner of his mouth. It's not really a smile, but more of a snarl, and when I try to pull my arm back, he tightens his hold enough for me to know he's not letting me go.

What's his problem? I want to be here less than I'm sure he wants me to be.

My eyes dart either side of him before returning his stare. Couples dance around us, oblivious to the cloud of hostility hovering above. "I was just going to the bathroom."

He ignores me, pulling me into his arms and lifting my hand to his shoulder before picking up the other. "Dance with me. I have some questions for you."

Exhaling loudly and with no other choice, I follow his lead. We sway to a pop song the string quartet plays, neither of us speaking. My eyes wander the room, searching for Romeo. There's a burning sensation in my chest when I come up empty. *Did he leave with her?* My eyes sting when it dawns on me. Of course he did, and he's using his cousin to distract me.

Dropping my eyes to Massimo's chest, I murmur, "What did you want to know?"

There's confidence in his voice when he replies, "I

doubt you'll give me the answer to my most pertinent question, but I have others."

I cock a brow, silently telling him to just ask whatever it is he wants to know.

He brings us to stop in the middle of the floor. "Where is your father?"

Rolling my eyes, I sigh, taking a step back. Massimo tightens his grip and brings me flush with his body. The air is knocked out of me and I can't hide my frustration and annoyance when I reply, "I've already told Romeo. I. Don't. Know. Where. He. Is. And the quicker you get that through your thick skull, the better. Francesco won't be coming for me."

Massimo loosens his hold, keeping his narrowed eyes on me as he looks into my soul. "But you know *something*, right?"

My brows tug together, and I open my mouth to ask him what exactly he thinks that might be, but his body is ripped from mine as Romeo pulls him back with a growl. He stands between us, fisting the collar of Massimo's tux jacket as he walks him back. Their faces are inches apart; Romeo's screwed up in anger and Massimo's relaxed and split into a grin.

"You might be my cousin, Massimo, but don't *ever* touch what's *mine* again," Romeo hisses, his voice dangerously low.

His?

Couples within earshot turn to watch, their dances long forgotten in favor of the free entertainment. Heat fills my cheeks at the attention, and I stumble back, needing to distance myself. I turn and hurry from the room, uncaring whether my guard is following. With every step, I feel the eyes of everyone in the room on me. *Why did he have to do that after practically ignoring me since we arrived?* Maybe he doesn't care how he makes me look.

In the quiet of the hallway, blood rushes in my ears, and I seek the sanctuary of the bathroom. The heady scent of roses and bergamot hits me when I push through the door. I'm vaguely aware of the opulence of the room before I rush into a cubicle, locking it behind me.

My breaths come in hushed, heaving pants, and I turn in small circles, unsure of what to do. The alcohol was a bad idea. Stopping to talk to Massimo was a bad idea. But not running from my apartment when I had the choice was probably the worst thing I've ever done.

Well, I'm not going back out there. If Romeo wants to talk to me, he can come and find me. I put the toilet seat down and drop onto it, holding my head in my hands and rubbing at my temples. Two toilets flush in quick succession on either side of me, the cubicle doors opening and falling closed with a dull thud.

The tap runs, and a feminine voice speaks. "Did you see the woman Romeo arrived with?"

My chest squeezes, and I sit up straighter before leaning forward to hear them. *How many Romeos can there be at one gala?*

Her friend must nod or something in acknowledgment because she continues, "It looks like Massimo wants her. He's been watching her all night while you've kept Romeo busy."

So that's why he came over. She must have gone to the bathroom, and he finally decided to pay me some attention.

There's a laugh on the other side of the door, and as I lean to the side, I can see a sliver of her through the gap in the door. She reapplies her red lipstick before pushing up her breasts and smoothing her hands over her curves. "As delectable as Massimo is, you've got to love a man in charge. I will say, let the best woman win. But I'd put my money on *moi*. He hasn't paid her any attention all night."

Oh, you want to turn this into a competition? Bring it on.

Yanking open the stall door, I keep my head held high when I march toward the basins. I roll my lips together to keep my smirk at bay when they both gasp in surprise, too slow to hide their reactions. Ignoring them, I rinse my hands before drying them on one of the warm towels and straightening my dress. Fussing with my hair, I meet their wide eyes in the mirror before sauntering from the room, calling, "Ladies."

My body sags as soon as the door closes behind me, the bravado slipping as I leave what was supposed to be the safety of the bathroom. There's nothing I dislike more than a woman who thinks it's acceptable to steal another woman's man. *Even if he isn't actually my man.*

Angelo falls into step behind me. "Everything okay?"

I look over my shoulder, surprised that he's actually spoken. His face lights up as he smiles at me before he clears his throat and drops his mask back in place. I didn't think he had any vocal cords. He's ignored any attempts I've made this evening to talk to him.

"Yes, everything's fine, thanks."

Angelo steps around me, holding the door to the main hall open. Movement in the corner of my eye draws my attention back to the bathroom door as the woman in the gold dress walks out, trailing behind her friend. She averts her gaze, her confidence from earlier apparently gone.

Good.

With my chin held high, I cross the threshold, an idea forming when I see Romeo. He's seated at our table. A restless energy rolls off him, hitting me from across the other side of the room as I move my way around the edge, one eye on the door.

As if the gods are looking down on me, the crowd parts when the woman from the bathroom walks in. I move across the room toward Romeo. With every step, his heated gaze follows me and I add an extra sway to my hips. He remains seated, waiting for me as he swirls the liquid in his glass.

I'm confident that my plan will work because it's a win-win. If my father is here and he sees what I'm about to do, well, there'll be no mistaking that Romeo and I are together. And if he isn't, then the woman in the gold dress gets to see me claim my man.

But he isn't mine.

Romeo's legs are wide when I reach the table, and I step between them like it's the most natural thing in the world to do. He discards his glass on the table as I bend at the waist, running my fingers through the curled hairs at the back of his neck. His hands come up to rest on the backs of my thighs and I don't *think*, I just *do*. Closing the distance between us, I brush my lips over his. Once, then twice, before I pull away, and his eyes search mine.

His fingers tighten a fraction and he brings one hand up to hold the back of my head as he claims my mouth and devours me. Desire pools in my core, and I grip the strands of his hair, needing more. *Why can't we be at home?*

Romeo's tongue demands entry to my mouth, and I give it up freely, tangling my own with his. He tugs me forward and I fall into his lap. His hands roam over my body before a loud cough breaks through the haze. We pull apart, our labored breaths mingling in the small space between us. Up close, his blue eyes are as dark as the deepest depths of the ocean, and I find myself wanting to dive back in and drown. It would be a blissful death.

Romeo's hand smooths a path up my bare thigh and I fight against the urge to widen my legs for him. "Were you a little jealous, *bella*?"

Tucking my head into the crook of his neck, I reply, "Not at all." The vibration of his chuckle makes me smile before I catch myself and add, "You said yourself that everyone needs to believe that we're together. It's the only way my father will be lured out."

And I had a point to prove.

He pulls back, searching my eyes. "Right, and it's not because you didn't like seeing me talk to Miss Wentworth?"

I straighten, half-heartedly wiping my lip gloss from his lips, unable to bring myself to look him in the eye. "No. I've got no reason to be jealous of you talking to anyone, especially when you aren't mine. Just like I'm not yours."

Romeo's fingers dig into the flesh of my thigh, and he rests his forehead against mine as he growls, "Yes, you *fucking* are."

A thrill races through me, and I bite down on my bottom lip.

Oh God, I'm in too deep.

Chapter 23

Romeo

The pleas of a man begging for his life echo around the room, falling on deaf ears. We found this *ratto* following us on the way to the helicopter pad from the gala. Daniele clocked onto him and after shooting a text to Massimo, we diverted and collared him in a dead end near a deserted warehouse. It didn't take long for him to start begging for his life, and now, as I stand behind Aldo with Massimo beside me, his whining is starting to grate on my nerves.

Not long ago, Aurora was in this room and far more accepting of her fate than the coward before us. We haven't even started yet and the stench of urine permeates the air.

I shrug out of my jacket, handing it to Aldo as I slide past him. Meticulously, I roll up the sleeves of my shirt, circling the guy—*Giorgio*—as he sits, bound to the chair. He was very forthcoming with the fact that he's a nobody from a rival family. Still, everybody knows *something*; it's just going to be a case of figuring out if he has anything of significance.

Wide, watery eyes meet mine when he pleads, "Please, Mr. Bianchi, I have a family. I'm not who you think I am."

Walking to stand in front of him, I hold my hand out to the side expectantly. Aldo places a pair of pliers into my palm. I keep my face neutral, tilting my head to the side as I look down at him and ask, "So, you do not work for Elio Morretti?"

Elio is the head of a rival family. Sometimes, as Massimo's father did with Elio's, we can reach an agreement to keep the peace. When each man sticks to his business, we can save ourselves a lot of hassle, but rumor has it Elio is spiraling. Word was sent last night from Sicily that Elio had taken out the head of a family on the West Coast without a care for the consequences. He's moved himself to the top of our suspect list. It would make sense that he'd be working with Francesco. After all, before Elio's father passed, Francesco was the go-between for the families.

Giorgio's eyes dart around the room to Massimo and Aldo. *Nobody will save you.* When his focus returns to me, he finally stutters, "Well, I mean...yes. I do, but I don't know anything. I just do as I'm told and keep my head down. I'm barely a blip on his radar."

Moving to stand behind him, I keep my voice steady when I say, "The thing is, Giorgio, I'm the head of a family, I know as well as anyone that a man of your position knows more than you're letting on."

He seems to consider what I've said for a moment, the tremors still wracking his body. "I swear. I don't know anything and even if I did, if I told you, I'm a dead man."

Exhaling heavily, I reply, "The problem is, you're a dead man either way. You have a choice. Either you tell me what you know and I'll make it quick and painless. Or you don't and you'll wish you had."

Holding onto his nose, I force his head back, stuffing the pliers into his mouth. Giorgio thrashes around as much as his bindings will allow. The chair moves under his weight, the metal scraping on the concrete floor. A few solid yanks, and I pull the pliers out, his molar held in the clamps. A mix of blood and saliva drips from it as I drop it into the metal tray Aldo holds out, ringing out a satisfying tinkle as it hits the base.

Giorgio wails, blood running down his chin, mingling with the tears as he begs, "Please. I don't know anything about Elio's operations."

Ignoring him, I roll my neck and bend to look him in the eyes. "Did you know, the average human has thirty-two teeth? Some of them won't be as easy to pull as that one, Giorgio. In fact, I had a guy in your position once, the tooth had grown into the jaw bone and he kept passing out from the pain. Of course, we'd stop and wait for him to wake up because it's no fun when you don't feel every yank and twist. Unfortunately for him, it did mean that the torture went on for days instead of hours."

Straightening, I circle him again, watching as his shoulders reach for his ears and he tucks his chin. Smirking, I come to a stop in front of him, pocketing one hand. "I'll ask you one time and one time only. Who placed the order on my family?"

Giorgio squeezes his eyes shut. His skin is clammy, and he flinches when I slam the pliers on the arm of his chair, demanding an answer. Stammering, he cries out, "I don't know anything."

"*Cazzate!*" My hand flies from my pocket, wrapping around his throat and applying enough pressure for his eyes to bulge. His mouth opens in a silent scream and his head rears back, pushing the chair onto its back legs. I stuff the pliers into his mouth, the metal clanging on his teeth. Muffled cries fill the room, his limbs fighting against the restraints, keeping him tied to the chair.

With as much force as I can, I pull out a canine this time. I ease up on his throat, holding the tooth up for him to see. "Thirty-one teeth, Giorgio. Tell me the truth and I'll consider letting you leave."

We both know it's a lie.

A cocktail of Giorgio's blood and saliva lands on my white shirt when he spits at me, his face transforming from fear to hatred in the blink of an eye. "*Vaffanculo!*"

Releasing him, I drop the pliers and his tooth into the metal tray before turning toward Massimo. He cocks a brow, and I crack my neck. Grabbing between the buttons of my shirt and ripping it open.

I turn back to Giorgio, shrugging out of my shirt and

leaving me in nothing but my undershirt. With a calm that portrays none of the disgust and fury rushing through my veins, I say, "It's clear you have nothing of use to tell me. So, here's how it's going to go. Aldo will slit your throat." Giorgio's eyes bulge, his breaths coming in rasping pants. "You'll sit here until you take your last breath and then he'll dissolve your flesh in hydrochloric acid. When all that's left of you is bone, he'll grind them down and Massimo's gardener will make use of you. Your existence will be erased from this world and your family will be left wondering where you are until they, too, no longer exist."

Giorgio cries out, begging and pleading as I walk from the room. Massimo is hot on my heels, a dark chuckle falling from his lips as muffled screams follow us back upstairs.

"I really thought he'd break after the first tooth. Maybe next time, I can take a crack at it?"

Grunting in reply, I push through the door into the main house. It closes behind us, blanketing the house in silence. The beginning of a headache pounds behind my eyes and I let out a heavy sigh.

Sensing my mood, Massimo doesn't say anything else as we move through the house. In less than an hour, a man will be dead and we'll be no closer to finding out who is targeting the family, much less what their end goal is.

Massimo strides into the office ahead of me, making a beeline for the drinks trolley. Pressing two fingers into my temple, I move them in small circles before taking a seat in front of his desk and staring out of the window at the rose garden. A three-finger pour of scotch is thrust under my nose, and I take it, slinging back the contents.

"I'll have Aldo grab a couple of men and stake out the house again. It feels like our next best lead."

It's our only lead, but I don't need to point that out to him. "We'll need to put someone on Elio too. Reach out to Callum and have him do some digging to find him."

Massimo nods, his mood just as dark as mine. This is a lot more tangled than it appeared when I first arrived. I have no doubt that Francesco built the bomb, but *somebody* ordered the hit. Somebody with enough sway to convince others that their plan will work. When he worked for Massimo's family, Francesco was nothing more *di un soldato*. He followed instructions; he didn't issue them. I don't buy that he'd have the presence to pull off something like this.

I can't help but feel like we're missing a piece of the puzzle.

Chapter 24

Romeo

Aurora's asleep, the curves of her body visible beneath the sheet when I walk into our room. *Our room.* The thought sends a possessive urge through my body. She's mine and even though I know I shouldn't have let her get this close, I do care about her.

I'm tempted to wake her and lose myself in her body, seeking out a release so I can rest. Having her so close, knowing how good it feels to have her heat wrapped around me, and not being able to have her has been my own personal hell. Every day I'm taunted by the memory of the taste of us on my tongue.

Dio, our cum is my new favorite flavor.

Needing a moment to get my body under control, I move toward the window seat I've found her in every day this week; absorbed in the pages, the pad resting on her lap as her pencil glides across the paper.

205

I come to a stop in front of the window, her pad calling at me from its place on the cushion. Lifting the corner of the cover, I check on her sleeping form. It feels like an invasion of privacy and although I'd tell her I have every right to look at whatever it is that she's drawing, there's still a weight settling on my chest when I peel back the cover.

A detailed sketch of the view from the window at sunset stares back at me. My brows lift as I take in every minute detail. The drawing could rival the ones Massimo has hanging on his walls that cost five figures. Light strokes of oranges and pinks depict the skyline, and in the distance, green firs dot the scenery. A portion of the west wing of the house is visible along with the gravel driveway and the disused fountain, except water erupts from the cherubs dotted around it.

I fall into the armchair beside the table, picking up the pad, and flipping the page, enthralled by what I find. Portraits of a woman with features similar to Aurora stares back at me. It's so lifelike that it could easily be mistaken for a photograph. There's a familiarity to her as I study every aspect of her face. The gray-scale images show her with an array of emotions, from happy to sullen and then to resigned.

Turning the page, my body tenses and I shift in my seat. The colors are the same as the previous page, but there's an obvious undercurrent of darkness to this one. These aren't drawn with love or even fondness. The hurried strokes from the pencil speak of a fear that jumps out at me from the faceless man that covers the page. Some drawings show him with a hood up, others show him with it down, and the unfinished features of his face visible.

One in particular draws my attention and has my nostrils flaring. He's holding a gun, pointing it at the observer. A water smudge is next to the drawing, and my chest tightens as I picture her crying as she sketches him out.

Who is he, and what has he done to hurt her?

"Rome." Her voice is soft and filled with sleep, breaking through the haze of anger and concern. It's the second time she's called me that, and I have to admit, I like the way it sounds on her tongue.

Like a child that's been caught with their hand in the cookie jar, the corner of my mouth lifts in some semblance of a sad smile when I look at her. Concern laces her words when she asks, "Is everything okay?"

She sits up in bed, the covers dropping to pool around her waist. My chest blooms, an urgent desire to claim her taking up root in the pit of my stomach. She has a wardrobe full of clothes, and yet, she's wearing *my* T-shirt to sleep. With her hair mussed, she rubs her eyes before pushing back the covers and swinging her legs over the side of the bed. Her steps are tentative as she walks toward me.

My eyes drop down to the pad in my hands, continuing to study her work like she might snatch it away and restrict me from seeing this side of her. I expect her to do just that when she reaches me, but instead, she kneels between my legs. Her familiar scent wraps around me in a comforting cloud.

Moonlight shines through the gap in the curtains, illuminating the soft features of her face. One hand rests on my thigh, moving back and forth until I cover it with mine and slowly soothe my thumb over her smooth skin.

"Who is this?" There's an edge to my tone. It demands answers and doesn't hide the fact that whoever it is will be dead by morning as soon as I have his name.

Aurora shrugs, dragging her eyes away from the page to meet mine. "I don't know. He's appeared in two of my nightmares. In the last one he said 'if only you'd have listened' and then pulled the trigger and I woke up. I don't know what he meant but I've not had the dream since we've..." She pauses, looking around the room. "Since we've been sleeping in the same bed, I've not had that dream again. I try to draw him, to see if I can figure out who he is and what he might have meant."

"And you haven't?"

"No. I close my eyes, force my mind to bring him up, and then all I see is his outline and what's on that page."

Aurora flicks the pages back to the portraits of the woman. "I know who this is. This is my mom." Her fingers glide over the paper, careful not to smudge the drawings. "Back home, I have pictures of her hanging in every room and I really miss seeing her face, so I've drawn her. She died when I was sixteen. I didn't know how until two years later. It was the day after my eighteenth birthday. She disappeared, and I went to live with my aunt and uncle in Long Island because my dad wasn't in the picture anymore.

"But he turned up out of the blue, asking me to come and stay with him. He said it wasn't safe for me because he was in the mafia. I told him I'd have been safer if he'd done us both a favor and stayed away." Her eyes go glassy and she swallows, looking away. My thumb rubs small comforting circles on the back of her hand until she continues, "I told him that I never wanted to see him again, and he walked away. Just like that, he accepted my decision and I haven't seen him since."

My chest tightens at the look of devastation on her beautiful face. I lean forward, unsure of how to comfort her. A sad smile tugs at the corners of her mouth, and she drops her eyes to her knees. "My father told me she committed suicide." Swiping angrily at a lone tear that tumbles down her cheek, she straightens her spine, running her finger over the sketches. "She kissed me good night, walked out the front door, and *apparently,* threw herself off the Manhattan Bridge. What makes it worse is her body was never found, so I never got to say goodbye properly."

I cup her cheek, my thumb swiping away the tears. "You don't believe him?"

Shaking her head, her watery green eyes meet mine, and she whispers, "No."

A weight settles on my chest as we sit in silence. I want to tell her that I'll find him and get the truth for her, but that's not how this works. My job is to look out for *la mia famiglia* and I need to remember that, because the more time I spend with Aurora, the harder it's getting to do.

She sighs heavily and despite knowing that I should put a stop to this conversation and find another room to sleep in, I still find myself asking, "What was she like?"

Aurora's face lights up and it's nothing short of spectacular. "Amazing. The best mom a girl could ask for. I felt nothing but love from her, and she protected me with a fierceness that gave me my own strength." The light in her eyes dims, and she looks down at the pad still in my lap. "She made me the woman I am today, and the day she died, I guess a part of me did too. You want to know why I'm so accepting of death?"

I nod, because it's the one thing about her that I haven't been able to figure out, although now I have an idea.

The corner of her mouth lifts. "Of course you do. The police came knocking on our door at three am that day, but long before they did, I knew she was gone. I was supposed to be asleep, but I woke up around midnight and I couldn't find her anywhere. For an hour and a half, I was calling her cell nonstop until I realized she was gone and that's when all the light left me. There's no color anymore and I've just been existing ever since. I can't find joy in anything because the world is just black and gray."

I want to ask her if she hopes to join her mother in

whatever afterlife might exist, but I can't force the words past my lips. Instead, I listen to her tell me about the woman who raised her, the strength of their relationship clear in every story she recounts.

Aurora chuckles, lifting her gaze to the curtain-covered window. "Oh, and there was this one time I was being bullied and came home from school with a torn shirt and bruised pride. She asked me what had happened, but I didn't want to tell her. I thought the girls who had done it would do something worse if they got in trouble with the teachers.

"The very next day, my mom marched me down to school, stormed into the principal's office, and threw my shirt at him, demanding to know what he was going to do about it. She hadn't listened to a word I said on the way, and because it happened on the way home, the school had no idea about what she was talking about."

"I bet you were a firecracker." An image of her pouncing on me the other day pops into my mind. "Actually, you kind of still are. I'm surprised I don't have the bruises to prove it." My voice is husky and amused.

Aurora huffs out a laugh, looking at me from her position on the floor. "That's because you're twice my size and threw me around like I weighed nothing."

She sucks in a breath and my tongue darts out, wetting my lower lip at the reminder of what came *after* her attack. I've been far too lenient with her, but anytime I'm around her, I find myself wanting to experience pleasure rather than cause her pain.

Lifting the pad from my lap, Aurora puts it on the table next to us before standing. "It's late. We should get some sleep."

She turns toward the bed, but I grab her hand and tug her toward me, until she falls into my lap, landing with a gasp. I grit my teeth as she wriggles, trying to right herself, her ass grinding over my hardening cock.

My fingers dig into the flesh of her thighs, and she stills, her chest rising and falling. Neither of us says a word when I reposition her to straddle my lap. As if I'm watching another man touch her, my eyes follow my right hand as I smooth it down the center of her chest and over to her hip. It's hard not to miss the heat emanating from her pussy or the way her nipples pebble through the fabric.

Delicate fingers dig into the arms of the chair as she hovers above me. Every time we've come together, her consent has been there, bubbling beneath the surface. My eyes search hers, seeking it out again.

Only when I find it do I forcibly pull her hips forward, pushing her down onto my confined cock as I thrust up. Her mouth opens a fraction, and a moan spills from her lips. There's a beat where everything is still and the last echoes of her moan drift off, leaving behind a charged silence. Her hips roll, sparking to life an urgency within me. Pulling her T-shirt over her head, I throw it on the floor beside the chair. She sits back in nothing but barely there panties and a heat in her eyes that's calling to me.

Sirena.

My fingers dig into her bare thighs. My words are gruff and demanding. "Undress me."

Aurora lifts the hem of my shirt, pulling it up my torso at a torturous pace. I lean forward so she can drag the material over my head and throw it to the floor next to hers.

Reaching out, I cup her breast in my hand, massaging the flesh. Her head tips back and she pushes herself further into my palm. I twist the right bud of her perfect dusky pink nipple to the point of pain and growl, "If you want more, you need to finish what you started, *bella.*"

Her head tips forward, heady and half-closed eyes meeting mine. *Fuck.* When she looks at me like that, having her do what I demand doesn't seem so important. My chest rises and falls in a chaotic rhythm. It's like my body is fighting with my mind, but they both want the same thing, just in different ways. *For her to surrender.*

In the end, it's my body that wins, pulling me under the waves of arousal until I can think of nothing else but burying myself in her and coming undone. She must feel some semblance of what I do because we crash together, our lips meeting in a rushed and hungry manner. Wrapping an arm around her waist, I lift her enough to undo my slacks and free my rock-hard cock.

Our mouths are still fused and I'm vaguely aware of Aurora pulling her panties to the side before I sink inside of *heaven.* Buried to the hilt, I move away from her mouth a fraction and suck in a much needed lungful of air.

Aurora rests her forehead on mine, her hair falling forward in a curtain, hiding us from reality. The only sound in the room is that of our heavy breathing in the small space between our mouths.

God, I'm fucked, and this needs to stop.

Wide eyes meet mine before she breaks out of the trance we both seem to be under, her hands resting on my shoulders before she moves. She starts with a tentative, gentle rocking of her hips before she gains confidence and seeks out her release. Our moans mix in the air, a cocktail of lust and arousal only heightening my senses.

"Romeo," Aurora calls out, her head thrown back as she massages her breasts.

My grip tightens on her hips, digging into the soft flesh as I grind out, "No. Don't call me that."

Her eyes meet mine, confusion clouding them before my demand is understood. Cupping my face, she leans into me, bringing her mouth to within an inch of mine. "Rome," she breathes before capturing my lips.

Cazzo!

She's intoxicating. This is nowhere near what this is supposed to be. She shouldn't even be in this room, let alone naked, and with my cock buried so deep inside of her, I'm not sure where she starts and I end.

With every moan and whimper, she's pulling me deeper and deeper under the current, and no matter how hard I try, I can't seem to get out. So I do what I do best. I take back control, moving her hard and fast along the length of my cock. My balls tighten with each stroke and the sound of our skin slapping together echoes around the room.

Breathlessly, she cries out, "Rome, I'm so close."

Me too.

Through gritted teeth, I demand, "Fucking come. Come for me, Aurora."

Resting her hands on my knees, she leans back, thrusting her chest up, and I tweak her nipples as she bounces on my cock. My eyes drop to the space between her legs, mesmerized by the sight of me stretching her pussy, my length glistening with her juices every time she moves. Wrapping my hand around the lacy material of her panties, I pull until it snaps and falls away, landing on my thigh.

Aurora gasps but doesn't slow down, not until she physically can't keep going and her body tenses around me. The spasms start small, rippling around my cock until her walls strangle it, setting off my orgasm.

I wrap my arms around her body, pulling her into my chest to stop her from falling, before I bury my face into her collarbone and grunt. My teeth graze over the soft skin as my hips keep jerking until our combined release seeps from her pussy and over my cock.

Greedily, I lift her and force her up my body. Aurora gasps, her fingers clutching onto my shoulders when a string of cum falls from her pussy and drops onto my bare chest.

"Rome," she calls, concern etched into her tone.

I can't speak, the need to clean her up all-consuming.

When she's positioned above me, with her hands pressed to the wall behind me and my fingers digging into the flesh of her hips as her knees rest on my shoulders, I tip my head back. Our cum slides out of her dripping pussy and into my open and waiting mouth. The first hit is like a drug I've been craving for decades.

It's not enough. Growling, I tighten my grip on her thighs and force her onto my face until her scent is all I can smell. My tongue laps her up, the taste of our cum intoxicating. The fingers of one hand claw at my hair while the other presses onto the wall behind us. She tries to get away from the ministrations of my tongue, but I don't let up. I can't.

My name is ripped from her lips on breathy moans that increase in volume the longer her orgasm builds and when she tips over the edge, her fingers painfully pull on the strands of my hair. Aurora rocks her hips with a ferocity that has my chest puffing out.

I want more of this.

More of her moans, more of her orgasms, and more of *her*.

Her body goes limp, and I press a hand to her chest to keep her upright. It's only when I'm certain that she's cleaned up that I help her climb down.

Nestled in my arms, she offers me a soft smile and chuckles. "I'm just going to need a second before I can move."

Licking my lips, I fight back the grin that threatens to slip free. "Put your arms around my neck."

She does as I ask, wrapping her legs around my waist when I stand from the chair. With her head resting on my shoulder, I carry her to the bed. It feels like the most natural thing to do. She's a distraction I can't afford and one I don't know I can stay away from. Not when she's everywhere I turn.

I set her down on the mattress and take a step back, needing to put some space between us. "Get some sleep."

Too much is resting on my shoulders for me to succumb to her temptations.

This has to be the last time.

Chapter 25

Aurora

My body aches, but there's a lightness to my mood that hasn't been there in a very long time. I throw an arm over my eyes, not bothering to hold back the giddy smile that breaks free and stretches over my face. It felt so good to talk to someone about my mom, and Romeo listened attentively, his touch soothing me even when I got upset.

And then there's what happened in the chair. Heat engulfs my body and I wriggle under the covers, desperate for his touch. I know I should be putting walls up between us, but last night felt *different*.

Doesn't change the fact that he kidnapped you.

Right, and it probably won't stop him from killing me, but for a moment last night, I forgot who he is and how we met. I know we don't have a future, but at least for the time I'm here, there can be peace between us and I can enjoy how my body explodes under his touch.

Resolute in my decision, I throw back the covers and swing my legs over the edge of the bed. I'm mid-stride toward the bathroom when my eyes land on the open bedroom door. My brows draw down, and I tilt my head as my eyes dart around the room.

This can't be happening.

Sucking in a breath, I hold it as I tiptoe toward the door. *Is this a trap? I walk out that door and get shot?* My hand goes to my stomach, urging the nerves bubbling away under the surface to calm down. Okay, so maybe I don't go out and I divert back to the bathroom and get ready for the day.

"You're up."

My heart slams against my rib cage, and I spin toward Romeo. He's leaning on the doorjamb, a towel wrapped around his waist and another around his neck, catching droplets of water from his wet hair. Steam billows out of the bathroom and around him. The only hint of danger emanating from him are the dark tattoos covering his upper body.

Swallowing thickly, I feign innocence and push the door closed before replying, "Yes. Just got up." The sound of the latch falling into place ricochets around the room.

Romeo quirks a brow, pushing away from the frame and walking toward me.

It was a test.

I knew it and I still failed, miserably. *God, what an idiot.* I should have known better. He comes to a stop in front of me, and I hold his stare. It feels like it takes the force of my entire body to keep my brows low and mask my surprise when he cups my cheek. He dips his head, capturing my lips with his own before sliding his other hand around my waist and pulling me against his body.

Instinctively, I stand on my toes, melting into him as I wrap my arms around his neck. The hardness of his cock presses into my stomach and I moan against his mouth.

Romeo pulls away, his gaze heated when he rests his forehead on mine. "*Dio*, what I wouldn't give to stay in here with you all day."

I dart my tongue out to wet my lips. I know it's not right or normal that he can turn me on so quickly, or that he can say things like that and I don't immediately feel terror at the prospect. What's worse is that it sounds like heaven to spend the day with him and get lost in each other.

He continues, grabbing my ass with one hand and pulling me into him. "You can move around the house and gardens, but if you try to escape, *bella*, Massimo's men have been instructed to shoot you on sight. *Capisci?*"

I nod, my mind racing in sync with my heart.

"Good." He tucks a strand of hair behind my ear before releasing me and walking into the closet, as if what he's said is completely normal.

I guess to him it might be. But is that it—I get some semblance of freedom so long as I don't try to run? *There has to be a catch.* I look over my shoulder at the closed door, wanting to test if what he's said is true. It's calling to me, begging me to pull it open and cross the threshold.

Sucking in a breath, I blow it out slowly and force my body to relax. I'll get ready for the day and then, if I find the door locked, I'll know this has been some sort of cruel trick. If it's still open, then I'll use my time wisely, because as lost as I'm getting in Romeo Bianchi, he's still my captor. He'll still kill me without batting an eye when this is all over.

Thoughts of what lies beyond the door occupy my mind as I move around the room getting ready for the day. I've seen some of the house during my time here, but since that dinner, over a week ago, the only time I've left this room was to attend the gala.

Excitement thrums through my body and when I'm ready, I stand in front of the door, smoothing my sweaty palms down the front of my floral mini cami dress. I suck in a sharp breath before resting my hand on the doorknob. The metal feels cool in my heated palm and when I turn it, I huff out a sigh of relief before pulling the door open and peering into the hallway.

The coast is clear, but I still find myself creeping along the corridor, my back pressed to the wall like I don't have permission to be here. When I come to a stop at the top of the stairs, I shake my head and exhale heavily. *What am I doing?* I don't need to sneak around like I'm doing something I shouldn't. If anything, it's going to draw more attention to me if I come across somebody. Pushing my shoulders back, I stride down the hallway, stopping occasionally to test the handles of doors along the way. I stumble upon the library after five tries, my relief palpable when the door swung open.

I can only imagine what secrets must be hiding in this house if, after five rooms, the library is the only door unlocked. These men are dangerous and the one I share my bed with is the most dangerous of them all. *I shouldn't forget that.*

But they do have good taste in books. My fingers run over the spines neatly lined up on the shelves. The titles are in Italian, but the authors' names are not. It's a collection of classics and there's no mistaking the value. I pull a hardback edition of *To Kill a Mockingbird* off the shelf, turning the leather-bound book over in my hands.

"Are you lost?" an accented voice asks, and I yelp in surprise.

I turn to face the man, a nervous smile on my lips when I'm greeted by his stony face. *He was at the dinner table last week.* Something twists in my gut, and my smile drops. There's a darkness to this guy, one that's not entirely to do with the world he finds himself in. Carefully, I slide the book back onto the shelf and clasp my hands together behind my back.

"I, uh, Romeo said... I'm free. To go around the house at least." Clearing my throat, I hold my hand out and take a step forward, my mouth tipping up at the corner. *Maybe I've got him all wrong.* "I'm Aurora."

He looks me up and down, barely concealing his contempt before he grinds out, "The library is off-limits."

I pull my hand back, looking around the room. It's literally the only door that was open. How can it be off-limits? When my attention returns to him, his eyes narrow with impatience.

"Oh." Walking around him, I head toward the door. "I'm sorry, I didn't realize. I'll, uh, just get out of here, then." Pausing on the threshold, I face him. "Are there any other rooms I should stay out of?"

"I suggest you keep your exploring to the ground floor and garden. Anything you stumble upon up here is likely to get you killed, Aurora." His tone is cold and sends a shiver running down my spine.

With a jerky nod, I step out into the hallway, not bothering to close the door behind me. It's only when I reach the top of the stairs that I look back. I don't expect to find him watching me, his hand resting on the holstered gun at his hip in a silent threat. I fly down the stairs, his message chasing after me.

It's only when I reach the bottom step and slip into the entertainment room that I allow myself to breathe. Every nerve ending in my body is alert and not in the way that it is whenever Romeo is near. These are firing on all cylinders with a desire to protect myself from harm.

Note to self: stay clear of him.

Slightly dazed and confused by the interaction, I stand in the middle of the room, my shoulders slumped and my brow furrowed. It's only when the ringing in my ears has stopped and I've shaken off the disorientation of the conversation that I continue with my self-guided tour of the *ground floor* of the house.

Chapter 26

Aurora

"Oh, I couldn't eat another bite." I push my plate away with one hand and hold up the other to keep Alma at bay. She's been feeding me nonstop for the last hour. I'm starting to wish I was still locked away in my bedroom because, although the food is delicious, there's only so much one person can eat.

Alma *tsks*, dropping another heavenly slice of home-made ciabatta onto my plate. Steam rises from the bread and my mouth waters, imagining it slathered in butter. "You're nothing but skin and bones, *signorina*. You need to keep up your strength."

I open my mouth to respond, but Haven, a house-keeper, pushes back her chair and admonishes Alma. "You shouldn't force-feed people, Alma. Especially when they've told you they've had enough." Walking toward the door, Haven calls, "I'll show you how to get to the garden, Aurora."

After exploring the house this morning, I stumbled upon the kitchen. Or rather, my rumbling stomach led me here when I got the first whiff of fresh bread. I've spent my afternoon with Alma, Massimo's chef, Maria, his head housekeeper, and Haven, her daughter. They've been so welcoming and made me feel at ease. *Unlike the man I ran into in the library.* Just the thought of the way he said my name sends a shiver down my spine.

Pushing back my chair, I gather up the dishes, but Maria stops me, smacking away my hands. She carries them to the kitchen sink, talking to Alma in rapid Italian and effectively dismissing me. With a shrug of my shoulder, I swipe up my pad and pencils and follow Haven as she walks from the room.

In the quiet of the corridor, she leans in, her voice low and conspiring. "Don't worry about them. You'll get used to their pushy nature in no time, just don't be afraid to tell them no or you'll end up in some *really* compromising situations. Believe me. My mom is the worst when it comes to pushing things on people."

I clutch my pad to my chest and try to keep the hurt out of my tone when I reply, "I don't think I'll be here long enough for that to happen."

The corner of Haven's mouth twitches and her brows shoot up before she composes herself and lifts her chin. "If you say so."

A heaviness settles into the pit of my stomach, but I narrow my eyes and affirm, "I do."

Soon, Romeo will have no use for me and he'll either follow through on the threats he made when we first met or return to Sicily and leave me behind without a thought. I'm not sure what will be worse.

Haven pushes through a set of doors that open up into the garden and I gulp in a much needed lungful of air. A peacefulness falls over me as I look out at the lush lawn that stretches for miles in front of us. A light breeze blows the strands of my hair into my face as I walk to the edge of the patio.

"I've seen the way he looks at you." Coming to a stop behind me, Haven softens her voice, drawing my attention to her. "Part of my job is to be invisible. But it does mean that people let their guards down because they think they're alone." She rests a hand on my shoulder. "Just know that if he didn't feel anything for you, you wouldn't be here. The men that occupy this house aren't the kind to do favors or make decisions just for the sake of it."

Sighing heavily, I look out over the landscape. "I'm not naïve enough to believe that." My voice is small and gets carried away in the breeze. "This"—I wave my arm at the garden before us—"is nothing more than him rewarding me for behaving. I know that if I so much as breathe the wrong way, he has the power to snatch away this little slice of freedom."

We stand in silence, the weight of my words hanging

between us and tarnishing the late afternoon brightness. The sound of a motor starting up cuts through the tension and I lift my face to the sky, closing my eyes and basking in the warmth of the sun that somehow feels foreign on my skin after the last few weeks inside.

Haven clears her throat. "I should get back to work."

Without looking back at her, I keep my head tipped back and sincerely reply, "Thank you, Haven."

The door clicks as she shuts it behind her and after five minutes of soaking in the tranquility. My movements are unhurried as I kick off my sneakers and bend to pick them up.

I walk out onto the lawn, my bare feet sinking into the grass. It's dewy from the rain this morning, but I won't let it deter me, not with the all-consuming need to make this moment feel real fueling me.

With the sun not due to set for another hour or so, I walk further out into the center of the lawn. I'm waiting for the moment someone jumps out and tells me it's all been a trick. For someone to shoot me for trying to escape.

My eyes land on a burly guy walking the perimeter to my left and I come to a stop, unable to pull in any air. His machine gun is cradled in his arms like a sleeping baby and my stomach drops, the butterflies erupting and taking flight when his eyes shift to mine. My body is tense, bracing for the moment he turns the weapon on me and fires. Within seconds, he breaks the contact, continuing on his walk like nothing ever happened. I exhale, my heart thumping a galloping rhythm in my chest.

Maybe I need to take Romeo at his word. He said I was free to explore the garden. What reason would he have for having me taken out now? I should be enjoying this moment for as long as I have it.

Shaking away the dark cloud hanging over my head, I stroll across the lawn, toward the back of the garden. The grass is bouncy beneath my feet and offers me a refreshing reminder of mother nature. Ever since I've been staying in Romeo's room, every morning, I've looked out of the bathroom window to the walled garden at the back. If I had to guess, from what I've seen, it looks like to be a rose garden that might provide me with some new drawing inspiration.

Anticipation skates down my spine when I push through an old wooden gate and into the separated garden. Greenery fills six large but equally sized flower beds and the buds of all different roses are visible.

Walking down the gravel path in between the first row of beds, I touch the leaves, careful to steer clear of the thorns. The weight on my shoulders lifts with each step, and I inhale deeply the smell of the earth; fresh and invigorating. Although the roses aren't in bloom yet, the buds are forming and my imagination fills in the blanks with the scent. There's a familiarity to the space, but I can't quite put my finger on why that is.

Gravel crunching signals the end of my time alone. The steps grow hesitant, stopping and starting before someone speaks, "We grow a lot of different varieties of roses here, but they won't be in full bloom until May and June."

I turn toward the voice, coming face-to-face with an older man, lines of a life well lived covering his face. His salt and pepper hair is barely concealed beneath his worn plain black baseball cap. He's grasping gardening shears in one hand and a pair of thick canvas gloves in the other.

He looks nervous, the hand holding the gloves shaking slightly. "I'm so sorry. I didn't mean to disturb you. It's been a long time since anyone came here. Not since..." he trails off, his eyes narrowing a fraction.

My gaze drops to the shears and I take a step back, clutching my pad to my chest. "I'm sorry. I was told I could draw in the garden." He doesn't say anything so I add, "I should go."

He drops the shears into the bed next to him, taking a large step away for good measure and holding up both hands before removing his cap. "You can draw here. I'll go. My curiosity got the better of me."

We stare, both unmoving. If I want to leave, I need to pass him and I'm not sure what his intentions might be. He seems harmless enough, but then so do a lot of things that could kill you.

"Who are you?" His question comes out quietly and coated in curiosity. I'm not sure he meant to ask it, but it doesn't stop my brows from pulling together. I thought everyone would know who I am.

With a neutral expression, I straighten my spine and reply, "My name is Aurora Costa."

His eyes bulge, and his mouth parts slightly. He shuffles toward me, squeezing his hat in his hands with his gloves. "Aurora? Is it really you? I mean, I thought you looked familiar, but it's been years and well..."

"Who are you?" I demand, thrown by what he's saying to me. It makes no sense. I have never seen this man before.

Shaking his head, he presses a hand to his forehead. "Of course, you wouldn't remember me." He smooths a hand down the front of his shirt, standing taller, his sincere gray eyes locking on mine before he speaks. "My name is Andrea Pesci. I worked with your mother."

"At Dunlocks?" My question rolls off of my tongue. I only ever remember my mom working at a department store. She'd take me in around the holidays and I'd get to pick whatever toy I wanted. As I got older, that turned into makeup and clothes.

"No." Andrea looks around, the bill of his cap now completely crushed in his hand. "We worked together here."

My thighs hit the back of one of the flower beds. What he's saying doesn't make any sense. I would have remembered if she ever worked for the mafia. *Right?* She'd have told me. *We didn't keep secrets from each other.* No matter how much certainty I inject into my tone, there's a hint of questioning in my statement when I declare, "My mom never worked here. She doesn't know these people."

Andrea puts his cap back on, before he stuffs his gloves into the back pocket of his worn, dirty jeans. "It was nearly twenty-five years ago, but yes, she did. She left when you were four... after your accident," he replies softly.

My accident?

I run a hand over my forehead and I look away, trying to process what he's saying. So many things are falling into place and yet remain unanswered. That sense of familiarity of the garden from earlier returns with a force. "What do you mean *my accident*?" I ask, my words barely audible over the rushing in my ears.

Andrea's eyes fall over my left shoulder and I glance back at the empty open space beyond the flower bed I'm standing in front of.

"There used to be a fountain over there. You were playing hide and seek with the boys and had snuck in here to hide. Your father had asked Mr. Marino to keep it off-limits *per i bambini*. He was worried you'd get hurt on the thorns, but he never imagined what actually happened. You must have tried to hide inside the fountain, but you were little and the inside was slippery. Massimo came running back to the house, frantic, telling us that Romeo had pulled you out of the water. He said you weren't moving." Inhaling sharply, Andrea clears his throat before continuing, his eyes glassy. "You stopped coming around after that. *Tua madre* left that day and we lost touch."

I don't know what to do with this information. Everything I thought I knew was a lie. The scar my mom said I got from falling from the jungle gym wasn't from that at all. She was part of this life. Hell, so was I. And yet I got on my high horse when I told my father to stay away.

This is all too much.

In some ways, it makes sense. My father was in the mafia, he must have worked with Romeo and Massimo's family, but to think that *I* knew them? That I grew up with them and did such mundane things like playing hide and seek? *That's* inconceivable.

How different would my life have been if I'd never had that accident?

My pad falls from my numb fingers, grazing my leg as it falls to the floor. The ground tilts and my breaths come in quick, shallow pants as I race from the garden, ignoring Andrea's pleas to stop.

Chapter 27

Romeo

Her body collides with mine when I step into the hallway that connects the one from Massimo's office with the main entryway. Fresh air and jasmine fill my lungs.

Without looking down at her, the press of her gentle curves against the hard planes of mine tells me exactly who it is. My hands hold her arms and Aurora looks up at me, her watery, sea-green eyes filled with confusion and hurt. Somewhere in the depths, there's a pleading before she blinks and it's gone.

My nostrils flare as a cocktail of fury and protective-ness sweeps through me. Holding her at arm's length, my eyes roam her body, searching for any injuries. "What's happened?" My tone is harsh and grating as I struggle to contain the desire to snap the neck of whoever put this look on her face.

Aurora sucks in a breath and aggressively yanks

234

herself out of my hold. Her voice is shaky and uncertain, her gaze darting around the quiet corridor. Trepidation fills her features, and in a broken whisper, she mumbles, "I'm sorry."

She brushes past me, racing toward the front of the house before she disappears. It takes everything I have inside me not to chase after her and I clench and unclench my fists, willing the unfamiliar, protective sensation in my gut away. In the distance, the sound of our bedroom door slamming echoes around the house.

Forcing myself to relax, I blow out a breath and unlock my jaw. I need to find out what's happened and *then* I can speak to her. *And make whoever has hurt her pay.*

Turning in the direction Aurora came from, I stride forward. The double doors that lead to the garden are wide open, giving me an indication of where she must have come from. I cross the threshold, my eyes scanning the vast garden. The cool afternoon breeze does little to soothe the heat flushing through my body.

Andrea approaches the house from the rose garden and my eyes narrow when I spot Aurora's pad in his grasp. I widen my stance and clasp my hands in front of me, waiting for him to reach me.

He briefly meets my eyes before dropping contact and offering up a nervous and apologetic smile. Holding out her pad, he shuffles his feet, making the gravel crunch beneath his work boots. "I'm sorry. I didn't realize she didn't know, Mr. Bianchi."

I don't take the pad. There's a deathly calmness to my tone when I ask, "Didn't know what, Andrea?"

He drops his arm to his side, lifting his face to mine. His brow furrows and I watch his mouth open and close as he thinks about how to answer my question. "That her mother used to work for Mr. Marino Sr., and... that she had an accident in the rose garden?" He ends his statement on a question, looking for reassurance.

I don't give it to him. Instead, I nod slowly, scrubbing a hand over my jaw. Masking my annoyance that *I* wasn't the one to tell her, I reply, "Okay."

He holds up the pad again, his shaking hands the only physical sign of his nerves. Andrea has worked for Massimo's family for nearly four decades. His father worked for us before him. He's part of our family and that's why I won't kill him. I know he meant no harm in telling Aurora about her past, but it doesn't abate the frustration that's still bubbling away in my gut at the thought of her not being prepared to hear it.

I should have told her the moment I found out, but it doesn't move us forward with finding Francesco, so I figured it could wait. *Dio*, it surprised me when Massimo brought it up. He said it so casually that I thought he was joking. Apparently, he'd had Aldo look into her mom and found out that she used to work for us. It was like the final piece of the puzzle for why there's been a familiarity about Aurora since the moment I first laid eyes on her photo.

Blinking away the distracting thoughts, I take Aurora's pad from Andrea and turn back toward the house without another word. I can't do anything about *how* she's found out, but I *can* do something to erase the pain that was marring her beautiful features.

It's not your responsibility.

Yes, it is. *She* is my responsibility. I took her, and that makes her *mine*. I owe it to her to keep her safe, even if it's from a past neither of us remembers. My steps are methodical as I move through the house, each one doing nothing to ease the dread that seems to be balling into a leaden weight in the pit of my stomach.

When I reach the bedroom, I stride in, only to come up short when I find it empty. Beyond the closed bathroom door, the tell-tale sound of water hitting tile draws my focus.

Throwing her pad onto the bed, I divert toward the noise, expecting the handle to give way when I push down on it. When it doesn't, I growl in frustration, pounding my fist on the door. A whimper sounds in response and I try to rid my tone of the frustration wrapping around my throat when I grind out, "Aurora, open the door."

Her voice is barely audible over the running water but I can hear the hurt loud and clear when she sniffs, "I'm fine. Please, leave me alone."

Bullshit, she's not fine at all.

Pounding my fist on the door again, I shout, "Open the goddamn door, Aurora, or I'll break it the fuck down."

She sobs the most pained and gut-wrenching sound

I've ever heard. It sends a sharp stab of pain to my chest. I don't wait for her to answer. Instead, I take a step back and kick in the door, uncaring of the damage. She startles from her position on the shower floor, pushing herself up the wall and into the corner when I storm in. Her eyes are wide and terrified, but through the mist of anger surrounding me, it barely registers.

My eyes flit from her head down to her toes and it's only when I can see that she's okay, my body relaxes. She's drenched, her dress molded to her body and wet strands of hair plastered to her face.

A shutter comes down over her features and she angrily swipes at her cheeks before hitting me with the full force of her glare. "I told you I was fine."

Running a hand through my hair, I tug on the strands to keep from reaching for her. "And I can clearly see you have no issues with lying to me."

Her features soften before she moves toward me, coming to a stop when she's within touching distance. My eyes bounce around her face. I can't ignore the dim light in her eyes and I press my lips together at the sight of it. This morning, that light shone so brightly that I thought it might blind me.

Reaching out her hand, she drops it before she makes contact, no doubt thinking my irritation is aimed at her. Round, red, pleading eyes look up at me. "That's the only thing I've ever lied to you about. I swear."

The tension seeps from my body, and I force my features into some semblance of neutrality. I close the distance between us, tugging her into my arms, uncaring that she's soaking wet. My hand soothes up and down her back, and I murmur into her hair, "I know."

She leans back, her teeth chattering as she searches my eyes. "I really mean it, Rome. I have no reason to lie to you."

I want to believe her, but in my world, trusting someone who isn't from it, can get you killed. And although Aurora might technically have been born into it, she's spent too much of her life out of this world for me to be able to trust her. So, I only nod, releasing my hold on her. "Let's get you out of these wet clothes and warmed up."

My hands reach for the hem of her summer dress, pulling it up and over her head. A wet thud sounds when I drop the sodden material to the tiled floor. Bending, I hook a finger into either side of her panties, sliding them down her legs. She rests her hand on my shoulder as she steps out, and I discard them as well.

I watch as she removes her bra before ushering her toward the still-running shower. "Warm up under the water and I'll get you some dry clothes."

When I turn to leave, she grabs my hand, halting me. Looking at her over my shoulder, I wait for her to talk.

She releases me, her voice quiet when she stutters, "D-do you think someone could have killed my mom?"

Facing her, I pick up her hand, squeezing it as I say the only thing that I know to be true. "I don't know, but I'm going to find out."

Blinking up at me, she takes a step forward, her hand coming up to rest on my chest. Her eyes are wide and filled with gratitude. "You will?"

Tipping my head back, I stare at the bathroom ceiling, steam clouding it from my vision. When she looks at me like I can solve all of her problems, it's so damn hard to remember that it's not my place to. Still, I find myself justifying why my mind is telling me that because this is important to *her*, it's important to *me* and so, easily and without thought, my answer rolls off my tongue. "Yes."

She moves into the shower and under the spray. The action is a reminder of the day of the restaurant shooting and how she shut down on me before I forced her to feel *something*.

"Aurora," I call, the authority in my tone clear. "I'll find out who killed her and I'll make them pay, but you have to promise me something."

"Anything," she breathes.

Inhaling sharply, I look away before forcing my focus back to her. I need her to know how important it is that she does this. "Want to live?"

A crease forms between her brows. "I do want to live."

I chuckle softly, shaking my head because she's far too accepting of death for someone who *supposedly* wants to live. "I've never met a person so at peace with having their life taken. I know that you miss her but you have your whole life ahead of you."

She goes quiet for a moment, dropping her attention

to the floor as water cascades over her body. There's a swirl of emotions in her green eyes when she lifts her head again. "Do I? Because when this"—she motions between us—"is all over, you're going to kill me."

Cazzo.

A heaviness settles over us as we silently stare at each other. I want to tell her that plans change and that the more time I spend with her, the less appealing it's getting, but I can't give her that hope. Instead, I wipe my hand over my stubbled jaw, my teeth grinding before I say, "Get showered. I'll leave your clothes on the bed."

A muscle in her jaw jumps but I don't stick around to see any more of her reaction. The lines between us are becoming increasingly blurred, and if we aren't careful, we just might implode.

Chapter 28

Aurora

I've been awake for twenty minutes, reliving the events of yesterday as I watch Romeo. He's asleep next to me, his features relaxed in the soft orange glow of the morning light spilling through the gap in the curtains.

I don't know where he disappeared to after he left the bathroom, but I didn't see him again last night. When he didn't join me for dinner in the kitchen like he has for the past week, I ate alone before dragging myself to bed. It wasn't until hours later that I felt the bed dip next to me and he wrapped his arms around me.

Rolling onto my back, I blankly stare up at the ceiling. It still doesn't seem real that my mom worked here. She walked these halls, worked for this family, and knew what they were involved in. How could she have not? It's not like anyone keeps it a secret. Jeez, Romeo told me the day we met that he is the head of the mafia.

Well, not the day we met, because apparently, we've known each other for years.

Did she leave to protect me? I know in some small way she must have because of the accident, but she could have come back. *Is her leaving the reason my parents got divorced?* My mom told me they grew apart, but was that just her trying to shield me? I wish I had someone to turn to for answers. Somebody who knew her, that she confided in. But the truth of the matter is, they all disappeared from my life the day she died.

My mind races with all the questions I don't know I'll ever get answers to.

Rolling to face Romeo again, I rest my head on my hands before pulling one out and reaching forward to brush away a curl that hangs over his forehead. A large, warm hand darts up and grabs my wrist before I can reach my destination. Stormy cobalt-blue eyes pop open and the air in my lungs vanishes.

We stare at each other, his eyes a mask, as usual. For a moment in the shower yesterday, I thought he cared. I thought that the feelings that have been weaving their way into my heart since he took me were reciprocated but whatever I thought I saw was quickly replaced with a cold hardness.

"Did you know?" The question tumbles from my mouth, and I bite my lip, wishing I could take it back. What difference does it make if he did know my mom used to work here or that he knew me?

For a moment, his brows tug together before

smoothing out. He's still holding onto my wrist and uses it to tug me into his arms and under his body in one swift movement. I don't have a chance to react or protest. When he's situated between my legs, he releases his hold on me, resting his elbows on either side of me.

His voice is low and sends a frisson of need racing down my spine before my mind can register his words. "Yes, and no. There have been things that felt familiar about you, but it wasn't until the other day, when Massimo told me, that I knew for certain."

I try to fight him, his words somehow feeling like a betrayal. My palms rest against his bare, solid chest, pushing at him. He doesn't budge; instead, he smooths a hand over my hair.

Hurt fills my voice as I beg, "Let me go."

"I can't do that, Aurora."

He can't or won't? My head twists to the side, forcing his hand away, and I suck in a lungful of air, blowing it out with a grunt.

Gripping my chin almost painfully, he forces my face back to him. "It doesn't matter if I knew, when I knew, or even that your mother worked for my family."

My tone is sharp and my words loud when I reply, "It does." Still, I try to fight him, turning more and more desperate with each push on his chest. "To me, it matters. That she worked for you *and* that she was involved in this world."

"Why?"

The simple word holds so much confusion, but doesn't stop my frustration from bubbling beneath the surface. *How can he not understand?* She was *all* I had. When she died, it broke me. And now I find out that she was involved with *these* people? That she was tangled up in the twisted darkness of their lives. Does he expect me to just accept that and not question everything I thought I knew to be true?

A certainty fills me, swirling with a venom that's been festering inside for years. It's been there ever since my father came clean, rooting itself in the periphery of my consciousness. "Because someone in *your world*," I spit the words out, my eyes growing hot, "took her from *me*."

I've always known that she would never kill herself. I was a kid and accepted what I'd been told, but her death has never made sense. There were never any signs, and we were so close that I would have seen them. *I know I would have.*

Romeo's eyes search mine, for what, I'm not sure. After what feels like an eternity, he rolls off me, his hand squeezing my hip. "I believe you, Aurora. And I meant what I said yesterday. I'm going to find out what happened to her but it's going to take some time."

I don't know if I should believe him, but I want to. After all, if anyone can figure this out and give me the truth, it's going to be Romeo. Nodding, I pull out of his grip and move to sit on the edge of the bed.

"I hope you meant what you said too, Aurora. This is

a two-way street. If you want answers, you have to keep your end of the bargain." *To want to live.*

My body stiffens. I'm not sure I can do that. Especially if I have to go through the pain again that I've had to live with since her death.

Chapter 29

Aurora

It's been two weeks since Romeo told me he would find out what happened to my mom. Each day has been more tortuous than the last.

It's taken everything in me to not ask him for an update whenever I see him. The rational side of me knows that when he has news, he'll tell me, but the desperate side of me... well, I've voiced my question a million times in my mind.

To keep myself busy, I've immersed myself in sketching, spending hour upon hour in the garden with my pad from sunrise to sunset. I don't know how much more of this I can take.

Tonight, after sitting across from him for an entire hour as I forced myself to eat, I excused myself and escaped to our room to run myself a bath. Haven handed me a magazine with sympathy shining in her eyes and

I've spent an hour in the tub, hoping it will distract me. But all I've come away with is wrinkled skin and a rundown on New York's most eligible bachelors, which Massimo is apparently one of.

Romeo strides into the room as I'm walking out of the bathroom, rubbing lavender-scented lotion into my hands. He shrugs out of his jacket, throwing it on the end of the bed before he starts to unbutton his shirt. I watch him from my spot in the doorway, leaning against the frame. When he turns to face me, his eyes flit down my body, and a welcome heat blooms in my core. My eyes drop to the ink swirling on his chest as he pulls the fabric apart. *I don't think I'll ever get tired of staring at him.* The thought surprises me and I push it down, forcing my attention away from his body and to my hands.

"Massimo reached out to a contact at the police station. They pulled the file on your mother's death and spoke to the detective in charge."

Ignoring the fluttering in my stomach, I move toward him, trying in vain to keep the eagerness from my tone. "And?"

When he speaks, there's a hint of hesitation in his voice. "They provided us with the name and address of the person who called it in. I sent Daniele to check it out today."

My eyes grow wide and I blow out a breath. "What did they say?" *Oh God, what if they're dead too?* Desperation coats my words as they rush from my lips. "Did he find them?"

Standing in nothing but his slacks, with his buckle undone, Romeo holds his hand out for me. I go to him without question. He cups my face with a large, warm palm, his thumb stroking the curve of my cheek in a gesture that is far too intimate and caring. There's an emotion swirling in the depths of his inky-blue eyes that I can't quite name. I don't know how we got here, to a place where being affectionate with each other was normal.

"He found him." He pauses and I'm glad he does because his next words are like a punch to the face. "She didn't kill herself, Aurora."

Air rushes past my lips and my legs give way, but Romeo's right there, banding a strong arm around my waist, pinning me to his chest. Instinctively, I wrap myself around him, burying my face in the thick column of his throat. "What *exactly* did they say?" I murmur softly.

Romeo sits us on the edge of the bed, dropping his hands to my thighs and smoothing the exposed skin. "There was a man on the bridge that night with a woman that matched your mother's description. They couldn't see his face but said he held a gun and forced her to climb over the railings."

A sob gets lodged in my throat. *She must have been terrified.* "They—they made her jump?" My voice sounds foreign on my own ears.

Sincerity coats his words when he confirms, "I'm so sorry, Aurora. It looks that way."

How could a person be so cruel?

On edge and with so many emotions vying for first place, I try to climb out of Romeo's lap, but he only tightens his grip. Tears tumble down my cheeks, falling with abandon onto his smooth inked skin and my nails dig into his biceps as each sob hammers home the reality. I'm furious with myself for showing any weakness and grief-stricken that my mom was forced to end her own life. But somewhere in the depths of my soul, I also feel a sense of relief that I was right. That I knew her.

Where do I go from here? How do I get justice for my mom when I don't know this world? Will Romeo help me or am I on my own in trying to figure this out?

Each unspoken question falls away unanswered. I might not know what happens now, but I do know that I won't rest until the person responsible for my mom's death is found. Inhaling deeply, I thrust out my chest and force my emotions down. I don't want to be dragged into the darkness again, not yet.

Romeo swipes his thumb over my cheeks, and I suck in a shaky breath, blowing it out as I shift my gaze to the space between us. I'm hyperaware of the way I'm strad-dling him and the gentleness he's shown when we both know that he shouldn't.

A heaviness hangs in the air when our heated eyes meet. It's filled with a need that's always present when-ever we're together. He hasn't touched me since the day I attacked him, and I would be remiss if I didn't admit to missing the feel of his hands on my body. Hell, I've missed the way he fills me, but most of all, I miss the way he devours me afterward, like I'm his favorite meal.

My eyes flare a fraction before I blink rapidly to clear the surprise from them. How has this happened? How has Romeo Bianchi come to mean something to me?

I see nothing but heat and a hint of compassion in his expression. He doesn't realize how deeply he's rooted himself into my soul. God, he's given me a reason to want to wake up each morning, and that is far more dangerous than anything he could have threatened to do.

I want to tell him how much I care for him, but the fear of rejection holds me back. Instead, we move in sync, doing the one thing we're best at. Romeo drags his thumb under the hem of my bathrobe, pushing the fabric further up my thigh. I move my hands up his arms, smoothing them over his shoulders and into the hair at the nape of his neck.

In the blink of an eye, our mouths crash together, teeth clashing and tongues tangling. In one smooth movement, Romeo slides a hand around my throat, holding onto my thigh with the other as he flips our positions so that my back is pressed into the mattress and he's hovering above me.

Pulling away, he rests his forehead on mine, dragging his hand down the center of my chest before undoing the knot of my robe. "Tell me what you want, Aurora." His voice is throaty and authoritative, sending a ripple of need racing down my spine.

"I want you. I need you, Rome," I plead.

Romeo rocks his hips into me, lifting my thigh higher on his waist to grant him greater access. I throw my head back, pushing my chest out and exposing the expanse of my throat.

I pull him into me and cup his face, ghosting my lips over his as I try to tell him how I feel without saying the words. Silently pleading with him to feel the same way.

He pulls away, searching my eyes, and for a moment, I'm afraid I've given away too much. The intensity of his gaze bores into me and I look away, needing him not to see any more than I've already shown him for one night.

I need to feel him.

To feel something good, in the midst of all of this heartache and pain.

My hands make light work of pushing his slacks and underwear down. Romeo kicks them off and they land with a dull thud on the carpeted floor.

Wrapping my fingers around his cock, I drag my hand up and down the length of him. Air hisses through his clenched teeth when I swipe my thumb over the pre-cum leaking from the tip.

"Be careful, Aurora. Or this will be over much sooner than you'd like," he grinds out.

Dusting kisses over his jaw, I breathe, "I just want to feel you inside of me, filling me to perfection."

My words must set off something inside him because he pulls away, turns me on my side, and positions his body behind mine. Lifting my leg, he runs the tip of his cock through my slit, coating his head in my juices before slowly easing inside. Muffled groans fall from my lips and into the comforter. My body stretches around him, welcoming the intrusion. *Why does he feel so good inside of me?*

When he's seated, he bands an arm around my torso and pulls me into his chest before resting his chin on my shoulder and gently rocking his hips. With him wrapped around me, I feel safe, even as he stokes the fire of desire inside of me. I moan loudly at the torturous feel of him.

It's both not enough and exactly what I need, leaving me feeling frustrated and needy.

Romeo's lips touch the shell of my ear, his breath hot and his words hushed. "You take my cock so well, *amore mio.*"

My mind is foggy and his praise barely penetrates the haze. Every nerve ending in my body is coming alive with each gloriously deep and methodical stroke. *How does he have the power to control my body like this?*

The hand on the arm he's using to keep my leg raised starts slow, torturous ministrations on my clit. I dig my nails into his thigh, my hips rocking with him, urging him on.

Breathlessly, I moan, "Rome, please."

"Please, what, *bella*?" he growls.

"More, I need more."

Romeo burrows his nose into the crook of my neck, inhaling deeply. The arm banded around my body squeezes me tighter and he murmurs Italian words that I don't understand. I hold onto the hope that maybe he's feeling just as consumed by this as I am. The low rasp in his voice and the way he sounds almost pained to be saying whatever it is he's saying only turns me on more.

Keeping a steady pace, Romeo cups one breast, rolling my hard, achy nipple between his fingers. With the attention he's paying to my clit added in, I don't know how much longer I can hold back from coming undone. I'm on the edge of losing all control, the tingling at the base of my spine forewarning what's to come.

His tone is biting when he grinds out, "I can feel your greedy little pussy trying to milk my cock. Don't you dare come until I say you can, Aurora."

There's a hint of warning in his tone, but I don't heed it and even if I wanted to, my body betrays me. "I can't hold back. It's too much." I barely get the words out before I explode. My vision blurs and my body tenses before white spots fill the darkness and my eyes flutter closed.

Romeo growls, biting my shoulder. The pain barely penetrates the haze of euphoria that's blanketing me. My entire body trembles, the aftershocks too much to handle.

A groove forms between my brows when Romeo pulls out and stands from the bed. There's a distinct lack of wetness between my legs and a weight settles onto my chest as I stare up at the ceiling. I was so caught up in my own orgasm and how only he can make me feel that I didn't consider his release.

Leaning on my elbows, I nibble my bottom lip.

Romeo turns away from me and I watch him inhale and exhale, the muscles of his back contracting and releasing. When he turns back to me, he grabs my ankles and forcefully tugs me to the end of the bed. I gasp at the roughness of his touch; a direct contrast to the care he's shown up until this point.

He spreads my legs, standing between them and pushing them even further open at the knees. His cock juts proudly and he grips the base, running it through my slit. I shake at the contact as he glides it over my clit before lining up with my entrance.

Teasing me, he eases in half an inch. "Are you ready?"

I nod, not fully aware of what I'm agreeing to, but if it's more of him, I will always be ready.

Satisfied with my response, Romeo repositions my legs to rest against his chest and circles his arms around my thighs. He holds me, my ass hovering off the bed before he slams into me. Inhaling sharply, I fist the sheets in each hand and hold on. Every thrust reminds me of his size, the stinging sensation only heightening my arousal.

"I told you not to come, Aurora. Clearly, I shouldn't have..." He pauses, searching for the right word. "*Fatto l'amore*." His eyes darken.

When he moves again, his thrusts are punishingly painful, but I still feel the familiar winding in my core as he stokes the flames.

Within a handful of jerky, skin-slapping thrusts, I'm

racing toward the edge of release *again*, my walls spasming around him.

"Don't you *fucking* dare."

Romeo throws one of my legs to the side and slaps my pussy. The pain is unexpected, and for a moment, it distracts me from the ecstasy I was seeking. Thrusting with jerky and uncontrolled movements, he races after his own release as I fight to keep mine at bay.

"I can't hold back," I cry.

His heavy pants and my breathy moans fill the room, ricocheting off the walls and colliding with the sound of our skin slapping together. It doesn't matter if anyone can hear us. Nothing else matters more than this moment.

"Come," Romeo roars.

He stills as I relax my body and give in to the orgasm that I've been teetering on the edge of. Blindly, I reach for him, dragging my fingers down his stomach as my walls contract and he fills me with his release.

My body goes limp and when he pulls out, his focus drops to the space between my legs. I can imagine what he's seeing because I can feel it—our combined release seeping from my pussy. He drags a thumb over my entrance, pushing the liquid back inside, and I close my eyes. Despite my sensitivity, I still luxuriate in the feel of his hands on my most intimate parts.

His eyes meet mine and he sucks his thumb clean before holding his hand out for me. There's a softness in his tone when he speaks. "Come, let's go get cleaned up. It's been a long couple of days."

His words are a reminder of another question that has been plaguing me for weeks. I don't have the will to voice it, worried that if I asked him how long I'll be kept here, he will shut me out. Or worse yet, take it as me wanting to leave when, in fact, I'm not sure that I do anymore.

Chapter 30

Romeo

C *azzo!*

I've fallen in *love* with her.

Chapter 31

Aurora

A slip of paper floats from the pages of my sketchpad, landing on the plush carpet by my feet. I stare at it blankly for a moment, my brow furrowed as I try to remember when I put it there before realizing I didn't.

Slowly sliding my pad onto the table, I bend to retrieve it. My scalp prickles and the hairs on my forearms stand to attention. Everything inside me is screaming for me to leave it alone.

This is going to change everything.

I pause before opening it fully. A leaden weight settles in the pit of my stomach as my heart pounds frantically in my chest.

Something tells me, there's only *one* man this note is about and our relationship is... Christ, what we were three short weeks ago and what we are now are polar opposites. I yearn for him in a way that I know I shouldn't. My body craves his nearness, and he's more than willing to offer himself up.

With each passing day, he's shown me another side of himself that I wouldn't have thought possible from a man like him. After all, how can a man who's so ingrained in his world feel compassion, affection, and, dare I say it, *love* for another human being?

Moreover, this house is starting to feel a lot less like my prison because, in his arms, I feel at home.

Of course, I'd be a fool to brush off the circumstances of how we met. But I feel the safest I've ever felt with Romeo.

I run my fingers over the paper, my mind consumed with thoughts of him. It's only when my finger catches on the edge, the pain bringing me back from my daydream, that I remember what I was doing.

Sucking on my index finger, my mouth fills with a metallic taste as I flip the note over. The paper is expensive and thick but not card and there are no other markings on it.

I inhale sharply and, without a second thought, lift the fold to open the note. My eyes scan over the words in front of me, the air leaving my lungs and failing to come back.

This can't be right.

My legs tremble and buckle beneath me as I sink into the chair behind me, my stomach plummeting to my feet. *How is this real? It can't be.* I read the words again and again. Blinking and rubbing at my eyes before my hand covers my mouth as bile burns my throat.

This is some cruel joke. *But who would think this was funny? How did it even get into my pad?* I've been in this room, in the vicinity of it, all day. Was it... It couldn't be... but even as I dismiss the thought, I know that somebody in this house has got to have done this. Which means that somebody that Romeo knows, and trusts, is willing to take him out. *But why?* My throat grows thick, and no matter how much I try, I can't swallow past the lump.

This isn't real.

I blink away the blurriness distorting my sight, focusing on the words again.

If you want to
keep Romeo
Bianchi alive be
at the
Strawberry fields
at 8PM tomorrow.
COME ALONE.

Shifting in my chair, I throw the paper onto the table and bring my knees up to my chest, resting my chin on them as I stare at the offending note. I don't want to think about what will happen if I don't follow their instructions. There's no way I'm not going, but getting out of this house and to Strawberry Fields in Central Park is going to be difficult. Exhaling heavily, I squeeze my eyes shut, trying in vain to sort through the whirlwind of emotions that are drowning me.

If I'd been asked a week ago what I would do, I'd have said he's made his bed and in his world, you get what you get. But things have changed. Somewhere along the line, I've handed him a piece of my heart.

My eyes pop open and my focus shifts to the bed. As if it's a scene from a movie playing out in front of me, I can see Romeo and I lazing in the sheets.

Romeo's hand traces over my waist as I lie cocooned in the crook of his arm. We're a tangle of limbs and racing hearts. In moments like this, I can pretend that what we have is normal. That our circumstances don't matter because when I'm with him, everything is perfect.

He's staring up at the ceiling, lost in his own head. The heaviness in the air and the slow tensing of his body tells me something is wrong. As if sensing my eyes on him, he turns his head on the pillow, our eyes locking as we stare at each other. The only sounds around us are the gentle patter of rain on the window and our breathing.

I reach my hand up between us, smoothing out the furrow between his brows. "What's wrong?"

He takes hold of my wrist, bringing my hand to his

mouth as he places a soft kiss on my open palm. "Nothing, bella."

He's lying.

I don't know how I know, but I do. Somewhere along the line, I've become attuned to him and the different moods that make up Romeo Bianchi. Right now, I know something has him worried. "You don't need to protect me."

Rolling on top of me, he settles between my legs, dusting kisses over my collarbone. My eyes flutter closed and my fingers dig into the flesh of his biceps. Just like I know when something is up with him, he knows just how to distract me.

His voice is throaty and hypnotic when he murmurs, "Ah, but that is where you are wrong, Aurora. I do need to protect you. There are people out there who would hurt you just for having been seen with me. Which means it is on me to keep you safe."

My fingers bury into his hair, forcing him to look up at me. Diverting his distracting mouth away from my body.

"Who protects you? Who looks out for you when there are threats?" I demand.

Romeo chuckles, his teeth flashing as the corners of his eyes crease. He brushes away a strand of hair from my cheek, dragging his finger down my throat and along my chest. "I have many, very skilled men that protect me with their lives, bella. I'm in a privileged position. You don't need to worry about me or what is going on in my world."

We stare at each other, a silent argument taking place

between us. I don't open my mouth to vocalize it though, because I know he'll win. And as much as I want to push my point that people being under your rule is not the same as someone willing to risk it all for you, I'm in no position to argue with him.

The sound of chatter in the corridor drawing closer to the open bedroom door pulls me back into the present. Romeo and Daniele come to a stop in the hallway, just in my line of sight, talking in rapid Italian. Romeo's back is to me, and with them occupied, I slip the note back between the pages of my pad.

I know what he'd want me to do, but I can't bring myself to do it. If I show him the note, he'll go to confront whoever sent it, and what happens if he doesn't come back? A sharp pain hits me in the chest. I can't bear to think about that.

I've fallen in love with Romeo Bianchi and that's why I need to find a way out of this house and into the city.

I could lose my life by escaping. Hell, I know Romeo gave his men the green light to kill me if I try, but if it protects him... then I'll do just about anything.

Chapter 32

Aurora

I *have a plan.*

And if Romeo trusts me like I hope he does, then it just might work. It *has* to work. The alternative doesn't bear thinking about. It's why, after a restless night's sleep spent staring at his handsome face, I've gone over every possible reason I can come up with to get into Manhattan without worrying him or coming clean.

The faith I have in my plan working doesn't stop the worry gnawing in my gut. It twists and turns in the pit of my stomach as question after question runs on repeat in my mind.

What if I do this and they hurt him anyway?

Am I making the right decision?

What happens if they kill me?

Would it be better if I told Romeo? Two minds are better than one, after all, and this is his world, not mine.

Resting my hand on my stomach to calm my nerves, I

read over the note again. I hate the idea of lying to him, but in this instance, I'd rather ask for forgiveness than permission. His refusal, if I came clean but said I wanted to go, would no doubt be instantaneous.

Straightening my spine, I push my shoulders back and force down the anxiety clawing at my throat. *I have to do this*. Losing him is not an option, not when he's made me *feel* again. Not when he holds my heart in his, without even knowing it. Romeo might be used to losing people as part of his job, but I don't think I could survive it if I lost him. Being kidnapped just might have been the best thing that ever happened to me.

Folding the note and slipping it back between the pages of my pad, I rip out a sheet, writing one of my own. If the worst-case scenario does happen, I want him to know the one thing I've not been brave enough to say. My eyes sting as my hand moves across the paper. When I'm done, I open my pad, drawings of my mom staring back at me as I lay the note on top and close the cover. Resting my hand on top, I blow out a breath before forcing my body to move.

I take my time getting ready, every action taken like it might be my last. There's a gloominess hanging heavy on my shoulders, pulling my already melancholy mood down. It matches the gray, thunderous clouds filling the sky. My eyes drift to the window each time I pass through the bedroom as I get ready.

Is this a sign of what's to come?

God, I need to get out of my own head. There will

still be people in Manhattan. Hell, even in Central Park at 8 pm. It's spring, the days are getting longer, it won't even be dark. It's going to be fine. I'll find out what they want and then come back and discuss it with Romeo. *Easy.*

Pulling open the bedroom door, I head to the kitchen for breakfast with Romeo. We've fallen into a routine these past few days. If he doesn't wake me with breakfast, I meet him in the kitchen and we eat together, chatting over my plans for the day—which usually consists of drawing in the garden or reading a magazine Haven picked up for me in the entertainment room. Romeo doesn't share much of his plans and I don't press him.

Maybe I should have.

I move through the house on autopilot, every step fueling the fire of anguish burning inside of me. My palms are sweaty as I rub them over my denim-clad thighs. By the time I arrive in the kitchen, the nausea has taken over and the magnitude of what I'm about to do and the fallout that could ensue hits me like a freight train.

Pausing on the threshold, I stare at Romeo as he chats with Maria. My eyes roam over him, cataloging every detail, from the hair that curls at the nape of his neck to his neatly trimmed fingernails. The morning newspaper is stretched out in front of him and there's a lightness to his demeanor that wasn't there when we first met.

Is that because of me?

This man has taken my grief and my darkness and

made me see that I can be happy without feeling guilty for living. That's something I *never* thought would be possible.

Unshed tears threaten to spill and the idea that he might not forgive me chokes the air from my lungs.

"Are you going to stand there all day, *bella*?"

Heat creeps into my cheeks and I duck my head, hiding my face behind the curtain of my hair. Exhaling out all the emotions that have been weighing heavy on my mind, I move across the room and take a seat at the table. I offer up a smile, just like I have each morning we've eaten together, praying that he doesn't notice how forced it feels.

"Good morning. How did you sleep?"

A grin splits his face, leaving me stunned at his beauty. I take a mental picture, unsure how long it will be before he graces me with a smile again. No matter how certain I am that my plan is the right way forward, Romeo will be pissed and I don't know how that will be channeled. Will he send me to the basement without hearing me out? Or will he be rational and listen to my reasoning? Or worse yet, will he kill me?

The unknown has a lump forming in my throat, and when he closes the newspaper and turns toward me, I squirm in my seat. There's a searing heat in his inky blue eyes, begging me to come closer, to give in to him.

"You know full well how I've slept, Aurora. And Maria doesn't care what we get up to in the privacy of our bedroom, so you don't need to be coy around her."

My lips part and I dip my chin to hide my surprise at him confirming our relationship. *If that's what you can call it.* I want to squeal, jump around, and ask him to say it again, but I settle for biting my lip to keep the smirk at bay. Despite what he's said, I lean into him, keeping my voice low when I tease, "So, not too much sleep then."

Romeo shakes his head, moving closer until his mouth is less than an inch away from mine. "Maybe I should bend you over this table and show you how little of a fuck I give about other's opinions."

I suck in a breath, my eyes dropping down to his mouth as I chew on my bottom lip. *Oh. Yes, please.*

He pulls away, looking down at the newspaper and chuckling. "I think you'd like that far too much, *bella.*"

Maria arrives at my side and I shake my head to rid it of the naughty thoughts whirling around inside it.

Setting down a bowl of fresh fruit in front of me, she pats me on the shoulder. "Buon appetito." There's a twinkle in her eye, and as heat fills my cheeks, I turn my attention to the bowl.

Needing a distraction, I pick up a fork, stabbing at a piece of melon, and bringing it to my lips. Before I pop it into my mouth, I inject as much casualness as I can possibly muster into my tone as I ask, "So, what do you have planned for today?"

Romeo watches me as I slide the melon into my mouth, his eyes darkening when my tongue darts out to swipe up the juice left behind on my lips.

Clearing his throat, he picks up his espresso and takes

a sip. "It'll be business as usual. What are you going to do?"

Laying my fork on the placemat, I smooth my hands over my thighs, trying to keep the nervous twinge in my throat away. I *need* him to say yes without asking any questions. *Here goes nothing.* "I was hoping to go to Manhattan and pick up a few essentials. There's a store I'd like to go to and pick up a dress for that thing next week, but I want to try it on first."

He doesn't speak for the longest time and it takes everything in me to stay still and not show any outward sign of the turmoil swirling in the pit of my stomach. My hand trembles as I pick up the fork and stab at a cube of pineapple. I squeeze the metal so tightly in between my fingers that I'm surprised it doesn't bend.

He's going to say no.

Romeo stands, stuffing his hands into his pockets and drawing my eye line to his crotch. *Do not get distracted, Aurora.* I watch him from under my lashes, sliding the pineapple into my mouth and slowly chewing it. It tastes like cardboard.

Throwing a black card onto the table, he clears his throat before he speaks. "There's no limit on the card, so get whatever you want, but make sure it's easily accessible. I'd hate to have to ruin it."

He wraps his fingers around my throat, forcing my head back to meet his as he bends to kiss me. My arms reach up, wrapping around his neck as I deepen the kiss, needing more of him. More than he can give me right now, anyway. *Later*. We'll have all the time in the world for more when I get back. *If I get back, if he forgives me...* He has to. When I tell him why, he'll forgive me. God, he *has* to.

Releasing my lips, he rests his forehead on mine, his eyes searching for something I refuse to show him. I look away, forcing his hold on me to drop. Lying to him doesn't feel good, and it's on the tip of my tongue to come clean, but he stands tall, cupping my cheek and forcing me to look at him again. A groove forms between his brows, and I know that my demeanor is worrying him.

Swallowing down the bitter taste of my deceit, I force a smile to my lips. "Have a good day."

His eyes narrow a fraction before he nods and replies, "Enjoy your shopping. I'll have Angelo meet you in the lobby in an hour, so enjoy your breakfast and maybe have a *cornetto*."

My eyes track him as he strides from the room and it's only when I can be certain that he's gone that I exhale and collapse back into my chair.

That's the easiest part of my day over and done with.

Chapter 33

Romeo

The bleak weather from this morning is gone, replaced with a brightness that has a lightness in my step when I stride into Massimo's office. *Who the fuck am I?* Streams of sunlight flood through the window as I cross the room to stand in front of the window, stuffing my hands into my slacks.

Although my mood is better than it has been for a long time—thanks to Aurora—I can't seem to ease the niggling feeling in the pit of my stomach. There was something wrong with her at breakfast. *Should I have let her go to Manhattan? Probably not. Will I do anything she asks of me? Within reason, yes.*

Over the last few weeks, I've come to know her in ways I never thought possible. Sure, there are intimate and physical ways to get to know a person, but I know her down to her *core.* From the little moods she gets into when her mind isn't communicating with her hand as she sketches. Or the way she likes to take a long bath when she's had a particularly hard day remembering her mother. To her favorite breakfast being fruit because she likes to kick her day off with something sweet, but she wants the balance of being 'healthy'.

Dio, I know her better than I know my cousin.

In the reflection of the window, I see Massimo talking to Aldo, their heads bent over the screen of his laptop, deep in conversation. Neither of them acknowledges me, which is to be expected, given our current circumstances. There are three shipments due next week, each scheduled a day apart, and there will likely be another attack because we're no closer to finding Francesco. But this time, we'll be prepared.

We're in a better position now, even if we don't know exactly where Francesco is. Daniele and Leonardo are out, keeping eyes on Elio Morretti because I'm not convinced he isn't somehow involved in this. We'll have confirmation either way soon. I tune back into the conversation, turning to face the room.

Massimo leans back in his chair and taps his finger against the edge of the desk. "And the dummy shipments have been arranged? For an hour before the actual ones are due in?"

Aldo has been at this longer than Massimo has been alive. If I'm being honest with myself, I don't know how Aldo puts up with him. There's only so much of Massimo and his unpredictability that I can take. There's a hint of frustration in Aldo's tone when he replies, "Yes, Massimo."

It's quiet for a moment before Massimo nods. The squeak of his chair echoes around the room as he leans forward. "I know I don't need to tell you just how important this is, Aldo. If we fuck it up, that could be it."

Massimo is right to be pressing Aldo on this. We shouldn't have lost anyone in the first place, but we can take steps to make sure we don't lose more. In the next week, all of our shipments will be preceded by a dummy shipment under an umbrella company. Our men will be waiting in the containers. We'll have more stationed around the docks, and we've upped our protection nearly tenfold. Whoever is trying to take us out won't stand a chance.

Aldo straightens, inclining his head to Massimo. His shoulders look tense and there's a slight tick in his jaw. If I wasn't watching him so closely, I'd have missed it. The stress of it all is starting to get to everyone.

"I'll make sure everything goes without a hitch," he confirms.

Picking up a pile of files from Massimo's desk, Aldo strides from the room. I amble my way over to take a seat, silently observing Massimo. He leans back in his chair, heaving out a sigh. It's a sound I'm familiar with. Being a leader in this business means you have the weight of the world on your shoulders and lost lives on your conscience as everybody waits for your next instruction. At times, it can be draining. He looks exhausted, with dark circles under his bloodshot eyes and the muscles in his face drawn from a lack of sleep.

I scrub a hand over my mouth before setting it on my thigh and resting my ankle on my knee. "Have you heard from Leonardo?"

He lifts his phone and looks at the screen. Scrolling through the notifications, he replies, "Yeah. He said he'll call us tonight with a proper update, but it's looking promising."

"Good."

My focus shifts to the shelves behind Massimo. They're filled with trinkets his father and our grandfather collected over the years. Our grandfather, for a long time, had gone between Sicily and America, but as his health declined, he started to delegate to his son—my father—and his son-in-law—Massimo's father. At the forefront of what we do, preserving our grandfather's legacy is paramount.

Returning my attention to Massimo, I remind him, "Protecting everything our family has worked for should be our main priority and guide us in everything we do."

Massimo bangs his fist on the table, erupting out of his seat and pressing a hand to his forehead. "Christ, Romeo, this is *my* fucking family too. I know *exactly* what our grandfather sacrificed to make sure we were always on top. Don't sit there and act like I've done anything that would have you questioning where my fucking head is."

Grinding my teeth, I force myself to remain calm. It'll do us no good to get into an argument. And he's right. I didn't need to remind him because, although we've all been working around the clock, Massimo has pushed himself further and harder. *Anything to protect the family*.

He collapses back into his chair; the fight having left him. "I apologize. This whole situation is frustrating. It's nearly been a *month* and we're no further forward. I'm fucking tired, man."

Exhaling heavily, I say, "We haven't ruled out the fact that someone in your house could have been feeding Francesco information."

Massimo stares at me blankly, running his tongue over his teeth before he replies, "I don't think anyone has."

"Have you had Aldo do a sweep?"

"Yeah, and nothing turned up."

Nodding, I look out the window as I run through possible scenarios. "They could have removed it. Nothing's happened since the night of the restaurant attack, so it's plausible."

When the only sound that can be heard is our breathing and that of a phone ringing somewhere in the house, I sit forward, needing Massimo to hear what I'm about to say. "If all roads lead to it being one of your men behind this in *any* capacity, I, and the rest of your men, need you to not hesitate. I don't care if all they did was feed them the information without realizing what they would use it for. An enemy is an enemy, even when they mask themselves as a friend."

We stare at each other, a silent war waging in our locked gazes. He wants to argue the fact, but he knows I'm right. There have been many times in history where an enemy has taken out a rival by befriending them. Nobody is truly ever on your side.

Relenting, Massimo offers a quick, sharp nod. "You have my word. I'll do anything for the family."

I lean back, flicking my wrist and tugging on my cuff. A knock at the door draws our attention and when Massimo calls for them to enter, a timid-looking woman enters, her fingers nervously fiddling with a dustcloth. Her wide eyes look glassy as they dart around the room, looking like we might kill her for the interruption.

When she doesn't speak, Massimo demands, "What is it, Haven?"

She looks at the floor before swallowing and lifting her focus back to us. "I'm so sorry. I've just taken a call on the housephone, Mr. Marino."

Her eyes dart to mine for a second, and my stomach clenches. I know what she's about to say before the words pass her lips.

I never should have let her leave this house.

"Miss Costa has been taken."

Chapter 34

Aurora

I 've been traipsing from store to store for the last two hours and have yet to make a single purchase. Most of my day has been spent trying to distract myself from the meeting tonight.

After breakfast, I tracked down Angelo and asked to push our leaving time to the afternoon. He shrugged and grunted before walking off so I took my things and went into the garden. I spent the better part of five hours trying to sketch out the landscape before giving up.

Haven caught me on my way back into the house and invited me to a late lunch with her and Maria. I wish now, as a knot of nerves sits on my chest, that I'd spent more time going over my plan. Although I had the foundation—get into Manhattan—I didn't even consider how I'm going to get away from Angelo. His mood has darkened with each minute that's passed as I've forced him into each store.

We're in a boutique just off Fifth Avenue. It's the ideal location for me to sneak out, access the park where I'm meant to meet the writer of the note, and hopefully make it back before raising any suspicion. *It's now or never.* I can't keep up this charade for much longer, especially when there are only thirty minutes until the meeting time.

Sucking in a breath, I pull nervously on my ear and stand taller. My voice comes out sounding a little too high-pitched when I ask the sales assistant, "Where's the restroom, please?"

She smiles, oblivious to my inner turmoil. "Go through the double doors." She points to the back of the store before continuing, "And then it's at the end of the corridor. You can't miss it."

I chance a glance at Angelo, his attention shifting from the window to me. He might get in trouble because of me, but I'm sure that when I get back and explain everything, Romeo will forgive him. I swallow down the nausea stuck in my throat and lift my chin. This is the *right thing* to do, no matter the consequences.

"I'll be right back." Turning to the saleswoman, I add, "Maybe I can try the red and blue dresses when I come back?"

She nods, her curls bouncing from the force. "Of course, take your time and I'll get everything set up for you in the dressing room."

If only she knew how long I'll be.

Every movement of my body feels short and jerky as I

walk toward the back of the store. Trying not to look back, I force myself to slow down and keep a leisurely pace. My hands tremble as I raise them and push through the door that leads to the employee only area.

When it swings shut behind me, I rub my sweaty palms over my thighs, looking around the space to make sure it's clear before I release the tension in my shoulders. I lean against the wall, closing my eyes and sucking in several deep breaths in a bid to calm my nerves.

I feel dangerously out of my depth.

At the end of the narrow hallway is an emergency exit, and I send up a silent prayer of thanks that at least *this* part is easy.

Eventually, they'll notice that I've gone and alert Romeo. But I'm counting on having enough time to at least get to the park before they send out the search party. I just need to meet with this person face-to-face, find out what they want and then I don't care if they find me. The entrance to Central Park is two blocks away. If I run, I'll have enough time.

I hurry down the hallway, throwing furtive glances over my shoulder as I go. Coming to a stop in front of the door, my hands rest on the bar and I grit my teeth as I read the writing printed across it in big block letters. I didn't even consider the door might be alarmed. *Fuck.*

I don't have a choice. Bracing for a jarring sound, I press down, prepared to run and not look back. Too much is riding on me making it to Strawberry Fields *alone*. It's only when the only noise is that of the city seeping through the gap that I breathe a sigh of relief. My eyes sting with unshed tears, but I push the emotion down and quietly close the door behind me.

Everything happens so quickly.

I turn to run but collide with a solid body. I'm met with a skull mask covering the face of a bulky man when I lift my eyes to his. I take a step back, but he grips my arms, his fingers digging painfully into the flesh.

"I'm sorr—" A hood is thrown over my head, cutting off my words and plunging me into darkness.

Confusion clouds my mind, but I know whatever this is, it's not right. My heart pounds a wild beat in my rib cage. Praying that Angelo can hear me, I scream as loud as I can, but it doesn't deter them. Tears tumble down my cheeks and my body shakes as fear takes hold. Heavy arms band around me, squeezing me tightly and minimizing any impact I might have as I thrash my body around, fighting with all my strength. *This is bad. Really bad.* I might have been welcoming of death when Romeo took me, but it couldn't be further from what I want now.

I want to go back.

I don't want this.

I want to be in Romeo's arms.

Why is nobody helping me?

When he growls, "Shut up, you stupid bitch," I realize I've been crying the words out loud.

I'm thrown into a vehicle. My body jolts at the hard metal floor and I knock my head against something. For a moment, I feel the pain before everything goes black.

Chapter 35

Romeo

Adrenaline courses through my body, and over the pounding in my ears, I can't hear a thing. *I'll fucking kill them.* Whoever has taken her, I'll kill them. Jolting out of the chair, I swipe my hands over Massimo's desk, knocking everything onto the floor. A guttural roar rips from my lips and I fly across the room, punching the wall. The vibrations rattle the painting hanging there and I'm barely aware of Haven leaving or Massimo coming to stand next to me.

"Rome." He rests his hand on my shoulder and pulls me away from the wall.

"If Angelo's stupid enough to return, I want him in the basement." I fist his shirt in rage.

Massimo holds up his hands, setting them over mine as he tries to pry my deathly grip away. "I get that you're angry, Romeo. But let's find out what he has to say before you start pulling his teeth."

Disgusted, I shove away from him and he smooths down his crumpled shirt. Pointing a finger in his face, I mock, "'I'll do anything for the family, Rome. I won't hesitate, Rome.' Did you not say that moments ago?"

He sighs heavily. "Yes, and I *will* do anything for the family."

Keeping my tone low, I take a step toward him, my eyes boring into his. "She is *my* woman, Massimo, and *he* lost her. For that, he owes me his life. If you were in my shoes, you would demand the same. Have him brought to the basement."

Standing toe to toe with me, he draws himself up to his full height. "No."

"This, right now, is the *anything* and if you fail to do your part, I'll have no issues with following through on mine." The threat is clear in my tone.

He huffs out a laugh, rubbing his hand over his jaw and with a shrug, he replies, "But she's not family."

Without a second thought, I connect my fist with his jaw. His head jerks back and his eyes flare in surprise.

"Fucking say it again. I dare you," I bark, spittle flying from my mouth.

His hand soothes over the spot I hit. "I shouldn't have said that, but you have to know that I don't think Angelo would be behind this."

Clenching my fists, I stare out of the window, hoping the greenery will tame the rage coursing through my body. "Why? Because it's not in his nature?" I sneer.

Massimo sighs. "He was at the dock the night of the bombing, and his twin brother was killed."

Cazzo.

The red haze on the edge of my vision dissipates marginally. If he wasn't involved, he's still responsible. She was under his watch and should have never left his sight.

A creak sounds behind me and I picture Massimo sinking into the chair behind his desk. There's a hesitancy in his voice when he asks, "Do you think she might have taken the opportunity to run?"

She was hiding something at breakfast this morning and yet I ignored my concerns because I wanted to trust her. With everything I've come to know of her over the past few weeks, the intimacy we've shared, and how she's been so forthcoming about her life... she didn't run.

"No." My answer tumbles from my mouth, certainty coating the word. I don't for a second believe that she *wanted* to leave. *Someone has taken her to get back at me.* I shouldn't have let her go and no matter how much I want to blame Angelo, this rests squarely on my shoulders.

Moving to the drinks cart, I pour myself a glass of scotch, throwing back the contents before pouring another. The burn does nothing to soothe me. "When will Angelo be back? Who called the housephone?" I ask, turning to Massimo, my glass raised to my lips.

He flicks his wrist, checking the time on his Rolex. "His text five minutes ago said he'd be back in about twenty minutes. He's got the CCTV from the store and the surrounding area." The silence hangs heavy in the air before he adds, "We'll find her, Rome."

Dio, I hope we do. I'm not sure what I'll do if we don't get her back. I can't live without her.

Leaning forward, I demand, "Who called the housephone?"

"Haven said they didn't give a name. They just said they've got her and that they'll call again."

"Why didn't they call you or me?"

Shrugging, Massimo replies, "I don't know. I guess they didn't have our numbers, or they called the one they've used before."

A knock on the door cuts off any further conversation and Massimo stands, calling out. Angelo enters seconds later, a grave look on his face.

Chapter 36

Aurora

I groan, squinting my eyes as I try to open them and get my bearings. My head is pounding, and it's not until I inhale deeply, the unfamiliar stench of chemicals assailing my nostrils, that I remember the guy and the van. *Oh God, and the note. Was it all a ploy to kidnap me? Romeo was never in trouble?*

Blinking, I try to clear away the fuzziness clouding my vision and mind. *How did this happen?* Nobody would have known we were in that particular store, let alone that I was going to be leaving through the emergency exit. My eyes widen, and I bite down into the flesh of my lower lip.

Was Angelo behind this?

He didn't know we were going to that particular store until I dragged him inside. *But that doesn't mean he couldn't have told someone.* Unlike me, he has ways of communicating with people. Maybe he figured I would make my escape out of the fire exit and gave them a heads up. If he was aware of the note, then it would have been an obvious exit.

Rubbing my eyes, I exhale through the pain that seems to be coming from every muscle in my body. Right now, I need to focus on finding a way out, not on how I got here. Tentatively, I sit up on the cot before collapsing back when the room tilts. Nausea engulfs me and I blow out a steady stream of air in a bid to ease it.

Okay, that's not going to work.

Turning my head on the lumpy, polyester-filled pillow, I scan the room. There's not much in here. Four gray cinder block windowless walls surround me, with a closed rusty metal door in the center of one. A silver, rust-stained bucket sits in the far corner with half a roll of toilet paper haphazardly thrown on the floor next to it. There's a heaviness weaving its way into the pit of my stomach.

I *knew* this wasn't my world, and yet I thought I could handle it. *How could I have been so stupid?* I should have told Romeo the second I read that note. He could have sent someone else, someone more equipped to handle whatever *this* is.

He won't come for me.

Rubbing at the dull ache in my chest, I blink away the tears and exhale a shaky breath. *What if he thinks I've run away? I don't want to die here.*

The sound of the door unlocking echoes around the room. I need to buy myself some more time to figure out who these people are. Praying that there isn't a camera in the room and cursing myself for not having checked, I close my eyes and feign unconsciousness. A stiffness seeps into my body and the position feels unnatural and forced.

On the other side of the door, I can hear unintelligible and urgent chatter before it opens and their voices become crystal clear. They don't seem fazed by my presence, comfortable to continue their conversation as they walk into the room. I listen intently, trying to place their accents.

"She wasn't supposed to get hurt. He said to bring her in, in one piece," one of them admonishes.

"She is in one piece, and anyway, I'd hardly call a knock on the head 'getting hurt'. She's got worse coming to her later, so what does it matter?"

Oh God.

I bite my tongue to keep my whimper at bay, swallowing it down with the bile that rises at their words.

If I had to guess, I'd say they're from somewhere in Eastern Europe, but I couldn't say where. I hold my breath, fighting to keep the despair at bay. I don't have a clue who Romeo's enemies are. It's not like he shared that kind of information with me and now I'm here with no idea what they might want from me. I doubt they'll be as forgiving as Romeo, and when they realize I can't help them with the information they want, they'll kill me.

Panic rises in my throat, threatening to choke me, but I keep my breathing steady and continue to listen.

A dull thud sounds, skin hitting something padded and then feet shuffling on a dusty floor before the second one exclaims, "Hey, what was that for?"

The first guy speaks. He sounds older and annoyed. "She clearly was hurt, *durak*, or she would be awake by now. The Italian was clear; we need *her* to lure Bianchi out and she can't do that if she's dead." He pauses before there's more shuffling. "I won't hesitate to lay the blame solely at your feet if she doesn't wake up and he demands answers." The threat in his tone is clear.

There's a heavy silence before they leave, the door banging shut behind them. It's only when the sound of their footsteps disappear that I allow myself to relax.

I replay their conversation, analyzing every sentence. They want to lure Romeo here and use me as bait. There was never any chance of me finding out what they wanted and returning to him. This was their plan all along.

They're going to kill Romeo.

And it'll be all my fault. I smack a hand over my mouth, smothering the sob ripped from my lips. If I'd just shown him the note, none of this would be happening. Squeezing my eyes shut, I picture Romeo at breakfast this morning and the smile I put on his face before *lying* to him. *Was that our last kiss?* I don't think I could bear to never see him again, to feel his presence near me or have a part of him touching me. Sliding my fingers into my hair, I massage my scalp to ease the throbbing from hitting my head.

I feel so helpless.

There's no getting through this because I can't take another heartache. A single tear falls from the corner of my eye and runs down into my hairline. I don't bother to catch it. Instead, I turn onto my side and wrap my arms around my waist in a vain attempt to hold myself together. I can't fall apart now, not when he needs me to stay strong and fix this mess.

Think, Aurora.

What else did they say?

Something about an Italian. It's possible that it's Angelo, but even with his grumpy demeanor, I don't think it is. Besides, when they realize I've gone, he'll be in so much trouble.

If he hasn't run away because he's involved.

Dismissing the thought, I wrack my brain. Could there be someone else from Massimo's house who is helping these guys? I don't know any men aside from Massimo, Romeo, Daniele and Leonardo. Can I rule them out?

What about... No, it can't be. Romeo said the guy from the library—Aldo, I think it was—has worked for Massimo's family for years.

This is pointless.

I don't know anything about the people in that house, not really. What I need is a plan; a way to warn Romeo of what they intend to do, and at the very least, a way to get out of here, preferably alive. I sit up, leaning back against the wall and resting my head until the room stops spinning. The swell of nausea is still there but is manageable.

It feels like a lifetime ago that I was working as an emergency dispatcher, but those years of answering calls have to be of some use now. What would I tell someone to do if they called 911? *Stay hidden*. We're a bit past that. *Be compliant and take in as much of your surroundings as possible.* Great advice when you have the emergency services on the other end of the phone and know that help is on its way.

I could try and fight them.

And they'd probably snap my neck quicker than I could land a punch. In any case, there are two of them and only one of me. Or at least two that I know about.

My gaze jumps around the room, desperately seeking anything I can turn into a weapon. There's no way I can break a piece of the bed off. I could use the sheet to suffocate one of them. But that's reliant on there only being one of them and the likelihood is they'll overpower me anyway. Maybe I can tie the sheet to the bucket. It would give me the distance to at least get a couple of blows in.

Who am I kidding?

In every scenario I can think of, I end up dead. Which is what I've been begging for Romeo to do all this time.

Except now, that wish to die couldn't be further from the truth.

Chapter 37

Romeo

Angelo shifts in the seat in front of Massimo's desk. It's the only sign of any effect my cold, unwavering stare is having on him. The rage I'd tempered earlier is bubbling beneath the surface, waiting to be unleashed. Angelo locks eyes with me and sets his jaw as animosity fills the room, hanging heavily in the air.

Massimo leans on the front of his desk, his ankles crossed and his arms folded across his chest. As if he's asking a toddler how they hurt themselves, he asks, "What happened?"

Shifting his focus to Massimo, Angelo scrubs a hand over the back of his neck, looking almost guilty. He should feel shame. In fact, he should sacrifice himself for what he's let happen. "I honestly don't know. One minute she's asking for the bathroom, then ten minutes passed and she hadn't come back, so I went looking for her. There wasn't any physical sign of her having left or a struggle."

Massimo meets my gaze over his shoulder before exhaling heavily and turning back to Angelo. It's taking everything inside of me not to drag him down to the basement and make him pay for having lost her, but I promised Massimo we would hear him out. Once he's done explaining though, all bets are off and I can take my time, ripping him limb from limb.

I move until I'm standing behind Angelo. He straightens in his chair, rolling his neck and clearing his throat, his fear palpable.

Before he can react, I hook an arm around his throat, grabbing my wrist with my other hand and tightening my hold. His feet kick and as I pull back, he lifts from the chair. His fingers grip my arm and although he could reach my face, he doesn't retaliate. Why would he? He knows better than to try.

"Rome," Massimo calls, but I ignore him.

There's nothing he can do to stop me. If Angelo valued his life, he should have protected what belonged to me.

So should I.

Cazzo! I should have done a better job at protecting her. I shouldn't have let her go. I release him and Angelo crumples back into his chair. There is nobody more at fault for whatever happens to her than me. Punishing Angelo will not bring her back.

I move to the couch, dropping into it and holding my

head in my hands, rage and fear swirling around inside me like a tornado about to obliterate everything in its path. "Show me your phone," Massimo demands.

I lift my head, watching as Angelo unlocks it and hands it over without question. Massimo searches through it. Lifting his eyes to mine, he doesn't hide the sympathy in his gaze. "There's nothing there, Rome. Not a single call or message to the number that called the house. Or anyone outside of our men, for that matter. The last message he received was from Aldo asking where he was because he needed him to cover Dante."

I slump back, my head knocking on the back of the couch as I stare up at the ceiling. My mind runs through every scenario before I speak, "Have Callum go through it."

A knock on the door cuts off Massimo's protests. When he calls out, Aldo enters. Angelo seizes the opportunity to leave, placing his phone on Massimo's desk as he passes. I let him walk away because I can't trust myself not to kill him right here and watch his blood spill across Massimo's office floor. Right now, I need to focus on finding Aurora, then I can make sure Angelo gets what he deserves.

Aldo inclines his head before handing over a manila folder to Massimo. "I've found something, boss."

Hope blooms in my chest, my eyes darting between Aldo and the folder in Massimo's hand. "About Aurora? Do you know who's behind this?" I hate how desperate I sound.

He doesn't meet my gaze, his focus firmly on Massimo as my cousin opens the file. "This is about the rat."

I watch the surprise register on Massimo's face as he slams the file shut, his eyes widening and his jaw going slack. His fingers bend the edges of the folder where he's gripping it so tightly, and when I move toward him, he pulls it to his chest. There's something in that folder that he doesn't want me to know. And I suspect it's something to do with Aurora based on the way my stomach has hit the floor.

Massimo clears his throat, shaking himself out of his stupor. "Thank you, Aldo. Can you find Leonardo and Daniele and ask them to come here?"

Without a word, Aldo leaves, the door clicking shut behind him. I close the distance between us, tapping my knuckles on the mahogany desk. "What does the file say, Massimo?"

He pinches the bridge of his nose, exhaling heavily as he meets my stare. "I'm so sorry, Rome." Running a hand through his hair, he drops back into his seat, sliding the folder onto the desk in front of him.

"What are you sorry for?" His eyes fill with an emotion I can't name, urging me on. "Is she dead? Did they kill her?"

Surely they'd have made a demand? If they wanted to get to me, they'd have—

Massimo's words cut off my inner rambling. There's a

harshness underpinning his words when he huffs, "No, but you might."

A groove forms between my brows, and I can't quite put the pieces together. My frustration at Massimo and his lack of explanation overflows and I growl, "I need you to tell me what the fuck is in that file. Now."

Reluctantly, Massimo opens it and removes a piece of paper from the top, sliding it toward me. "There's call data from the housephone and CCTV stills of Aurora making a call the night you took her out to dinner."

I pick up the sheet, collapsing into the chair as my eyes bounce over the text. Blinking, I lift my focus to him. "Who did she call?"

He doesn't answer me. Instead, he's looking at the picture in front of him, keeping me from seeing it. Banging my fist on the desk, I demand, "Who did she *fucking* call, Massimo?"

Swallowing thickly, he blows out a defeated sigh, finally lifting his eyes to mine. "It looks like a number connected to the Bratva. The call lasted thirty seconds. I'm sorry, Rome."

He's sorry because the woman I brought into this house, the one I couldn't bring myself to kill, is the one that's fucked us over. On more than one occasion. That realization is more painful than any bullet I've ever taken. She's played me. I've fallen for her feigned innocence like a fool.

Everything's been a lie.

Every single moment we shared was a lie.

But there's one thing I know for certain: if the Bratva don't kill her, I fucking will.

Chapter 38

Aurora

The cell door creaks open, and I roll my head in the direction of the sound. A burly man enters, a skull mask covering his face. His presence is menacing and I bolt up, swinging my legs over the edge of the cot to be better prepared for a fight—not that I stand a chance.

He stands on the threshold, one hand resting on a gun holstered on his hip. "Stand. Hands on the wall," he barks, his tone gruff and commanding.

This isn't either of the guys that came by earlier. His accent is much thicker and there's more of an edge to his words. Aside from kidnapping me, there's something off about him.

On shaky legs, I stand and face the wall, pressing my hands to the coarse brick. His footsteps are like a countdown to impending doom and with each step he takes, my body tenses even more. When he's standing behind me, I can smell the vodka and feel a sense of foreboding before he yanks a hood over my head. The force has his hands slamming into my shoulders and my knees buckle beneath me before I catch myself, pressing my body into the wall.

He runs a hand over my hip and tugs me back into his crotch. I bite down on my bottom lip to keep a sob from spilling free. *Please don't let him do what I think he intends to.*

A shiver trickles down my spine when he groans in my ear and grinds into me. His grip is harsh, trapping me between his body and the wall. He chuckles, as if my fear is exciting for him. "I wonder if they'll leave me to enjoy you when they've finished. *If* you survive what they have planned."

If he's the prize for surviving, I hope I don't make it through this.

His fingers wrap around my bicep, digging painfully into the flesh as he spins me toward the door. I stumble over my feet, thrown off balance and disorientated by the darkness of the hood. There's no consideration given for the difference in our strides as he drags me down the corridor. *Why would there be?*

Unable to see, I listen as we walk, counting the creaks of doors and any other noises that might give any sign as to where the hell we are. Within a matter of minutes, I'm forcefully pushed into a chair. The hood is whipped off, pulling on the strands of my hair as it goes. I hiss at the unexpected pain, squinting as my eyes adjust to the natural bright light filling the space and blinding me.

I scan the room, trying to take in as much as possible. Exposed stone walls surround us, and above, a rusted tin roof rattles with each gust of wind, mingling with the pitter patter of rain falling on it. There's nothing notable in here except a table, some chairs and a camera, all of which are facing me.

Dark black spots are splattered sporadically across the floor, forcing me to wonder how many other lives might have been taken in this very room. We're clearly in a warehouse, but I wouldn't have a clue if we were still in America, let alone in New York.

Another man approaches, also wearing a skull mask. He smells like he's bathed in aftershave and I frown, trying to place where I've smelled that particular scent before. It's right there, on the edge of my memory, but I can't quite grasp it. I'm still trying to place it when he grabs my wrist and ties it to the arm of the chair. The rope is so tight it burns my skin and every move I make only has him pulling it tighter until it's digging into my flesh.

The door at the other end of the room creaks open, and a woman enters, her long blonde hair tied back, showing off her makeup-free face. If I passed her on the street, she wouldn't draw my attention. She looks *normal.* The fact that she isn't surprised to see me tells me all I need to know. *She's here for me.*

My curiosity gets the better of me, and I find myself

watching her as she walks across the space. She inclines her head to the masked men as she strides toward me, her head held high, an aura of importance around her. She comes to a stop at the table, throwing the gym bag in her hand on top. Our eyes meet and the corner of her mouth lifts before I drag my gaze away.

Six men stand, dotted around the room, each with an automatic gun cradled in their arms ready to shoot. For a second, I wonder if I'll get out of here alive if I just comply and give them what they want, but I dismiss the idea almost as quickly as it forms.

They clearly have plans to kill Romeo and want to use me to do it. But what they probably don't count on is the fact that I'd rather die than know that Romeo is gone because of *me*. My eyes sting before I force the emotion away and sit taller in my seat, ignoring the way the rope rubs at my skin. I want to prove to myself that I'm strong, that I can love even after all the heartache. To sacrifice my life for his. I want to make him proud. And the only way to do that is by being strong for *him*.

My focus shifts back to the woman who is pulling items from her bag, but from my position, I can't make out what they are.

When she's done, she moves across the room, a calmness emanating from her that I wish I could embody. Instead, the pounding of my heart feels like it's echoing around the room for all to hear. I focus on the tangible things, like the black jeans she's wearing with rips in the knees and the white oversized shirt that probably wasn't a good idea for today. Unless she's in charge and one of the men will do her dirty work.

"Do you know why you are here?" There's no trace of an accent, and the lack of one throws me off slightly.

I lift my chin, holding her stare with a bravado coated with indifference that's all for show. "Yes." She tilts her head to the side, folding her arms and jutting out a hip. "You intend to kill Romeo Bianchi, and you're under the impression that *I* mean something to him."

She raises a brow. "Well, aren't you a smart cookie?" She pauses, no doubt for dramatic effect. "I'm sorry to disappoint you, Aurora, but we're smarter. Did you really think we would make a move without all the facts? You may have started out as a pawn in his plan, but you quickly moved into his bed. Very quickly, might I add. I have no doubt that he will come for you and when he does, these men will be ready." Turning away, she moves toward the camera.

"I won't do it. Whatever it is, I won't be complicit in it. You might as well kill me now," I scream.

Chuckling, she prowls back to me, a dark look swirling in her gray eyes. *I think I might have made a mistake.* Her hand shoots out, fisting my hair and pulling it back with force. I roll my lips to keep from calling out at the unexpected pain.

She's calm and her tone is deadly when she says, "You won't have a choice, Aurora." She leans closer, her perfume enveloping me. "I know a million ways to bring you to the brink of death. You'll be begging me to make it stop, and the only way will be for you to do what we ask. And don't think that just because your uncle is paying us that we'll spare your life."

My uncle?

A groove forms between my brows and I open my mouth to voice my question, but I'm cut off.

"Now, now, Anastasia, don't get carried away just yet. You'll ruin the fun."

Where did he come from?

I've been so caught up in what she's doing to me that I didn't notice another person enter the room. I need to keep my wits about me if I want to stand a chance of getting out of here alive.

Anastasia releases me and my focus shifts to the man that just spoke. I take him in, moving from his polished shoes, over his navy suit pants and up to the matching double-breasted jacket covering his broad shoulders. When I reach his face, there's a hint of familiarity. He has an air of authority about him, and in my periphery, I don't miss the way every man in the room stands a little taller.

"I can see the cogs turning in that pretty little head of yours, Aurora." He shrugs out of his jacket, carefully draping it over the table. As he walks toward me, he rolls up the sleeves of his baby blue shirt. "It's been a long time, *bambina*. I don't blame you for not recognizing me." He comes to a stop in front of me, his hand reaching for me before he drops it back to his side and he regards me. "You look just like your mother."

My voice comes out small and disbelieving. "Dad?" I

feel foolish the moment the words leave my lips. Of course he's not my father. It's been a long time but not *that* long since I last saw him.

He chuckles, taking a seat in a chair one of the other men places behind him. "No, Aurora. I'm your *zio*." At my questioning stare, he clarifies, "Your uncle."

Shaking my head, I reply, "I don't have an uncle."

He smooths a hand over his rounded stomach and leans back in his chair. "*Oh, cara*, I see your parents kept many things from you. Well, I'm sorry to be the bearer of bad news, but your father is dead." He flicks his wrist, indicating over his shoulder. "Floating somewhere in the Hudson River. Or at least that's what my sources tell me."

He winks and I know his sources are *him*. *Romeo has been chasing a ghost.* My stomach drops, knowing my father is gone for good this time. And my 'uncle' is responsible for his death. I swallow down the nausea and chew on my lip as the grief I didn't think I'd feel at this news wraps around me.

Did he have my mom killed too?

My throat constricts, and a stabbing pain takes up residence in my chest. I want to cry and demand an answer to my question, but I don't want this *monster* to see the effect he's having on me. Schooling my features, I welcome the numbness that seeps into my body as my uncle—if I can even call him that—lays out his plans for me.

His demeanor is casual and his tone level, like he's

recounting a shopping list rather than his murderous plan. "I've been working with the Bratva"—he waves his arm, indicating to the other men in the room—"for the last six months. It all just happened, really. They want a bigger piece of the pie and I want to go home. I'm getting older and so returning to Sicily to take over the operation there makes sense.

"I see your confusion, Aurora. Decades ago, it was *our* family that ran the mafia. We're only righting the wrong that was done. I have no interest in an American arm of the operations, so once Massimo and Romeo are gone—along with most of their men—the Bratva will take over New York."

All of this is over territory and greed.

The thought that I could die, that *Romeo* could die, because my own flesh and blood wants to have it all, is sickening. This is too much, and it's all my fault. Had I not kept that note from Romeo, I wouldn't be here and he wouldn't be walking into a *trap*.

My uncle's voice pulls me back into the moment. "So, you see, that is how we've ended up here. We've drafted in the lovely Anastasia. She's... what would you call it?" He taps his finger on his chin before holding it up as a sinister smile spreads across his face. "Ah, yes, a contractor. Romeo will watch as Anastasia inflicts a great deal of pain on you." Standing, he stares down at me and adds, "I don't want to ruin all the surprises. You can use that imagination of yours to figure out how this all ends. But don't be mistaken, you won't be leaving here alive."

My mind works furiously to figure out a way to make this reality not be true. At each turn, I come up empty. There is no getting out here or making this right. My uncle walks away to the table where Anastasia is laying out more items and my attention shifts to the camera.

Like a lightbulb going off, an idea forms. It just might be the only hope I have of protecting Romeo and getting a message to him so he doesn't come for me.

Chapter 39

Aurora

Blood runs down my chin, dripping into my lap as my head lulls forward. I try not to move. The excruciating pain radiating from my cheekbone only gets worse whenever I do. My fingers dig into the splintered wood on the arms of the chair, the stabbing sensation a welcome distraction.

Sucking in a lungful of air, I fight to contain the grimace of pain that shoots through my body. Every inch hurts from the assault I've been subjected to.

I'll hand it to her; Anastasia has been brutal with the onslaught of blows she's forced me to endure. My face is swelling, and despite my pleas, she's remained uncaring. When she crouches in front of me, I notice through my swollen eyes, the latex gloves on her hands covered with specks of my blood. She changed into white overalls before getting to work on me, a cap covering her hair. "Have you had enough, Aurora?"

Yes, God, yes.

Lifting my head, I meet her eyes before spitting the blood pooling in my mouth onto her black boots. "Is that all you've got?" I taunt.

Throwing her head back, she lets out a throaty laugh as she stands. "Oh, babe, you haven't seen anything yet. If I wasn't under strict instructions to keep you alive for him, you'd already be dead. I don't make it a habit to play with my food." Turning away, Anastasia walks over to the table, lifting up objects and putting them back down as if deciding what to use on me next. With a casual air to her command, she says, "Get her up and in the chains."

Two men come forward, their faces hidden by the same skull masks. They untie the rope from my wrists and roughly force me to stand. My legs buckle beneath me as a numbness seeps into them. The room spins as they yank me around like a doll. The taller of the two comes to stand behind me, pushing my arms together and caging me in. With my wrists outstretched, the other binds them and I jolt forward from the force when he tightens it.

As much as my mind is telling me to run, my body is too weak from the abuse it's suffered. God, I *wish* I had strength to fight them off. Or at the very least, try to make a break for it, but I feel so out of it and woozy from the pain and blood loss that I can't concentrate on even the smallest of things, let alone dodging the inevitable gunfire.

My arms are yanked above my head, and the cool

metal of a hook slides against my skin. Disorientated, I tip my head back, staring at the chain hanging from a low beam in the ceiling. They winch me up until my feet hover just above the floor. The pain as my arms pull at the sockets is momentarily distracting. At least until the panic overcomes me and my feet scramble to touch something solid.

Anastasia comes to stand in front of me, a mask now covering her face, leaving only the blonde of her hair and a slither of her eyes. There's an emotion in her eyes that looks like... *regret?* That can't be right. My brow furrows, and I blink, trying to focus, but it's gone.

I'm definitely imagining things, because there is no way this psychopath is empathetic toward me. *Who even does this sort of thing for a job?*

Shaking my head to clear the thought, my focus drops to the metal bar Anastasia is holding. She moves around me, dragging it across the floor behind her. The noise it makes is grating and an unwelcome reminder of the circumstances I find myself in. *And the pain she will inflict.*

Stay strong, Aurora.

I won't beg.

An image of Romeo pops into my mind. He's smiling at me, the love I feel for him reflected in his inky blue eyes. *I'd give anything to be back in his arms.*

The first blow of the pipe hits the back of my thighs. Despite being aware of the weapon and her intentions, the contact is still unexpected and the pain unbearable. I cry out, my body thrashing around. The confines of the rope pull harder on my arms, the burning sensation almost enough to mute the rest of the pain in my body. I suck in a breath as I fight to suppress the bile clogging my throat and the need to beg her to stop that sticks to my tongue like a poison I refuse to spit out.

With my eyes closed, every muscle in my body tenses, and I hold my breath, waiting for the next hit. When it doesn't come, I crack open one eye to find Anastasia walking across the room to the camera. She removes the lens cover before nodding to a guy I hadn't noticed before sitting with my uncle and a few of the masked men behind the camera. He's sitting in front of a laptop and after a few quick keystrokes, a red light illuminates on the front of the camera.

"Thank you for joining us on such short notice, Mr. Bianchi. I believe I have something of yours." She steps to the side, and I lift my head, looking into the camera as best I can through eyes that are swelling.

My tongue feels heavy in my mouth and the bruise forming on my jaw hurts when I speak. "It's a trap. Please, Rome, don't come." My words come out small and unintelligible.

I drop my head, urging my body to garner the strength I need for him to hear me. When I raise it again, my mouth parts, the words on the tip of my tongue before they're stolen by a fist connecting with my jaw. I cry out as nausea crashes over me.

*Ts*king, Anastasia admonishes, "No talking to our guests, Aurora, or I'll cut out your tongue."

She presses a knife onto my lower lip, tracing it over my chin and down the center of my chest. I can't hold back the tears that tumble down my cheeks when I feel the pressure of the blade on my thigh. An agonizing scream is ripped from my lips as she presses the knife harder until it slices through my skin.

Tremors wrack my body when she pulls the bloodied blade away and holds it up to the camera. My eyes flutter closed and my head lulls forward as I try to breathe through the dizziness. Behind my eyelids, starbursts pepper my vision.

I sense Anastasia step forward, crowding into me. Squinting, I bare my teeth, my mind unable to focus on any one particular area of pain. Her hand fists my hair and she forces my head back. The harshness of her gesture doesn't match her words when she keeps her voice low for only me to hear. "You shouldn't bleed out, but when you get back to your room, wrap it up tightly."

My brows tug together at her concern. It feels so out of place with what she's done to me, but I don't have time to digest it. She releases me and turns toward the camera, the knife covered in my blood still held up.

Romeo's words cut through the quiet of the room. Even through the laptop speakers, they hold an air of authority. "What do you want?"

I don't know how long I've been gone, but I miss him more than my freedom. My chest compresses as I exhale heavily, disappointment seeping into my bones. *I've failed him.* Because of me, he's going to come here and they'll kill him. I close my eyes, biting down hard on my tongue to keep from crying out for him.

Anastasia throws the knife onto the table, picking up a rag and wiping her hands as she moves to stand back in front of the camera. "The people that have hired me are asking for you to shut down your operation. *In its entirety.*"

Romeo huffs out a laugh and I can picture him lifting his chin and straightening the cuffs of his shirt. "My family has been in this business long enough for me to tell you *that* will not happen. Do whatever you want to her." He pauses, my shock barely reaching the surface before he continues, "And *Aurora...*" He spits out my name like it revolts him. "I hope they make your death brutally painful."

He fires off something in Italian that I don't understand, my mind unable to even contemplate trying to translate it. *Was he hoping I'd understand?*

The guy on the laptop looks alarmed. "He left the call." His words hang in the air, an eerie atmosphere settling over the room.

Panic swells within me, wrapping around my throat and choking me. This is just Romeo making sure they understand that I mean nothing to him, so that they let me go. So that they give up on the idea that I can be used to get to him. He doesn't mean what he said.

He can't mean it.

My uncle stands, his chair falling to the floor behind him. The shock on his face is quickly masked by a look of indifference as he rounds the table. There's a venom in his tone, speaking volumes of the control he's losing when he says, "It looks like you might have been telling the truth after all." He inclines his head toward me. "Take her back to her room," he demands.

Two men rush forward, unhooking me. My body crumples to the floor, every inch searing in pain. I flinch when a large hand wraps around my arm and I'm pulled up forcefully. The hood is thrown over my head again. I want to tell them that it's pointless; I have no strength to leave and I can barely see, but I keep my mouth shut.

As we move, I hear Anastasia ask my uncle, "What will you do now?"

I don't hear his response; a metal door clangs shut behind us, cutting off their conversation. It doesn't take a genius to work out that I'm of no use to them now. Their plan has failed, and I doubt they'll just let me go.

It feels like an eternity before we arrive back at my cell. I'm thrown inside, falling to the floor without the strength to keep myself upright. It's only when I can be sure that I'm alone that I curl in on myself, allowing the tears to fall with abandon.

He's leaving me here to die.

The more I think about it, the more it becomes reality. *What purpose would he have for telling them that they can kill me?* He doesn't know where I am or who's holding me, aside from what little information Anastasia gave away.

He's taken the foundations we've built and set them on fire, content to watch them burn to the ground. Whatever I thought we shared, it didn't mean a single thing to him and I've risked my life for someone willing to leave me here at the hands of depraved monsters.

How can I love a man that is willing to abandon me so easily? Especially after my dad did the exact same thing.

Should I, by some miracle of God, make it out of here alive, I'll put the entirety of the Earth between us. No country will be far enough away.

I'm furious at myself for allowing him to encourage me to want to live. For being naïve enough to think that what we had might bloom into something more. But what I'm most angry at myself for is for fantasizing that we might be something and that it was worth existing for *him*.

There's one thing I'm certain of, and that is that Romeo Bianchi is no longer worthy of having a piece of my heart. *He doesn't ever get to own any part of me.*

Chapter 10

Romeo

I mages of Aurora's bruised and bloody face are tattooed in the forefront of my mind. Seeing her like that—defeated and broken—would have pulled on the strings of even the coldest of hearts. But she betrayed me and that makes whatever happens to her necessary.

Or at least that's what I tell myself.

Sipping on the scotch I'm nursing, with unfocused eyes, I look at the wall in front of me in the entertainment room before tipping my head back and staring up at the ceiling. It's been three days since she was taken. Three days since I've felt anything other than rage.

No, she left.

Three days since we uncovered her dirty little secret.

I'm ashamed to admit to myself that I didn't see it coming. Her deceit stings far worse than any I've ever experienced. *My nonno was right*. Of all the betrayal I've witnessed in my life, this one feels the most deceptive and it's all because I let her into my life. I want to find her just so I can put my hands around her neck and take back everything we had.

Dio, I should be celebrating the fact that my enemy is taking care of her for me. As much as I gave Massimo shit about pulling the trigger for the family, I don't know that I would have been able to do it to her. If she'd have looked up at me with those wide, sea-green eyes full of fear, as she begged me to spare her, *I would have.*

"You okay, boss?"

My head rolls to the side on the back of the couch. Daniele stands on the threshold, his features morphed into a look of concern. I feel like I've been caught doing something I shouldn't have, and in some ways, I have. It's three am, I should be asleep, or better yet, tracking down the *figli di puttana* she's been working with.

I throw back the remainder of my drink, the sting a welcome distraction from the heavy weight traveling the expanse of my body. Pushing my empty glass onto the coffee table in front of me, I rest the bottom of one foot on the edge. Ignoring his question, I ask one of my own. "Why are you still up?"

Daniele steps into the room, closing the door behind him. His body is tense and his movements stiff. I watch as he seems to catch himself and force his muscles to relax. He doesn't reply as he strides across the room to the bar in the corner. Finding a glass, he pours amber liquid into it, the sound filling the quiet.

When he's done, he holds up the decanter, inclining his head toward it as his eyes meet mine over his shoulder. With a shake of my head, I refuse a refill. There's no point in continuing to drink when I'm not enjoying it and it's only marginally numbing the ache.

Waiting until he's seated on the couch across from me, Daniele brings the glass to his lips before saying, "Something isn't adding up."

I lean forward, desperate to take on something that might distract me from the dark path of my thoughts. "With what?"

He swirls the liquid before taking a sip. "Aurora. Something isn't adding up with her being behind this. She—"

Lifting a palm, I stop him. "I don't want to hear it, Daniele. We should be grateful the Bratva are taking care of her for us. Besides, I've seen the evidence, and it's pretty damn obvious she was behind this, even if we never saw it coming. She might not have been the mastermind, but she was involved and that makes her just as guilty."

He shakes his head, his mouth thinning into a flat line. He slides his glass onto the table, linking his fingers in front of him. "First of all, where did she get a phone from? We checked her over before she got in the car. Secondly, how could she call someone to come to a restaurant she had no idea you were going? And why would she have someone shoot up the place when she could have been killed herself? It just doesn't make sense and those are just two pieces of the puzzle that don't fit for me."

How fucking dare he? My anger consumes me, and I stand, needing a release for the pent up energy. Towering over him, I point my finger in his face and bellow, "Because she's a master *fucking* manipulator, Daniele. We might never know why she did what she did, but regardless of that, she's involved in us losing the men we have and our firearms being taken. That should be enough for us to want her dead. You need to remember where your loyalties should lie because if they're with her, I'll hand you over to the fucking Bratva to be with her."

Picking up his glass, he leans back, mimicking my pose from moments ago. Saluting me with his glass, he says, "Problem solved, I guess. *Especially* because the Russians *will* kill her after you practically threw her at them. Even if she isn't involved."

I stare at him for the longest time, trying to figure out what his point is. Whatever it is, it doesn't change the facts and it won't fix what she's broken. He sips on his drink, unaffected by the intensity of my gaze.

Scrubbing a hand over my face, I exhale heavily, my shoulders sagging with exhaustion. "Go to bed, Daniele. We have a meeting with Massimo in the morning because, in case you've forgotten, we've still got a mess to clear up. One that she's caused."

With a shake of his head, he stands, placing his

tumbler onto the coffee table. "If it's okay with you, I'm just going to look into a couple of things."

I know what he's going to say, but I still ask, "What things?"

"Things that aren't quite adding up for me."

"You're asking to take *annual leave* in the middle of a *fucking* war? I hate to break it to you, Daniele, but this isn't a nine to five. The answer is no."

His stance widens, and I know I won't like whatever he's about to say. "Not quite, Rome. I'm telling you, things aren't making sense and I think someone is trying to shift the blame onto Aurora." He pauses, searching my eyes. "If you aren't going to step up for your woman, then as your underboss, I will. It's my job to protect you. *And her.*"

My head rears back at his comment and I huff out a surprised laugh as my brows lift to my hairline. "Given how long you have worked for me, I'll forgive the casual nature in which you've just spoken to me. But I will say this..." I lower my voice, leaning into him so the message is clear. "You will be at that meeting tomorrow morning or you'll find yourself digging your own grave. *Capisci?*"

His shoulders stiffen before he nods. "Yes, boss."

When he leaves, I collapse back onto the couch. *How dare he question me?* The last time I checked, I was the head of the family and what I say goes. Clearly, I'm not the only one Aurora has infected. She's dug her claws into this family, and worst of all, she's softened my ruthlessness.

Well, it's time that changed.

My body convulses, making the box springs on the metal bed frame squeak from the violence of the movement. Clenching my teeth, I wait for the pain that will inevitably follow.

Some time ago, with Anastasia's words ringing in my ears, I dragged myself from the floor and onto the cot. Tearing off a strip of the sheet, I wrapped it around my thigh, but I don't think it's tight enough. Blood is starting to soak through the fabric, and I feel weaker with every second that passes.

Have I been left here to die?

Nobody has been to check on me. Or at least I don't think they have. I've been falling in and out of consciousness ever since I was brought back. Hell, I don't have the strength to try to escape, but moreover, I don't have the will to. This is me officially giving up. This is me breaking the promise to Romeo because... *how could he do this to me? How could he be so callous as to leave me here?*

Because that's who he is.

The devil.

A sob breaks free, but I do nothing to stop it. The tortured sound reverberates around the room. I only wanted to protect Romeo, but he's willing to leave me in the hands of his enemies to die.

Now more than ever, I wish he'd pulled the trigger the day he broke into my apartment. If he had, I wouldn't have drowned in what I thought was love. *I can't believe I was so stupid.* What we had was lust, pure and simple, and hidden behind it, was an evil darkness cloaked in deception. Just like the man himself. Romeo used me for his own agenda and the second he no longer needed me, he disposed of me. And he's letting someone else do his dirty work.

The only person who has ever shown me *real love* is my mom. I was content to simply exist, waiting for the day I'd die so I could finally be reunited with her and bask in that kind of love again. It was lightness and laughter, wrapped in the warmest of hugs.

I close my eyes and turn onto my side, angling my head to relieve the pressure on my cheekbone and jaw. I'll be back with her soon and then I can finally be rid of the memories of Romeo Bianchi.

Swallowing thickly, my throat contracts painfully. It feels like days since I last had a drink.

Opening my eyes, I give up on the delusional idea

that I can slip away into nothingness. *This isn't how this stuff works.* It's not like the movies where everyone seems to die within seconds. My death will not be quick.

With my eyes fixed on the wall in front of me, I trace my fingers over the bricks. The course texture scrapes over my sensitive flesh and is a reminder that this is real. Sure, the pain my body feels with every breath is also a reminder, but there's a numbness seeping into my bones as I accept what this is. *The end.*

The sound of a key jangling on the opposite side of the door forces me to roll over. I wince with every movement, but the need to see who's coming urges me on. Holding my breath, I send up a prayer that will no doubt go unanswered, begging for it to be anyone but the man who wanted to violate me.

A young boy—he can't be any older than fifteen— juggles a tray in one hand as he pushes the heavy door open with the other. Briefly, he meets my gaze before his eyes widen and he drops his head. When he reaches the end of the cot, he carefully slides the tray onto the mattress before darting another glance at me.

Sitting up, I hiss at the slicing pain that shoots through my body before reaching out and loosely gripping his arm. "What is going to happen to me?" My voice is barely a whisper.

His eyes dart to the door and his voice is hushed, like he knows he'll get in trouble for talking to me. "I don't know."

Of course he doesn't. Why would he? For a moment,

I consider trying to overpower him. He's left the door open—he's skinny and looks like he's barely eaten a meal this week himself. A twinge in my thigh reminds me of the state of my body, and I dismiss the idea. I won't be doing much other than bleeding out on this uncomfortable mattress.

Releasing him, I pull the red plastic tray he's left toward me, dismissing him. It's hardly a nutritious meal. Something resembling porridge, an apple, and a bottle of water. *Great, no spoon.* I guess they figured I might use it as a weapon. Which is laughable because what damage can really be done with a spoon.

When I open the bottle of water and bring it to my lips, he turns to leave. On the threshold, he watches me as I drink down the room temperature liquid, half hiding behind the door.

I don't understand why he's not left.

I keep my tone low. After all, I don't know who could be on the other side of the door. "What's today's date?"

"The twenty-seventh."

Okay, that means it's been four days since I was taken. Four days of being held captive with no hope of ever making it out. I swallow down the helplessness that's threatening to drive me insane. "Have they left?" I ask.

He shakes his head.

What are they waiting for? Romeo isn't coming. I'm of no use to them now that he's disowned me.

"Do you have a pencil?"

His brows pull together before he shakes his head

and steps back. I'm not fast enough and my legs aren't strong enough when I push up from the bed and stagger the six steps across the room.

The door closes with a bang, a reminder of my prison. Collapsing to the floor, I bang my fist on the door and cry out, "Please. I just want to leave a note."

I don't want to die and be forgotten.

I need to leave behind something that shows I *existed*, even if it's never found. Someone has to know I was here before my body ends up in the Hudson River, just like my father.

And my mom.

Chapter 42

Romeo

I glance at my watch when Daniele strolls into Massimo's office. *He's thirty minutes late.* If last night's conversation hadn't happened, I wouldn't think twice about it. I'd have trusted that he had a damn good reason for holding us up. As it stands, a man I've considered a brother for the last fifteen years has just guaranteed himself a painful death.

Dropping a manila envelope onto the desk, he chances a glance at me before nodding to Leonardo who's positioned behind Massimo. Daniele drops into the seat next to me as Massimo reaches for the envelope. The way he leans away ever so slightly pisses me off, because we both know there's no getting away from what's to come.

Aurora has him wrapped around her little *fucking* finger. Too bad she's probably already dead. A tightness pulls at my chest and my throat thickens as I swallow. *She only has herself to blame.* If she hadn't betrayed us, I'd have done anything to get her back. But she did and so, for the family, I know I did the right thing.

Massimo flips the envelope over in his hand, his thumb poised on the opening. "What's this?"

Daniele clears his throat. "It's your evidence. I worked with Callum and we hacked the systems. It's proof that whatever information you were given that Aurora was behind *any* of this was doctored."

Massimo's brows tug together before he calmly tears open the envelope. Tipping it upside down, papers fall out onto the desk and Massimo's eyes widen a fraction as they bounce around the scattered documents.

My breath halts when I pick up a log of calls to the house, my eyes scanning the page. It looks similar to the one Aldo showed us, but there are clear differences. There's a fluttering in the pit of my stomach, but I ignore it, refusing to allow the hope in. *Not yet, anyway*. Because with the hope, the guilt will inevitably follow. "How can you be sure *this* hasn't been manipulated?"

Daniele holds my stare, his defiance clear. "I know it hasn't." His attention moves back to Massimo before he continues, "No offense to your guy, Aldo, and whoever gave him the information, but I had a hunch and I needed to follow it for my own peace of mind."

A muscle ticks in Massimo's jaw when he picks up a photo. He hands it to Leonardo.

Massimo turns his focus to me. "Anything for the family?"

"Of course."

"Deal with her, Leonardo. Take her upstate, and when you come back, break the news to Maria. Don't do it before. I don't want the drama," Massimo commands.

Leonardo's Adam's apple bobs as he swallows. "Yes, boss."

Whoever is in that picture has clearly betrayed us and I know that he'll do what his boss is telling him to do, even if he doesn't want to. After all, he knows better than anyone that there is only one way to deal with disloyalty.

Leonardo leaves us, a stiffness in his walk, and when the door clicks softly behind him, I return to looking over the papers spread out on the desk. A photograph shows Aurora in the living room, dressed in the skimpy outfit, with overdone hair and makeup from the night we went to dinner. Her back is to the room as she looks out of the window, but in the corner of the image, you can see what looks like an arm. My stomach rolls and a sour taste fills my mouth.

With a hoarse voice, I ask, "Do you have the actual footage?"

I already know what it will show. *Her innocence.* Smoothing my hand over my chin and down my neck, I tug on the collar of my shirt. The guilt hits me in the chest, leaving behind a tightness that will stay with me for the rest of my life.

There's no judgment in his tone when Daniele replies, "I do." He pulls out his phone, flicking through the screen before holding it at an angle for us to view.

The recording plays, showing Aurora standing at the

window in the living room, her arms wrapped around her slender waist. There's no sound, but when she jumps and turns to look over her shoulder in the direction of the phone, I can hear it ringing.

I feel Daniele's eyes boring into me when he says, "It was an incoming call. Which is consistent with the data I got directly from the phone company."

Aurora makes no move to get it, instead her attention shifts over her other shoulder before one of Massimo's housekeepers enters the frame. She looks vaguely familiar, but I wouldn't be able to name her. I've seen her around the house but... she's the one that told us Aurora had been taken.

Dio.

The housekeeper picks up the phone, her back to Aurora as she puts it to her ear. Thirty seconds later, she puts it down and scurries from the room. The video continues to play and I see myself stroll in. Not once did she move to make a call.

A muscle in my chest contracts and no matter how much air I try to drag in, it's not enough to fill my lungs. I cover my mouth with my hand. I should have known that she wouldn't betray us. Wouldn't betray *me*. Nothing she's done since I took her has indicated that she would, and yet at the first sign of trouble, I've abandoned her. I don't know that she'll forgive me, but I have to hope that she will. *If she's still alive.*

Cazzo!

My eyes grow hot before I rub at them and let the

regret wash over me. It settles on my chest, heavy and incessant.

I've killed plenty of people in my life and given orders for others to do the same. I couldn't tell you how many people have died because of me, but if she is one of them... *I'll never forgive myself.* I should have trusted that she wouldn't do something like this. And because of me, she's most likely dead.

Clearing my throat, I reposition myself in my chair and squeeze the bridge of my nose. A pounding behind my eyes only intensifies with every second that passes until I can't take it, or the feeling of guilt, anymore.

Standing, I wrap my hand around the base of the lamp on Massimo's desk and launch it at the wall. The porcelain shatters, falling to the floor as I turn, looking for something else to throw. *Anything to get rid of this feeling.*

My fingers grip the heavy crystal paperweight before a hand lands on my shoulder, gently squeezing. "Rome, I need you to stop destroying my office."

Turning toward him, my voice cracks. "I told them to kill her." My eyes widen as I recall my last words to her. "I told her that I hoped they'd make it as brutally painful as possible, Massimo. There's no getting her back."

"I know what you said but you have to hold on to the hope."

My breaths come in heavy pants, the panic clawing at my lungs. Massimo turns me toward the chairs, pushing me to sit. Leaning against his desk, he says, "Look, I'm sure you took them by surprise and they're regrouping, trying to figure out a way to get back at us. It's what we would do. So, if we're going to get her back, then we need you to be the levelheaded one."

But what if they've already killed her?

The question tastes bitter on my tongue, but I can't force it out. Instead, I suck in a breath and push down the emotions. If I want to get her back, I can't drown in this feeling of hopelessness and guilt.

I have to find her and bring her home.

Chapter 43

Aurora

The boy hasn't been back. He must have told them about our interaction. *Snitch.*

Between losing consciousness and calling for help, the hours are blending together. And no matter what I try to keep track of how long has passed, I still don't know what day it is.

I need the end to come.

I need the grand finale in an *extraordinarily* boring life to arrive sooner rather than later.

My cut hasn't stopped bleeding for longer than a few minutes and if it wasn't for another tray of food being dropped off earlier, I'd think they'd left me to die. Hell, I'm not sure why they're feeding me at all, to be honest. Especially since the last monster who brought me food responded to my pleas for something to staunch the bleeding with a disgusted grunt. He threw the tray onto the floor by the door, spilling half of its contents.

332

I forced myself to crawl across the room to ease the hunger pangs. The scraps did little to help, barely giving me enough strength to sit up, let alone make it back to the cot.

My eyes feel heavy and with my back propped up against the wall and my head rolling against the exposed brick, I allow them to flutter closed.

There are what feels like two seconds of darkness before a familiar voice calls out, "Hey, baby."

My brows tug together and my eyes sting from unshed tears. Emptiness fills my body, but the pain in my chest only amplifies. *I miss her so much*. Blinking my eyes open, I search the room for her, calling out, "Mom?"

She's been coming to me more often these past few days. Appearing in snippets, like a hologram. Now, she crouches in front of me, her hand brushing away the hair that the sweat has plastered to my forehead. I close my eyes at the familiar touch. It feels so real.

"It's me, sweetie." She moves to sit next to me on the floor, wrapping an arm around my shoulder and pulling me into her side like she did when I was a kid.

Tremors race through me and I tighten my arms around my waist as I lean into her touch. I feel clammy and hot, yet I can't stop shivering. *Is that because I have an infection?* The first aid training I got as part of my job doesn't exactly cover past the time it would take a medic to get to the scene.

Well, nobody's coming for me.

With all this extra time on my hands, I've reflected on

how much I've messed up with purely *existing*. There was so much I could have done that wouldn't have involved the extremes of mafia life, but instead, I chose to do *nothing*. As if that was any better, or even what my mom would have wanted for me.

I should have traveled the world or opened an art gallery. Instead, I hid away and worked. *And what exactly do I have to show for it?* I missed out on love... on lust and the feeling of being wanted so much by another person that they'd sacrifice it all for me. That fills me with a sadness far worse than the thought of never getting out of here and being forgotten ever could.

A tear slips free, and I hiccup, "Nothing makes sense anymore. I miss you so much."

"You have to hold on to the hope, Aurora." She dusts kisses into my hair and her familiar scent fills my nostrils.

She's not real.

My eyes flutter closed and I wince from the pain I feel down to my bones. It's so hard to keep fighting when I'm not even sure what I'm fighting for. To get out of here? And then what? Go back to living the life I was before all of this because I know nothing else?

Cutting through my ruminations, her words are hushed and filled with certainty. "He's coming for you."

Blinking rapidly, I pull out of her hold, turning to look into her eyes as I try to process what she's said. "Who is?"

"Romeo's coming, baby," she soothes.

Oh. There's no point in asking her how she knows

about him; she's just my subconscious telling me things I want to hear. I want it to be true so badly because, despite the hurt that he's caused me, I have utter faith that he would be able to get me out of here. But I know he's not coming and I can't feed those dying embers of hope. If I fan the fire, I'll only be disappointed when reality douses its flames.

Looking up at her, my vision blurs around the edges as I try to memorize the small details I thought I'd forgotten. The more I look at her, the more I question whether I want to leave this room. "I don't want him to."

She squeezes my hand, sadness coating the features of her face. *Why does it all feel so real?* "He's your happy ever after, Aurora. You were always fated to be together."

"He left me to die." My voice cracks.

Her hand slips from mine and I feel the loss of her all over again. My eyes dart around the room, but I come up empty. "Mom. Please, Mom, come back." The words are raw, coming out in a tortured whisper as darkness surrounds me like a blanket and my eyes flutter closed. *Don't leave me here alone.*

Shouting and gunfire penetrates the quiet somewhere in the distance. The noise is only getting louder and more persistent. *This isn't a dream.* My brow furrows and I force my heavy eyes open, dragging my body across the room. The instinct to protect myself, urging me on. Each breath as I move feels labored and sends shooting pain through every inch of me.

When I reach the cot, I use the last reserves of energy

I didn't know I had and push the bed further down the wall. Crawling into the space I've made, I make myself as small as possible, my eyes trained on the door. My heart beats at an erratic rhythm as I wait to be found.

Please, God, let it be help.

Chapter 11

Romeo

With my back pressed against the brick wall of a warehouse just outside of Brooklyn and my M4 Carbine secure in my arms, I watch our men get into position on the far side of the lot. They bunker down behind cars and containers, ready to catch anyone coming out of the building that we might miss. There won't be a single person spared. Anyone who thought they could take what's mine and get away with it will die.

Unbeknownst to me, Daniele had hooked Callum up with a link to the live stream and for a hefty—but well worth it—fee, he traced the IP address. I've never been so grateful for another person's incompetence. I'd have considered sparing the guy's life if it wasn't for the fact that I'm typically not that way inclined.

Somewhere behind me, Aurora is waiting, and based

on the last time I saw her, she's seriously injured. *I just hope we aren't too late.*

The place is surrounded. Massimo is on the south side of the building with Leonardo on the east and Daniele on the west. IEDs have been attached to blast open the walls and our plan is to attack as one. Once we're in, we shoot, taking out every man who crosses our path. The element of surprise is on our side, given there doesn't appear to be any security.

My earpiece crackles and Massimo's adrenaline-laced tone checks in. "Marino in position."

Leo is next. "Rossi in position."

Then Daniele. "Ferro in position."

"Bianchi in position." The line crackles before I hold down the button again. "Stay safe, have each other's backs and kill every last one of these fuckers." My tone is sure and authoritative when I command, "Breach."

Explosions go off at all four points and we move quickly through the smoking hole. Almost immediately, the sound of gunfire and shouting permeates the air. I tap the shoulder of the guy in front of me and signal for him to go left as I go right. We each lead the way for five men.

My gun is primed and ready to use. Adrenaline rushes through me when I breach a room a few feet into the building. A brute of a man stands frozen in the middle of it, his eyes wide and a burrito hanging from his mouth. He reaches for his weapon, but he's not quick enough and I fire off a shot, hitting him between the eyes.

There will be no questions asked today.

Not a single soul in this building—aside from Aurora's—deserves to be saved.

We move down the corridor, coming up empty in the next two rooms we hit. This morning, there was a determination fluttering in my chest, but with every room we clear, it gets heavier, a weight settling onto it as it morphs into disappointment. If we don't find her alive, I'm not sure what I'll do.

My fingers tighten around my gun as we move to a set of double doors at the end of the corridor. We line up, three men on each side with our backs to the wall. When everyone's in position, I look through the small glass window. It's an open space, bodies lie on the floor and some of Massimo's men move around pulling out boxes and furniture.

Pushing into the room, we move further into the space, keeping our wits about us. Just because it looks like everyone's down doesn't mean they are.

Angelo walks in from the other side of the room. Two of his team drag in an older guy with a bullet wound in his leg. Dragging a chair into the middle of the room, he indicates for the man to be seated. I move forward, popping a brow in question as I reach them.

"We found him trying to hide in one of the rooms. He tried to run."

Now that I'm closer, I can see this guy isn't Russian. My radio chirps and Massimo's voice fills my ears, cutting off my question to Angelo on why he's still alive.

"Rome, I've got her." He pauses, and I can hear the hesitation. "She's... she's not looking good."

I'm moving in the direction I know he would have entered, even as I question, "Where are you?"

My scalp prickles and a tightness in my chest twists and tugs with every step I take. It feels like an eternity before I pull open the door and see Massimo standing at the end of a long corridor. A metal door to his left is propped open, and as I get closer, he moves to stand on the threshold and my eyes bounce around the features of his face. He opens his mouth to speak before he thinks better of it.

"Is she still alive?" I rasp.

His body is blocking the room so I can't see in. He rests a hand on my shoulder, but I shrug it away, my teeth grinding. Massimo meets my gaze, his words soft and his tone sounding more mature than I've ever heard him. "She's alive, Rome. But she's in really bad shape." I push him out of the way, clutching onto the doorframe to keep myself upright when my eyes land on her.

All that matters is that she's alive.

She's propped on the edge of the cot, with one of Massimo's men crouched down in front of her, wrapping a cloth around her thigh. On the floor is a blood-soaked sheet. Her right cheek is puffy, and her eye swollen shut. Dried blood covers her face and the T-shirt she left wearing five days ago. Every inch of exposed skin has evidence of her ordeal covering it. *I want to burn the world to the ground just so I try to give her some semblance of justice.*

There's a pounding in my ears and I dig my fingers into the metal of the doorjamb to keep myself from doing something I shouldn't. I clear my throat and Massimo's guy stands, his eyes widening a fraction when they meet mine. He moves to the side and Aurora lifts her chin. It trembles and even from the other side of the room, I can see the tears welling in her eyes.

She's unsteady when she stands and I push the strap around my body, dropping my gun onto my back as I move further into the room. She limps toward me, landing against my chest with a soft thud that causes her to hiss. I wrap my arms around her, careful not to squeeze her as tightly as I want to before I gently place kisses on the top of her head. My hand soothes up and down her back and I breathe in the scent of her hair, the smell reminding me of the torment she's been through.

All because of me.

Pushing out of my arms, she steps back, a look of surprise on her beautiful but bruised face. She rolls her eyes before shaking her head. Muttering to herself, she asks, "What am I doing?" Her brows furrow and a harsh look takes over her features. "You left me here to *die*."

I reach for her, but she takes another step back.

"*Amore mio*, I'm here now."

The corners of her mouth lift in a disbelieving smile and she scoffs. "And that makes it all better?"

Ignoring her question, I hold my arm out and take a step forward. "Let's get you to Doc and then we can talk."

She shifts her weight off her injured leg. "I don't have anything to say to you."

I'm vaguely aware of Massimo's man hurrying from the room when I say, "Just let me get you taken care of. I'll spend the rest of my life righting my wrong, Aurora. I promise you that." My tone is low and cajoling when I continue, "Come, I'll help you. You won't make it more than a few steps on your own, *bella*."

I hold out my hand, and she stares at it for the longest time before reluctantly slipping her own into it. Some of the tension leaves my body at that small sign of acquiescence. I know the fight to keep her isn't over yet, but whatever she wants, I'll give it to her.

Even if it means losing her?

Chapter 15

Aurora

Romeo wraps his arm around my waist and I lean into him for support, while trying to keep as much of my body away from him as possible. His clean scent is like a balm to my aching heart, but it's one I need to resist. If these past few days have taught me anything, it's that my priorities have changed and I need to figure out *my* future. The one I wasn't sure I'd get.

The one without him in it.

The thought has a sharp sting forming at the back of my throat, and I press my lips together as I force it away. I've cried enough over the past couple of days to last me a lifetime. Wallowing in my self-pity hasn't gotten me very far and now that I have a second chance at life, I'm going to grab it with both hands.

Romeo moves us across the room slowly and when we reach the door, my eyes meet Massimo's before I avert them to the floor. Something suspiciously close to sympathy shines in the depths. Of all the people here, I don't want or need him to care about me. In fact, the sooner I can get away from both of these men, the better.

Massimo straightens and addresses Romeo, "Angelo said that the guy they've got is claiming to be Aurora's uncle and that he was taken by the Russians too."

Romeo's fingers flex on my hip and he exhales heavily through his nostrils. Curiosity coats his words when he asks, "Why would they have taken her uncle?"

My voice is quiet and grating on my vocal cords when I try to speak. "They didn't. *He* had them take me. It was all part of their plan."

They share a look before Massimo drops back. With a hushed tone that only gets quieter the further down the corridor Romeo moves us, he speaks into his comms. Romeo's thumb smooths back and forth over the back of my hand. Any other time I'd have found the gesture comforting, but it's just a reminder of all he's put me through.

When we step out into the open room they tortured me in, my uncle screams out. Pleading words tumble from his lips and I stiffen at the sound of his voice. I can't help but take one last glimpse at him as he struggles with the men tying ropes around his wrists and ankles. Pulling out of Romeo's grip, I hold on to a pillar we're passing for balance and watch as they secure him to the chair.

This man—I can't even call him family—killed my father and took away any chance of me ever having a relationship with him. I can't be sure that he wasn't involved in my mom's death and I need answers. As far as I'm concerned, he's going to get what he deserves. Hell, he was going to kill Romeo, and he was very close to killing me.

With their guns trained on him, Angelo and another man surround my uncle when the ones tying him to a chair step back. My eyes land on the 9mm holstered to Angelo's hip. Even as I feel Romeo's presence moving closer behind me, I keep my focused stare on the gun, running through every possible scenario of what could go wrong with what I'm about to do.

Here goes nothing.

It's only when I can trust myself to stand without toppling over that I move forward. A strength I thought I'd never feel again fuels every step. My fingers are swift and I'm holding the gun before Angelo can react. I point it at my uncle.

Fascinated, I watch as his face transforms from fear to certainty. It's like watching a different person enter his body. His posture is relaxed, a confident grin stretching across his face. "*Bambina*, you don't have it in you to pull that trigger."

I ignore his comment, because it really doesn't matter if I do or not. We'll all find out sooner or later. The thought makes my chest feel light and with the gun still aimed at him, I ask, "Did you kill my mom?" When he doesn't answer me, I stab the gun into his forehead and scream, "*Did you kill her?*"

There's a look on his face and it tells me what I

already know, but I need him to say the words. I reposition my hand on the gun, swallowing down the grief that threatens to consume me. "Why?" I croak.

He doesn't speak, instead continuing to sit there with that same look on his face. Daniele steps up behind him, grabbing a fistful of his hair and yanking his head. My eyes meet his and he nods before pulling out a knife. I want to scream at him to not kill him, to tell him that *I* want to be the one that does it, but when I open my mouth, nothing comes out.

I suck in a breath, staggering back a step before I catch myself. Daniele plunges the knife into my uncle's shoulder and pulls it down the front of his chest to his armpit. He screams out in pain, sobbing as Daniele pulls it free and aims for the other shoulder.

"Answer her," he growls.

A dark patch appears in his lap, spreading out as he stutters, "Y-y-yes." His bulging, watery eyes meet mine. "I ordered your mother's death. She was pressuring your father to leave and cooperate with an FBI investigation. *That* isn't how this life works."

I swallow down the bile at his words. My mom was no doubt trying to protect her family, and he thought he'd destroy it. Taking a step toward him, I press the gun into his forehead again. A sense of power overcomes me, knowing that he can't hurt me. *If he wasn't tied up, would I still be pointing this gun at him?* Probably not. Daniele releases him and moves to the side.

A flare of panic ignites behind my uncle's eyes. "We are famil—"

"*Fuck you.* We're not family. Families don't kill each other."

I pull the trigger, the resulting sound near deafening. Pain jolts through my body and my arm falls limply to my side. My heart pounds in my chest as I stare at my uncle's lifeless body, his blood pouring from the hole in his forehead, onto the floor.

Dazed, I look around for a way out. I can't process any of what has happened right now. My body moves on autopilot. I need to get out of here, to be as far away from all of this mess as I possibly can. It doesn't feel as good as I thought it would. Killing the man who killed my mom. *And my dad.* I blow out a breath, blinking away the emotions inside me.

"Aurora." Romeo calls out for me, his authority clear. *As it always is.*

I keep walking. He's part of what I need to leave behind. I'm not cut out for this life and I certainly have more respect for myself than to be with a man so willing to think the worst of me.

His hand lands on my shoulder, forcing me to a stop. I turn toward him, automatically pulling my arm up and aiming the gun that is still in my hand at his head. The sound of every gun in the warehouse being lifted and cocked echoes around the room. It doesn't scare me, even knowing they are all aimed at me.

Unfazed by the gun pointing at him, Romeo doesn't flinch. A single tear falls down my cheek and I swipe it away angrily. "I hate you," I spit out. Sniffing, I flex my fingers around the gun, setting my jaw as I continue, "I'm going to walk out of here and you aren't going to follow me. You're going to let me leave. I didn't ask for *any* of this."

Shrugging a shoulder, he scrubs a hand over his jaw before confidently saying, "We'll get you medical attention first and then you can go."

I scream out, the sound guttural and raw, laced with my frustration and pain. I'm *done* with not being listened to. *With not being heard.* I press the barrel of the gun into his forehead.

He holds up his hands, his eyes never leaving mine even as he commands, "Put your weapons down."

"Do you think I won't pull the trigger?" I swallow, a sudden wave of nausea throwing me off. "Did you not see what I just did to my *so-called family*? Do you think that just because you gave me a few *orgasms*, you mean *anything* to me?"

A fire ignites in his eyes, turning the inky blue depths even darker. "I saw, *amore mio. I fucking saw.* And if it would make you feel better to hurt me, then go ahead."

I blow out a breath through my nose as spots appear in my vision. Adjusting my grip on the gun, I tilt my head. My voice comes out small and distant. "You think that's what I want?"

It irritates me that it's the last thing I want to do to

him, but I also can't stand to look at his face. *I just want to leave.* I want to never have met him.

"I don't know what you want, Aurora, but if you tell me, I'll make it happen."

It feels like such an effort to keep upright. Waves of dizziness and exhaustion crash into and my arm falls as my attention shifts to the buttons of Romeo's shirt.

Why are they moving?

Lifting my hazy gaze to his, I see the concern in his eyes. My brow furrows as a whimper escapes my lips and confusion clouds my thoughts.

What's happening to me?

I lick my lips and open my mouth to speak, but nothing comes out. The room sways and everything goes black.

Chapter 46

Romeo

I lunge forward, wrapping an arm around Aurora's waist and tugging her into my chest before she can hit the ground. Her body is limp and weightless in my arms. *Cazzo*, she's so fragile and it's only been a few days. Blinking down at her, I don't question my actions before repositioning her in my arms and striding out of the warehouse. Inhaling sharply, the faint scent of jasmine comforts me, even as it feels like my entire world is imploding.

My sights are set on the convoy of SUVs discreetly parked on the opposite side of the lot. Daniele approaches from the right, jogging ahead to open the door of one before I can reach it. He holds it open, not saying a word as I climb inside with her still in my arms. When Daniele gets behind the wheel, we speed off through the industrial area.

It's only when he pulls onto the highway that he

speaks. "Massimo said he'll take care of the warehouse and I've got Doc meeting us at the house."

I don't reply, instead, I smooth Aurora's hair back from her face. Cataloging every detail like it might be the last time I have the opportunity. There will be nowhere the woman who did this to her can hide. Every connection I have will be utilized, and every favor called in until she's dead.

Daniele navigates the roads, pushing the speed limit to get us back to Massimo's as quickly as possible. She needs help and I couldn't give a shit if we pick up a ticket or two to get her it.

Aurora stirs a couple of times during the one-hour journey, but she never opens her eyes. When we pull up outside the house, I have my door open before Daniele can put the car in park.

Cradling her in my arms, I climb the steps, calling out to Daniele, "Show Doc to our room."

Without waiting for him to respond, I stride into the house and head straight for the stairs. I'm no more than two steps up when my eyes meet Aldo's. His blow wide when they land on me from his position on the landing.

He pulls on his earlobe and steps to the side as I pass. "Is she... will she be okay, Don?"

My voice is strong and sure, conveying none of the uncertainty that's churning in my gut when I affirm, "Yes. She will."

She has to be.

I continue to our room, where I lay her on the bed

before pulling off her shoes. My mouth is dry, and I run my hand over the back of my neck, squeezing it as I stare at her. *She should be awake*. It's not right that she isn't.

A knock sounds at the door and I bark out for Doc to enter. He crosses the threshold, his medical bag in hand. He looks disheveled in a pair of slacks and an untucked, creased white linen shirt. My brow furrows at his state and I look at my watch to check the time. *How is it nearly midnight?*

Doc lightly grips my arm, forcing me to step back. "Let me see the patient."

I move to the end of the bed, closing my eyes and pinching the bridge of my nose as I blow out a heavy breath. Guilt fills me, but I focus on Doc as he lifts Aurora's wrist, checking for a pulse and making a note on a chart he's pulled from his bag. When I know she's going to be okay, I can figure out how to make this right for her. Until then, I'll have to live with the regret and the guilt that is eating me alive.

Under my scrutiny, Doc pulls on his gloves and carries out his examination. After a few minutes of quiet work, he looks at me over the rim of his glasses and says, "I instructed one of my nurses to bring around some equipment. Her name is Callie Brunswick. She should be here soon."

Inclining my head, I pull my phone from my jacket pocket and shoot off a text to Daniele. His response comes within seconds, confirming he will alert the front gate and escort her up when she arrives. I throw my phone onto the bed and run a hand through my hair as I stand tall.

Doc pulls off his gloves, throwing them onto the suture kit he's been using that is laid out on the bedside table. He turns to me, his worry evident in the wringing of his hands. "I've stitched up her leg. It doesn't look to be a deep cut, but when the items arrive, I'll hook her up for some general antibiotics and an IV to get her hydrated. I'm worried, considering how long she's been with this open wound, that there could be a serious infection there. I've taken some blood, but I'll need to get it tested in the lab so that we can pinpoint if they gave her any drugs. We'll know more once the bloods come back. The good news is, I've done an ultrasound, and she's clear of any internal bleeding."

"Put a rush on those tests, Doc." My tone is gruff and slightly frustrated.

He sighs heavily, putting the equipment he used back in his bag before closing the clasp. "Of course." Coming to stand in front of me, he implores, "She needs an X-ray. Without it, I can't confirm any broken bones, but from what Daniele told me, it's likely that she'll have a few broken ribs. And it feels like she's broken her cheekbone, but, again, I can't say for certain. Then there's obviously the extensive bruising. Unfortunately, she's going to be in a world of pain when she wakes up and the adrenaline has worn off, but I'll have the nurse administer some painkillers to help with it."

I scrub my hand over my jaw, ignoring the tightness

in my chest. "Was she…?" I can't bring myself to finish the question.

Doc squeezes my shoulder, a softness relaxing his face as he offers me a sympathetic smile. "There's no evidence of it." He turns to look at Aurora. "I guess a saving grace would be that whoever tortured her knew what they were doing and everything has been done to hurt, not maim or kill."

As if that offers any level of comfort.

"When will she wake up?"

"There's no telling. Her body has experienced extensive trauma and with these kinds of things, it's hard to put a definitive timeline on it. When she does wake up, she's going to need to rest for a while. Callie will fit the IV and stay with her overnight, and then I'll pop back again tomorrow afternoon after surgery hours."

I fix my focus back on Aurora. "Thanks, Doc."

Clapping me on the shoulder with the familiarity of a friend, he squeezes it gently. "She'll be okay. You got to her in time."

She might survive this, but I'm not sure *we* will.

Chapter 17

Aurora

A hand soothes over my back and I burrow further into the familiar warmth by my side. Romeo's signature woodsy scent fills my nostrils as my nose brushes over his bare chest. *It feels so real.* I squeeze my eyes before fluttering them open and staring at his toned chest. A groove forms between my brows at the sight.

Something about this is off and I don't know why.

I stretch my body out, pushing my chest into his and luxuriating in the rich cotton on my skin. Moaning as my nipples brush the coarse hair on his chest, it quickly morphs into a gasp of pain when a jolt rips through my body, hitting every limb and forcing me to relax.

It wasn't a dream.

Breathing through the pain, I hold still, waiting for it to dissipate as I let memories flood my mind. *I held a gun to Romeo's head and told him I hate him, so why am I in his bed?* None of this makes any sense. At best I should be in hospital, at worst I should be six feet under.

Romeo's arms tighten a fraction. "You're awake." Concern, laced with relief, coats his words.

Pushing at his chest, I try to move back and put some space between us so I can think, but Romeo holds steady, his arms banding around me like a vise. Struggling in his arms, everything hits me at once, from how I tried to save him, to how he left me to die. And then the fact that I'm now a murderer. I killed my uncle because he killed *my mom,* but that doesn't make what I did right.

My hands form into fists and I pummel Romeo's chest until he relents and loosens his hold enough for me to fully break free. Air rushes through my teeth as I move to sit up, the skin on my thigh pinching and pulling.

Shoving away the covers, I move to the side of the bed. There's a needle in the back of my hand and I stare at it for a moment, confused as to who would have put it there before I remember what Romeo had said about Doc. *I should be in the hospital, not Romeo's bed.* In fact, I don't want to be anywhere near him, despite the reaction my body just had to his proximity. I wasn't fully awake. *At least that's what I'll tell myself.*

Blowing out a breath, I pull at the tape holding the needle in place. When I have it lifted, I slide it out of the back of my hand before sticking it to the bedside table. I close my eyes before standing, putting most of the pressure on the leg that wasn't sliced by my *psychotic* torturer.

A wave of dizziness assails me, but I rest my hand on

the table and breathe through it. Every inch of me still hurts, but if I can make it through the assault I was subjected to, then I can get the hell out of this house.

Romeo rounds the bed, coming to a stop in front of me. His hands reach out to grab mine, but I pull them away, glaring at him. He takes a step back but keeps his hands outstretched, no doubt so he can be ready to catch me if I fall. *What a hero.*

"I can help you to the bathroom. The doctor said you have to rest, at least for a week, Aurora. I'm here to help." Concern fills his voice.

A week? I can't help but scoff at the notion. Yeah, I'm not staying here for a second longer than I have to. Determined, I move around him and hobble toward the closet, aware of Romeo's presence behind me every step of the way.

"Aurora, you need to get back into bed. Whatever you need, I can get it." His tone is authoritative, but there's also a hint of pleading in there.

If the idea that he cared about me wasn't so laughable, I'd be turning back toward the bed and asking him to stay with me. Begging him to take back what he said and to love me just as much as I love him. *Correction, loved.*

On the threshold of the closet, I face him, supporting myself on the frame. "You said if I told you what I wanted, you'd make it happen. Well, what I want is to *never* see you again. You should have left me to die because it would have been preferential to being in your presence for a second longer." My voice is calm, but the fury swirling beneath the surface wraps around us, suffocating any hope of a second chance we might have.

He steps forward, and I step back. My leg buckles out from underneath me and my arms flail, looking for something to hold on to. A growl echoes around the room, the sound drowning out the pounding in my ears.

It's going to hurt.

When I hit the ground, it's going to hurt.

Romeo grabs me, and pulls me in tightly against his chest. I suck in a breath, holding it and refusing to fall under his spell, *again*. Sliding one arm behind my knees, he scoops me into his arms and carries me back into the bedroom, heading for the bed. "You're going to rest for a week. It's the doctor's orders, not mine." I watch the column of his throat as he swallows. "If you still feel the same way by the end of the week, then I'll let you go. But you need to heal first."

Folding my arms, I look away from him and roll my eyes. They sting as I hold back an emotion that has no right to be there. I don't say anything, simply because I can't. If I try to, I know I'll cry and I've done enough of that over him.

At my silence, Romeo lays me on the bed, taking a step back before he adds, "I'll run you a bath and call the nurse to come and put the IV back in."

It's only when his back is to me that I inhale sharply, my lungs burning from the lack of oxygen. I don't know what drove him to rescue me or why he has a look of guilt on his face, but whatever it is, I won't allow it to wash away the hurt and the pain he's caused me.

We'll never come back from this. Leaving someone you love to die isn't something that can be redeemed, regardless of whether you *eventually* rescued them.

Love?

That's laughable. Romeo Bianchi isn't capable of love and even if he was, it isn't an emotion he feels for me. *That* I can be sure of. I'm going to spend this next week regaining as much of my strength as I can before I leave.

I need a fresh start, maybe somewhere far away from New York.

Far away from *him* and all these painful memories.

Chapter 48

Romeo

I stride into the bathroom, closing the door behind me, my fists clenched and barely concealing the anger I feel toward myself. My eyes meet my reflection in the mirror, the haunted look on my features a stark reminder of the guilt that's been sitting like a heavy weight on my chest ever since we found out she'd been set up.

Will she ever forgive me?

I can't blame her if the answer is no. *Dio*, I wouldn't forgive someone for what I've done, but I have to try. *How do I make this right?* Because aside from taking care of her, I don't know how to get us back to how it was. Sure, I could force her to stay, but that will only make her resentment toward me grow.

I turn toward the bath, turning on the faucet. Water spills out and into the tub, the sound filling the room. As it runs, I search the bathroom cabinets for something soothing to put in it. I find a bottle of vanilla and honeysuckle bubble bath under the basin and pour a hefty amount in. Standing back, I watch the clusters of bubbles form and grow, my mind wandering back to the woman I love in the other room.

Will she always see me as the villain?

I know the answer to the question before it comes to me. *Of course she will.* Ever since the day I took her, she's only ever seen me as the devil and at the start, I played into that notion. But when things changed between us, I can't be sure that she was just tolerating me to have an easier life. I should have told her how I was feeling when I realized, but my *nonno* and my parents taught me to bury my emotions, to keep the walls up to protect myself. It served me well, but now I'm wondering if it's fucked me over.

Shaking away the thoughts of the past and what I should or shouldn't have done, I turn off the faucet and head back into the bedroom. Aurora's still sitting on the edge of the bed, her fingers fiddling with the hem of her T-shirt.

Her sea-green eyes meet mine, flames flicking in the depths as she grinds out, "Who changed me?"

I lean against the doorframe with my thumb hooked into the waistband of my silk boxers to keep from reaching for her. "The nurse. She's been taking care of you. I'll call her while you bathe."

Taking a step toward her, I stop mid-stride when she

holds up her hand. "I don't need your help. I'm capable of undressing and bathing myself."

Shrugging a shoulder as if her refusal of my help is of no consequence to me, I walk around the bed, unplugging my phone from its spot on the bedside table and calling the nurse. Aurora stands from the bed and my eyes track her as she hobbles to the bathroom. Her presence in my room is a teasing reminder of what I've lost.

"Mr. Bianchi, how can I help you?" The nurse's motherly tone pulls me back into the moment, and I turn away from watching Aurora.

"Aurora needs to have her IV reinserted."

"I'll be right over. Shouldn't be more than fifteen minutes."

Rubbing at my eyes, I reply, "Make it thirty."

I cut the call, make a pit stop in the closet to throw on some clothes before crossing the room and knocking on the bathroom door. When there's no answer, I lean in and try again, listening intently. There's not a peep coming from the other side. No sound of water or movement. My mouth goes dry as worry settles into the pit of my stomach.

Testing the handle, I push against the door. It gives way almost instantly, and I fall into the room. Aurora is naked, standing in front of the mirror, a pained expression clouding her face. When her glassy eyes meet mine, a tightness pulls at my chest. Her entire body is covered in tiny cuts and huge bruises. I grind my teeth at the sight of her, running a jerky hand through my hair to keep from reaching for her.

She's the first one to move, turning away from me and climbing into the bath, careful to keep her leg elevated and her dressing dry. *I can't be here right now*. Not when she's a constant reminder of my mistakes. "The nurse will be here in thirty minutes."

With her head tipped back against the roll top tub and her eyes closed, I allow myself one last look before I turn and leave, closing the door behind me.

Marching across the bedroom, I pull open the door with more force than necessary. It bangs against the wall, no doubt leaving a mark.

Cazzo!

I exhale and crack my neck, forcing the tension out of my body. There's still work to be done. We need to find out who doctored the information Aldo gave us and find the woman who tortured Aurora.

Daniele is typing on his phone, as he waits for me, his head lifts at the sound. *And I still have to deal with him*. When I turn toward the stairs, he falls into step beside me. Out of the corner of my eye, I can see the concern etched into his features. "How is she?" he asks quietly.

I sigh heavily, running a hand over the back of my neck. The lack of sleep from the night before weighs down my limbs as I push through, forcing my body to move. "In pain, angry, exhausted, the list goes on. But she's healing, and that's the main thing."

Daniele stops, resting a hand on my shoulder and forcing me to turn to him. "And how are you?"

Isn't that the million dollar question? Being honest with myself, I'm feeling all the things she is, but for an entirely different reason. "I'm fine," is all I can tell him.

Daniele's grip tightens. "Right, and I'm the tooth fairy. I thought we could be honest with each other, Rome."

I shrug him off, the anger I felt only days ago returning with full force. "You mean like how you went behind my back after I explicitly told you not to?"

"And I wouldn't change a thing because if I hadn't, she'd be fucking dead." Arrogance and defiance mix together.

Grabbing the collar of his shirt, I pull my fist back, connecting with his jaw. "Don't forget who the fuck you're talking to, Daniele," I spit. "I'm still not sure if you'll be digging your own grave in the States or back home."

Releasing him, I turn and head to Massimo's office, done with him and his clear lack of respect. I know deep down that he's right and that the anger I'm directing toward him is just a projection of how I feel about myself for having nearly cost her her life. This burning feeling of guilt won't *ever* go away. Even when she's better and living her life, I'll always have that seed in the pit of my stomach. I don't think a lifetime of apologies will make up for me having left her.

Changing the past isn't possible, but making sure *we*

have a future is and to do that, I need to sort out everything else. There's too much to be done, like confirming it was Aurora's uncle behind the attacks. We'd be fools to take the situation at face value, especially in our world. It wouldn't surprise me if there was more than one character at play.

Daniele walks into Massimo's office shortly after me. He rubs at the red spot where I hit him, asking, "Is Leonardo joining us?"

Massimo, who is already sitting behind his desk, shakes his head, his attention on his phone. After a minute, he slides it onto the table and leans back in his chair. "No, he's gone back upstate to take care of the housekeeper."

My brows furrow and I look at Massimo in question. "Apparently, he didn't get to finish up because of the raid. He'll be back in a week or so," he explains.

The room falls quiet, a heaviness hanging in the air as the gravity of what has happened over the last twenty-four hours blankets us. We were lucky to not have lost any men yesterday, but we aren't really any closer to a resolution.

Scrubbing a hand over my jaw, I ask, "Has Angelo finished at the warehouse?"

Massimo cracks his neck, stifling a yawn. "Yeah, they came in around four in the morning. I did a debrief and he let me know what her uncle had told him when they were tying him up." As if he knows I need confirmation he adds, "Leonardo has verified what was said."

I lean forward, my curiosity piqued. "What did her uncle say, Massimo?"

He sucks in a sharp breath. "That I have a rat in my house."

I reply, "Well, *I* already knew that."

Resting an elbow on the arm of his chair, he runs his fingers through his hair. "I know. And Leonardo is taking care of that, but if what Mattia said is true, there might be another one. Someone who has been a part of this family for a *very* long time. So, for now at least, everything stays between the three of us and Leonardo."

I nod in agreement, running through the names of every man who might have an inkling to do something like this.

"He also told Angelo that Elio was financing the whole operation, because he wanted us out of New York. Which is nothing new really. We've been dealing with his shit for years. Apparently, he set up the connections to some Russians he knew, and they weren't Bratva, just men who wanted to have some excitement in their lives."

I huff out a breath. "What's the plan in terms of next steps?"

"Well, for the rat, we'll have to set a trap, but it could take some time to weed them out. For Elio, I have a source that's told me he's going to be at his house in Manhattan on Friday. We could attack then. The only risk will be the NYPD and getting out of the city once alarms have been raised. I can have them delayed, but it won't be for long."

I smooth my hand down the front of my shirt. "And what about the woman?"

Daniele steps forward, knocking his knuckles against the desk. "I'm on it. She won't be able to hide forever. Callum is analyzing the footage and running what we know about her through every database he can. When Aurora's up for it, we'll need to talk to her and see if she can shed any more light on her."

As much as I don't want to make Aurora relive her trauma, we need her to find this woman. *And what if she refuses to help?* Then I'll do what I should have done all along, trust that she's doing the right thing, and protect her with my entire being.

Chewing on the inside of my cheek, I consider everything else that's been laid out on the table. These aren't things that can be fixed quickly. It's going to take time. *And what will that mean for me and Aurora?* If she wants to leave, I'll have to let her go. But I won't be sticking around. I'd rather put four and half thousand or so miles between us than occupy the same country and not be able to have her.

Massimo cuts into my thoughts as he rests his elbows on his desk. "I know you'll want to get home, Rome, so if it's okay with you, maybe Daniele can stay and help us out? Then you can take Aurora and give her another view from the one in your room."

Without bothering to correct his assumption or give Daniele the courtesy of a glance, I reply, "Sure. But I'll be staying, at least until Aurora's healed enough to leave." *Hopefully, with me.*

"Of course, I wouldn't expect anything less." Massimo pauses before adding, "How is she?"

Running my tongue over my bottom lip, I stare out of the window. "She's going to be fine. It'll take her time to come to terms with what she's been through, but I know she will."

Massimo chuckles and I shift my focus to him, catching the smirk lifting the corner of his mouth. "She sure surprised me back at the warehouse. You might just make a made woman out of her yet."

I'm fucking *proud* of what she did. She took back her control and there was no way in hell I was going to stop her. Holding his stare, I reply, "It wouldn't have been fair for anyone else but *her* to have killed him. Not after what he's done to her family."

Massimo and Daniele both nod. The reality of what Aurora's lost hits us all at once. She's the strongest person I know and if she gives me another chance, I'll spend the rest of my life making sure she doesn't forget her strength and resilience.

Chapter 19

Aurora

My body is relaxed and in a perfect, hazy slumber right before I wake up. I luxuriate in the feeling of Romeo's warmth surrounding me. It's the only time I allow myself to forget what he's done. *To forgive him.*

This is the second morning that I've woken up like this. His bare chest pressed to mine and his arms holding me with a gentleness that brings tears to my eyes. And each time, I blink my eyes open, press my hands into his chest, and force my way out of his embrace. He rolls onto his back, an ugliness filling the surrounding air. It's getting harder and harder to push him away and it's only been two days since I returned. It should be easy. I should be able to remember what he did—*what he said*—and fan the flames of my anger. But it's not working, especially when I wake up with the reminder of what we had.

Why can't it be easy to hate him?

369

Because I love him.

This morning, Romeo exhales sharply and throws the covers off before climbing from the bed and walking into the bathroom without a word. I stare up at the ceiling, listening to the sounds of him getting ready for his day.

I don't want to love him. I *want* to hate him because I don't like how weak I feel by giving in. *Why am I doing this to myself? I should leave.* There's nothing keeping me here, after all. Even Doc said my leg was healing nicely and if it continues to, then he'll be giving me the all clear at the end of the week. *So why not just walk out of the door? What are they going to do, shoot me?* Besides, if I stay any longer, I might do something as stupid as giving in to my heart when my head is screaming at me to run.

Sitting up, I swing my legs over the edge of the bed, searching the room for my crutch that Callie brought over yesterday after she caught me walking on my own. It's safe to say I'm motivated to get back on my feet. I prop my crutch up against the bedside table so I can reach it, but this morning it's resting on the chair by the window. *Great.* Romeo must have moved it.

With one hand on the bedside table and the other on the mattress, I push up. I'm halfway to standing when the bathroom door opens and Romeo strides out, a towel wrapped around his waist and his wet, bare chest on full display. I avert my eyes and drop back down onto the mattress as I listen to him pad across the carpet. *I'll try again when he's gone.*

He comes to stand in front of me, holding out the

metal stick. My hands feel clammy as I reach for it and I pray he can't see the way my body is trembling as I wrap them around it. I hate that he has this effect on me. All he has to do is be half naked and I'm a melting puddle of need. It's pathetic.

His deep timbre rolls through my body, sending bolts of desire shooting to my core when he says, "Callie will be here in an hour to check on you."

Callie isn't supposed to be coming today. I frown, brushing off the unwanted desire as I finally meet his gaze. "Why?"

"I've asked her to. She'll take you into the garden and bring you back in. I thought you might want to do some drawing and get out of this room."

My mouth forms into an O shape before I close it and nod. It *would* be nice to get outside and do some sketching. I feel his eyes on me, but neither of us speaks, and when he heads into the closet, I exhale a heavy breath before standing and heading into the bathroom.

———

A chill has settled into the air and the sun has long disappeared between the heavy gray clouds that have rolled in. I've been putting off going inside, the fresh air enough to keep me out, even if the hairs on my arms are standing on end.

Pushing my pad onto the table in front of me, I pick up my crutch and awkwardly stand from the chair, the blanket Callie placed over my lap falling to a pile on the floor at my feet. A drop of water falls from the sky, landing on my nose and I turn my face up, breathing in deeply as I wait for more to come. There's something calming about the rain.

A knock on the window behind me pulls my attention and I turn to find Alma gesturing animatedly behind the glass. I watch as she rushes to the door a few steps away before bursting through it and crossing the patio toward me.

"What are you doing? You should call for help," she admonishes.

I can't help but chuckle and the first genuine smile I've felt since I was taken tugs at my lips before my face crumples and tears tumble down my cheeks. Rain falls in a sheet soaking me through and yet I still don't move. Alma pulls me into her arms, squeezing me tightly as she mutters hurried Italian words that I don't understand into my shoulder.

We're both getting soaked as she hooks her arm into mine to help me into the house and through to the kitchen. By the time we enter the warm room, my teeth are chattering and my eyes have dried up. Maria is at the sink, her back to us and a stiffness that I know all too well in her posture. She doesn't turn to acknowledge our presence and something about it fills me with unease. Alma settles me into a chair at the kitchen table and shuffles across the room to the refrigerator.

I watch as she moves around the room preparing tea,

before darting into the laundry room and returning a moment later with a pile of towels. She hands one to me before returning to the two cups of tea on the counter. I don't miss the way she runs her hand over Maria's back in a comforting gesture.

Something's happened.

It's obvious by the straining tension that's hanging in the atmosphere. Questioning eyes lift to hers when Alma places a mug of tea on the table in front of me. She smooths her palms down the front of her apron before sliding into the chair next to me and enveloping my hand in hers.

"Haven is missing." Her words are said on a whispered breath, a fear of reality coating them.

My eyes widen and my jaw goes slack, certain that I must have misunderstood her. "M-missing?"

Alma nods, leaning forward and keeping her voice lowered as Maria quietly sobs by the sink. "She won't be coming back."

My brows tug together at her confusing statement. "So, she's not missing?" Alma stares at me, deadpan until all the pieces of the puzzle fall into place. "They've..." I can't bring myself to finish that sentence. Tears well in my eyes and I choke out, "Why?"

Alma looks away, her eyes becoming as glassy as I'm sure mine are. Her voice cracks when she speaks, like she can't quite believe what she's saying is true. "She betrayed the family."

What? That doesn't make any sense. *Why would she*

do that? My hand grasps Alma's. "You and I both know that's not true, Alma. What have they said? What lies have they told about her?"

Her fingers fiddle with the delicate chain around her neck. Squeezing my hand, she opens her mouth to speak, but a harsh bark of her name cuts her off. "Alma." It's a warning and meant to silence her.

My eyes dart to Daniele standing in the doorway. Alma slips her hand free from mine, leaving it to fall to the table with a dull thud as she stands, walking over to Maria before escorting her out of the kitchen.

Only when they've gone does Daniele move into the room. He walks to the refrigerator, pulling it open and staring at the contents. I shake my head in disbelief at his callousness before using my crutch to stand and walk toward the door. None of this should be a surprise to me after what I've been through.

I come to a stop, holding onto the doorframe for support as I look over my shoulder. "What did she do?"

He rolls his neck, the ink tattooed across it stretching and contracting with the movement. "It doesn't concern you."

I scoff. "Wow. It's really like that?" When he doesn't respond, I add, "No offense, but I don't really trust any of you to make a call on what happens with someone's life, given my own *personal* experiences." He tenses, and I know my jab hit the mark. "What *exactly* are you accusing her of doing?"

He widens his stance, squaring his shoulders. "I won't repeat myself, Aurora."

Turning to face him, I hobble back into the room, hating how weak I must look with the crutch. "Fine, I'll leave it. But let's just hope that you don't leave another innocent woman to die."

The sooner I can leave this place, the better, especially when I know exactly who would have made the call to have her *dealt* with. What's worse is that even if I wanted to stay, I'd be at risk of being put in this exact same situation again, and I don't know if I'll be lucky enough to make it out a second time. I might not be fully fit to leave just yet, but there is something I can do to give myself some much needed respite.

"I will need your help moving to another room," I demand, my mind made up.

Daniele narrows his eyes as he asks, "Has Romeo said it's okay?"

My spine stiffens and I take a step forward, momentarily forgetting about my leg. I grit my teeth against the jolt of pain that slices through me and spit out through gritted teeth, "It's none of his *fucking* concern. *I'm* none of his concern. There have to be at least a hundred spare rooms in this place and either you help me move into one or I do it myself."

He regards me for so long I'm certain he's going to say no, and as I turn to leave, his words pull me to a halt as he calls, "I'll be up in thirty."

Without a word, I leave the kitchen. Helping me is

the least Daniele can do and he should count himself lucky that I'm not asking him to drive me to the nearest damn airport. But most importantly, screw Romeo Bianchi, and any man in this house who thinks they get a say in where *I* sleep.

I'm rounding a corner at the end of the hallway, heading to the living room, when I bump into Massimo. *Just what I need.* His hands land on my shoulders to steady me and his eyes drift over my body. "Are you okay?"

Shrugging him off, I go to move past him, but his tight grip wraps around my elbow.

"I'd like to speak to you." He pauses, loosening his hold a fraction. "If that's okay."

Huffing out a breath, I tug my arm free. "I don't have anything to say to you."

He glances around the hallway before lowering his voice and taking a step closer. "It's about Haven."

I lift my chin, narrowing my eyes at him before I sneer. "Unless you're going to tell me what she's supposedly done or show me the evidence, I'm not interested."

"I'd like you to look over the video and give me your side of the story."

My lips part, but nothing comes out. *What does he mean by my side of the story?* I want to tell him to go to hell, but if it helps Haven, I can't walk away. I don't want anyone to have to go through what I did if they're innocent. Sighing heavily, I reply, "Okay."

Massimo heads down the corridor he came from,

leaving me to trail behind. As we walk, I think over every interaction I've ever had with Haven, so that I can make sure he has the full picture. Deep in my heart, I know she wouldn't hurt a soul, let alone betray her family.

When we enter Massimo's office, he directs me to take a seat in front of his desk. A laptop sits open on top of it, and after tapping away on the keys, he turns it to face me. An image of myself in that *stupid* dress Romeo had me wear stares back at me.

Reaching over the screen, Massimo presses play and I watch the video, trying to take in every detail. When it finishes, he presses the lid closed and leans back in his chair before asking, "What did she say on that call?"

Shrugging, I reply, "Nothing."

Massimo sighs heavily, as if my perceived defiance is tiresome. "You can't protect her, Aurora. We know it was from a number associated with the Russians. And possibly the ones involved with your uncle."

"I'm not protecting her. She literally said nothing," I implore. "Well, not nothing. She said 'hello' a whole bunch but I don't think anyone was on the other end."

Exhaling, Massimo runs his hand through his hair. "Okay, thank you."

As I stand, I lean toward him, resting my hand on his desk. "I don't think she had anything to do with what happened to me. She's my friend and if she isn't already..." I shake my head, unable to get the word out. "I just ask that you don't do it. If she's still alive, let her go."

He runs his tongue over his teeth, before turning his

laptop back to face him and opening it again. "That's not how this works."

I dig my nails into the palm of my hand. "I'm *very* aware of that."

"Even if it did, it's too late."

With tears brimming in my eyes, I leave Massimo's office, my mind swirling with images of a lifeless Haven.

I'm not cut out for this life.

Chapter 50

Romeo

My body and mind are exhausted. In fact, *everything* is tired. I want nothing more than to climb into bed, pull Aurora into my arms, and fall into a dreamless sleep. But I know that I'll be awake until the early hours, running through plans and trying to figure out how best to approach the situation with Elio as I steal glances of her in our bed.

Time is running out. Both with getting to Elio while he's in New York, but also with trying to gain back Aurora's trust. The latter feels more and more impossible with each day that passes. Yes, she lets me hold her in her sleep, but come the morning, her walls go right back up.

I rub my fist over the throbbing in my chest, dismissing the idea that I might have to let her walk away. *Not a fucking chance. I can't let her go.* I'll take what I can for now but come the end of the week, I need a plan that doesn't revolve around me locking her away.

Slowly pushing open the bedroom door, I slip into the darkened room. Immediately, I sense something isn't right. There's a hollowness that hangs in the air like there isn't a living, breathing soul in the room.

The curtains hang slightly ajar, and the moonlight casts a beam of light across the bed. *The empty bed.* Every muscle in my body tenses at the sight before I rush through the room, checking the bathroom and closet for any sign of her.

She's gone.

One of her drawing pads sits on the table by the window and I move toward it in the hopes it might hold a clue. Flicking through the pages, my breath halts when they reveal two pieces of folded up paper. I snatch them up, sinking back into the chair. Carefully, I unfold the first, my eyes widening as I take in the typeface.

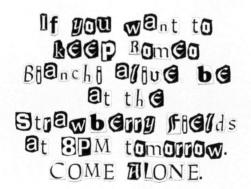

If you want to keep Romeo Bianchi alive be at the Strawberry Fields at 8PM tomorrow. COME ALONE.

This is why she left? *Cazzo.* She was trying to protect me? I throw the note onto the table, opening the second slip of paper. Her neat handwriting greets me and my eyes scan over the words.

> *My darling Romeo,*
> *If you've found this note, I'm assuming I'm either dead or you've discovered that I've gone. I promise I'll try my best to return to you, but if I don't, I need you to know that what I did was for you. I love you and you'll always hold my heart.*
> *Love, Aurora.*
> *Forever and always x*

I move quickly, storming from the bedroom as I pull out my phone and call Daniele. It rings out before going through to voicemail. Nausea claws at my throat as I try him again. My phone vibrates against my ear as his voicemail connects. Pulling it away, I disconnect the call and bring up our message thread.

DANIELE
She's in one of the spare rooms.

I was just with him and he decides to wait until he's in the safety of his room to tell me this shit? This has gone too fucking far. Stopping in the hallway, I dial him again.

When he doesn't answer, my fingers fly furiously across the screen.

> ROMEO
>
> Which one?

DANIELE

She said she would do it herself if I didn't help.

Said she needed some space.

Maybe you can talk to her tomorrow?

Who the hell does he think he is? I head in the direction of his room, my phone to my ear as I call him again. *Keep digging your fucking grave, Daniele.*

> ROMEO
>
> Answer the fucking phone.

I dial his number for the fifth time, pressing my phone to my ear and daring him to ignore me again. He picks up on the first ring, sighing heavily.

"Which room is she in?" The words are barked out, my patience gone.

"Romeo, maybe—"

My fury consumes me and I sink into it, a welcome departure from the guilt that's consumed me since she came home. I bellow, "Don't you fucking dare. You're on thin ice, Daniele. In fact, it's cracked around you and I'll be damned if I save you. Tell me where she is. Now."

Defeated, he replies, "She's on the third floor, in the

room at the end of the corridor on the west side of the house."

As far away as she could get from me, in other words.

"I'll deal with you later." All the anger I feel is contained in that sentence. There have to be consequences for his actions. He's been crossing the line too often recently. *Especially when it comes to her.*

Disconnecting the call, I head for the room. It feels like everything is spiraling and I need to get a handle on it all. *Starting with her.* Even now, when she's moved herself to the opposite end of the house, I can't help but hold on to the delusional hope that she'll stay. The words in her note have to mean something. Those kinds of feelings can't just be shrugged off or taken back. Deep down, she has to still feel something for me. There has to be a shred of hope that we can make it back from all of this.

When I reach her door, I twist the handle, intent on slipping in and under the covers. Hell, I'd take sleeping on the floor beside her bed. Anything to be close to her. The doorknob doesn't shift and I chew on my lip in confusion.

She expected me to react like this. To hunt her down and force myself into her room. I let my head fall against the door. *Dio.* I've never been this consumed by another person and I can't seem to control myself.

Taking a step back, I lean against the opposite wall, going over my options. I could get the master key and let myself in. *Or respect her decision and return to my room.* The idea tastes bitter on my tongue and makes up my mind for me. I'll be sleeping in the hallway tonight. Sliding down the wall, I cross my legs at the ankles and relax back.

I've slept in less comfortable places.

My limbs feel heavy, and I smother a yawn as I close my eyes and settle in. A door closing further down the corridor has my eyes springing open. Daniele appears at the end of the passageway with a pillow and blanket in his arms.

He looks sheepish when he approaches me, holding out the items as a peace offering. "I figured you could do with these. And I needed to apologize."

Handing them over, he slides down the wall, taking a seat next to me as I position the pillow behind my head. He has a lot more than apologizing to do, but then again, so do I with Aurora.

Tugging on the back of his neck, he lowers his gaze before continuing, "I shouldn't have disobeyed you, but I stand by my decision. Something wasn't adding up and if I hadn't listened to my gut, she'd have died *alone* in that room."

I blow out a breath because he's right and I am grateful for what he did. "I can't let what you did go unpunished."

He nods, fully aware that I would respond like that. "I accept responsibility for what I did, and I'll take whatever punishment you think is warranted. Everything I've done has been for you, Romeo. It might not seem like it, but you're like a brother to me and sometimes you need protecting from yourself because I know you never would have forgiven yourself if you'd lost her."

He's both wrong and right. I've already lost her and I won't ever forgive myself for what she went through. At my silence, Daniele stands and leaves me alone to stare at her locked bedroom door.

Chapter 51

Romeo

A tapping on the bottom of my shoe rouses me from sleep. Everything aches from my awkward sleeping position and I crack my neck as I push through the fog clouding my mind. My eyes land on a pair of sneaker-clad ankles, traveling up the smooth bare legs. Pausing momentarily on the white dressing on her thigh, I'm hit with the familiar cocktail of regret and guilt before continuing on to meet Aurora's frustrated gaze.

She juts a hip, sighing heavily. "What are you doing?"

I clear my throat and stand. "I wanted to be here in case you needed me."

Every night since she returned, she's had a nightmare. Her body trembles and she cries out. The only way I've found to soothe them was for me to hold her, but I don't think she knows that.

She huffs out a breath and mutters something I can't make out before dismissing me, turning to walk down the corridor with her crutch. Like a lost puppy, I follow behind.

Praying that she can hear the sincerity in my voice, I say, "I know my words won't make any of this right or fix us, but I'm sorry, Aurora. For everything I put you through and for not believing you when you needed me to. If I could take everything back, I would."

She turns to face me, her eyes glassy. "You're right." Her tongue swipes over her bottom lip. "It doesn't fix anything. You can't unsay what you said. *You* broke us. And as far as I'm concerned, your apology is as useful as a punch to the face and I took a fair few of those. Now, if you'll excuse me, I have an appointment with Doc."

My stomach plummets and I reach for her when she goes to walk off. A spark of electricity races from the tips of my fingers straight to my heart, but I ignore it. "Is everything okay?"

She tugs her elbow away. "Yes. It's just a checkup to make sure I'm on track to have my stitches removed in a couple of days," she replies dismissively.

Right. Because in four days, it will have been a week and Doc will give her the all clear. And I haven't got any reason for her to stay. Desperation claws at my throat, but I've had a lifetime of masking my feelings, so it's easy enough to push down.

Waving an arm in front of us for her to continue

walking, I look at her pointedly when her eyes narrow with suspicion before she starts moving again.

Shrugging, I say, "I don't have anything going on this morning, so I'll come with you."

I nearly barrel into her back when she comes to a stop in the middle of the hallway, spinning to face me with panic pulling at her features. "You don't need to do that."

"It's not an issue."

Her knuckles turn white as she tightens her grip on her crutch. Stopping short of stomping her foot, she huffs, "I don't want you to come."

I fight to hide the twitch of my lips, scrubbing a hand over my jaw and forcing my mouth to relax. "Well, I need to see him anyway."

She steps forward, her mouth open slightly. Her eyes bore into me, daring me to lie to her face. "What for?"

Rubbing at my right shoulder, I reply, "My shoulder. It's been playing up ever since the restaurant."

"Do you think I'm stupid?"

I narrow my eyes, unsure where she's going with her question. "Not at all."

"It kind of feels like you do." I open my mouth to respond, but she holds up her hand, cutting me off. "The bullet *grazed* your left shoulder, Romeo. In case you forgot, I was there."

Cracking my neck, my chest expands and with a firmness to my voice I reply, "I fell on my right shoulder and it's been playing up." It's not technically a lie. I *have* hurt my shoulder, just not at the restaurant.

388

Instead of questioning me further, like I expect her to, Aurora sighs and turns back to walk away, ignoring me for the remainder of the way to the room Doc uses for consultations on the ground floor.

I have four days until the week is up and I'm not ready to let her go, even if that's what she wants. For the first time in my life, I'm not sure how to get her to stay. Forcing her isn't an option. I did that once before and look how well it turned out.

No, I need to earn back her trust and make her *want* to stay.

Chapter 52

Aurora

I t's Friday and today is my penultimate checkup with Doc, which means I'm one step closer to my freedom. To putting all of this behind me and packing up my life to move to New Zealand. The furthest possible country from *him*.

Why does the thought of leaving fill me with dread?

A pressure builds in my chest, hurting my heart. I should be feeling elated, even happy at the prospect of my future. *It shouldn't feel like this.* I know that leaving is the right thing, but I can't shift this heaviness and the feeling that this might not be the right decision.

I know Romeo is truly sorry for what's happened. I *know* that he's trying. But is that enough for me to forgive and open my heart back up to him? And risk something like this happening again? I honestly don't know. It feels like the obvious answer should be no, but it feels like the wrong one.

Doc cuts through my thoughts as he turns from the counter and flicks through the chart in his hands. "Okay, let's get you up on the table."

My eyes dart to the clock above the door, double checking the time. *He's late.* Closing my eyes, I blow out a breath and shuffle onto the paper sheet covering the table. It doesn't matter if Romeo's here or not. In fact, all it does is add another point to the leaving side of the mental chart I'm making.

Pulling on a pair of white gloves, Doc asks, "Please, can you lift your dress so I can examine your thigh?"

Distracted, I do as Doc asks, lifting the hem of my dress to reveal the large cut on my thigh. It's only when my eyes drop to the ugly mark that I pull out of the haze. *It's going to leave a scar.* A constant reminder of what happened to me. *But at least it'll be hidden.*

If I leave, I know that over time I might forget Romeo and the feelings he stirred within me, but I'll always have a reminder marking my skin of the horrible words he uttered that could have ended my life.

Doc places his hand on my thigh, examining the wound, and I jump at his touch. *God, focus, Aurora.* Romeo isn't even here, and yet he's consuming my thoughts. *He promised me he'd be here.* Have I learned nothing?

My eyes burn, and I tip my head back, blinking rapidly. *What a fool.* I thought he was trying, in his own way, to make an effort but I was wrong. Even if his actions for the last few days have said otherwise. Each morning, I've found him asleep outside my door, he's walked down to the kitchen with me and eaten breakfast in silence by my side. He even left me some drawing supplies and a cell phone. But none of that means he's trying to... I guess, *win me back.*

I don't know what it means, and that annoys me the most.

Doc's examination takes no more than fifteen minutes, but the entire time I can't help but watch the door, praying that Romeo will walk through it.

Finishing up a note on my chart, Doc says, "The cut has healed nicely, Aurora. I think you can ease up on your use of the crutch and slowly start to get back to your normal activities. I'll see you in two days to remove the stitches and then you should be good to go."

Go. Two little letters, but together, the word feels so final.

Swiping a finger under my eye, I ask, "When will I be able to travel?"

Doc gives me a soft smile, pulling off his gloves and moving back to the counter. "Whenever you like, you can even have another doctor remove the stitches if you're planning to leave before the end of the week. I've heard Sicily is nice this time of year."

I smooth down the hem of my dress. "No," I hesitate. "I'm going to New Zealand."

As soon as the words leave my mouth, I want to take them back. Not because I'm worried Doc will tell anyone, but because I don't know that I really want to leave. I've only ever known the States. What waits for me in New Zealand aside from some beautiful scenery? *Absolutely nothing.*

Doc stiffens. "I must have misunderstood."

Misunderstood what? I want to question him further, but I know he won't tell me whatever it is that he knows. Nobody ever does in this godforsaken place. *And just like that, my anger is back.* I climb down from the table. "Is that all?" I ask, my tone sharp and accusatory.

"Yes, thank you. Enjoy your trip."

I could be traveling into the pits of hell and it would be more preferential to this place and the secrecy that comes with it. Storming out of the room without my crutch, I head in the direction of the kitchen. Alma promised me a homemade cookie after my appointment and I intend to cash in on it. It could be the last one for a while, after all.

When I enter the kitchen, I head straight for the island, swiping up the warm, gooey chocolate chip goodness and stuffing half of it into my mouth. *How can a cookie make everything that little bit better?* My frustration eases out as I chew on the deliciousness. Alma walks in from the laundry room, chuckling at my moans of delight.

"Don't eat them all."

Snatching up another one, I hold it close to my chest. "I can't promise that. They're delicious."

I watch as she moves around the kitchen, preparing lunch. She places a glass of milk in front of me and I wrap an arm around her waist, pulling her into my side as I mumble a grateful 'thank you'. If every day was like this, no darkness infecting the light, I'd stay. There's a homeliness that I've found in Alma, Maria... and Haven. Staring up at the ceiling, I blink back the tears that well in my eyes. *Since when have I been such an emotional mess? Maybe I need to find a therapist when I get out of here.*

The peacefulness of the kitchen is shattered when one of Massimo's men barrels into the room, a panicked urgency filling his voice as he rushes, "Alma, we need towels. Doc needs towels."

My eyes flare, watching Alma as she springs into action, grabbing up the clean towels she'd placed on the kitchen table. She hurries from the room and I follow after her, a desperation to know what's going on fueling me.

We enter the entryway of the house and Alma hurries through to the room I left moments ago. I come to a stop in the middle of the space, my focus landing on the convoy of cars visible through the window on the side of the door. They race down the driveway and I watch, mesmerized by the speed they are traveling. The gravel has barely settled before the front door slams open and four men carry a bleeding and unconscious man through the space. His blood leaves a trail on the marble floor as they rush past me.

Suddenly there's a hive of activity surrounding me as the entrance fills with men, all in different stages of disarray. I look around the room, desperately searching for him. *Where is he?* One by one, the men leave and I'm left standing alone, my breath coming in short sharp pants. Resting my hand on my collar, I double over, trying to catch my breath.

Why is he not here?

Rocking my body back and forth, I try and fail to drag in enough oxygen. My body trembles, and a sob is ripped from my lips as the unbearable weight of the worst possible thing being true settles on my chest. *Why didn't I just forgive him?* Tears stream down my cheeks, dropping onto the floor and mingling with smeared blood tarnishing the once pristine flooring.

Chapter 53

Aurora

Brown wingtip shoes appear in my line of sight, and a hand lands on my back, rubbing in soothing circles. Immediately, I know it's not Romeo. I'd know it down to my core if he was touching me. Hell, I'm so aware of him that I'd have known if he was in this house.

Daniele crouches in front of me, worry flooding his hazel eyes as they search mine. "Aurora?"

Standing straight, I squeeze my eyes shut and pivot away from him. If he's going to tell me that Romeo's gone, I don't want to hear it. *I can't handle that.* Shouldn't I have felt him leaving, like I did with my mom?

Daniele follows me as I move toward the still-open front door. His hand comes to rest on my shoulder as he forces me to face him. "Hey. What's wrong?"

Shrugging him off, I cry out, a gut-wrenching pain ripping the words from my lips. "Why did you leave him?" Pointing to my chest, I shout, "I need him, Daniele." Pain seeps out of every inch of my body, and I wrap my arms around my waist to keep myself together.

Solid warm arms pull me in, the act giving me the safety to let go. Daniele rubs his hand up and down the center of my back. "Hey, hey, it's okay, Aurora. We didn't leave him. He's okay, he's here."

Pulling away, my eyes bounce around his face, searching for the truth. I want to believe him, but if that's the case, then why isn't Romeo holding me? My voice is hoarse when I demand, "Where?"

Daniele's grip on my shoulders tightens a fraction. "He's in the rose garden." When I make to leave, he holds me still as a somberness coats his features. "It was a tough one, Aurora. We lost some good men. It always hits him hard and he just needs a moment to himself."

I won't disturb him, but I just need to see for myself that he's really okay. Tugging free of Daniele's grip, I brush past him as I race through the house and out into the garden, ignoring the throbbing in my thigh. I'm sure Doc didn't envisage me running when he said I could get back to my 'normal' activities.

My lungs burn as I pound across the lawn and the harsh wind stings my eyes, making them water as I push through the pain. It's only when I can see his stoic figure in the rose garden, his hands stuffed into his pockets as he looks out over the rolling hills, that I slow down. I approach him gently, like he's a wild animal that I might scare away. My eyes catalog every inch of his back, taking in the stiff set of his shoulders and the dirt covering his jacket.

God, I'm so glad he's okay.

Blowing out a relieved breath, I continue toward him. My body is drawn to him like a magnet, closing the distance between us. My sneakers crunch on the gravel and he looks over his shoulder at me, a streak of blood on his cheek. Without thinking about it, I step up to him, wrapping my arms around his waist and pressing my body into his back. I squeeze my eyes shut, willing the hotness behind my lids to ease up.

I could have lost him.

"I thought you'd..." I choke on the words, a whimper leaving my lips as I cry softly into the fabric of his jacket.

Romeo rests his hand on mine. For a moment, his thumb smooths back and forth before he breaks the clasp of my hands. He turns to face me, cupping my cheek as he offers me a small, sad smile. "*Mia amata.*"

Never have two words sounded so loaded. There's a wealth of hurt and apology in them. He drops his chin to his chest; the motion filled with defeat, and when he lifts his dark blue eyes back to mine, there's a cocktail of acceptance and resignation swirling in the depths.

"I'm so sorry, *amore mio.*" He brushes his thumb over my cheek before dropping his hand and leaving me bereft. "We should have had this conversation a long time ago. I found the notes, and it wasn't until I read them that I truly understood what you were willing to sacrifice for me. I've never had a love like that, Aurora." He pauses, sucking in a breath and forcing out his next words. "It pains me to say this, but I'm giving you back your freedom. If letting you go is the sacrifice I have to make for you to live, and I mean *truly* live, then I'll do it. You deserve so much more than what I can give you."

His eyes grow glassy before he looks away from me and stares off in the distance, a muscle working in his jaw.

I jab my finger in his chest as I scream, "No!" The force of the word gets lost in the swirling wind.

Romeo crowds me, bringing his hand up to cover mine, flatting my palm against his chest. His warmth seeps into me, the steady beating of his heart a reassurance I didn't know I needed.

Sadness hangs over us like a dark cloud and he closes his eyes before opening them and staring down at me. The emotion that was swirling in them is gone and his shutters are in place. "Just walk away, Aurora. *Please.*"

Turning away from him, I take three steps before I spin to face him again. He's not looking at me, his focus on the flower bed closest to him. My words come out hoarse as I scream, "I can't *fucking* walk away from you because I love you." Emotion clings to my words as I continue, "Even after what you did—leaving me with those monsters—I can't let you go. Despite everything that's happened and how much I've tried to *hate* you, my heart always seeks you out."

Shaking his head, he scrubs a hand over his jaw and walks through the gap between two flower beds. When he turns toward me, he shrugs. "It would be better for you to just walk away, Aurora."

"And I'm telling you that I can't." My voice cracks, the weight of my emotions consuming me.

Romeo takes a deep breath before blowing it out. "You need to leave. I promise that you'll be safe wherever you decide to go. We're hunting her down and she won't be able to hurt you again. You have my word."

A breeze blows through the garden, lifting the strands of my hair and whipping them around. I wrap my arms around my waist as a shiver runs down my spine. There's something heavy in the air, patiently waiting for a realization to dawn on us. "You hurt me far worse than they ever could when you told them to keep me, and yet, I can't..." My voice breaks, clogged with emotion before I clear it and continue, "I don't want to let you go."

He's the one.

"Letting you go is the last thing I want to do, *mia amata*. I don't want to live another moment without you, but I won't hold you prisoner. I won't take away your freedom or your choices. If you stay with me, it has to be because you are choosing to."

Nodding, I gnaw on my bottom lip. "And if I don't want to leave, what happens then?"

"Then I won't ever let you go."

He says it so matter-of-factly that a fluttering of hope ignites within my chest. I take a step forward and then another until I'm standing in front of him. Our chests brush and I tentatively bring my hands up to hold onto the lapels of his jacket.

I know what I'm signing myself up for if I stay and we still need to work on the foundations of this relationship, but the cracks *are* repairable. Besides, nothing else matters if I have him by my side.

My voice is small, but I know he can hear the certainty when I say, "I don't want to go. I want to stay. I *choose* you, Rome."

Romeo's eyes search mine, his hands gripping my hips and squeezing the flesh gently. He drops his head to mine, closing his eyes, and I take the opportunity to cup his face.

"But," I wait for him to look me in the eye before I continue, "It's going to take me some time to forget everything that's happened and move on fully."

"I don't want *us* to forget, Aurora. I want your forgiveness and your love, but I don't want you to *ever* forget my mistakes. Promise me you won't ever forget them."

"I promise," I breathe. The words lift the heaviness from my chest, allowing it to drift out into the wind.

Romeo growls before capturing my lips in a searing kiss. A familiar heat coils in the pit of my stomach as my pulse pounds in my ears before he pulls away and rests his forehead on mine.

Our breaths mingle in the space between us and although his words are quiet, for only me to hear, *his* promise is clear. "I love you, Aurora. And I'll love you until this life ends and we're far into the next one... *Dio*, I'll love you until we're nothing more than two distant memories that existed as one in *every* lifetime." He pulls away, cupping my face and smoothing away the hairs before continuing, "You have me. All of me, from the top of my head right down to the soles of my feet and the blood pounding in my veins. There will only ever be you, *amore mio.*"

And just like that, the heat I felt moments ago turns into a fluttering. My arms circle his neck and I stand on my toes as I whisper, "I love you."

Romeo bends to lift me into his arms. He carries me into the house, all the while devouring my mouth. Later, I'll tell him all the ways I love him, but for now, I'm going to show him.

Epilogue

Romeo

It's been a month since Aurora told me she loved me. A month of having her back where she belongs, in my arms and my heart. I was ready to let her go, because after seeing five of Massimo's men being killed, I was resolute in not bringing her any further into this darkness.

But then she gave me her heart, and with it, I'm earning back her trust. I'll do everything within my power to protect her from the ugliness of this world. We returned to Sicily a week after the attack on Elio's place, needing a change of scenery that wasn't a reminder of the mistakes I'd made.

Daniele is still in America, working with Massimo and Leonardo to find who tried to set up Aurora. Before I left, we determined that Mattia, Aurora's uncle, was responsible for the bombing at the docks and at least one of the other attacks, but we've had no luck finding the woman Aurora confirmed went by the name Anastasia. Daniele has been keeping me updated, but there hasn't been much progress.

I've spent my days since we returned showing Aurora her new home and checking in on the various operations that make up both the legal and illegal sides of the family business. It's been good to be back here, with her by my side and a new hope for our future.

Aurora's asleep next to me as I finish up some emails in bed. We spent the day at a private beach a short walk from the house and it was good to unwind and relax, but I could tell she was exhausted when she nearly fell head-first into her soup at dinner.

My phone vibrates across the bedside table, and I snatch it up to stop it from waking her. Massimo's name flashes across the screen. Closing my laptop, I set it on the table as I climb from the bed and move across the room. I only connect the call when I'm halfway down the corridor with the bedroom door closed behind me. It's three am my time, so that makes it... nine pm his time.

"Cousin, how are you?" he slurs.

Loud music sounds in the background and I move further down the corridor as I raise my voice to be heard over the noise. "Where are you, Massimo?"

Chuckling, he replies, "At my bachelor party, believe it or not."

I press a finger into my ear, sure I've misheard him. "Your what?"

"My bachelor party. I'm getting married, Rome."

Disbelief drowns his words, as if he can't quite believe it's happening. *You and I both, cousin.*

Tugging on the ear my phone isn't pressed to, I try to hide the confusion I'm feeling when I reply, "Congratulations. I didn't know you were seeing anyone."

"I'm not." He sighs. The music dies down and I imagine him heading to his office. He's got to be in his club; it's weirdly his safe space. "It's a long story, but someone owed me and now I have a wife. Well, I'm *going* to have a wife."

Sounds like a recipe for disaster.

A groove forms in my brow as his words register. "Someone owes you and you're going to have a wife you don't want?"

I imagine him rolling his eyes when he speaks, as if the answer to my question is obvious. "I always collect on my debts, Rome. He owed me, and after some persuasion, he offered her to me."

I rub my hand over my forehead. "And what exactly will you do with her?"

"I don't fucking know. Look, I called to see if you'll come for the wedding?"

My eyes widen, and I blow out a breath. I never thought I'd see the day. "When is it?"

"I don't know."

Chuckling, I reply, "How can you not know? Don't people usually have a bachelor party when there's a set date?"

"Fine." Massimo pouts. "It's more of a 'drowning my sorrows' kind of party."

Shaking my head, I pull my hand down over my jaw. *This is Massimo to a tee.* Without the stress of a war, he's letting loose and back to his old reckless behavior. "When you sort out a date, let me know. I'm sure we can make it over."

"Thanks, Rome. Look, I have to go, Candy's just arrived, but… I'll catch you later."

Disconnecting the call, I return to the bedroom, rubbing at my eyelids. I never thought I'd see the day when Massimo Marino would call me to say he's getting married.

My eyes land on Aurora as I step into the room, the soft glow of the bedside light illuminating her beauty. All this talk of marriage… One day, I'll give her the wedding she's always dreamed of and then I'll give her anything else she asks for.

When I climb under the covers, Aurora snuggles into me, throwing her leg over mine. Her face is upturned and I bend down to dust a kiss over her lips.

Sleep fills her voice when she asks, "Who was on the phone, *amore*?"

"Go back to sleep, *amore mio*. It was just Massimo."

She leans up on her elbow, a hand pressed to her chest to keep the sheet from falling. Her hair hangs in a curtain around her face as she looks down at me, a furrow in her brow. "Is everything okay?"

"Yeah." I smooth her hair back, a smile pulling at the

corners of my mouth. "Believe it or not, but he's getting married."

Her eyes blow wide and the sheet falls to pool around her waist. I can't stop my eyes from dropping to her bare breasts, the globes begging to be touched.

"He is? Wow, never thought that would happen. I thought we'd be married before him."

My eyes dart to hers as I sit up. "*Mi sposi?*"

Aurora tilts her head, her teeth working the fullness of her lower lip. She drops her eyes to her lap before looking at me through her lashes. "I... What does that mean?"

Clearing my throat, I pick up her hand, turning it over to drop a gentle kiss into the palm. "Marry me."

Her jaw goes slack before she catches herself and she looks away. "Are you only asking because Massimo is getting married?"

Cazzo.

"Never, *amore*. Never. It was always my plan. Make you my wife and fill you with my babies. This has nothing to do with Massimo. I just didn't know if you were ready for that next step. I know I still have work to do."

Biting her bottom lip, Aurora climbs into my lap, cupping my face. In between kisses, she says, "I think I've been ready since the day I met you." Pulling away, she swipes her thumb over my bottom lip before adding, "Well, since the day you broke into my apartment. I just didn't know it. You saved me, Rome. You took all of my broken pieces and put them back together. It would make me the happiest woman on Earth to be your wife."

I capture her lips with mine and roll us until she's underneath me. We spend hours getting lost in each other, declaring our love with each kiss.

The End

Links to leave your review, pick up a sneak peek of Marino and, to pre-order, can be accessed here.

Also By

<u>Addison Tate - Dark Romance</u>

<u>Sinful New York Series</u>

Bianchi

Marino - Coming 2025

<u>Anthology</u>

Title To Be Revealed - Violence and Virtues: Vol. 2

<u>KA James - Contemporary Romance</u>

<u>Breaking The Rules Series</u>

Don't Tell Anyone

Don't Fall In Love

Don't Make Promises

One Date

<u>Standalones</u>

To Be Revealed - Coming 2025

Acknowledgments

First and foremost, I want to extend a huge thank you to all the beta and alpha readers who joined me on this journey to the dark side. Your energy and love for the characters in this new world has been inspiring.

Thank you to Sarah from Word Emporium for your thorough work with editing Bianchi. Without you, he wouldn't be as polished as he is today, and I can't wait to work with you again.

To Jasmine, my PA. Without you encouraging me to write a darker book, this would never have happened, so thank you because I had the best time writing Romeo and Aurora's story.

What is for you will not pass you. I truly believe that and so I would be remiss if I didn't give a massive shout out to TL Swan and the rest of the Cygnets. I found you at the start of my journey and it has been a whirlwind, but you've all been there to offer support and guidance, which has been much needed.

Finally, a massive thank you to my boyfriend Ryan and our dog Mia. Thank you for encouraging me every day to do what I love.

About the Author

Addison Tate is an author of dark romance. She lives near London, UK and also writes under the pen name KA James.

Outside of writing, Addison works in HR. She has been in this field since finishing school, but her passion has always been writing. She wrote her first book (where everybody died) when she was fourteen years old.

 Addison hopes you enjoyed reading Bianchi. She is currently writing the next book and you can stay updated through her social media or newsletter. Be sure to follow along on one or more social media channels to be kept in the loop.